Where the River Takes You

A Greyson Gap Novel

By

Sophie Sinclair

To Lisa, thank you for dragging me out to a small mountain town in the middle of the Smokies. This book wouldn't have happened without you.

I'm only dealt the cards I'm dealt.

A strong woman knows she has strength for the journey, but a woman of strength knows it is the journey where she will become strong.

–Unknown

Chapter 1

The Mayonnaise Melee

Blakely

SWEAT BEADS ON my brow as I rush up to a woman fanning herself with the menu I personally crafted. All the places are set for lunch and I can't figure out why she's sitting down in the tent. The food won't be served until after the state senator speaks.

"Ma'am, can I help you? Are you feeling okay?" I ask.

"I'm feeling queasy." She looks pale and kind of green around the gills.

"Let me help you to one of the bathrooms." I will be furious if she gets sick all over the beautiful table I've painstakingly set. She takes my hand but wrenches it free after a few steps forward.

"I'm going to throw up." She lurches to the left while I desperately look around the tent for a trash can or bag. I eye her big purse and wonder if she'll get upset if I shove it under her mouth. I can't have the senator's luncheon ruined. I spy my work tote across the room and stride over to it.

My business partner Liz rushes into the tent, her mouth in the shape of an O, her eyes wide. "Blakely! People are vomiting all over the rose garden! What on earth is going on?"

What is she talking about? Irritated, I shove a plastic bag I found in my tote at the woman just in the nick of time.

"Blakely, answer me!" Liz clenches her fists at her sides.

"I don't know," I shout back, losing my cool.

Typical of Liz to think this is my fault. She's half owner of Polished and Posh Events. Perhaps she should know what the heck is going on. I can't be everywhere at once. She's constantly putting the responsibility on me, never taking the blame when there's a mishap, but always first to take credit when things are good. Wiping my hands on my pale pink sheath dress, I try to regain my composure. I don't understand it. I had every possibility of something going wrong tied up with a pretty bow. Everything but this.

The lead caterer rushes into the tent. "Ms. Mayfield, I think we have a problem…"

What else could possibly go wrong?

"What is it? I'm a little busy." I hand the woman who just threw up a bottle of water from the table before hurrying out of the enclosed tent with Liz and the caterer on my heels. Women and men are hopping up from their seats and scurrying like fleas on a dog, rushing to the designer port-o-johns I had set up on the outskirts of the botanical rose garden. Some guests are throwing up in the bushes.

"Oh my god, what is happening?" I look around, slack-jawed. I need to do something—call for help, call an ambulance. These poor people are dropping like flies.

One pretentious socialite, Victoria Von Meade, vomits in her Louis Vuitton bag. Even through all the chaos, I can't

2

help but feel a small sense of satisfaction. She hired us a few months back for a charity luncheon over the holidays. She was an absolute beast to work for. I've never met someone who insisted on two thousand yards of freshly strung cranberries and popcorn garlands for her gated entrance, only to change her mind as soon as we hung them. Not only were they too kitschy for her liking, but she decided the squirrels and birds would eat them and poop all over her driveway. My fingers were raw and stained for weeks from threading three hundred pounds of cranberries and popped corn.

"Uh...I don't know how to say this," the caterer says, ducking his head.

"Just spit it out. Obviously, I have a crisis on my hands," I snap, horrified by the scene unfolding in front of me.

"The mayonnaise we used for the hors d'oeuvres was spoiled." The caterer blanches as I turn toward him. "At least, that's what we think."

"Mayonnaise?"

"Yes—mayonnaise," the caterer mumbles. "From the watercress sandwiches and crab tarts we served earlier. Is she okay?" he asks Liz.

I'm in a bad horror film. All I can picture is mayonnaise. It's everywhere, dripping off chairs and rose bushes. There are sandwiches covered in globs of mayo littering the rose garden. People are slipping in mayonnaise, and it's all over their faces and in their hair. It's one big hurl-fest of Hellmann's.

This event was going to be the icing on the cake for our business. I slaved for almost six months to make this luncheon perfect. The senator promised me she would recommend us to her colleagues if everything went off without a hitch. She has a long reach, but now... It looks as though all my hard work and credibility as a well-founded event planner is about to go up in flames.

All because of fucking spoiled mayonnaise.

A camera crew for the local Atlanta news films the chaos. I scan the crowd for the senator and gasp when I see her two assistants trying to hold her up while one wipes her brow.

"Oh my god, that's two hundred people who possibly have food poisoning?" Liz screeches beside me, but I've gone numb. Everything turns black right before I crumple to the ground.

Chapter 2

The Mechanic

Blakely

THE TIRES CRUNCH over gravel, skidding, as I turn the wheel of my Infinity SUV sharply. I slam on the brakes, slip-sliding over the road.

"Oh God, I don't want to die today!"

I close my eyes and pump the brakes, praying I don't careen off the side of the mountain. My heart crashes into my ribcage while the SUV lurches to a stop. White knuckles return to their normal skin tone after I loosen my vise-like grip on the steering wheel. If I had been looking down at my phone a second longer, I would have plowed right into the elk casually walking across the road. I force my heart rate to slow to a steady beat while waiting for the giant creature to mosey on across.

"Welcome to the fucking middle of nowhere," I mutter to myself, wondering for the hundredth time if I made the right decision to come to the mountains of North Carolina.

I need to pay attention to where I'm going and stop thinking about the fight I had with Liz. *You're an embarrassment to the company*, her voice echoes on loop in my head.

It's killing me I screwed up so badly. Like an onion layer peeled away, I've been left raw and exposed. And hurt. I'm incredibly hurt she called me an embarrassment. Not only has it damaged my pride, but it makes me question everything I've done up to this point. Which is why I agreed to take some time away from the business.

The map on my phone redirects me back to the highway, but that's not the way I need to go. I feel like I've been circling the same route for the last thirty minutes. Ignoring my Waze app, I turn left off of the main road onto Greyson Farm Road. I'm not sure if this is right, but at least I'm not heading back toward the highway this time. Pastures blur past me in a green haze for a few minutes until I spot an old barn up ahead. I peer through the windshield and see a man working on a truck. Hopefully he can help me with directions.

I pull off onto the dusty gravel road and cross my fingers this guy isn't a murderer. Armed with my little bottle of pepper spray, I wipe my hands on my white skinny jeans and turn off the engine, sliding out of the SUV. I check my key chain to make sure my spray is unlocked, just in case.

He's shirtless, bent under the open hood, tinkering on an old white Ford truck. Faded Levi jeans hug an amazing ass, his tanned muscular back bunching while he cranks on something. He pulls out a long dipstick and wipes the oil off, standing to his full height. I catch a glimpse of light-brown hair under a red ball cap turned backwards.

"Are you going to stare at my ass all afternoon or are you going to ask me for help?" he says, wiping his hands on a bandana he stuffs into the back pocket of his jeans before turning around.

"I…" The words quickly die on my tongue. My gaze travels from his bright green eyes to his eight-pack, down to his scuffed cowboy boots. His well-defined chest glistens with sweat from the afternoon sun. "I think I'm…" I swallow thickly before finding my voice again. "Lost."

"That's pretty obvious." He chuckles. He reaches up to turn his hat around, shading his eyes.

I can't stop myself from ogling him because he looks just like Mr. April, hanging on the wall at my esthetician's office. *He's talking to you, Blakely. Pay attention! Get your eyes off his abs!*

"The highway is ten miles east of here. Take a right on Kitcher Road and it will get you back." He lifts his chin in the direction I just came from, giving me one last curious glance before he turns back around to fiddle with his hunk of rust.

Two cats lay casually in a spot of sun by the entrance to the falling-down barn loaded with junk, tinny country music playing on an old radio. Chickens and some kind of turkey-looking things peck the ground behind the barn. Fields in the distance stretch to meet the Smokies on the horizon, but I don't see any houses in the distance. Or a town, for that matter.

"Um, I don't need to go back to the highway." I step closer, shading my eyes, my Sam Edelman heels wobbling a bit on the rocky ground. "Hello? Are you even listening to me? What I *need*—"

"Oh darlin', I'm sure I got what you need." He smirks over his shoulder.

My hand tightens on my pepper spray. *Did he seriously just say that to me?* I need to shove the dipstick up his ass, is what I need.

"What was that?" he asks.

"I didn't say anything," I bite out.

"I know… I felt it with your eyes."

I cock a hip, annoyed by his smug attitude. "Can you help me or not?"

He straightens, turns around, and walks over to me with a cocksure grin on his face. He's tall compared to my five foot seven inches; he's got to be well over six feet. I suck in a breath as he gets close. His dazzling smile, dimples, and grass-green eyes make my heart stutter in my chest. His eyes flicker to the pepper spray gripped in my hand.

"Anything for a pretty little lady."

My lungs collapse as I blow out the breath I was holding. "FYI, 'Little Lady' is probably one of the most hated, not to mention completely demeaning phrases in women's history," I grit out.

He folds his arms over his chest, his muscles bulging. He arches an eyebrow, waiting for something. It's unnerving.

"What?" I flap my arms out in exasperation.

He chuckles again, looking off down the road. "I'm not a mind reader, Susan B. Anthony. I'm waiting for you to tell me where you need to go."

"Oh." I look past him, flustered by his bare chest, dimpled smile, and muscular forearms. Definitely *not* something Susan B. Anthony would let distract her from her cause. I'm so disgusted with myself. "I need to find Willow Drive over in Greyson Gap. Do you know where that is?"

He looks me over from head to toe and grins. "Well, you're already in Greyson Gap. Willow Drive is down by the river. Head out on this road and take your first right at the O'Mallys' house with all the chickens. You're going to go about five miles past town. Willow Drive will be the second road on your left near the old settlers' fort and Eluwei River. You'll see the Weitzels' goats."

"Chickens, town, fort, river...goats?" I nod and chew my bottom lip, knowing I won't find the place. Maybe if I get into town, I can ask a normal human being for directions. Not this shirtless, sweaty, sexy mechanic staring me down with his gun show on full display. "Don't you people have street signs...or shirts?"

"You people?"

Flustered, I just blurted out what I was thinking. I quickly look down at my phone. "So, um, am I not going to have good cell service up here?"

I swear I hear him grumble, *damn city girl*. I quickly peruse his features. His nose has a slight bump in it like it's been broken before, dark slashes drawn together in a scowl over light-green eyes. The planes of his face are hard lines and sharp edges. His cheekbones slope down into a squared jaw and chin. He drags his tongue over his full lips and my stomach flips. I'm completely mesmerized by the lip-wetting porn show he's giving me.

"Is it hot out here or is it me?" Chuckling deliriously, I fan my phone in front of my face, creating zero wind draft.

He shakes his head and takes off his hat, smoothing down his sun-streaked brown hair, before he puts it on again. I notice the ends curl a little under his hat and it looks silky.

I bet that hair would be amazing to run my fingers through…

No, Blakely! Gah, I don't need a sweaty mechanic to distract me right now.

"So, left at the chickens…"

"No, I said right at the chickens. Who doesn't have a map in their car?" he grumbles, turning on his heel. "Look, if you get lost, go to The Greyson Gap Pub in town and ask for Whit. She'll take you to your place."

"Who's Whit? Wait, I don't even know your name!" I yell at his retreating back.

"Are you asking me to dinner?"

"What?" I squeal. *Is this guy insane?* I stomp my foot in frustration. "No! I'm just trying to be polite!"

"That's a shame." He waggles his eyebrows, looking at me over his shoulder.

I stand there with my mouth hanging open. The nerve of this asshole! He returns to the hood of his car and flips his hat back around.

"You… I…" I stumble, flapping my arms wildly at him.

"If I were you, I'd stop standing there looking at my ass and get a move on because we're about to get some rain."

I look up at the baby-blue sky with white clouds innocently scuttling across. I'm tempted to spray him with my pepper spray for my own satisfaction, but I don't want to waste it on this egomaniac. "I hope the town of Greyson Gap doesn't rely on your crappy weather forecasting skills because they stink and so do your directions…and so does…so does your personality!"

I spin away from him, ranting while I stomp back to my

car, furious he's made me lose my composure. "Ugh! Turn left at the chickens. Who the hell says that? When the rooster crows, make a right." One of the turkey things is standing by my car. "Shoo! Go!" It squawks at me and pecks my back tire. I wave my arms frantically. "Shoo, you stupid bird!" I slam my car door shut and peel out in reverse, kicking up so much dust I can't see out of the windshield.

Asking him to dinner, puhlease! I wouldn't ask him out if he were the last available man on the planet!

I pray there isn't another car coming down the road. Or—*bang*! A loud thud hits the back taillight, making me scream. *Shit-shit-shit*. Please, baby Jesus, don't let it be the turkey thing.

I stop and glance out my rearview as the dust settles. I don't see anything and I'm not about to get out and look, giving this guy more fuel for the fire. I throw the car in drive and hightail it out onto the main road, fishtailing over the gravel as I speed off in the direction he showed, not daring to look back one last time.

Ten minutes into the drive, the sky opens up.

Chapter 3

Rest and Relaxation

Tucker

I WIPE DOWN the mahogany bar before placing fresh beers in front of Ike and Uncle Beauford.

"Thank you kindly," Ike says, while Beauford shoots me a dirty look.

My sister Whitney sidles up to the bar. "Thanks again for covering, Tuck."

"It's no big deal. I'm happy to help."

"I know, but it's your day off and you're probably tired and have a million things going on. The last thing you want to do is be here until midnight. I don't understand why I can't keep a bartender."

"Probably because you've slept with half of them," Uncle Beauford grumbles loudly.

"Jesus Christ, Beau. He doesn't mean it, Whitney!" his best friend Ike shouts a few barstools down from where we're standing.

"Yeah, I do," Beauford crossly gripes. "First there was Tony, and then there was that fruit loop Tad or Ted who always wore purple. Then there was—"

"Okay, Uncle Beau, we all get the picture." Whitney rolls her eyes at me and I arch an eyebrow in return.

"I mean, the ornery bastard does make a strong case. You dated both Tad and Ted."

"Shut up." She giggles. "I'll find someone. I need two IPAs and a Coke."

I get busy pouring the drinks when Ike whistles softly behind me. "Lookee here, Beau. Now she's a Betty Boop."

Looking over my shoulder, I almost shoot soda all over the back of the bar. It's the aggravating woman from this afternoon. Is aggravating the right word to describe her? She definitely got under my skin earlier. I purposely taunted her because I liked watching her cheeks bloom the pretty peachy rose when she would lose her cool.

"Good evening, ma'am," Ike says behind me. I chance a quick glance in the mirror lining the back of the bar. She casually puts her purse down, sitting down on a stool, and smiles at Ike.

"Good evening." Her voice pours out smooth and raw over my nerves like honey. She looks around the pub and pulls her phone out.

I bring the drinks over to my sister and whisper, "This is the woman I was telling you about earlier."

"Hmm, she has style, looks to have half a brain, and she's pretty. Not your usual type."

I give Whitney a flat stare. "She's a nuisance and she's high maintenance."

"I take it back. She's exactly your type." Whitney's eyes flicker back to me and her smile grows. "You like her."

"I don't."

13

"Uh, huh. Be nice, she's a paying customer. Besides, once word gets around there's a stunning woman at the bar, the men will be driving in circles on Main Street to cram into the parking lot."

I give her a doleful look. She pats my chest and winks before heading off to deposit the drinks. I turn my attention to the dark-blonde at the bar. Her eyes widen, watching me approach. I make a point of glancing at my watch.

"Hey, darlin', did you just now manage to find your way into town? It's been about four hours since you tried to run over my guinea hen." I wink at her and she scowls back.

"What are *you* doing here?"

"I'd say it's pretty obvious…"

"At least you're wearing a shirt," she grumbles, opening the menu in front of her face.

"Can I get you something?"

Her eyes narrow as she lowers the menu. "A glass of rosé, sparkling if you have it."

God, she's making this way too easy for me. I stick a toothpick in my mouth, fold my arms over my chest, and lean against the bar. "This ain't the country club, Smiles. Sorry, we're plum out of sparkling rosé, but I think I might have an old wine cooler in the back."

She rolls her eyes at me and looks around the pub. "What about a mojito? Crushed ice please with extra mint, and make sure you muddle the mint. I hate it when bartenders lazily throw it in."

I bite my cheek and smirk. "Try again, darlin'."

She stares at me for a beat. She picks up the menu, pretending to peruse it, and sighs. "What's the special tonight?

I'd kill for a filet."

Taking the toothpick out of my mouth, I point it at her. "Well, sorry ma'am, we don't have filet, but the special tonight is some kind of stew. I think the chef caught a rattler earlier or maybe it's squirrel? Hard to tell."

"The buffalo burgers are good," Ike pipes up from a few stools down. "Or you could go over to Surf and Turfs—"

"Okay, boys. Last one tonight, Uncle Beau, okay? Ike, you think you can get him home?" I quickly cut Ike off before he sends her running over to my cousin Jason's restaurant.

"Sure thing, Tucker."

Beauford grunts, tapping his beer bottle on the bar. Leaving Smiles, I reach down and pull a beer out of the cooler, sliding it toward my uncle Beau. He's a cantankerous, stubborn son of a bitch, but he's family, so we put up with his grumpiness and let him hang out here.

In my peripheral, I notice a preppy guy I've seen around town come over and sit next to her at the bar. I think his name is Garrett. She smiles at him and my ego takes a hit, wondering why she doesn't smile at me like that.

"What can I get you?" I gruffly interrupt right before he introduces himself to her.

"Oh, uh, hey, Tucker. I'll have a Bud Light, thanks." His attention returns to the blonde. She arches an eyebrow when I don't move to leave.

"Garrett, let me introduce you to our out-of-town guest. This here is Smiles. She likes drinks with muddled mint and getting lost in the rain. Go easy on her, though. She might try to pull her pepper spray on you or run you over with her car." I wink at her, pull a bottle out of the ice chest, pop the top, and slide it toward Mr. Preppy Pants. "That will be three-fifty."

"Don't listen to him, *Garrett*." She turns to him and smiles brilliantly. "He's whining like a little schoolgirl because he can't work up the nerve to ask me out." She folds her arms over her chest and looks at me coolly. "I secretly think he has little dick syndrome."

I grin wickedly at her while Preppy Pants Garrett coughs up the beer he just swallowed.

"Don't listen to Smiles," I counter, leaning in, keeping my eyes on hers. "She's just prickly because she asked *me* out to dinner, but I politely declined. Oh, and she can't keep her eyes off my butt."

"You're ridiculous," she seethes.

"I know." I wink at her and give her my signature smile.

Garrett looks back and forth between us. "Yeah, I don't know what's going on here, but I'm good." He grabs his beer and hurries back to his table.

"Ugh! You're infuriating!"

"Yeah. So what's it going to be, darlin'?" I slide the menu over to her and notice her cheeks pink up.

"First, I'm not your *darlin'* so you can cut the good-ole-boy country crap."

Ike does a low whistle, which makes me smirk. "Well, I'd call you by your name if I knew it."

"Why don't you ask me for it like a normal human being?" she gripes, picking up the wine menu.

"Simmer down there, Smiles. I was gettin' there."

"Please, do us both a favor and don't call me anything."

She looks over her shoulder to see where Preppy Pants ran off to. Her brown-sugar eyes burn with contempt as she returns her gaze to me.

"Let's start over. Hi, I'm Tucker." I hold my hand out to her. "You ran into my grandaddy's tractor this afternoon while you were eyeing my butt."

"I...what? No! I..." she splutters, my grin widening. "I couldn't see because of the dust. I'll pay for whatever damages I may have caused." She ignores my hand, so I slide the rag off my shoulder and wipe down the bar.

"For that old bucket of rust?" Beauford grumbles.

"That thing hasn't run in twenty years," Ike chimes in.

I shoot Uncle Beau and Ike a mind-your-business look and they return their attention to *So You Think You Can Dance* on television.

"Tuck, stop harassing this poor woman and get her a drink. I need two chardonnays, a cab, and three amber ales." My sister arches an eyebrow, throwing her notepad in her apron. "Ignore my brother. He thinks he's the cat's meow. Hi, I'm Whitney." My sister holds out her hand, which Smiles immediately shakes. Indignance pools in the pit of my stomach because she looked at my hand like it still had grease stains from earlier today.

"Nice to meet you. I'm Blakely." She aims a breathtaking smile at my sister, completely transforming her face. She's beautiful when she isn't scowling. Hell, she's beautiful when she *is* scowling.

"Welcome to Greyson Gap. Are you staying in town for the kayak festival this weekend?"

I snort. Blakely looks like she's going to a photoshoot in

her flowy sundress, not a kayak competition.

"What?" Whitney shrugs. "She might be a pro kayaker or photographer or reporter..."

"Actually, I'm here for a little rest and relaxation."

"Ah, yes, it's a great place to reenergize. If you like sauvignon blanc, we have an excellent one. Don't pay attention to Tuck and definitely say no if he tries to ask you out."

"I take offense to that," I shout at my sister's back as she walks away with her drink order, cackling.

"I feel bad for all the poor souls of Greyson Gap if you're the town ladies' man." Blakely snaps the menu shut. "I'll have the sauvignon blanc, and a small salad, as tempting as the stew sounds."

"Color me surprised," I mumble.

"Hmm? What was that?"

"I didn't say anything." I glance over my shoulder. Her narrowed eyes are throwing daggers at my back. I may never see this woman again after this weekend, but slinging insults with her is much more entertaining than talking to Ike and Uncle Beau.

"If you're only here for the weekend, I can show you how to rest and relax. That is, if you need help." I wink, pushing her wineglass in front of her.

"As tantalizing as your offer sounds, I'll pass," she says drolly.

"So, Blake—can I call you Blake? Why Greyson Gap?"

"No, you can't." She fidgets in her seat. "What do you mean, why Greyson Gap?"

"Well, there are hundreds of other mountain towns which would suit your needs better."

"And you know what my needs are?"

"Let me guess." I lean back, chew on my toothpick, and assess her. I know her type like the back of my hand. "You need someone to wine and dine you. You're independent, but still crave a man to make you howl in bed. You need to be in control, but secretly, you're begging for a man to take the reins and sweep you off your feet like a Disney princess."

She snorts, shaking her head, before peering over at Ike and Beauford to see if they're listening. I'd bet my life savings they are, even though their eyes are glued to the dancers on TV.

"That sounds ludicrous. Howl in bed?" She eyes me over the rim of her glass. "Let me guess. You are just the guy to do that, am I right?"

"Nah, you're not my type."

Her lips part, clearly offended by my statement. She quickly composes herself and folds her arms over her chest. "Well, you're not my type either."

I smile. *She's full of shit.*

She takes a sip of wine, eyeing me again over the brim. "You seem overly confident in your assessment."

"Just telling you how I see it." I pick up a beer glass and dry it.

"I see. So, you're Greyson Gap's beer-slinging Dr. Phil? How cute." She flattens her lips.

"Are you always this prickly?"

"Maybe I *am* here for the kayak festival," she says snootily, while picking imaginary lint off her dress.

I shake my head. "Nah, you don't seem like a river rapids kind of girl."

"Oh really?" She arches an eyebrow in challenge. "What kind of girl do I seem like?"

I set the glass down and lean into her space, placing my hands on either side of her at the bar. Her throat bobs and her pupils dilate. "You're more like a lounge by the pool, sipping on mojitos at The Ritz, kind of girl to me."

She rears her head back. "I can river rapids with the best of them."

I'm about to open my mouth when Stacy Reeger and her three girlfriends walk in. I snap my mouth shut. Great, this is all I need tonight. Stacy spots me like a heat missile finding its target, her eyes narrowing. With her fists clenched and snarl in place, she stalks over to the bar.

Stacy and I aren't exactly on the best of terms. Unfortunately, I made the erroneous mistake of kissing her a few months ago at my cousin's BBQ after having too much to drink. She became clingier than a dryer sheet, popping up wherever I was like an unwanted pimple. Not looking for anything serious, I apologized to her and made it clear I was only interested in being friends. Unfortunately for me, Stacy refused to accept. I made the mistake of smiling at one of her friends the other week here at the pub. It didn't end well for me.

"What are *you* doing here?" Stacy growls.

"What does it look like? Working."

"Do I have to look at your putrid face all night? If so, we're leaving."

Blakely snickers, her eyes pinging back and forth between us.

"Hmm, looks like it," I say, keeping my expression neutral. I turn to go get Blakely's salad, effectively ending my conversation with Stacy. Hopefully she'll make good on her promise, take her friends and leave. I don't need unnecessary drama tonight.

I return with the salad and silverware, annoyed Stacy is waiting for me. "What can I get you, Stacy?"

"I'll have a Moscato."

Great, she's staying. I try to smile politely, but it feels more like a grimace. I'm tempted to add new tires onto her tab since she slashed mine the morning after flirting with her friend, but my grandpa always taught me, if you mess with the bull, you'll get the horns. "One Moscato coming up." I quickly turn away from her. "Are you opening a tab?"

"I guess." Her nasally voice makes my skin itch. "If you go on break later, maybe we can play darts. I have the perfect target in mind."

"Hmm, maybe next time." I hand her the glass and quickly check on Ike and Uncle Beau. Stacy saunters back over to her friends. I make my way back to Blakely after checking on a few other patrons at the bar, her salad half eaten.

"From my brief observation, I can tell you're a real lady killer," she deadpans and puts a twenty down on the bar.

"I've been told by enough women my dimples make them melt." Her eye twitches as I push the twenty back toward her and grin. "It's on me, Smiles. Welcome to Greyson Gap." I turn my back on her and dry a glass, trying to hide my smile. When I turn back around, the only thing left at the bar is her twenty.

CLEANING THE LAST glass, I place it on the shelf, feeling wiped. The crowd picked up right after Blakely left and stayed busy until we closed at midnight. I also had to keep busy to avoid Stacy, who, for some strange reason, tried to talk to me while I slung beers. I guess she was hoping I'd forgotten about the tires. I haven't.

"Hey, Whit, I think I'm going to crash at the river house tonight instead of going back to the cabin." I make a mental note to meet the cleaning crew up at my place on my grandfather's ranch. "The renters are coming the day after tomorrow."

The cabin on the ranch is where I mostly stay, but I rent it out to families during the summer who are looking for the ranch experience. We initially built the river house to rent out, but then decided to keep it and use it when my cousin visits and so I have a place to stay in town when I need to be here for work or late nights like tonight.

"That's a good idea. No sense in driving twenty minutes through the mountains." She yawns while counting her tips. "Sorry it's so late." She hands me half her stack.

"I'm not taking your tips." I push the wad back to her. "And don't argue with me. You won't win."

She smiles up at me, her eyes tired. "Thanks, Tuck. I really appreciate your help tonight. This weekend is going to be insane with the festival. Luckily Kristen and Tiff are coming up from Asheville to help and Jason said he'd chip in tomorrow night."

"Okay, good. Well, if you need me…"

She pats my arm. "Thanks. Go home, get some sleep."

We lock up the bar, and I drive the five minutes to my river house in town. I text my cousin Jason and leave him a message to drop my dog Hershel off in the morning since I won't be able to get back up to the cabin until later. I unlock the door and disable the alarm system. I'm so exhausted I don't bother turning on any of the lights before heading straight to my bedroom, where I land face first on my bed.

Chapter 4

S'mores and Stuff

Blakely

THE EARLY MORNING light shines through the filmy curtains as I lazily stretch in my bed. I haven't had a full night's sleep in a long time. My best friend, Junie, was right. The mountain air does clear your head. She told me I needed to come stay in her little house on the river for the summer to get away from the chaos. Little is an understatement. Her newly built house is gorgeous. I'm staying in her room upstairs, which has a four-poster king-sized bed, French doors leading to a private balcony, and an ensuite bathroom. I step out on the little balcony and look down at the river sweeping along over smooth rocks. This is just what I needed—peaceful solitude. Coming here was the right decision. I can feel it in my bones.

I look over to the house left of mine and wonder if it's occupied. Junie did say this summer will be pretty busy with all the festivals in town. I brush my teeth and throw a robe over my pajamas. It's a beautiful morning to sit out on the back deck with a cup of coffee. I never let myself relax like this back in Atlanta. My schedule didn't allow it.

I head downstairs and open up some cupboards in search of coffee.

"Oh thank God," I mumble, pulling out a bag of pre-ground beans. I'll definitely have to make a grocery run into town and stock up.

I start the coffee pot and bang open more kitchen cupboards in search of a mug. The smell of coffee brewing is absolute heaven. Junie's house on the river is only a year old and it's beautiful with its modern sleek design, white cupboards, and marble countertops. Somehow, the clean lines work well against the pines and the river rustling by.

I came up here to get away from the fallout from the senator's event, to clear my head, and this is exactly what the doctor ordered. Literally, my doctor ordered me to take a vacation, but I didn't know where to go, so Junie shoved her keys in my face and ordered me to run out of town without overthinking it.

Watching the coffee drip, I contemplate my current situation. I've always been on the go, a bit too high-strung for most. I prefer order and predictability over chaos. My therapist thought it would be a good idea to take a sabbatical from my job as an event planner, and my business partner, Liz, readily agreed. My first instinct was to sell my half of the business and walk away from the company I helped build, but the thin thread of pride still tied to my ego wouldn't allow me to let go.

Even after what seemed like a thousand apologies to the senator and her staff, it wasn't enough. Clients canceled left and right after vomit-gate, and we became the fodder for gossip at all the social events. Seven years of sweat and tears, missed holidays and weekends spent catering to our clients' whims, washed down the toilet with one mishap. I never dreamed our friendship and business would dissolve over something as inconsequential as mayonnaise.

Drumming my fingers on the counter, I push everything to the back of my mind. I've never done something so frivolous as hightailing it out of town before. I didn't even plan outfits or color coordinate my bras and panties. Junie shoved clothes in my suitcase and threw it in my car before I changed my mind. There has to be a J.Crew or a Lululemon around here somewhere, if I'm missing things, right?

Stress tingles down my spine. *Of course, they have clothing stores here, you dingbat.* I could have organized and packed my suitcase blindfolded without my checklists, but Junie was on a mission. Pouring a cup of coffee before the tingles turn into a full-blown panic attack, I add a little cream and head to the French doors, which open up to the back porch overlooking the river.

I need to call my therapist, Dr. Cooper, and give her an update on my arrival. But the first thing on my to-do list is to enjoy the quiet morning, something I haven't done in forever. This is the start of the new me. I need to learn to solve the problem when it arises, not have everything so perfectly planned out that problems don't exist. My mind is an exhausting place to live.

A large brown-speckled dog jumps on me once I open the door to the back deck. Coffee sloshes all over my robe as I release a blood-curdling scream. He barrels past me and hops up on the couch, his tongue lolling to the side. I stay plastered against the door, afraid he might go for my jugular.

Where the hell did he come from and why is he in my house?

"Shoo! Get! Go on, get out of here!"

He looks like he could take my arm off with his sharp teeth. His big blocky head is the largest I've ever seen. His ears perk while he checks me out. Oh god, he's for sure going to turn me into beef jerky.

"What the hell is going on?" a man's gruff voice asks.

I scream, dropping my coffee mug when a shirtless man stumbles out of the downstairs bedroom. It's the guy I ran into yesterday, the bartender, Tucker. How the hell did he get in here and why is he stumbling out of the downstairs bedroom?

"What are *you* doing in *my* house? Are you following me?" I screech.

He scrubs his hands down his face. I desperately look around the room for my purse with my pepper spray keychain, just in case.

"*Your* house?" he bites out. "This is *my* house."

"No, this is *my* house. My friend Junie owns this house and is letting me stay here."

Tucker growls an expletive as he runs a hand through his hair. It irritates me to all hell that I can't take my eyes off his abs or control the urge to want to run my tongue over his body like a road map. I swear I've seen this man's naked torso more in the last two days than my ex-boyfriend's in the two years we dated. *What is wrong with me?* I should want to bludgeon this guy or pour my hot coffee on him, not stare at his incredible eight-pack—again.

Oh damn, my coffee. I bend down to retrieve my mug

and rush to the kitchen for a towel to clean up the mess, side-eyeing the dog on the couch who seems quite at home there.

"Junie is my cousin," Tucker announces. "We share this house. She forgot to mention she was sending a houseguest."

What? How on earth is the smart and talented Doctor Junie Thorton *cousins* with this imbecile? "You've got to be joking."

He grimaces. "I wish."

"But Junie is Korean."

"Junie was adopted. Didn't you say you were friends with her?"

"I mean, yes, but we never really talked about our families much."

"Clearly." He eyes me suspiciously, grabbing the carton of creamer out of the fridge.

I blot the coffee on the floor and wonder why Junie never told me she was adopted. I feel like that's something best friends should know, right? I tuck the small kernel of hurt and stupidity I'm feeling into a corner of my heart while I stare at the large dog on the couch.

"If that's your dog, he practically mauled me getting into the house."

"Who? Hersh? He wouldn't hurt a fly." Tucker ruffles his head. "What's your last name?"

I slam the door shut. "Mayfield. Blakely Mayfield. Check with Junie. I'm not some crazy person who broke into her house."

"Oh, don't worry. She is first on my list to call this morning," he says grumpily. "Get down, Hersh." The large brown-speckled dog hops off the couch and trots over to the water bowl in the kitchen. How did I not see that?

"What's wrong with his eye? Is he blind?"

Tucker peers down at Hershel. "What do you mean?"

"They're different colors."

"I take it you're not a dog person."

"I don't have a dog, no. I don't dislike them, it's just…they're messy."

"Ah, you're one of those." He smirks.

"One of what?"

Ignoring me, he pours himself a cup of coffee.

"Help yourself." I fling my arms out, exasperated.

"Thanks, I will, since it's *my* coffee," he grumbles.

I can't stop my gaze from trailing down his muscular back to his ass in his jeans. It's not fair having to look at this chiseled Adonis this early in the morning. *No, Blakely, you dislike this naked man. He's annoying and rude, remember?*

"He's a Catahoula."

"Who's a cata what?"

"Hershel, he's a Catahoula. Otherwise known as a Louisiana coonhound. Bred to hunt wild boar."

"Wild boar? Do *you* hunt wild boar?" I shiver, picturing wild boar heads mounted on the wall in his bedroom. Disturbing.

He looks at me over his coffee mug with a smugness I'd like to wipe off with the coffee-soaked rag I'm holding. "No."

I sit down on the couch in front of the enormous stone fireplace. "So, what are we going to do?"

"About what?"

Oh my god, this guy is dense. "About the house. Obviously, we both can't stay here."

"It's the kayak festival this weekend. Our one hotel is full." He sips his coffee and leans against the island separating the kitchen from the family room.

"Well, there's got to be another hotel—"

"Not in Greyson Gap. The nearest Hilton is an hour from here. People rent houses and cabins in our town, not stay at big chain hotels. They come for the week and take day trips or go hiking and fishing." He looks pensively at the floor. "My house on the ranch is being rented out tomorrow, which reminds me, the cleaning crew should be up there soon. Look, it's fine. There's plenty of room and you won't even know I'm here. I've got lots going on this weekend. By Monday, you'll be back in the city and life will be back to normal."

"Except I'm not going back Monday."

His piercing green eyes pin me to the spot. "When are you going back?"

"September."

He coughs on the coffee he just swallowed. "September? That's three months away! Junie said you could stay here until *September*?"

"Uh, well, to be honest, I probably won't last that long. I'm not exactly a mountain kind of girl."

"You don't say," he says irritably, giving me a quick head-to-toe glance. "I've got to get ready. I guess make yourself at home, but don't expect me to cater to your every whim. It's not like we'll be having cookouts, quiet walks along the river, s'mores and stuff."

Once again, this man has rendered me temporarily speechless as he turns and slams his bedroom door closed.

"*Rude!*" I whisper-shout. Hershel jumps up on the couch next to me, looking at me doe-eyed. "Is he always like this?"

He lays down with a groan, nudging my leg with his wet nose.

"I thought so." I reach out and stroke his spotted fur, causing him to grunt and stretch. So much for a nice, peaceful morning.

Chapter 5

Helpful Junie

Tucker

"JUNIE, ARE YOU fucking kidding me? Did you seriously send her here for the summer and not run it by me first?"

"Sorry, Tuck. Honestly, I wasn't thinking. She was desperate and on the verge of…anyway, I'm sorry. Can't you put her in one of the rentals?"

"No, I can't. It's the kayak festival this weekend. Everything is taken."

"Shit," Junie says, "I completely forgot."

"Seems like you've forgotten a lot since you moved away."

"Tucker, that's not fair."

I shake my head. I don't mean to take my anger out on Junie, but I'm frustrated she hasn't bothered to check in with me. Ever since she moved to Atlanta, she's distanced herself from the family. The big-city doctor from small-town America trying to make it on her own. *Go easy on her. You were the same way once.* "What do you plan on doing with Blakely?"

She sighs heavily into the phone. "Look, can't you stay

up at the cabin? Or better yet, have her stay up there."

"No. I've rented it out to families this summer, starting this weekend. Which was the whole point of building this house, so family could use it anytime during our busy rental seasons."

"You're right. I'm sorry I put you in this position. She needed my help and I didn't even think. Honestly, she's very high strung and I'm worried about her. She needs to slow down. She's one of my best friends, Tucker. Perhaps I can call Whitney and she can stay with her. Oh, or maybe you can stay with Jason. I know he's messy, but—"

"Whit's house is being remodeled and Jason has a new roommate." I sigh, not wanting this complication in my life right now. "It looks like I don't have much of a choice."

"She's a great roommate, obsessively neat. You won't even know she's there. I promise."

I peer into the living room where she's doing some sort of yoga pose with her ass in the air. I grind my teeth, unable to control the lust shooting straight to my dick while I watch her downward-dogging it in Lycra. "Yeah, I won't even know she's here," I mutter, hanging up on Junie.

This is the last thing I need right now. If I wanted a roommate, I'd have moved in with my cousin Jason. Teasing Blakely and getting under her skin was one thing, but having her as a houseguest all summer? Not exactly what I had planned. I like my privacy and I don't need some uptight city girl getting in my way.

I move out into the living room. "You know, there's a yoga studio in town. Perhaps you could do your stretches there instead of in the middle of my living room." *Stop fucking picturing her legs wrapped around your waist, you dickhead.*

"Oh, I'm good here. I really like the yoga videos on YouTube." She looks at me over her shoulder, stretching an arm out in front of her. "Are you looking at my ass?"

I fold my arms over my chest. "If I was staring at your ass, do you really think I would have asked you to stop? I would have just sat here like a pervert and watched."

"Which is precisely what you're doing." She twists her body, reaching up to the ceiling with one arm.

I guess I am a perv because she's completely mesmerizing. I shake my head, snapping my attention to the windows. Silence hangs thick in the air between us. "Do you always pretend you're better than everyone else?"

She blanches, and I know I've hit a nerve.

"Are you always such a dick?" She gathers her phone, her water, and yoga mat, effectively ending her session and our conversation. She doesn't spare me a glance as she runs up the stairs and slams her door shut.

"Point one for me." I exhale, running my hands through my hair. I don't have time to worry about hurt feelings or unwanted houseguests, though. Whistling for Hershel, I stride out the front door and head to the cabin to meet the cleaning crew, leaving my miserable roommate problems behind.

Chapter 6

Roommates

Blakely

I'M NOT SURE where Tucker has been all day, but I haven't heard from him since I slammed my door this morning. Embarrassed by my immature behavior, I went for a walk along the river to clear my head. It was exactly what I needed after the unexpected turn of events.

After showering and unpacking, I drove the short distance into town and went to the local grocery store for necessities. I bought Tucker the same brand of beer I saw in the fridge, my way of extending an olive branch. I cleaned the house, did some laundry, and even made his bed, fighting the urge to snoop around his room. Afterwards, I made him dinner as an apology for hitting the tractor. Yes, there's a nice dent in my rear fender. I'm just thankful it didn't break a taillight.

What baffles me the most is Tucker. When I look at him, I see a sinfully sexy man in his tight-fitting t-shirts and jeans, but when he opens his mouth...well, let's just say I've already done the cocky, chauvinistic thing with my ex, Charles. And the syrupy eye winks and darlins' he was throwing my way last night make me see red. I almost prefer him moody like this morning. He hit a nerve when he said I thought I was better than everyone else. My parents act like that and I swore up and down I'd never be like them.

Pouring myself a glass of wine, I take it out to the back porch and wait for my call-in time with Dr. Cooper. We agreed it would be beneficial to have weekly check-ins while I'm on sabbatical. I sip my wine and kick my feet up. I can't remember the last time I had a relaxing afternoon to do nothing. I'm thirty-four years old and have never taken a few hours for myself, much less a vacation. I breathe in deeply and exhale. Time for a change, Blakely.

The alarm on my phone dings, letting me know it's time.

"Blakely, I'm so happy to hear from you. Tell me, how you are doing?" Dr. Cooper's soft-spoken voice calms the errant thoughts racing around my brain like a soothing balm.

"Hi, Dr. Cooper. I made it to Greyson Gap. Right now, I'm sitting on the back porch with a glass of wine, enjoying the quiet."

"And how does that make you feel, Blakely?"

I sigh, because she knows me better than I know myself. "Jumpy, because there are a thousand things I could be doing right now."

"It will take some time. Close your eyes and breathe in deeply. Let go of all your mental to-do lists. Breathe and live in the moment. Tell me what else you are feeling."

I swallow, my eyes glazing over with tears, my nose smarting. "Lonely."

"Why are you feeling lonely? You live alone in Atlanta."

"I don't know."

"Blakely, I want you to take advantage of this time. Do things you would never have the opportunity to do in Atlanta. Meet new people—"

"Oh, I've met someone. He's rude, condescending, and thinks he knows everything. And to top it off, he's Junie's cousin. We're stuck together as roommates because the only hotel in town is completely booked."

"Hmm, interesting. How does that make you feel?"

"Like he's totally encroaching on my *me* time."

Dr. Cooper chuckles. "I'm going to give you an assignment, Blakely. I'd like you to keep a daily journal. Report back to me about how it's going. First order of business is to make a new friend."

"Dr. Cooper, please don't say I have to be friends with Tucker. There's no growth potential there."

"It doesn't have to be with your new roommate, although it might make your time there more enjoyable." I roll my eyes because she's never met him. "I also want you to step out of your comfort zone and try something new. A new life experience. Let go of the daily tasks which have held you back from experiencing spontaneity. Let's reconvene next week and talk about your assignments. Remember, Blakely, you're never alone. You can always reach out to me. I'll talk to you next week." Dr. Cooper ends the call after I promise to work on the assignment.

Thoughts jumble around my brain while I consider Dr. Cooper's suggestion. Create a new life experience? The river rushes by, reminding me I've never fished before or kayaked down a creek. The cloudless blue sky reminds me I haven't traveled since starting the business. There has always been too much work for me to take a vacation. I've never relaxed on a beach and soaked in the sun without a care in the world. The sound of children's laughter and wind chimes carry on the breeze a few houses over. I've never thought about having kids because it wasn't in my plan. Do I even want kids? They're so messy.

"I've had no life experiences," I say out loud, in equal parts wonderment and horror. My phone buzzes next to me. I groan when I see the caller.

"Hey, Mom."

"Ugh, Blakely, is that how you answer a phone call? Hay is for horses, and I thought we discussed this already. I prefer to be called Susan now that you're a grown adult."

"Right, sorry, Susan. Hard for me to get used to since I've always called you Mom."

Silence hangs thick over the line before she clears her throat. "Well, moving on. Listen, I heard about what happened the other week from Charles. Such a shame."

Why is my ex talking to my mom? "It was so awful—"

"Yes, I'm sure it was. You realize this could be very damaging to your father's and my reputation, being high-profile attorneys. We can't be known as the parents of the woman who started vomit-gate. Absolutely dreadful." She sniffs, and it's like a punch to my stomach. I've never gotten sympathy or support from her before, so I don't know why I expected this call to be any different. Yet it still hurts me to the bone she can't say, 'we're behind you, Blakely, and we love you.'

"Hello, Blakely...are you there?"

"Yes, unfortunately, I'm here."

"As I was saying, I hope you're on new medication. If

you need to call a psychiatrist, my friend Grace gave me the best recommendation."

I grind my teeth in irritation. "I'm fine."

"I'm glad, Blakely. Oh, my appointment is here."

I stare at the phone in disbelief, the call ending before I can say goodbye. God, my mom, I mean Susan, is such a piece of work. I gulp my wine, watching a family float down the river on a raft. They wave to me and I wave back. It must be nice for those kids to have loving parents who take them on fun adventures. My parents never had time for fun.

I've never let myself get drunk or lose control. I've never danced like no one was watching. In college, I always had my nose in books, too busy trying to be the best at every subject, trying to be too perfect. I was terrified of letting loose, screwing up, and feeling the wrath of my parents over it.

"I am the most fucking boring person in the history of ever!" I shout, as if yelling it confirms it. Charles said the same thing. No wonder he broke up with me. He said I spent more time with my planner than I did with him and he's absolutely fucking right!

I slam down my wineglass, march upstairs, fling open my door, and grab my purse. I pull out my beloved leather-bound planner and hug it to my chest. Dr. Cooper is right. I need to let go if I'm ever going to move forward from this mess and what better way than to snip the artery to my organizing heart? I kiss the soft calfskin and lovingly run my fingertips over the etched gold foil, spelling out my name. *Do it, Blakely, you'll be free*, the voice in my head chants. Before I can change my mind, I fling open my balcony doors and chuck my planner over the railing into the waters below.

"Wahoo! I'm free!" I shout into the wind, my eyes closed, breathing in the fresh pine trees surrounding the house. My heart is pounding, exhilaration and fear duking it out in a battle of wills over throwing away my lifeline. *Oh god, what did I just do?*

"Ow! Fucking A. What the hell?"

I squint one eye open and look down. Tucker is standing on the back porch rubbing his head with my planner at his boots. "Oh sorry, did I hurt you?"

"Why are you dropping books?"

"I wasn't dropping. I was trying to throw it into the river."

"Well, you need to work on your aim, and that's littering, by the way. The forestry service can fine our house if they catch us throwing stuff into the river." He leans down and picks up my planner.

"Oh, I wasn't thinking...sorry, I got carried away. I was trying to be free."

"Yeah, well, go be free near a trash can," he grumbles, walking into the house while rubbing his head.

I quickly check my appearance in the mirror before rushing down the stairs to find him standing in front of my daily chore chart I made, holding a cold beer in his hand. He's wearing a fitted black t-shirt with a Greyson Builders logo on the pocket, jeans, and dirty cowboy boots.

"I got you the beers as a peace offering since we're going to be roommates," I say, a little out of breath. Hershel runs up to me in greeting. I absently pat his head and move into the kitchen.

"What the hell is this?" He points to the posterboard I

have taped to the wall in the kitchen.

"It's a daily chore chart. Do you mind taking your boots off at the door? They look…dusty." His boots look like he's been roping cattle all afternoon. And if there's cattle, then there's manure. My nose wrinkles, wondering if he has manure on the bottom of his boots. I add 'sanitize the floors' to my mental checklist of things to do. He ignores me as he continues to stare at the chart. "Do you like it? I even color-coded it. You're blue and I'm green. Oh, and I made a spinner for Silly Sundays. We can spin for our chore. Isn't it cute?"

He runs his hand through his light-brown hair. "A chore chart," he says slowly, like he thinks it's the stupidest idea in the entire world. Maybe he's colorblind. It's brilliant, if I do say so myself.

"Yes!" I say brightly, trying to pump him up. "See here? On Mondays, you have dishwasher duty and bathroom cleaning. Tuesdays I have dishwasher, linen changes. Wednesdays—"

"No," he cuts me off, pivoting away from the chart.

"No? What do you mean, *no*?" I fold my arms over my chest in indignation. The nerve of this guy.

"I'm not following a chart. You have cleaning the bathroom up on the list three times a week."

"Your bathroom can never be too clean."

"No."

"I heard you the first time," I bite out.

"I don't think you did because we're still talking about it," he shoots back, making me gnash my teeth together.

"Are you always this rude?"

He sighs, leaning against the counter, and stares up at the ceiling. I follow his gaze, wondering if I missed a cobweb earlier. Hershel trots into the kitchen and laps water from the dog bowl. I bite my lip in distress when he walks away with water drooling out of his mouth all over the kitchen floor I just cleaned.

"Are you going to wipe his mouth off before he trails it all over the house, or God forbid, gets it on the furniture?"

"No, he's a dog." Tucker walks into the living room and sprawls out on the couch while he looks at his phone.

"Can you at least take off your boots, please?" I cringe. Jesus, I'm about to have a coronary and it's not even my house. Tucker ignores me while Hershel stretches out on the carpet, rubbing his mouth, head, and other unmentionable body parts along it. All I can think about is getting the steam cleaner out, pronto. I'm positive I saw one in the garage.

I march into the living room and clap my hands at Hershel to stop licking himself, but he continues, even throwing a groan in like he's having the time of his life on the carpet. *Gah!*

"What are you doing?"

"Trying to get him to stop licking his dingaling. It's really gross." I clap again.

"Hershel is a stud. He does not have male parts called dingalings, and your clapping in his face won't stop him. It's annoying."

I sigh in frustration. "Look, if we're going to live together, we have to share duties and lay some ground rules. It's only fair."

"What are we, twelve and at summer camp? Have you

ever had a roommate before?"

"Yes, in college."

"Did you have these rules for her, too?"

"Yes, of course," I scoff.

"Are you still friends with her?"

"Well, not exactly..."

"Because she requested a new roommate mid-year?"

"I... How did you know... You know what? Never mind. The point is, I don't want to get stuck cleaning every day or doing your laundry."

"I'm not asking you to do any of that, Blake. I won't be around much. If you need me to do something, just ask." He looks back at his phone. "But I can assure you, I'm not living my life by a chart and neither should you."

"It's Blakely, not Blake," I snap back. "And I don't live my life by a chart."

He picks up my planner off the coffee table. "Your organizer suggests otherwise. Do you really set aside a half hour every morning to brush, floss, and wear whitening strips? Isn't that an automatic? I mean, except for the whitening part."

"Give me that!" I pull the book out of his grasp and hug it to my chest. "Dental hygiene is extremely important. Your toothbrush probably hasn't seen toothpaste in a week," I say haughtily.

His perfectly straight white teeth blind me as he grins. He could be in a Crest commercial. God, I hate him.

I chew my bottom lip, staring back at him. As much as it pains me to admit this, he's right. Time to change things up.

"You know what? I can live without my planner." I slap

my book open and dramatically tear a page out, crumple it up, and throw it at him. Immature? Yes. Does he deserve it? Most definitely. The paper bounces off his chest onto the couch, and I immediately regret defacing my beloved book.

He gives me a bland look while he takes a drink from his beer bottle. I watch his Adam's apple bob in his throat as the beer travels down. Why do parts of this man, which shouldn't be sexy, turn me on so much? I grind my teeth while he arches an eyebrow. This silent standoff is driving me bananas. I break eye contact and sit primly on the chair, perpendicular to the couch.

"I made you dinner if you want some."

"Thanks, that's really nice of you, but I have plans."

"Oh, of course." *What the hell am I going to do with a huge pot of spaghetti and meatballs?* "I'll just eat it for the next ten days."

He smirks, making me want to throw a meatball at his face instead of paper. I hold out my holy grail to him. "Can you please dispose of this somewhere? If I keep it, I'll never get rid of it."

He leans forward to take the planner back, but I can't let it go. My grip tightens as he pulls.

"Blakely."

"Just...give me a sec." I close my eyes, the buttery-soft leather smooth like a baby's butt under my fingertips. Do I really need to give it up? It's so pretty and organized with neat little columns. I could keep it under my bed and pretend like it's not there...only drag it out for emergencies.

He clears his throat and tugs harder, the leather slipping from my fingers.

"Are you afraid you might forget to apply your Crest Whitening strips at eight thirty a.m.?" He flips open the book to a random page. "Or meet Trish at eight forty-five for your tennis lesson. Who's Trish? She sounds hot." His eyes travel down the page, sparkling when he looks back up at me. "Didn't peg you as the Brazilian wax type. That's—"

"Ugh, never mind, give it back, jerk," I growl, lunging for the book. He quickly moves it out of my reach. I'd have to straddle him on the couch to get it. Nope. Not going to happen in this lifetime.

"I'm just teasing, Smiles. I'll take care of it." He gets up and heads to his room.

"Where are you going?" I sound desperate to my own ears, so I dial it back to a casual nonchalance. "Not that I care, but in case someone calls for you or stops by, I like to be prepared."

"Everyone knows where to find me." He winks before he walks into his room.

Ugh, this man is infuriating! I dig my nails into my palms. "Sounds good!" I say with fake enthusiasm. "I've got lots to do myself."

He pokes his head back out. "Did you make my bed? With military corners?"

"Throwing a blanket over your sheets is not the proper way to make a bed."

"You're like Martha Stewart on crack." He shakes his head, walking back into his room.

"A bed made starts the day," I singsong obnoxiously.

"Is that on your schedule, Mr. Rogers?" He reappears, flipping through my planner, and I cringe. "Jesus Christ, I was kidding, but here it is in the seven-a.m. slot." He looks up at me in wonder. He closes his door, muttering something before I can think of a snappy comeback. Who cares what he thinks? Not me. Nope. This girl is cool as a cucumber. I pick up my wine and gulp it.

I'M CHUGGING STRAIGHT from the bottle, because why the hell not? Life is great. No, scratch that, life is fucking amazing! I need to make a chart of things to do. Right now! I tear down my chore chart and grab a Crayola marker from the set I used earlier, and start scribbling on the back of it.

I need to dance, right this minute! I'm going to put on some music and dance like no one's watching. No one is watching because I'm here all alone. This is the best! Pulling up Spotify, Lizzo's song, "About Damn Time", plays. *Yes, this is my jam.* It's like she wrote this song for me.

I strut around the room while shouting, because honestly, I can't dance or sing. Tripping over the coffee table, I crash down on the couch. Even though Lizzo is singing my song, it's not as fun when you're by yourself.

I pick up my phone and call Junie.

"Blakely, before you say anything, I'm so sorry about Tucker. I had no idea—"

"June-ee, are you there? Dr. Juniper Thorton, it's me, Blakely. Your best friend? I'm hammered!" I hiccup.

"You're what? Where's Tucker? I'm going to murder

him."

"Tuck, Tucker, Tuck-er…he's out. Hot date. I'm all alone. All by my lonesome. All by myself…don't want to be all by myself…anymore…" I belt out Celine Dion into the phone.

"Jesus, you shouldn't be left alone to your own devices, ever. Hey, Blakely? Stop singing for one sec. Blakely Marie!"

"Mother?" *Hiccup.* "Did I call you?"

"It's Junie. Do I need to come up there?"

"Junie! My bestie! You love me, right? You don't find me annoying, do you? Your cousin finds me annoying."

"Of course not. You know I love you." She giggles. "I don't think I've ever been around you when you're drunk. You always stick to your one-glass rule."

"Rules shmools. You'd drink and dance with me if you were here, right?"

"Without a doubt."

"Oh goody! Come up tonight." I take a healthy sip, stretching out on the couch. "Your cousin is a jerk. Jerk with an A."

"Don't you mean jerk with a J?"

"He's an ass-face."

Junie laughs. "Tell me how you really feel. Look, do me a favor. I know he's cute and all, but don't hook up with him. I love him like my brother, but he's a playboy, Blakely. You don't need that in your life right now. In fact, don't hook up with my brother, either."

"I would never. Ever, ever, ever…" *Hiccup.* "EVER hookup with your cousin. He calls me darlin' and thinks my chore chart sucks… Junie, are you there?"

"Yeah, I'm here. You gave him a chore chart?"

"He said no."

"I don't doubt it," she says with a laugh. "Just go with the flow, Blakely. Doctor's orders."

"Go with the flow… I can flow. Like wine."

"Uh-huh, maybe you should drink some water. Flow like water."

"Juniper, you're a buzzkill. Who drinks water?"

"People who want to live…and not have hangovers."

"Hey, how come you never told me you were adopted?"

"I don't know, it never came up. It's complicated."

"I understand complicated. What's that beeping noise? Oh, someone's beeping on the other line. Byeee."

"Don't forget to drink water and take two ibuprofens!" she yells before I disconnect.

"Hello?" I look down at the black screen before realizing the beeping is coming from the kitchen. I pick up the almost-empty wine bottle and drain the last possible drop down my throat. Stumbling to the fridge, I peer inside. "Why are you beeping? Ooh beer!"

I'm not really a beer drinker, but it's all I've got. Even though I got it for Tuck, aka Tucker the Fucker, he's not here to drink it. He's out having a grand ol' time living the life of a womanizing mountain man.

Gloria Gaynor's "I Will Survive" plays on my phone and I belt out the lyrics at the top of my lungs. Chugging the beer, I zigzag over to Tucker's bedroom and lean against the doorjamb. His masculine scent lingers, making me want to roll around on his sheets. I notice a t-shirt thrown casually on his bed. My fingers itch to go over and fold it nicely, or at the very least, throw it in his hamper.

No, it's not my responsibility. He is *not* my responsibility. I shake my head and turn back toward the living room.

I'm always by myself. No one ever wants to be around me because I have too many rules. At least that's what my ex-boyfriend Charles told me. I hiccup on a sob. I'm a lonely loser. Charles, my parents, my business partner...even Tucker the Tease doesn't want me.

Bawling, I realize what a fake I am. I don't want to be perfect anymore. I want to be messy and carefree! Throwing pillows off the couch, I knock a lamp over. The old me would have rushed over and straightened it. Nope, not the new me! I go into the kitchen and take a spoon of spaghetti sauce, flinging it on the floor. Grimacing at the mess, I say to hell with it, splattering more. I yell like I'm Mel Gibson in *Braveheart* leading his men to battle. Yes, this feels so freeing! I run into Tucker's bedroom and rumple his sheets. I throw his laundry all over his room. "Fuck being clean!" I shout to the empty house. "And fuck being perfect! Fuck this chore chart!" I rip the posterboard to pieces. "Freedom!" I battle-cry before I fall face first on his bed and everything goes black.

Chapter 7

The Bet

Tucker

"I'M NOT SURE what to do." I peel the label on my bottle while my cousin Jason wipes the bar down. He's helping my sister out tonight until her new hire can start. The pub is packed because of all the tourists in for the festival this weekend. "I need to crash on your couch tonight."

"Sure man, but it stinks."

"Yeah, I know it's lumpy, but one night won't kill my back."

"No, I mean it literally smells." He wrinkles his nose. "Not sure what happened. Anyway, what did Junie say?" He uncaps four beers for a server.

"Try to get along. Apparently, her friend Blakely hates disorder and nature. Junie's positive she won't last long up here."

"Is she hot?"

I eye him over the bottle. "She's hot, but high maintenance. Definitely uptight."

Jason chuckles. "Uptight?"

"She made a chore chart."

He snorts. "What the fuck is a chore chart?"

"You know, on Tuesdays I clean the bathrooms, on Fridays she empties the dishwasher. She even made a spinner to go with it for 'Silly Sundays', where we have to spin to see what chore we have to do."

"Dude."

"She left a Post-It note on the fridge asking me to wipe off fingerprints."

"I see what you mean."

"Yeah." I take a long pull from my beer. "I have enough on my plate, I don't need to worry about leaving fingerprints on the fridge or a dish in the sink, you know?"

Jason places another beer next to me. "Well, there's your answer. If you want her gone, drive her to the brink of no return."

I smile, but it doesn't sit right in my gut. "How do you propose I do that?"

"Drive her up the wall. Make her hop back in her car and hightail it back to Atlanta." He smirks as he pulls a beer. "You said she's a pushover?"

"I said she's a priss." I tilt my beer bottle back and relish the cool liquid bubbling down my throat, thinking about her full lips, which purse in irritation every time she sees me.

He shrugs. "Do what we used to do to Junie and Whit when we were kids."

"You want me to leave dirt and worms in her bed?" I grin.

"Take her fishing or kayaking…camping if you can stand it. Make it the most miserable time she'll ever experience." He grins at me. "Hang out at the house as much as possible and be a slob. Leave the toilet seat up. Women hate that shit."

"Is that why you're still single?" I smirk.

"Dick."

"The hardest part will be trying to convince her to do those things with me. She can't stand me. I've got annoying the shit out of her down pat."

Jason leans on the bar and laughs. "I think this is the first time I have ever heard those words come out of your mouth." His grin widens. "Hey, Grandpa, Ike, fifty says our boy Tucker gets a home run with the new city girl."

"No way. You should have heard her the other night. She hates him. He won't even make it to first base." Ike eyes me. "Sorry, Tuck."

"I don't bet on losers," Uncle Beauford says grumpily, his eyes never leaving *The Voice* on TV.

"Gee, thanks, Uncle Beau," I mumble, shooting Jason a dirty look when he bursts out laughing.

"I'll take that bet." Whitney flings an arm over my shoulder, startling me. "I believe in your charm, Tucker Greyson." She winks at Jason. "Give me five IPAs, please."

"Ah, hell. Fifty says he can't," Ike grumbles, sliding a fifty toward Jason.

"I'm with Ike." Jason takes out a tip jar and throws another fifty along with Ike's in the pot.

"Two minutes ago, you thought I could," I say incredulously.

"Ike changed my mind." He smirks.

"Well, I say he can." Whitney hands Jason a fifty.

I shake my head. "All of you are going to lose because

nothing's going to happen." Three more parties of people walk in. "Dude, I can't let you get swallowed up back there. I'm helping out."

"Thanks man, tonight is nuts." Jason wipes his brow as I get off my stool and settle in behind the bar.

I WALK INTO the house the next morning with Hershel and stop short. The kitchen looks like a crime scene and the living room looks like it was tossed. "What the fuck happened in here?" *Shit, were we robbed?* "Blakely? Are you home? Blakely!"

I hear a groan coming from the direction of my bedroom. I rush in there, scared she might be seriously hurt. Fuck, I knew I shouldn't have slept on Jason's couch last night. Not only did it smell like stale sweat socks and was lumpy as hell, but Junie would kill me if anything happened to her.

"Blake, are you okay?"

Picking up a beer bottle off my dresser, I look over to find her curled up on my bed covered in tissues. She sits up slowly, moaning. She's got green marker all over her face from where she fell asleep on her chore-chart spinner. Tissues are stuck in her hair and her eyes are puffy. I crouch in front of her. "Blake, honey, are you okay?" I try to wipe the grin off my face, but I can't.

"No," she whimpers.

I get up and grab a bottle of water and ibuprofen from the kitchen. "Here, take this. It will make you feel better."

She downs the medicine and drinks half the bottle. I arch an eyebrow and pull a tissue out of her hair. "I see you had a party last night."

"Yup, 'the new me party'," she moans and lays back down, closing her eyes.

"The new you?"

"Can you please stop yelling?"

"I'm not." I chuckle. I lean down and pick up a torn piece of her chore chart. Flipping it over, I see the word 'dance'. "What's dance?"

"Something I apparently suck at, that's what."

"Wanna talk about it?"

"No."

"Can you tell me why the house looks like a bomb went off in it and why you're in my bed?"

"You didn't come home last night," she whispers, pulling a piece of tissue over her eyes. For some inane reason, it tugs at my heart. I should be furious she trashed my house, but I can't find it in me.

"Did you have people over?"

"No. Pathetic, right?" she moans. "Party for one."

Relief courses through me. I'm not big on people I don't know showing up to my home.

"Well, I'd be super impressed if you managed to have a party on your second night in town." I gently bring a blanket over her. "Why all the tissues?"

"I got cold."

"You realize there was a throw blanket right next to

you?" Biting down on my lip to keep from laughing, I pluck the tissues off the bed. Junie had told me she was working through some stuff and now I feel bad for leaving her alone last night. *She's not your responsibility.* "I'm going to make you some coffee. I'll be right back."

"Okay." Her voice wavers as she pulls the blanket to her chin. I take one last look at her vulnerable state before I head into the kitchen. I look around at the chaos and sigh. She took being 'messy' to a whole new level. Spaghetti sauce is splattered all over the stove, walls, and floor, which Hershel is currently licking. Noodles crunch under my boots as I walk around the kitchen. Bits of posterboard stick to every surface. I don't have time to clean this up because I have to get down to the kayak competition early. My company, Greyson Builders, is the main sponsor.

She gingerly sits up when I reappear back into the bedroom with coffee. Her skin is pale and her hair is a tangled mess. "You know, when I said I didn't want a chore chart, I didn't mean for you to go apeshit crazy." I smile, handing her the steaming mug.

She grimaces, her cheeks staining pink. "I... Sorry. I got a little carried away."

I fold my arms over my chest, kicking myself for what I'm about to do. "You should come down to the kayak festival today. It's being held at the Greyson Gap Outpost Whitewater Center about ten minutes down the road."

"Thanks for the offer, but I'm not sure I'm in the best shape right now to make a public appearance. Besides, I have to clean up after my night of drunken debauchery."

I raise an eyebrow. "How often have you had a night of

'drunken debauchery'?"

She pulls the blanket over her head. "Never."

"That's what I figured." I pat her leg. "Come down to the festival when you feel like you're human again. Have a beer with the locals."

She groans through the blanket. "I'm never drinking again. *Ever.*"

I chuckle. "That's what they all say. I'll leave the directions and my phone number on the counter." I get up to leave.

She pulls the blanket down. "Tucker?"

I look over my shoulder at her. "Yeah?"

"Why are you being so nice to me? I destroyed your house."

I rub my jaw. Why *am* I being nice to her? I'm not sure and I sure as hell don't have time to think about it right now, so I put on my good-ol'-boy charm, which I've noticed makes her eye twitch. "Darlin', you're welcome to throw a party anytime. But next time, invite me." I wink at her before I turn back around, dropping my smile, and stride out.

Chapter 8

Barracuda Bhodi

Blakely

SWIPING LIP BALM across my lips, I grab a book off of Junie's shelf and head downstairs. I haven't seen Tucker in a few days, but I know he's slept here because the telltale signs of a roommate who doesn't clean up after himself are evidenced in every room. I pass by his open door, peeking in. His bed is unmade and he has clothes strewn across the floor. I wrinkle my nose in disgust. I haven't completely given up my orderly ways, but I'm consciously attempting to let things go.

The old me would have picked up the clothes and neatly folded them. The new me? Well, the new me is still repulsed by his slovenliness, so I shut his door and move into the living room where I spy his dirt-encrusted cowboy boots left haphazardly lying about. Someone could trip on them, *like me.* A cake of mud falls off one heel as I pick the boots up by my thumb and forefinger. They smell like manure. What the hell does he do during the day?

Plugging my nose, I quickly shuck them out the back door before sweeping up the mud. I write him a quick Post-It note explaining he left his dirty boots in the living room, *again*, and stick it on his bedroom door. I quickly scribble out another note asking him if he's having a hard time finding the dishwasher, since his cup never makes it in there, with an arrow pointing toward the dishwasher. I post a sticky note to the dishwasher and label it in case he doesn't know what it is.

I made it down to the kayak festival this past weekend, but it was so crowded and I was so hungover it wasn't worth sticking around for. I ended up walking into town, stopping at the cutest little stationery and gift shop owned by an interesting woman named Etta Bird. She was quite chatty while I perused her shop. She was born and raised in Greyson Gap and knows everyone and everything. If I needed information, Etta was the woman to get it from, for a small monetary fee, of course. I told her I'd keep that in mind. She had the most beautiful watercolor stationery of foxes and birds from England, so I bought two boxes. I also bought a journal by the same artist, following Dr. Cooper's advice. Etta asked me what I was going to write about, but I just shrugged and told her, "Life." She cackled and gave me another journal on the house. Even Etta Bird sensed I'm a complete mess.

New journal in hand, I step out onto the back porch and sit down in a lounge chair. Opening the cover, I write my name neatly in the corner. My heart stutters when I open the first page. It's blank, fresh, and starchy white. This is not the journal I looked at in the shop. That one had lined paper. Running my hand over the smooth white paper, it ominously stares back at me, causing my anxiety to ratchet up a notch. What if I write crooked? That would drive me bananas.

I could go back and exchange the journal even though I wrote my name on it, or I could put on my big-girl pants and make this work. Getting up I hunt down a pencil in a kitchen drawer. I use my other book to carefully draw straight lines across the page. Every day I'll have to draw lines before I write. No biggie. Proud of my handiwork, I sit back down outside and stare at the lines on the page. *What the hell should I write about?* Not wanting to mess up my first assignment, I pick up my phone and type *how to journal* in the search engine. A bunch of titles pop up: *How to journal like a pro; How to journal your feelings; How to write a self-improvement journal*...bingo!

First thing on the list: *Write down your goals, your problems, your stresses, what's the best thing that happened to you that day, and one thing you're grateful for.* I think of my relationship with my business partner, Liz, and my parents. Cringing, I realize I could easily write an entire book on both within an hour. Maybe I'll start with a simple entry once a day. No need to dive right into the hard stuff my first time journaling, right? Dr. Cooper wants this journal needs to be about my time in Greyson Gap and the people I get to know here.

Goal: Dr. Cooper suggested I make Tucker my friend.

Problem: I don't like him.

Stress: Having to pretend to like him to make him my friend so I can meet my goal.

What's the best thing that happened today: *Not talking to Tucker.*

What I am grateful for: He's been MIA.

I sign my name and date it. Sure, there's room for improvement, but it's a good start. I close the book and glance over at the porch to my left. A pair of bright sunflower-yellow Crocs sit on the railing drying in the sun. Beyond the Crocs, a shirtless man stands, stretching his arms up, groaning loudly. I haven't seen him before. The house seemed unoccupied this weekend. Apparently not anymore. He looks over at me and gives me a sheepish grin.

"Sup." He lifts his chin, acknowledging my presence.

"Uh, hello."

"Just got here. Haven't seen you before." He flexes his biceps and walks over to the railing.

"Um, yes, I arrived a couple days ago. I'm visiting for the summer. Do you live there?" Please God, don't let him be a permanent resident. Something about him screams annoying. Maybe it's the way his eyes keep drifting to my boobs.

He gives me a cheesy smile. "Yep, I bought this place last week. I can't wait to huck the falls later and get a gnar rapid…maybe make a run on a stout later."

"Uh-huh." I nod. I have no idea what the hell he's talking about. "That's nice."

"I'm what you call a weekend warrior, but decided to bite the bullet and spend more time up here in the summer. Now that I've met my neighbor, it was an excellent decision on my part." He waggles his eyebrows.

Ew, gross. Here's to hoping he's referring to the old guy living on the other side of him. I feel like I need to spray Lysol in the air between us. "Weekend warrior?"

"I usually head back to Atlanta for work during the week, but now I'm working remotely."

"Hmm, lucky me," I murmur. This guy makes Tucker look like Prince Charming. "What do you do?"

"I'm a numbers cruncher for a firm hired by Fleet's Sporting Goods. Pretty big deal. You heard of it?"

"Fleets? Uh, yeah, I think everyone who lives in the United States has." This guy is so full of himself. That's like asking if I've heard of Walmart.

"You on Viphut?"

"The dating app?" I wrinkle my nose in disgust and bark out a laugh. "Ah, no." Viphut is an acronym for Very Important People Hooking Up Together. I'd jump off a cliff before joining that app.

"Don't knock it 'til you try it." He winks. "Name's Bhodi Mills. My friends call me the Barracuda."

"Blakely." I frown, upset I had to divulge that precious piece of info. He's named after a fish?

He raps twice on the railing with his knuckle. "See you soon, Blake...Lee."

I smile and wave. "Not if I can help it," I breathe out, skipping down the steps of the porch and out of Bhodi's line of sight.

I take a walk, marveling at the peaceful sounds of the river rushing by, the leaves rustling in the wind, and the birds singing in the trees. It's so different from the blaring horns and cement sidewalks in the city. Not being on a schedule has been difficult for my brain to get used to. There's only so much I can clean at the house. I need a hobby like flower arranging. I've always wanted to take a course, but never found the time to do it. I have an eye for color and have rearranged plenty of centerpieces which weren't up to my standards for our events. Perhaps I can swing by the bookstore and see if they have flower-arranging books I'll like. Maybe check out the local floral shop.

Laughter floats up from the river, interrupting my thoughts. Tucker is on the river bank with Hershel teaching a little boy how to fish. I wonder who the boy is and what he means to Tucker. Is it weird I'm sharing a house with this guy and I know absolutely nothing about him? I duck behind a tree and peek my head around so I can watch them without being seen. He helps the little boy cast his fishing line out into the water and the boy squeals and claps his hands until Tucker hands him back the rod. It's the cutest thing I've ever witnessed.

A woman laughs as Hershel drops a slobbery ball at the boy's feet. She's sitting on a rock on the shore taking pictures of them, her strawberry-blonde hair shining in the midday sun. Her smile is wide and full of affection for the two playing in the water. I was so focused on Tucker, I didn't even notice her sitting there. Is he *married*? He doesn't wear a ring, but he's obviously familiar with this woman. He looks over at her and smiles, saying something I can't hear from my distance. This must be who he's been spending his nights with. I should be elated Tucker has a girlfriend, or wife, or whatever the hell she is, but I'm not. I'm...surprised, and maybe a tinge jealous? That's ludicrous. I don't even like him. Clearly, I'm not going to get any information from him, so I'll have to head to the woman who can tell me everything: Etta Bird.

Chapter 9

Etta Bird

Blakely

THE SHOP DOOR jingles as I step into the cool air-conditioned space. The cream walls and furniture showcase the beautiful stationery and other trinkets Etta has. An elegant diffuser with wood sticks holds court in the middle of the shop on a glass table. The shop smells like roses and rainwater. It's quiet in here except for a faint symphony playing in the background. I feel like I'm in an elegant library where you get reprimanded with raised eyebrows if you speak too loudly. It's exactly my type of place. It has order and rules, and if you don't like them, you can get the hell out. At least that's what Etta told me the first time I walked in. She's not too fond of tourists.

Etta is not your typical grandmotherly type. She's sharp as a tack with snow-white wavy hair cut to her chin in a stylish bob. Her hawk-like eyes track customers around the room with her cheetah-print readers perched on her hooked nose. She knows everything that goes on in the store, even when she's busy helping another customer.

She wears colorful capelets with chunky gemstone necklaces, bangles on her wrists which jingle when she walks. Silver rings adorn several fingers while she flutters about pointing out different styles of stationery to her customers. Her purple suede flats are sensible, yet fashionable, and her gypsy skirt screams boho hippy. In other words, Etta Bird is a touch unconventional.

"I'll be with you in a moment, dear." Her crisp, clear voice floats over to me. I turn and smile, touching a silk hand-painted scarf I was eyeing the other day. It's beautiful, but not something I'd ever buy for myself.

"No problem, Etta. I'm in no hurry."

"I suspected as much." Etta eyes me over her readers, making me feel slightly embarrassed she instinctively knows I'm a lonely loser. I pick up a candle and smell it while she wraps up her sale.

"Well, I hope you haven't filled up your two journals already." She waves me over like she's the Queen holding court after the other customer leaves.

"No, I'm here on a different matter." I smile, nervously wiping my hands on my shorts. I'm the lowly peasant begging her for a favor. "I'm wondering if you could give me some information."

"Information on what?" She side-eyes me while she folds the tissue paper back in the drawer.

"Information on who, not what," I hedge.

"Ah, I see. It's going to cost you."

Count on Etta to get straight to business. "Yes, of course. How much?"

She eyes me up and down. "I need someone to man the store a few days in the mornings."

I stumble on the plush carpet. "Etta, I'm not looking for a job."

"Hmm, I need help and you need information."

"Well, yes, but…I'm only here for a few months."

"Yes, dear, you've told me already," she says blithely, straightening the pens and stapler on her countertop.

"I think I'd rather pay you outright."

"No, dear, that's not the deal I'm offering."

Who doesn't take cash outright? I nibble on my thumbnail. The anxiety of things not going exactly as planned causes my heart rate to gallop. Do I really need information on Tucker that badly? The answer is no, but I am very curious…and bored. Let's face it, I'm extremely bored. Working in the mornings at this adorable store could break up the monotony. I really would like to reorganize her jewelry collection, and the candles could be set up differently. Etta crosses the room, her bangles jingling as she reaches for the scarf I was admiring earlier.

She walks over to me and wraps it around my neck, tying it in a loose knot, fiddling with the edges. "It suits you."

"It does?" I touch the silky material, turning to look in the mirror hanging on the wall. It's bright with bold flowers, something I would never pick for myself, but it is beautiful. The pinks brighten my skin tone and bring out the rosy hue of my cheeks and lips. "It's so pretty."

"Do we have a deal?" Etta must have cast a spell on me because before I can stop myself, I nod yes. "Now, don't expect a fancy salary or health benefits, but I pay fair enough and you get forty percent off anything in the store. The scarf is a gift from me. Now tell me what's so important, you took a job at a stationery store out of desperation."

"Oh, I didn't... I'm not desperate..." The words die on my tongue as she raises a steely-gray eyebrow. "Right. So, what's Tucker...oh gosh, this is embarrassing. I'm living with the man and don't even know his last name."

"Tucker Greyson? You *do* work your way around town fast." She arches a brow. "What would you like to know, dear?"

"Well, what's his story? I saw him down by the river with a little boy and a redheaded woman I've never seen before."

She walks past me and flips the sign on the door to closed. "Come on back where we won't be interrupted by pesky tourists wanting to use the bathroom."

I follow Etta to the back-office storage room and sit across from her at a little desk. "Would you like something to drink?"

"No, I'm fine, thank you."

Etta gathers her skirts and plunks down into her seat. "So, Tucker Greyson's family has been here for generations. Everyone knows the Greysons. Tucker was a baseball sensation. That boy could throw a ball faster than wind in a hurricane. He made it to the majors, which is difficult to do, especially for a small-town North Carolina mountain boy. He was plucked up right out of college. Played for the Braves for a few years and then got traded to the Astros." She waves a hand in the air, her bangles jingling. "He was magical out on the field, but ended up tearing his rotator cuff. Surgery could have gotten him back on the field, but his father was ill and his girlfriend was pregnant. He came back home to marry his girl, and take over the family business so that it wasn't a stress on his dad. Bless his heart."

"Oh, wow, I didn't know any of this."

Etta gives me a withering glare. "The mail lady could have told you this story. It's common knowledge."

I nod and drum my fingers on the table. "So…he's married?"

"No." She abruptly gets up from the table.

"Well, what happened?" I follow her back out into the shop and watch her switch the sign to open.

"I think that's something you need to ask Tucker Greyson, dear."

"But I came to you! I'm now working for you, for information I could have gotten at the local Gas N Go!"

"Well, maybe you should have gotten a job there, although you don't strike me as the beer-guzzling type. See you next week, dear."

Oh, this woman!

"That's it?" I fling my arms out in exasperation.

"That's it." She sashays by me, nose in the air. Her skirts make a swishing noise, leaving a rose fragrance in their wake.

"But…but…"

Etta turns and looks at me pointedly. "You can't wake a person who is pretending to be asleep, Blakely." She turns back around, dismissing me. *What the hell does that even mean?* As I reach for the door, she shouts, "Oh, and Blakely? Don't be tardy. I can't stand tardiness."

BY THE TIME I make it back to the house, I'm mentally exhausted from my go-around with Etta. I also stopped by the bookstore and picked up a book on flower arrangements, a cookbook, and some new self-help books. Let's face it, I need all the help I can get.

The sweetest woman named Laura Twinkle recommended the self-help books. Just hearing her name makes me smile. She moved here two years ago after an awful divorce and bought the bookshop. We chatted for about an hour. She was thrilled to meet another non-local and told me to stop by anytime. My first real friend in Greyson Gap and I'm finally feeling like the pieces are falling into place.

I trudge up the front steps and notice the bright yellow Crocs sitting on my new neighbor's front porch.

"Hi, neighbor!" Bhodi shouts, causing me to trip over the step and land hard on my knee, my bag of books spilling out on the porch. *Ow, motherfucker.* "Ooh, rough fall. Need me to look at it?"

"At my knee? No, I'm good, thanks." I gingerly pick myself and the books up. How I missed him stretching on his front porch boggles my mind because he's wearing a tight neon-green shirt, black biker shorts, and biker shoes. I don't want to talk to him again, but ingrained politeness makes me pause. "Going for a ride?"

"Yeah, thought I'd tear it up on the trails. Maybe when I get back you could join me for a soak in the hot tub? I've got one out back."

I look Bhodi over from head to toe. Physically, he's an attractive man with nice wavy brown hair and an impressive upper body, but something about him screams poser to me.

He has been nice, if not a little annoying, so I don't want to be rude. "Maybe another time, thanks."

"Raincheck, gotcha." He shoots the gun finger at me with a cheesy smile. I grimace, turning away from him. There will be no rain or checks with Bhodi…ever.

"Have a nice ride."

Hershel mows me down when I open the front door and drop my purse down next to a pair of muddy boots. I limp toward the kitchen. Great, my roomie is home.

Chapter 10

Roll Tide

Tucker

BLAKELY ENTERS THE kitchen, hobbling, with Hershel hot on her heels. She throws a bag of books on the island and turns to me with a frown marring her pretty face. I eye her over my iced tea bottle, Jason's words running through my head. The easiest way to get her to hightail it back to Atlanta is to make her miserable.

"What's up with you? Why are you limping?"

"So, is this how it's going to be? You think you can waltz in here when it pleases you and rummage through the fridge and drink my beverages?"

I smile, taking another drink, the cool crisp liquid sliding down my throat. Her eyes narrow. "I bought this on my way home."

"Pfft, on your way home from fishing down at the river?"

I arch an eyebrow. "Keeping tabs on me, Smiles?"

"What? No!" Her eyes dart nervously around the family room before they land on my gear out back. "Your fishing gear is thrown haphazardly all over the deck."

I look out the French doors to the gear in question,

which is neatly stacked in the corner. "Right, I'll make sure I get it cleaned up right away." Taking another swig of my ice-cold tea, I push off the counter and walk over to her. Her muscles tense when I place my hands lightly on her shoulders. I dip my head, waiting for her eyes to lock onto mine. "Relax. You know what we need to do?"

She swallows, her large brown eyes meeting mine. "No, what?"

The golden flecks in her irises catch in the afternoon light, completely hypnotizing me as her pupils dilate. She smells like fresh laundry and meadow flowers. I have the sudden urge to skim my nose along her neck and bite her earlobe. Toying with her until she pants with need. I squeeze her arms and quickly release her before I act out the crazy fantasy I just played in my head. *Stay the course, Tucker. You don't want or need a sexy new roommate.*

"We should go fishing."

"Fishing? I don't want to go fishing."

"Come on, Smiles, it will help you relax. You seem really tense and…"

"And?"

"Uptight."

She huffs, crossing her arms over her chest. "I am *not* uptight."

"You're strung tighter than a violin. Come on, roomie, we'll take the boat out and get to know one another. Maybe catch some dinner if we're lucky."

"That sounds gross. Lake fish?"

"Some of the best." I lean back against the counter and fold my arms over my chest. "What else are you going to do?"

"I have things…"

"What things? Did you forget to clean your toothbrush with your UV light case?"

"Have you been snooping in my bathroom?" she asks incredulously.

"No, Smiles, it was a lucky guess." I chuckle. "Let's go."

"Do I have a choice?" She chews on her bottom lip and it makes me want to tug on it with my teeth. I rub my jaw.

"You always have a choice. Come fishing with me," I say gruffly. Now it's not just about annoying her to death. Some small corner of my ego might crumple if she doesn't want to go with me. I shake my head, dismissing that crazy thought. "Come on, Hershel." I whistle loudly, causing Blakely to jump. "Load 'em up!"

"Are you talking to me or the dog?" Blakely's knuckles are white from where she clutches the island.

"Well, Hershel can't pick up the fishing poles. He's a dog." I flash her a smile, turning to go put on my boots. "Meet you out by the truck."

"But, I…what…ugh! Tucker, what do I grab? I don't even know how to fish! I'm tired and I need sunscreen. Tucker, stop ignoring me!"

Hershel follows me out the front door and I load him into the back of the truck. I poke my tongue in my cheek to keep from laughing while she trudges around from the back, trying to wrangle two fishing poles and the yellow tackle box I had sitting with them.

"Are you going to help or just stand there like a jackass ogling me?"

"You're doing great. You can put them in the bed of the truck." I follow her around to the back. "Here, let me get the tailgate for you."

"Gee, how kind of you," she grumbles, throwing the gear in the back.

"Hey, careful. Those rods aren't cheap."

She mutters an expletive as she trudges to the front of the truck. I step around to help her up into the passenger side, much to her dismay.

"I've got it," she bites out irritably while I shove her butt with one hand, causing her to pitch forward into the seat.

"Ooh, sorry about that." I make sure her legs are in before I slam the door on her protest.

"Don't you have to work tonight?" she huffs, buckling her seat belt. I maneuver the truck onto the highway, purposefully ignoring her. She wrinkles her nose. "What is that awful smell?"

She looks at me and I grin. "That, Smiles, would be Hershel."

She looks over her shoulder into the second row of seats, cringing when Hershel leans toward her, panting with drool dripping down. "Ugh, he needs a mint. Don't you brush his teeth? Oh wait, I forgot, you're not into dental hygiene."

"I give him dental bones, and for your information, I floss daily."

"Where are we going, anyway?"

"Almost there. My fishing boat is docked at an inlet down this road."

We exit the highway and drive a mile to a little gravel road which opens up onto Meadow Lake, a large beautiful blue lake filled with walleye, bass, muskie, and pike. The late-afternoon sun glints off the ripples in the water and I sigh in contentment. I park at the dock my boat is tied up to.

"Aren't you afraid someone will steal your boat?" Blakely asks, stretching. A sliver of tanned skin peeks from under her shirt, making my stomach dip.

"It's not Atlanta. Besides, everyone knows this is my boat. They wouldn't mess with it."

"What are you, the town mayor or something?"

"Or something," I mumble, reaching for a can of bug repellent. "Here, you might want to put this on."

"Ew, no thanks. Do you know how many chemicals are in that thing? Many which could cause cancer. I should have brought my citronella spray."

"What are you talking about? Look, lemon eucalyptus is the main ingredient. It's not like it has Deet in it."

"No, thank you."

"Suit yourself." I shrug and throw the canister back in my console. I grab the tackle box and poles and lead her down to the boat. Hershel almost knocks her over to get on the boat first. I give her my hand, which she gingerly takes, stepping down into the fishing boat. "Have you ever been on a boat before?"

"I've been on cruise ships and sailing boats, but not a dinghy." She stands primly in the middle of the boat, looking around like it's a gas station bathroom.

I nearly choke. "This is *not* a dinghy, Blakely. This is the top-of-the-line Bass Cat Puma FTD fishing boat. Sit down in the chair and put this on." She doesn't move. She's looking at the chair as if it has fish slime all over it. "It's a boat, Blake. You won't catch a disease from it." Without argument she puts on the life vest I'm holding for her.

"It smells like fish," she says, wrinkling her nose.

"You're very observant," I mumble, sliding one on myself while cursing Jason for his stupid plan. I'm not sure who's being tortured more…her or me. The wind whips her long ponytail across her back. She sits ramrod straight in her seat, her hands folded in her lap, careful not to touch anything. I chuckle to myself, because I know her type so well. I met plenty of uptight, pretentious women during my baseball career.

The lake is practically deserted this afternoon, so we have our pick of spots. I get the tackle box out and place a worm on my hook before reaching over and handing her a live worm. She looks at my outstretched hand like I'm handing her a snake.

"What do you want me to do with that?"

"Put your hook into it."

"What? No, no way. Why can't I have one of those pretty feather thingies?" She points to a lure in my box.

"Those feather thingies are for a different type of fish that's not in this lake. You'll get a good one with this worm." I drop the worm in her lap and she shrieks, standing up and shimmying it off. Hershel jumps up and down, barking. "Jesus Christ, Blake, sit down or you'll fall into the damn lake. It's a worm, for God's sake!"

"Well, you didn't have to dump it in my lap, asshole! I'm afraid of worms!"

"Who the fuck is afraid of worms?" I bite out, completely irritated with her. "Spiders, snakes, yeah I get that…but a fucking worm that can't see or bite? Jesus, even the four-year-old I was teaching today could handle a worm."

"Well, some people don't enjoy having worms thrown at them." She sits down on another seat and brushes off her thighs. I grab the worm and shove it onto the hook and then cast the line into the water. "Just hold this." I peel my life jacket and t-shirt off before casting my own line.

"Why did you take off your life jacket and shirt? Don't you need to keep those on?"

"No, it's hot. If you have a problem with it, then swim back to shore."

"Gladly. I don't even want to be here right now," she grumbles, looking out at the lake.

"Fine."

"Good." She takes off her life jacket and throws it down. I make a silent vow not to save her if she falls in. I sit down in the chair across from her and stare off in the opposite direction. I could sit and wait all day long, but not this one across from me. She has the patience of a squirrel. She taps her foot against the ledge, her chair squeaking while she swivels around. Sighing loudly, she opens a bottle of water.

I'm hoping this little fishing expedition will make her go running for the hills and I can have my house back without little Post-It notes tacked up on every surface, reminding me to clean my boots off or to wipe up Hershel's drool. I also won't have to watch her do yoga in those skintight leggings she wears. I have so much on my plate, the last thing I need is a distraction like Blakely Mayfield.

She slaps her skin, and I smile. Serves her right. Her chair squeaks.

"Is this it?" she asks, clearly unimpressed with this outing. "When do they bite?"

"This is it. Sit and wait until they bite."

"This is so boring." She sighs loudly, slapping her arm again.

"It's called patience, which you are severely lacking."

"I have patience. Just not with jerks like…"

"You gonna finish that sentence, Smiles?"

"No." *Slap*. "Damn mosquitos. So, you're a bartender at night and teach kids how to fish during the day?"

"No, I don't tend bar. I was helping my sister Whitney the night you came in. She owns the pub. I own a construction business with my cousin Jason. Today, I was helping a friend of mine."

"Your ex-girlfriend?"

I look at her over my shoulder, but her back is still to me while she plays with the reel. "Where did you hear that?"

"Everyone knows your story, Tucker Greyson."

I chuckle without humor. "Please indulge me with your version, because there are so many."

She peers over her shoulder. "I heard she was your ex-girlfriend and you have a baby together."

"Ah, I see." I turn around, fiddling with my line.

"Well?" Her chair creaks. My muscles bunch, feeling her gaze on my back.

"Well what, Blakely?"

"Is it true?"

"What do you care?"

She huffs in annoyance, "I don't." *Slap*.

"Good."

The silence stretches between us before her chair squeaks again. "God, you're so irritating!" she cries out, causing Hershel to raise his head and thump his tail. "Why are you so stubborn and annoying? I'm trying to get to know you and you're being rude about it."

I turn in my chair, exasperated with her. "Town gossip isn't the way to get to know someone. If you have a question about me, then ask, but don't assume everything you hear around town is the truth."

"I'm trying to ask you questions, but you're being evasive!" *Slap.*

This was a bad idea taking her out in the middle of a lake because I can't escape her prying questions. I don't want her to get to know me. I want to be left alone by this whole damn town. Tired, I rub my hand across my jaw. "What do you want to know?"

"Is the woman I saw you with down at the river today your girlfriend?"

I look up at her, surprised. "So, you were spying on me?"

"Yes. I mean no!" Her cheeks bloom a pretty pink. "Accidentally. I was on a walk and saw you."

"Yes, Annie was with me, but she's not my girlfriend."

"Is the little boy your son?" she asks so quietly I can barely hear her.

"No, he's not mine. I don't have any kids."

I'm suddenly angry at Blakely, at the town…at myself. It seems no matter where I go, my past smacks me in the face at every turn. I may be loved by the town because of my family roots and ability to play baseball, but small towns love gossip and I can't seem to shake mine.

Poor Tucker Greyson. He was a superstar until he had to come home because his daddy was sick and his girlfriend was pregnant. Poor Tucker Greyson. He gave up everything and the baby isn't even his. Poor Tucker Greyson, with his movie-star looks and charming personality, he lives like a monk up on his grandaddy's ranch. It's pitiful he can't find someone to settle down with. *Poor Tucker Greyson just wants to be left alone in peace.*

Sometimes I wish I could start over somewhere new where no one knew anything about my past.

"Oh…oh! Tucker, my line is tugging!"

I set my pole in the holder and go to help her. "Stay in your chair. Don't reel it in too fast." I lean over her and still her hand, winding the line back in with mine. "Easy, Blake, nice and easy, or you'll break the line."

Her eyes are bright with excitement, her teeth tugging on her bottom lip in concentration. Anger melts into lust, making me want to cut the line, pick her up in my arms, and devour those plump lips. *Damn, now is not the time to be lusting after Martha Stewart, you idiot. Keep your head in the game.*

She reels the fish in and it's small, but she doesn't care. "I did it! I caught a fish! This is so empowering!" The fish flops on the bottom of the boat.

I crouch down and smile up at her. "You still have to take it off the hook."

"What? Oh no, I can't. They're slimy and scaly and the one eye…ugh." She shivers.

"Blake, look. Just hold it like this." I hold the fish and grab her hand, wrapping it around the fish.

"Oh god, oh gross. I can't." She makes gagging noises as she looks away.

I chuckle. "How are you going to unhook it if you're not looking at it?"

She peels one eye open and Hershel, who has been patiently waiting on the other side of her, licks her face. "Ugh, god, I'm surrounded!" she cries out, making me laugh again.

"Watch me," I command, and her beautiful brown eyes immediately find mine. They're mesmerizing as I lose myself in their golden pools. I feel myself shifting my balance, leaning in to her. Her lips part, pupils dilating. Just one kiss. What's the harm in that?

No, Tucker, she annoys you. And kissing her would lead to liking her. And if you like her, you'll let her stay in the house because you'll want to be around her more. Liking her would lead to more than kissing. It would lead to feelings, and having feelings for Blakely Mayfield would be a monumental mistake. I shake my head, clearing the barrage of thoughts and quickly unhook the fish, throwing it back in the water.

"Wait, I thought he was dinner!" She watches the fish swim down in the murky water. "I didn't even get a picture with him."

"Blakely, the fish was four inches long. It wouldn't have been enough to feed Hershel." Hershel barks on cue and I ruffle his head. I look over at her and see welts rising on her skin. "I think we've had enough fishing for the day." Feeling guilty I didn't insist on the bug spray, I hand her a tube of cortisone cream before reeling in my line and stowing away the poles. I throw the boat in drive and head back to the dock.

We get to the truck and I load everything into the back while Blakely gets Hershel in the cab.

"Hey, Tucker, I'm sorry about earlier. It was really rude of me to ask you all those questions. I shouldn't have pried. I'm…I'm really sorry if I upset you."

I start the truck. "It's okay. I said you could ask me anything."

"Do you miss it?"

"Miss what?"

"Baseball."

I raise an eyebrow. "Have you been asking around town about me, Blakely May?"

"Ugh, please don't call me that." She turns the air vent in her direction. "I may have asked a question, which led to another. I had to make sure I wasn't living with a serial killer."

I put the truck in drive and decide if she's going to ask about me, it's best to hear it *from* me.

"I miss the competition, my teammates, the fans, the smells… I miss the game. But I don't miss the travel or the politics."

"Why'd you quit? I mean, I know you were injured, but it could have been fixed with surgery."

"I didn't quit, I retired."

"Seems kind of the same," she murmurs, looking out her window.

"Hmm, some might see it that way. I lived and breathed baseball since I was a kid. It was all I had, and I was good. I'm not saying that to be egotistical, it's just a fact. Then my dad got sick and I had to choose between my dream and my family." I shrug. "It was the cards I was dealt."

"I'm not sure I could have thrown away my dream."

"Have you ever played poker?"

She looks over at me and huffs out a laugh. "No, I've never played."

"So, in poker, you're dealt two cards to start. Sometimes you get crap cards like a two and a three and you throw your hand away and wait for the next game. Sometimes you get two aces and you know you've hit the jackpot." I look over at her to see if she's following. "Sometimes you gamble on mediocre cards and you lose, sometimes you bluff and win. That was baseball for me. I won a little, I lost a little, and I got out of the game when I knew it was time to fold. Family will always come first for me."

"I wish I had that foresight and had family that supported me."

"What is it you do?"

"I'm a...*was* an event planner."

I bark out a laugh. "That's so perfect for you."

She smiles. "You think so? I'm not so sure anymore."

I cock a grin. "I know so."

"My partner disagrees."

"Why, what happened?"

She blows out a breath while she scratches a mosquito bite. "I screwed up."

"Everyone makes mistakes, Blakely." I smile, thinking she's probably blowing it out of proportion. She runs her finger along the leather seat, hesitating.

"Everything that could go wrong went wrong. It was a luncheon for a senator campaigning in Atlanta. A fundraising event for her election and we were psyched we won the bid for it. We had celebrities, local women-in-business groups, campaign donators, the media…you get the picture. It was a big deal for our little boutique company. The day was unusually hot and humid, but we had already planned a tea in the botanical gardens. I had everything planned to a T. I knew this woman's likes and dislikes inside and out. Nothing was going to go wrong. I insisted on having crab tarts and cucumber watercress sandwiches for hors d'oeuvres because they were the senator's favorite. An hour into it, several guests started rushing to the designer bathrooms we had brought onsite."

"Oh no, I saw this on the news." I look over at her and she winces. She's shaking, so I grab her hand and squeeze it. "Hey, it's okay."

"Every single person at the two-hundred-person party got food poisoning from spoiled mayonnaise. People were vomiting and passing out left and right. We had to have ambulances come…and, of course, it made local and national news."

"I bet it was devastating."

"Devastating doesn't even begin to describe it. I don't know if you've noticed, but I'm a little Type A."

My mouth twists into a wry grin. "You? Doesn't everyone make chore charts for fun?"

She smiles ruefully. "Ha, ha. Anyway, the party sent me into a tailspin. I was so humiliated I failed, but also embarrassed I let my business partner down. I thrive on detail and getting everything as perfect as it can be. My therapist thought it would be a good idea to go on a sabbatical, to take some time to reevaluate. My partner, Liz, encouraged it, saying she needed time to salvage the business. Which was her polite way of telling me to get out of her hair. Junie gave me her keys and, now I'm here." She blows out a deep breath. "God, I can't believe I told you all of that."

"You couldn't have predicted food poisoning." I squeeze her hand. "You realize that, right? It wasn't your fault."

"I'm trying to."

"Do you miss it?"

She takes her hand from mine and puts it in her lap, looking out the window while we speed down the highway. "It's my job to predict what could go wrong. I miss…" She falls quiet, so I chance a glance. She looks completely lost. "Actually, I don't," she whispers. "I thought I did, but I don't. I got dealt a shit hand, but I didn't fold. I stayed in the game and lost everything."

"I'm sorry that happened to you." I pull into our driveway and look over at her. She scratches another bite on her neck. "I'm going to go have a beer and grab some dinner at the pub. Do you want to come along?"

"Are you asking me out on a date, Tucker Greyson?"

"Are you going to say yes, Blakely Mayfield?"

"No." She smiles and it makes a crack in the cement wall I've built around my heart.

"Then no, I'm not asking you out." I chuckle.

"If I wasn't feeling so grimy and itchy, I'd probably say yes, but I think I'm going to go take a long, hot shower."

My brain immediately switches to picturing her naked in the shower. Water sluicing over full perky breasts…shit. I bow my head and start thinking about business emails I need to answer and reports to go over with Jason to get her image out of my head. I shift uncomfortably in my seat. "Okay, I'll be back in a bit and we can—"

"Okay," she cuts me off, sounding relieved. Is she scared to be here by herself or is she lonely? Should I stay home with her? I think if she asked me to, I probably would.

"Okay," I say gruffly, making the mistake of looking into her eyes. Something instinctual and basic takes over, urging me to reach out and pull her to me. Her pupils dilate when I lean toward her, but she doesn't pull away. Her little pink tongue quickly darts out and wets her full lips. *Jesus Christ.* I want to carry her into the house and fuck her senseless. The feeling is so overwhelming it makes me dizzy.

She's not your type, she's too prickly. This would be a gargantuan mistake. You cannot have sex with your new roommate...with Junie's friend, who is here because she needs to reevaluate her life. She leans an inch closer. I reach for her seat belt and unsnap it, releasing her from the confines before I lean back against my headrest.

"Night, Blakely." My voice is thick and raw as I look up at the ceiling. I run a hand over my face. That was close...too close. I try to think back to the last time I had sex. A pathetic six months run laps around my brain. That's all this is that I'm feeling. A simple, basic need wanting to be met.

"Right, yes. Goodnight, Tucker." She fumbles with the door latch, practically falling out of the truck.

"Do you mind taking Hershel with you? It drives Whitney nuts when I bring him to the pub."

"Sure, no problem." She opens the back door. Hershel

groans and stretches out on the bench seat.

"Here pup pup. Come on, Hershel, time to go inside," she says softly.

"What are you doing?" I look over my shoulder at her.

"Trying to get him out of the back seat."

"He's not my grandpa. Be stern with him."

She puts her hands on her hips. "Come on, Hershel, get down. I mean it, mister. I'm going to count to three and you better be out of this truck."

I bite down on my lip to keep from laughing. "He's not a kindergartener, for fuck's sake. You've got to give it a little oomph. Tell him to move it and then scream yeehaw!"

She gives me a doubtful glare. "For real?"

"Yeehaw."

"Come on, Hershel. Move it…yeehaw," she says half-heartedly, her cheeks flushing pink. Hershel doesn't even lift his head. "Why isn't he getting out?"

"Haven't you ever gotten so frustrated with something you wanted to scream?"

"Yes, with you."

I chuckle. "Use that tone of voice. Put some oomph into it. Maybe do a little tongue roll and throw a yip in there or a coyote call."

"A coyote what? I don't even know what that is and I can't roll my tongue."

I shake my head. "You'll never make it as a rancher."

"I didn't realize I was auditioning to be one." She takes a deep breath and yells at the top of her lungs, "Move it, Hershel, goddammit! Get your ass out of the car! Move it! Yee-haw!" Her chest rises as she inhales deeply before closing her eyes. She puts her all into it. "Get out of the car now! You make me so mad sometimes! You drive me crazy, Tucker the Fucker...shit, I mean Hershel! Move it!"

Hershel lifts his head and I can't keep my laughter in. Her eyes are bright and her cheeks are pink from the exertion of yelling.

"I don't know what I'm doing wrong," she gripes, flopping her arms at her side.

"Did you really just call me Tucker the Fucker?" My grin stretches wide.

"What? No! What? You must have misunderstood me. I probably said something silly, like Tucker the *trucker*. I call you that sometimes. You know, because you have a truck..." She looks away, completely embarrassed, and I can't help but laugh harder.

"Uh-huh." I look back at my dog. "Hershel, roll tide."

He immediately jumps down from the truck and trots up to the front door. Blakely watches him with her mouth gaping. "*Roll tide?*"

"I'm an Alabama fan." I shrug. "It's my alma mater."

"That's all I had to say was *roll tide?*" she asks incredulously. "Not scream at the top of my lungs and yell yeehaw like a country hillbilly banshee?"

I smother my laughter with a cough, irritation sweeping across her face. "Just wanted to see if you'd do it."

"Ugh, you're infuriating!" She slams the door shut. "And the Crimson Tide suck! Georgia Bulldogs are the only team worth rooting for!"

"Those are some fightin' words, Smiles." I grin like a loon while she stomps off.

Chapter 11

Rhonda's Sweater

Blakely

HERSHEL PRACTICALLY RUNS me over to get to his food bowl after I unlock the front door.

"You're a traitor, Hersh, a disgrace to the dog community. No one should answer to the command *roll tide*." Hershel looks back at me dolefully, wagging his tail before returning to his food.

About to close the door, a car pulls up to Bhodi's house and a gaggle of twenty-something-year-olds stumble out of the Uber, laughing, clearly inebriated. I roll my eyes and shut the door. Thank goodness I didn't take him up on his hot tub invitation earlier. Who knows what he does in there. A mosquito bite on my neck itches and I'm reminded I need to take a shower and roll in cortisone cream.

Stupid sexy Tucker Greyson. If only I had taken his advice and used bug spray. When he took off his shirt on the boat, I almost passed out. His body is a chiseled work of art. He didn't get riddled with one bite. It's as if the mosquitos knew not to bother with him and mess up his perfectly tanned skin which stretches taut over well-honed muscles. I absentmindedly scratch at the welts on my arm, picturing Tucker with his shirt off. *Gah! Stop thinking about his sexy-ass-in body, you idiot!* I trudge upstairs to take a shower and hopefully alleviate the itching.

Lathering up with soap, my mind circles back to Tucker. He's such a conundrum. He's not the type of man I'm usually attracted to. I gravitate toward the preppy, perfectly gelled-hair types, who care about whether their loafers are paired well with their designer jeans. Tucker seems like he couldn't care less. He doesn't have to worry about what to wear because everything looks damn good on him. It blows my mind I spilled my most vulnerable moment to him in the car—a painful blip on my radar which caused a monumental breakdown. I was hanging onto my sanity by my fingernails and, with one prompt from him, I unloaded it all. He's so easy to talk to, or maybe it's because I don't care what he thinks of me. I don't, right? Perhaps a microscopic part of me does.

Stupid shirtless Tucker Greyson. He makes me want to do dumb things like kiss him in the cab of his truck. The disturbing part? I would have if he asked. I wonder what it would feel like to run my fingertips down the hard ridges of his abs and unbutton his jeans, sliding them down over his magnificent tight ass. He's probably an amazing lover who *could* make me howl in bed. That just chaps my hide.

I don't need to get involved with *anyone* right now, especially *that* guy. I need something to relieve some of this high-strung tension pumping through my veins, because he makes me think about sex far too much when he's around. Would it be going against every fiber of my being to imagine dirty, dark thoughts of Tucker Greyson while I showered? Yes. Am I gonna? Hell yes.

ONE SHOWER AND a pretty damn good orgasm later, I towel off and get dressed in comfy cotton pajama shorts and a tank top. I wrap my hair up in my towel and slather lotion on my arms. I count ten welts on one arm alone. Cursing Tucker Greyson for the millionth time, I apply cortisone cream to the welts. Bass thumps through the closed windows from the Barracuda's house next door. I hope he doesn't plan on partying late into the night.

Skipping down the steps, I head into the kitchen and get a container of cold pasta salad out of the fridge and pour myself a glass of white wine. The noise outside has increased in volume. As long as he doesn't interrupt what I'm going to watch on Netflix, I don't give a fig about what happens over there.

I sit down and get comfy, turning on the TV. I grumble in annoyance as loud squeals from next door interrupt my quiet solitude. It sounds like they're on my back porch. Hershel barks and whines at the back door.

"No, Hershel, roll tide," I snap before shoving a bite of pasta into my mouth and cue up my favorite binge show, *Tidying up with Marie Kondo.* I turn the volume up while he whines and scratches at the back door. I'm five minutes in when Hershel barks. And he Doesn't. Shut. Up.

"Roll tide, Hershel! Roll tide!" I scream at him while my favorite organizer gently tries to get rid of another hideous sweater the lady must have hoarded since the early eighties. She's explaining how special it is to her when Marie's eye subtly twitches. She never loses her cool with her clients who can't give up culottes and moth-eaten sweaters from decades ago. Marie is a saint to put up with the ridiculous attachment someone has to a chartreuse dress from the nineties they got at a garage sale and refuse to part with because someone once said they looked slim in it. Throw it all away is my motto.

Unfortunately, I'm not as refined as Marie. I'm about to lose my shit on Hershel and the party next door. I pause the show and stomp over to the French doors to let him out. The women scream and I roll my eyes, stepping out on the back porch, looking over at my neighbor's back deck. Rap music is blaring and he has red Chinese lanterns strung up all along the deck. Women are running around topless while Bhodi sits in the hot tub holding a glass of champagne while he alternates swapping spit with the two women he's wedged between. *Gross.* It looks more like the red-light district than a nice relaxing mountain retreat.

He takes a breath and notices me glaring, standing rigidly with my hands on my hips. "Hey, neighbor! Want to join in on the fun?"

"I'll pass, thanks. Can you turn down the volume a bit? All the noise is making my roommate's dog bark like a madman."

"Sure thing. The water is nice and warm and I have some bubbly." He waggles his eyebrows, as if that will somehow entice me into stripping off my bra and jump in.

"I don't do hot tubs…or orgies…not enough chlorine to kill the…yeah…" I watch while he sticks his tongue down the brunette's throat. "All right, well, thanks for keeping it down." I wave but no one notices me.

Hershel comes bounding back up the steps covered in the most foul-smelling gunk imaginable. It's like rotten fish, vomit, and spoiled milk all rolled into one. Gagging, I hold my nose. Oh god, I can't. I just want to watch Marie solve this woman's awful sweater dilemma and go to bed. I stick my foot out to prevent Hershel from barging back inside, but I don't stand a chance. He barrels past me, pushing me hard with his bulk into the side of the door.

"Hershel, no!" I shout, rubbing my bruised elbow, watching in horror as he gets up on the couch and rolls around on the cream plush blanket. *My* cream plush blanket. I grab him by his collar and try not to vomit from the stench as I pull him off the couch and into Tucker's bedroom to get to his walk-in shower I saw the other day cleaning. Hershel, of course, isn't having it and puts on the brakes as soon as we enter the bathroom. This task is more difficult than I anticipated. All I want to do is have a glass of wine and see how Marie will transform Rhonda's closet. Is that asking too much? I should leave him in the bathroom for Tucker to deal with.

"Come on, you stinky dog. Roll tide!" I push his butt and pull his collar forward simultaneously. He growls, but I don't care because I'd rather have my hand chewed off than have to sit and smell him for the rest of the night. I quickly turn and shut the bathroom door before he can push past me. Collapsing against the door, I breathe out a sigh of relief. His nails scratch along the door while he whines.

"Too bad, Hersh. This is your fault, not mine." I fold my arms over my chest while he bangs his body against the door. *He can't break it down, can he?* I look around for a chair to wedge under the knob while he barks. And it's not a sweet Tiny Tim, *please sir, let me out* kind of bark. It's high pitched, needy, and constant. I'm never going to relax with this ding-dong barking all night. His barks turn to howls. After a few minutes of trying to wait him out, I realize he won't be giving up anytime soon.

"Fine! You win, stubborn little mule!" Opening the door, Hershel backs up until I'm through before placing his giant paws on my chest, his tongue lolling out. "Ugh, get down, you stink."

After wrangling him into the shower, I belatedly realize I'll need to go in with him to turn the taps on. Tucker is going to owe me big time for this. Luckily for me, his shower has a detachable spray nozzle. Unlucky for me, he also has a rain showerhead which immediately turns on, soaking Hershel and me. I scream and practically jump out of my skin as I arch away from the freezing water. An eye opener I wasn't prepared for. Hershel barks and I rant about how much I hate his owner while we wait for the water to warm up. Running the nozzle over his fur, I wrinkle my nose as brown mud runs down the drain, which he promptly shakes off, spraying it all over me. I growl in disgust and frustration, wondering if pretreatment will remove the stains.

"I seriously hate you right now, Hersh." I lather him up with Tucker's masculine-smelling shampoo. He prances, tilting his head.

"Don't you do it, mister. Don't you dare—" He shakes and lathered soap flings everywhere. "No!" I shriek. "Ugh, you are a bad, bad dog."

I'm soaked, my white tank splattered with brown mud. I rinse him off and slowly open the glass door. He shakes again for good measure because apparently, I'm not wet enough. I grab him from behind with one of Tucker's big fluffy towels while he shimmies against the walls and rolls on the floor.

"What the hell is going on in here?" Tucker's voice thunders off the tile. Hershel jumps up on him in greeting and barks.

I look up and the first thought which crosses my mind is murder. Straightening up, I glare at him, throwing the towel on the wet floor.

"Well, it all started because our new neighbor decided to throw a party and Hershel here just *had* to see what was going on. All I wanted to do was watch Marie Kondo. *But no*, I couldn't because Hershel wouldn't stop barking. Then he rolled in something rotten and proceeded to rub his funk all over my favorite blanket. I tried to contain him in here, but evidently, he has a fear of small spaces. So, I had to give him a bath, which he is horribly inept at, by the way. I didn't get to eat my dinner. I have no idea if Rhonda is keeping her hideous eighties sweater, or how Marie plans on organizing her locker-sized closet, and now I'm covered in soap and mud and can't get the disgusting image of the Barracuda sticking his tongue down the topless brunette! Next time, he goes with *you*!"

Tucker's eyes flicker to my chest, then quickly back up to

my face. He stands there, speechless. I'm sure he's as disgusted and embarrassed with his ill-behaved dog as I am.

"Well?" My eyes practically pop out of my head while he ogles me. "Are you going to say something like, I'm sorry, Blakely, you had to wash my dog? I'm sorry he rolled in foul-smelling shit and got it all over your clean blanket and interrupted your night watching the queen of organization. And I'm *sorry* we have Hugh Hefner reincarnated living next door!"

"I..." His eyes flicker down and up again as he rubs the back of his neck.

"Are you going to answer me or just stare at me?"

"You might want to cover yourself up with this. I can see right through your tank top." He grabs a towel from the rack and hands it to me. I look down at my soaked white tank top and realize my nipples are standing at attention. They seem to perk up knowing Tucker is salivating right in front of me, staring at them.

Growling, I snatch the towel from his hands, silently cursing my traitorous body while sliding past him.

"What are you, twelve? It's a pair of boobs. I'm sure you've seen plenty." I march upstairs, slamming my bedroom door.

I take another quick shower, but instead of imagining Tucker Greyson bending me over, I'm now daydreaming about punching him in the nuts. Turning off the taps, I quickly dry off.

"Blakely?" Tucker's deep voice resonates behind my closed door.

I tighten my towel and open the door. "What?"

Tucker swallows, his eyes quickly flit over my towel-clad body. "Hey, I threw your blanket in the wash. I'm sorry Hershel rolled on it and ruined your night."

Dammit Tucker, quit being Mr. Nice Guy. "Okay."

"Are you coming back downstairs? I'll watch whatever you were watching with you." He pauses. "Uh, Hershel ate your pasta salad, so I can make you some popcorn…"

"Of course, he did." I sigh in defeat. "Fine."

After applying lotion, I change into shorts and a t-shirt and throw my hair up into a sloppy topknot. I reapply the cortisone on my welts and walk downstairs. Tucker has showered and changed into a tight-fitting t-shirt and joggers. His wet hair looks artfully tousled and dark, bringing out the green in his eyes. He smells like clean soap and detergent and it takes all my willpower to not bring his shirt to my nose and inhale. *Stop looking at him, Blakely, and for God's sake, stop smelling him.* I sit at one end of the sectional. He hands me a bowl of popcorn and a fresh blanket.

"Thanks," I murmur while he sets a beer down on the coffee table and grabs the remote. Instead of sitting on the other end of the sectional, he sits next to me. I look at him and scowl, annoyed because we have a large couch to spread out on.

"What are we watching?" he asks gruffly, settling back against the cushion. He casually props his bare feet on the ottoman in front of me. Even his stupid feet are sexy. Why can't he have hideous hairy feet where his toes are all wonky? I stare at his gorgeous feet, realizing it's quiet outside.

"What happened to the party next door?" I ask, munching on popcorn, starved since I only had one bite of pasta.

"Interesting neighbor we have. When did he arrive?"

"Oh, you met Barracuda? I'm not sure. A couple days ago, I think."

"Hmm. I told him to wrap the party up."

"Seriously?" I arch an eyebrow. "And he listened to you?"

"Well, there's a noise ordinance in Greyson Gap. I made him aware."

I side-eye him while he gets comfortable. The party was in full swing when I gave Hershel a bath. The fact I can only hear crickets outside astounds me. And there were naked women running around. I would think Tucker would want to join in on the fun, not sit here on the couch with me.

"So, what is this?" He presses play on the TV. "Who's this lady?"

I pluck the remote out of his hands and press pause, tucking my feet under my legs.

"Okay, so this is Marie. She's a master organizer from Japan. The other lady is her interpreter because she only speaks Japanese. She is in Rhonda's house, helping her organize her closet, getting rid of a lot of stuff she's held onto for forty-plus years. Oh, my god, wait until you see this lady's house. It's a disaster! Marie is a miracle worker. They should make her a saint. Like, legit sainthood."

He sighs and rubs his eyes. "Sounds...awesome."

"It is!" I press play and giddily snuggle under the blanket he gave me. He gives me a bemused smile, stretching an arm along the back of the couch. His other hand rests on his stomach. I have a hard time concentrating on my favorite show when my eyes keep sliding over to him. His profile in the glow of the TV is hard to look away from. I'd like to glide my fingertips over his sharp jaw, feel the scratch from his stubble. I want to straddle his lap and dive my fingers into his hair and run them down his sculpted chest. I'd kiss the spot right under his jaw where his pulse beats.

"Why is this lady so hung up on this sweater? It's hideous."

"Hmm?" His question snaps me back to the moment and I direct my attention to the show. I can't believe I zoned out, fantasizing over making out with Tucker Greyson instead of watching Marie Kondo. His foot accidentally touches mine, sending tingles along my skin. Bringing my knees up, I wrap my arms around them so there's no chance he'll accidentally touch me again. "Sometimes it's really hard to get rid of stuff if it has personal sentiment."

"If I were her husband, I would have burned that thing years ago. Nothing sexy about it."

"Not everything is about sex, Tucker." I roll my eyes, silently berating myself for calling him out about what I was just thinking. I'm such a hypocrite. Snuggling deeper into the couch, I cast a glance in his direction.

"Smiles, it's always about sex." He lifts his lip up on one side in an incredibly sexy smirk before leaning forward, reaching for his beer. I watch his back muscles bunch and contract under his t-shirt. "Cat got your tongue for once?" He looks at me over his shoulder. Our eyes meet. He's teasing me, but I'm at a loss for words because it hits me like a ton of bricks. I want Tucker Greyson. I want to run my lips over every inch of him. I want him to take me to bed and make me howl like he promised he could.

His eyes sober, losing their playful glint. They harden as

if he's resolved something in his mind about me. He stands up and offers me his hand. I look at it curiously, my hand sliding into his callused one, moving on its own accord. He pulls me to him, holding me close while he looks down into my eyes. Without a word, he runs his index finger down my cheek and over my lips. I gently bite his finger and then suck on it, his green eyes turning feral. His breath shudders when I release him from my lips. He runs his hands up my ribcage, so painstakingly slow, every cell in my body screams for him to touch me. His fingertips smooth over my breasts, cupping them while his thumbs roll over my pert nipples. I drop my head back and arch toward him.

"Yes, Tucker," I moan. He feels the weight of them in his palms while he bends and drops a kiss on my collarbone. I want his mouth on them. My breath comes out in a staccato rhythm. "More…" I whisper. He runs his tongue up the side of my neck and I pant with need. "Give me more."

"You're playing with fire, Blakely. Watch out or you might get burned," he whispers in my ear before he abruptly drops his hands, pushing me back down on the couch with a finger to my sternum before walking away.

A cold, wet nose nudges my hand. The smell of wet dog permeating the air. I sit up straight and let out a strangled noise when Hershel jumps up next to me, plopping down on the couch. I look around at my surroundings, rubbing a hand over my face. Tucker is stretched out on the couch, watching the show with his head propped in his hand.

"What happened?"

He looks over at me and smirks. "You made me watch this snooze-fest organizing show and fell asleep on me five minutes in. Rhonda kept the ugly-ass sweater."

I try clearing my head. What was real and what was fantasy? "Tucker, did we...did you?"

"Did we what?" He looks over at me and chuckles. "I'm not sure what you were dreaming about, Smiles, but I don't think it was about Marie and Rhonda's sweater dilemma. Lots of moaning...along with my name."

My cheeks feel like they are on fire. I grab a throw pillow and toss it at his stupid head. "I did not."

"Whatever you say." He grabs my legs, and I squeal in surprise when he pulls me underneath him. He leans over me, his biceps straining against his t-shirt. The smell of his soap mixing with his masculine scent makes my head dizzy. His eyes turn dark with desire, his lips hover agonizingly close to mine. "I promise you this, if anything were to happen between us, you'd remember every single detail of it."

"Tucker..." I hate how needy and weak I sound.

"Every. Single. Detail."

Before I can even blink, he hops up and heads to his bedroom, leaving me unsatisfied and wanting more. "Night, Blakely May."

Goddamn Tucker Greyson. I just showed him my stupid poker hand.

Goal: Make Tucker suffer with my sexual prowess.

Problem: *I don't have any sexual prowess whatsoever. What does sexual prowess even mean?*

Stress: *Having to pretend like Tucker Greyson doesn't have any kind of effect on me.*

What's the best thing that happened today: *Where do I start? *sarcasm* I have a hundred mosquito bites, my neighbor had an orgy in his hot tub even bleach can't scrub away from my eyeballs, and I missed my favorite show. Hershel is a sorry excuse for a dog because he ate my dinner and rolled in shit. I had a sexual dream about Tucker and apparently moaned his name out loud, and he has stupid sexy feet.*

What I am grateful for: *I didn't think about my old job today.*

Chapter 12

Huck a Waterfall

Tucker

EVEN THOUGH I showered earlier, I immediately turn on the taps and take another one. I jack myself off to images of Blakely and what I'd do to her if she wasn't my temporary roommate. I blame her for the dichotomous situation she's put me in. There's no question, I want her gone, but goddamn, when I got home and found her in my shower looking like she won a wet t-shirt contest, it took all my self-control not to throw her over my shoulder and take her to my bed. And then on the couch when she was moaning my name in her sleep, I was so hard and aching I almost came in my pants. Her smell drives me insane, her expressive golden eyes—the color of brown sugar, her smart mouth and even smarter mind.

She's completely the opposite of what I normally date.

Date? Jesus, I must be fucking out of my mind to entertain those thoughts. I don't have time for a girlfriend, much less get involved with someone who's leaving soon. Imagination and fantasies are what I'll have to live by until she goes back to Atlanta. I need to take my cousin's advice and drive her out of town. It's best for both of us.

She'll get back into the swing of things when she goes back to Atlanta, forgetting all about the town of Greyson Gap, and I can get on with my life.

I GROGGILY HEAD to the kitchen to grab some coffee. Blakely is sitting with her back to me at the island, flipping through a book. She's still in her pajamas from last night. Fishing didn't make her run for the hills, so it's the perfect time to initiate Plan B—be as annoying as possible.

"Morning, sunshine," I grumble and head to the cabinet to take out a coffee cup.

"Morning."

"Sleep well?" I pour the coffee and turn around, almost dropping my mug. "What the hell is all over your face?"

She self-consciously touches her cheek. "Oh, uh, I forgot I had this on. It's a green tea aloe soothing mask. I got a little sun on the lake, so I thought this would help."

"Jesus, warn a guy next time." I stare at the greenish-gray smeared all over her face. "I think you missed a spot on your chin."

"You're so original," she deadpans, not even sparing me a glance as she reads her book.

"Maybe from now on you'll listen to me."

"Highly doubt it," she grumbles. "Life must be so hard, being right all the time."

"At least you can admit it."

She rolls her eyes, sipping her coffee. "Do you need something, or is it asking too much to be left alone to enjoy my coffee and book?"

"Not a morning person, got it. Do you know what today is?" I ask.

"Great, he wants to chitchat." She shuts her book, the bored expression on her face priceless. My plan is working perfectly.

"It's camping day." I clap my hands together, causing her to jump. "We're going on a camping trip to-day. I checked the weather, no storms in the forecast. You'll need a swimsuit, some water shoes, a change of clothes, overnight clothes—"

"Yeah, no. I'm not doing that."

"Didn't you say you were a kayaking kind of girl?" I sip my coffee.

"I never said that." She looks at me blandly.

"I believe your exact words were, 'I can river rapids with the best of them'." I obnoxiously air-quote. "Isn't that the whole point of your 'new me' movement? To try things you haven't done before?"

She narrows her eyes. "You can't walk around here without a shirt."

I look down at my bare chest. I love that it bothers her. "Most women wouldn't complain." I smile at her cheekily while I rub a hand over my abdomen.

"I'm assuming we're not talking about the women in this town."

"Tell you what"—I smirk—"I'll put my shirt back on as

soon as you get dressed for our camping trip."

"I don't respond to flagrant attempts at blackmail, but nice try." She gets up to put her coffee cup in the sink. I turn to get out of her way, but we step in the same direction. We immediately step in the other direction, doing our own little tango. She growls in annoyance as I grab her arms. The look in her eyes tells me she's seconds from kneeing me in the balls.

"Settle down there, Sasquatch, and let me get out of your way."

"Sasquatch?" she shrills, which is way too much for my eardrums first thing in the morning.

"Jesus, crank the siren back down. It was just an endearment." I move out of her way and sit down at the island.

"Ugh, you're so rude and—"

"Disarming? I get that a lot." I wink.

"I was going to say obnoxious."

"Hmm…whatcha reading?" I pick up the book she was thumbing through. *"He's the Reason You're Slowly Dying Inside."* I look up and arch an eyebrow. "Nice light reading for a Saturday morning. Is it a romance novel?"

"Give me that." I ignore her outstretched hand and she huffs in annoyance. "It's about women in the workforce."

"Suuure it is, Smiles." I wink at her. "Let me guess. Some guy crushes her heart, so she has to escape from the city and hide out reading self-help books in a cabin in the woods until she can face him again." I turn the book over and pretend to read the blurb on the back. I know I'm being a complete dick, but it's all part of the master plan. "Perhaps even getting him out of her system by sleeping with the hunky ex-baseball player turned builder who happens to own the cabin she escapes to."

"If you find him, let me know." She stalks over and rips the book out of my hands.

I take a sip of my coffee and stare at her. Her eyes narrow, her nose doing this cute little bunny-rabbit twitch.

"What?" she snaps.

"I'm waiting for you to get dressed so we can go camping. What other books do you have in here?" I open the bag to take a peek. *"Anchoring your Happiness Within."*

"Ugh, fine!" She swipes the bag off the table and stomps upstairs muttering, "Stupid egotistical jerk-head."

"I can hear you, Blakely May."

"Good, and it's *just Blakely!*" She slams her door. I chuckle, knowing I hit my ball into the outfield. This is going to be easier than I thought. She'll be hightailing it out of Greyson Gap by tomorrow. Unplugging my phone from the charger, I notice a missed call from Annie last night and listen to her voicemail.

'Hey Tuck, thanks again for taking Ben fishing. It's so nice having you help...well, you know. Anyway, maybe we can get together this weekend. Dinner at my place? Let me know.'

I shoot her a quick text saying I'll be unreachable until Sunday. Annie's become super clingy in the last couple of months. I don't want to send her mixed messages that I'm interested. I will always care for her, but friendship is all I can offer. It breaks my heart Ben's dad didn't stick around, but I'm not going to keep living in the past, and Annie is definitely not what I see in my future.

Grabbing my coffee, I go back into my bedroom to toss

clothes in my bag. I text Whitney and Jason about my plans and ask Whit if she can watch Hersh. Jason gives me a thumbs-up and airplane emoji. Whitney sends me ten hearts. I shake my head and laugh. If she really knew how much Blakely hated me, she never would have taken the bet.

I load up the truck with camping gear and pack a cooler of food and drinks, then head back inside to yell for Blakely when she strolls downstairs with a large tote.

"Ready?"

"I guess." She grabs her phone and sunglasses.

"What's in the bag?"

"Well, I wasn't sure what the weather would be like, so I packed shorts and a tank if it's hot, three t-shirts if I get too cold or one gets wet, four pairs of different length socks, a long-sleeve shirt with pants, my favorite yoga...what?"

I drag my hand down my face, trying to contain the laugh bubbling out. "We're going tubing and hiking. For *one* day. You only need a change of clothes and a swimsuit."

She hugs the tote to her chest. "But I like to be prepared."

"Leave the tote bag behind. I have a backpack if you need one."

"Yes, I'll need one." She fishes out a smaller bag. "But I'm bringing my makeup and toothbrush, oh and of course the emergency kit with Band-Aids, sunscreen, and hydrocortisone."

"Of course. Don't forget the whitening strips and ACE bandages."

My sixth sense tells me she's giving me the middle finger behind my back as I go into the hall closet and grab a backpack for her. She takes her time, neatly refolding her clothes, debating what to take and what to leave behind.

"If you keep going at this rate, we'll get there by midnight."

She grumbles something under her breath before neatly placing the clothes in the backpack. Zipping up the bag, she stalks past me toward the truck without another word. I whistle for Hershel and he comes running and jumps into the back. I throw the cooler, my tent, and bag in the back.

"Hershel, too?" she asks, exasperated.

"I'm dropping him off at my sister's. Although he loves camping."

"Guess I'm the odd man out."

"Hey, neighbors! You going camping?"

The douchebag from last night is blatantly eyeing Blakely while he loads his kayak on top of his car.

"Yes," I begrudgingly answer, grabbing her bag.

"Awesome! Mind if I tag along?"

I press my lips together. Before I can tell him that I do mind, Blakely chimes in.

"Not at all. The more the merrier, right Tucker?"

"Cool, bro! Let me grab my bag! I'll follow in my car. I'd love to have someone take a picture of me doing a boof, maybe huck a waterfall." He quickly turns and runs into the house.

"I have no idea what he's talking about," she says.

"He's a fucking poser. What were you thinking, saying he can come with us?"

"Well, maybe you two should just go and *huck a waterfall* together." She smiles sweetly.

I side-eye her and shut the tailgate. "Nice try."

She sighs and reluctantly pulls open the door. Bhodi comes running down the front steps. "Ready bro!"

"Do you have a tent?"

"Nah, I'll sleep in my car."

"Good." I'm furious we got roped in with this toolbox. Maybe I can lose him on the back-mountain roads.

Chapter 13

Wild and Free

Blakely

I TAKE MY journal out of my backpack and stare down at the empty white page. Dammit, I'm going to have to write without lines. I take a deep breath. *You can do this.*

"What's that? Another self-help book?"

I hold the pages to my chest so Tucker can't see it. "It's my journal."

"Like a diary?"

"No, like a journal. Each day I write a new goal and solutions on how to obtain said goal."

"What's your goal today?"

"Not to get arrested for murdering you."

"Ah, I see. You've set the bar high."

Smirking, I stare back down at the page. I write *goal* out as neatly as I can. Tucker's truck bounces over something and my pen skids off to the right. Ugh, no! I bite my lip in frustration. *Just let it go, Blakely. It will not ruin your journal or your day.* Taking a deep breath, I count to ten like Dr. Cooper taught me to do in stressful situations.

I think about where we're headed, and although I'm

really nervous because there isn't a plan in place, a little part of me is thrilled by the unknown. I've never tubed or camped before. The company isn't exactly desirable, but I have to remind myself I'm in it for the experience.

Goal: *Be adventurous.*

Problem: *I don't like the unknown.*

Stress: *Not knowing exactly what will happen today and not being prepared for what may go wrong. I like having a plan.*

What's the best thing that happened today: *Pissing off Tucker by inviting Bhodi the Barracuda.*

What I am grateful for: *Distractions and adventure. I haven't thought about how badly I screwed up at my old job for the past week.*

Satisfied, I snap the book closed and stuff it into my backpack. "So, what's our plan?"

He looks over at me, but his eyes are hidden behind his wayfarers. His light golden-brown hair ruffles in the wind from his window. It annoys me how badly I want to run my fingers through it. I sit on my hands to squelch the temptation.

"No plan. We can head up to the falls, do a little hiking. Maybe rent some tubes and go down the river. Relax, camp out. The day is ours to do whatever."

"Do whatever." I chew on my thumbnail, stressing over the term 'whatever'.

"Relax, Smiles, it's going to be fun." He looks over at me and gives me a devastating grin. "What do you like to do?"

"You mean for fun?"

He chuckles, returning his gaze to the road. "Yeah, for fun."

I bite my lip while I try to come up with something I enjoy doing for fun. "I play tennis...ooh, I like to organize my friends' pantries and closets."

"That's your idea of fun?"

"Having an organized pantry is very rewarding."

"I'll take your word for it." He blows out a breath. "What I'm trying to ask is, what makes you excited? What gets your blood pumping?"

I give him a quizzical glance. "Organizing."

He laughs and shakes his head. "Wow, okay then. The secret to getting into Blakely's heart is through organization."

I suck in a breath as his words wash over me. Does he want to get into my heart? I look over at his profile. No, no way. Remember what Junie and his sister said. He's a player. I brush over his comment.

"What about you, Tucker Greyson? What gets your blood pumping?"

"That's easy. The crack of the bat when it meets the ball. Nothing is more satisfying. Well, besides sex."

I try to steady my thundering heartbeat, the cab of the truck suddenly a touch claustrophobic. It should be illegal for Tucker Greyson to utter the word *sex* out loud, dropping it in a sentence so casually, like he does it every day after brushing his teeth. Who am I kidding? He probably does.

I clear my throat and try to erase the image of Tucker brushing his teeth naked while I wait for him, tangled in his sheets. "I've never been to a baseball game."

He shakes his head. "Jesus, were you raised by wolves? That's completely un-American."

"Not wolves, just very career-driven parents who accidentally had a baby. I wasn't exactly planned and I wasn't a joyful surprise."

"Sorry, that doesn't sound like a happy childhood."

"It wasn't great, but it wasn't terrible either. I had everything a child could want. Toys, weekly field trips to the zoo and library, my horse, wonderful nannies..."

"Wonderful nannies? Jesus, sounds depressing."

I shrug and look out the window. "My parents were rarely home. It's one reason I'm so Type A. I followed my mother's rules religiously so I could fit in and not rock the boat when they were home. My nanny always used to tell me, *be seen, not heard, Blakely*. There were rules and expectations to be met. All I wanted growing up was to please them so they would accept and love me." I huff out a laugh. "Even after years of therapy, it's still hard to break free of that."

Heavy silence hangs in the air. I chance a glance over at him, wondering what he's thinking. His expression is stony. My confession of my childhood sinks my heart like an anchor keeping its vessel from beating. *I can't believe I just blurted out I'm basically a complete nut job who depends heavily on her therapist. Real winner here. Typical privileged girl who grew up with a silver spoon in her mouth and now is boo-hooing because she didn't get enough attention from her parents, so she's enrolled in a lifetime therapy membership.* I roll my eyes at my stupid verbal vomit while I stare out the window.

He looks over at me, his expression softening. "If you

could do one rebellious thing, what would it be?"

I chuckle nervously. "Oh, gosh, I don't know…" We pass a lake to the right and the idea slams into me like a wrecking ball. "I've always wanted to go skinny-dipping. It seems so freeing and kind of daring. Completely naked, floating in the water with nature…scandalous if you get caught." Heat spreads across my cheeks when he doesn't say anything. "It's silly." Shaking my head, I busy myself by looking in my bag.

"No, it isn't. If that's your one rebellious thing, then you should try it while you're here. YOLO."

"What does YOLO mean?"

"Jesus, woman." He shakes his head. "You only live once."

"YOLO." I roll the acronym over my tongue, testing it out while I stare at the scenery flying by. "What about you? What's one thing you wish you could try?"

"Falling in love," he says, keeping his gaze straight forward. "I've never been in love before." My mouth hangs open as I gawk at him. That was the last thing I anticipated coming out of his mouth. "What?" He swings his head a fraction in my direction.

"Nothing…I just wasn't expecting you to say you've never been in love." A beat of silence passes between us. "You weren't in love with the woman I saw you fishing with?"

"Annie? I loved her, but I wasn't *in* love with her. I was more in love with baseball than I was with her. We were childhood friends and it was kind of expected we would end up together."

"I've never been in love either. I thought I was in love with my ex, Charles, but I was blinded by my checklist."

"Your checklist?"

"He checked off everything on my list. My parents adored him. He had a good job, was well educated, handsome, a great tennis doubles partner, and dressed nicely. But there was always something off. He was too perfect, too slick."

"He sounds like a douche."

I chuckle. "Yeah, he was. A narcissistic one. He said I was..." My cheeks heat for the millionth time while I replay the words Charles said. I definitely don't want to put the image of a cadaver in Tucker's head. "He said I was too stiff and boring."

"Nah, you just need to expand your horizons...live a little. Go skinny-dipping, have crazy wild sex, go to a ballgame and eat a hotdog. Shout into the wind. Fall in love..."

"Who says I haven't done those things?"

"Something tells me you're not a shouting-into-the-wind, wild-crazy-sex kind of girl." He flashes his signature sexy smile my way. "I don't know, just be wild and free."

"Wild and free, huh?" I chew on my bottom lip. "YO-LO," I whisper.

"Exactly...YOLO. And Blakely? Burn your checklist."

Chapter 14

One Croc

Blakely

I'VE NEVER SEEN anything more majestic than a natural waterfall. The larger one cascades down into the smaller one perpendicular to it against black craggy rocks. I take a deep breath and close my eyes, the sound of the pounding water taking over my senses. If Bhodi wasn't with us, I'd probably strip down to my swimsuit and dive in.

But he *is* with us, much to my dismay, and I totally blame myself. Well, ten percent is Bhodi's fault for being alive and annoying, inserting himself into every damn conversation Tucker and I try to have. I'll admit, inviting him along was a knee-jerk reaction to annoy Tucker for dragging me on this trip.

After the dream I had of him last night, the sexual tension brewing between us is palpable...well, at least to me it is, and it makes me nervous. When he leaned over me last night, my head kept screaming *yes, yes, yes*! This morning, when he sauntered into the kitchen, shirtless, I had to will myself not to lie down on the kitchen island and offer myself up like a breakfast buffet. *No, no, no*. Bhodi seemed like a good buffer the instant he asked to come along. I completely regret that decision now.

He has a kayaking story for *everything*. I would mention rainbows and he had a *fascinating* story about the time he hucked a waterfall in the rain and saw a rainbow. Or Tucker mentioned having carrots in his bag if I needed a snack and there was this *awesome* bit about how he hucked a waterfall and saw a vision of a woman with carrot-colored hair in the water. Turned out to be a leaf. I wish he'd huck right over the edge of a waterfall and never come back. How about that story, Barracuda?

The first thirty minutes on the hike, he wouldn't shut up after he discovered Tucker used to play for the Braves and the Astros. You would have thought Tucker's curt one-word replies would have given him a hint he wasn't interested in discussing his baseball career, but no, the questions kept coming. It got really awkward when Bhodi asked him why he would give up all the pussy in the free world to return to Greyson Gap. I'm pretty sure Tucker wanted to punch him more than me.

He insisted on helping me over every single rock which could be deemed sweet by some, but not to me. The two-foot rock I could walk over blindfolded? Yeah, I got it, thanks, Bhodi. I honestly think he was looking for an excuse to touch me. *Cue the hand sanitizer.* And if I hear one more kayak or mountain-bike slang word or the word 'bro' or 'bruh', I might try to knock myself out with a river rock.

Tucker is taking it all in stride as he guides us along the river and trails. There's something kind of sexy about a man who feels at home in nature. Don't get me wrong, I'm not looking for the guy to quit showering and start eating berries off a tree or anything, but his confidence and knowledge of his surroundings is definitely a turn-on.

"Let's head back to the truck, grab lunch, and then go floating. Sound good?" Tucker looks back at us over his shoulder. Okay, so another plus about this hike is I've been staring at his ass for the last hour. It's a magnificent ass. Thankfully, I'm wearing my sunglasses, so he can't see my eyes are glued to his glutes.

"Sounds good." I smile.

"Bro, I'm a no-go."

"Oh no, really? That's too bad," I say flatly.

"Yeah, think I'm gonna rip the cord."

"Sounds intense, whatever the hell that means." I roll my eyes, again thankful for my sunglasses.

"If we cut through this trail, it will take us about fifteen minutes to get back." Tucker points to a trail leading to the left.

"Bro, I'm looking at the map, and I think we should go right. We have to cross the creek, but it looks like a shortcut."

"No offense, Bhodi, but I think I'm going to trust Tucker, who has hiked this before."

Bhodi scoffs. "Typical woman. Where's your sense of adventure?"

I bristle, seconds away from pushing him off the ledge we're next to. Tucker steps between us.

"Bhodi, that's not a creek, that's a class-four rapid. I don't feel comfortable making Blakely cross it."

Bhodi surveys the map. "Nah, she can do it, it's marked

as a creek on here. She can always hop on my back."

Ew, ew, ew, please God, no.

Tucker smiles at me. "You know what, Bhodi? You take the creek and we'll take the trail. Let's see who's right."

I hide my smile, pretending to look up at the sky. Clever, Tucker. He knew Bhodi's ego could never pass up a challenge.

"Care to make it interesting?" Bhodi volleys right back.

Tucker shrugs. "What do you have in mind?"

Bhodi lifts his chin in my direction. "If I win, I get to spend the rest of the day with Blakely, and you return home."

"Uh, wait a minute—"

"And if you lose?" Tucker asks coolly while I mentally spiral out of control. An afternoon and evening alone with Bhodi? I'd rather slather my skin with Hershel's rotten mud for eternity.

"Excuse me? Don't I get a say in this ridiculous, immature, sexist little bet?"

Both men stare each other down, ignoring my stomping feet and waving hands.

"If I lose, I'll return home after kayaking."

Tucker nods his head in agreement. Bhodi drops his backpack, strips off his shirt, and tucks it into the waistband of his shorts, purposefully flexing his muscles while he winks at me.

"Later losers! Blakely, get ready to get your kayak on!" He jogs down the trail to the right.

"Tucker, what the hell was that? What if he wins?" I'd tell them both to go huck a fall if I knew how to get home.

"I am not kayaking with him!"

He shrugs. "Trust me, Smiles, he's not going to win. He's wearing bright yellow Crocs, for fuck's sake. Let's go." He jogs off to the trail going left.

"But…but what if…wait, what do his Crocs have to do with it—Tucker!"

"Come on, Blakely May, you're losing precious seconds stammering back there," he shouts over his shoulder.

"Ugh, you're so infuriating!" I follow him on the trail. "And it's *just Blakely*!" I clench my fists.

FORTY-FIVE MINUTES LATER, Tucker and I clean up our trash from lunch and make a plan to drive to the little stand we saw down the road to get our tubes. Our tent is all set up, and although I had misgivings about sharing a tent with him, it holds eight people, so there will be plenty of room for the two of us to be on opposite sides.

A wet, squishing, squelching sound diverts my attention from folding my chair. A water-logged Croc squeaks with each step over to us. It takes all my self-control not to burst out laughing as Barracuda hobbles up to us, soaked to the bone.

"Oh my god, Bhodi, what happened to you? You're missing a shoe, and where's your shirt?"

Tucker turns and smiles. "Wow man, how was crossing the creek? I was about to call in a search party."

"Turns out I was reading the map wrong. That wasn't a creek. It was a beater. It wouldn't have been bad, except for the undercurrent knocking me on my ass when I was waving to some girls on the other side. I slipped on a rock and it pulled my shoe right off. My t-shirt was tucked into my shorts because I was trying to even out my tan, but it got carried away before I could regain my balance. I almost lost my backpack with my keys in it."

"Hmm, tough break."

Bhodi shakes his head like a wet dog. "Is that your tent?" He pokes his head into the tent Tucker erected.

"Remember, you lost."

"Right, right. Calm down bruh, I was just asking. Mind if I change in it after I kayak? Going to hit the gnarly rapids in a bit before heading back."

"Yeah, sure…"

We get into the truck, look at each other, and burst out laughing.

Chapter 15

Misery Loves Company

Tucker

I CHUCKLE AS Blakely's tube gets stuck on a rock ahead of me. She tries to lift the tube off while remaining in it, but it's not budging.

"Do you need help? I'm right behind—" The current is faster than I expect and I slam right into her, causing her to tumble into the water.

"Oh my god, it's so cold!" she shrieks. I grab her tube and wrap my arm around her waist, hauling her up onto me so I don't lose her in the swift waters. She's splayed across my legs and I can't help but laugh at her incensed expression.

"Quit wiggling." I chuckle.

"Well, let me up!"

"Wait until we get up here and the current is slower."

"Floating down the river with my face in your crotch wasn't what I had in mind when you said, let's go tubing," she snaps.

"This isn't ideal for me either," I grit out, shifting my body. "For the love of God, Blakely, please stop squirming." Of course, I have a hard-on since her head is in my lap, her wet skin slick against mine. God, give me the strength not to pull her up and smash my lips to hers.

"Well, if you hadn't tried to be Mr. Macho Hero, you wouldn't have knocked me off. I was about to get my tube unstuck," she gripes while pressing down to leverage herself up. I grunt in pain while she involuntarily squishes my balls, shoving off me. Hissing out a breath, my mind goes completely blank, the pain traveling up my abdomen into my throat, making me feel like I'm about to vomit. She jumps over onto her tube, completely oblivious she crushed the family jewels, almost ending the lives of my future children in one fell swoop.

She looks back at me, her eyebrows rising when she sees my hunched posture. "Are you okay? You look kind of ashen, like you're about to pass out. Oh crap, I'm not equipped to handle a situation like this. I don't even have my first-aid kit. Can somebody help us?" she shouts, her arms flailing wildly as she tries to get a nearby floater's attention.

"Stop yelling. I'm fine," I grind out. "Meet you at the end."

"Are you sure?"

"I'm good. Just go. Please."

I sit back in my tube waiting for the pain to subside and look up at the clouds lazily plodding across the blue sky. My mission on this trip was to make her so miserable she would run screaming back to Atlanta. *Guess who's miserable now, you fucking idiot?*

Why on earth do I keep trying to help her? I should have let her cross the river with dipshit Bhodi the Barracuda. I should have dunked her ass under the cold water and left her in my wake.

I run a hand through my hair and sigh, the pain finally dissipating. I can't run her out of town because I'm not that kind of guy. Being jerky and annoying is exhausting. And dare I say, I've actually enjoyed her company on this trip. She definitely entertains me...

I curse the clouds, floating down the river as I begrudgingly accept the fact that I do like her and I'm definitely attracted to her. The last thing I need in my life right now is Blakely Mayfield. She isn't part of my plan.

"WOW, THIS WATERFALL is beautiful!"

I look up at the water cascading over rocks into a beautiful blue pool of water.

"Yeah, only the locals know about this spot. The water isn't as cold as the river water. Want to go for a swim?"

"Right now?" She looks around nervously. "Right here...with you?"

"I'm not gonna bite." Why does she make it sound like I'm the last person in the world she'd be caught dead swimming with? I have to admit, it stings my ego just a touch. I survey the area. "Come on, it'll be refreshing." I strip off my shirt and toss it on a rock. She folds her arms over her chest and averts her gaze.

"Have we checked if—"

"Jesus, Blakely, stop overthinking everything and live a

little. Get in the water!" I run and cannonball off a ledge. She's standing over the ledge with her hands on her hips when I breach the water. I smile up at her. "What?"

"Did you even check the depth of the water? You could have been paralyzed! You could have hit your head! It doesn't look very deep, and if you injured yourself—"

"YOLO, Blakely."

I swim away from her, ignoring her tirade, pissing her off even more. I stand up under the falls and let the water sluice over my tired muscles. The pounding pressure of the water feels incredible on my shoulders and back. Out of the corner of my eye, I spy Blakely shimmying out of her shorts and tank top, slowly climbing down the rocks into the water. She's beautiful in her little navy polka-dot two-piece. Her curves make my fingers itch to pull her to me and run my fingers over the soft swell of her breast and down around to squeeze a handful of ass.

She'll be leaving soon, and although I wouldn't mind a quick romp in the hay with her, I have a feeling it would affect her more than it would me. The least I can do is show her how to let loose a little. Reluctantly, I turn my back to her and tilt my head up into the rushing water. The feeling is freeing, figuratively washing all my sinful thoughts away.

Chapter 16

The Parkers

Blakely

I'M WAIST DEEP, watching him stand under the waterfall, the water beating down on his broad shoulders. The afternoon sun bakes down on us, making the water refreshing, if not a bit on the cool side, but nothing compared to the icy-cold river. He turns his back to me and reaches up, clasping his head while he points his face directly into the water. The man is a human Greek god, a marble slab cut to perfection. He's Apollo, relaxing his tired muscles after a day of battle. I want to wrap my arms around his waist and lick his shoulder blade. I want to dip my fingers into his swim trunks and grab a hold of his thick...

"Earth to Blakely!"

I jolt in surprise, my eyes refocusing on the man swimming toward me.

"Are you okay?" His brown hair is slicked back and his green eyes shine wickedly as he stands in front of me. I can't tear my eyes from his eight-pack or the droplets of water dripping down his biceps.

"Uh-huh." It's all I can manage.

"Well, are you going to swim?"

"Uh-huh."

He smirks, waving a hand in front of my face. "You sure you're okay?"

An impulsive decision cements in my brain. "Turn around."

"What?"

"Just do it…before I lose my nerve."

He turns around and I quickly pull off my bikini bottoms and undo the string of my bikini top. "Keep your eyes closed." I put them on a nearby rock.

He chuckles. "Okay…you're making me kind of nervous."

"Trust me, okay?"

"Okay," he says quietly, causing goosebumps to break out along my arms. I swim toward the waterfall and look back over my shoulder to make sure he isn't peeking. He's grinning goofily with his eyes closed. I stare at his beautiful face for a beat before I stand up and let the waterfall beat down on me. It's such a rush to swim completely naked with no restrictions dragging me down. It's so taboo and thrilling. I shake my hair out and sink back down into the water.

"Okay! You can open your eyes."

In four quick strokes, he joins me next to the falls. I quickly cover myself with my arms, but it's too late. He's right next to me, grinning. "Check that off the list."

"Ha, yes, well…this would be a good time to exercise my new YOLO motto, right?" I squeak.

"Right." He leans down and pulls his swim trunks off.

"Oh, my god!" I try to cover my eyes, but then realize in

127

doing so I've left my boobs exposed. I quickly place my arm across them again, keeping my eyes closed tight.

"You're beautiful, Blake, I won't judge you," he whispers right next to my ear, his chest grazing my shoulder.

I freeze like a deer in headlights, unable to move or speak. Pulling in a deep breath, I open my eyes. His gaze holds mine, a deep pool of emerald inviting me in to test the waters. His hand gently wraps around my waist, pulling me closer. Gliding his thumb gently back and forth over my hip bone is the only movement he makes. I'm drowning and I can't breathe, just from his touch.

He's so patient with me as I slowly trace a water droplet with my finger as it races down his chest. Feeling brave, my fingers glide over his pecs. I look up into his eyes and he shudders, a swirl of molten green piercing me to the spot, an arrow hitting its mark. My lips are inches from his as he whispers against them. "So beautiful."

Like a lion circling his prey, he taunts me, his fingers lazily gliding up my ribcage. My breasts grow heavy in anticipation of his hands possessing them. He's clearly cast a spell over me, because he's all I can see, smell, and hear. My body willingly readies itself to give in to him. Our legs brush and I suck in a thready breath. The need to wrap my legs around his waist is so intense it scares me. He pulls back, a mischievous smile curving his lips right before he dunks me under. I sputter and choke while he laughs and swims away, the spell broken. All I can see is his pale ass before he goes under.

"Tucker Greyson, you're going to pay for that!" I shout at the empty swimming hole, scanning the area where I saw him dive under. Lust is quickly replaced by mixed emotions. I'm glad he stopped whatever was happening between us, but also a little disappointed. The thrill of swimming naked made me daring and vulnerable, but I was exposed in more way than one. Any other guy would have taken advantage of the situation, but not Tucker.

Seconds quickly turn into a minute, and I anxiously worry the longer he stays under. What if a tree log snags him? What if there are alligators in here? Shit, I didn't even think about that! Do they have alligators in the mountains? I don't think so, but what the hell do I know? I'm a city girl. "Tucker?" my voice is shaky and unsure.

Something grazes my ankle, and I shriek, kicking my foot out. It connects with hard muscle and I scream again when Tucker rises for air. "Jesus, you scared the shit out of me!" I yell, and he grins sheepishly.

"Thanks for kicking me in the chest." He rubs a fist over his heart.

"Well, you deserved it." I don't want to smile, but his grin is contagious, making my own lips twitch. Damn him. "So, uh, quick question. Are there alligators in these parts?"

He barks out a laugh, making me feel foolish. He sobers when he realizes I'm serious.

"No, Blakely May, there are no alligators living in the mountains. The bears ate them all."

I splash water in his face and swim back over to the falls. He quickly catches me, grabbing hold of my ankle, dragging me under the water. Water rushes up my nose, causing it to burn before I break free of the surface, gasping for air.

"Are you *trying* to drown me?" I pinch my nose to ease

the burning sensation.

He laughs and I want to hold him in a headlock under the falls. Unfortunately, he's twice my size and undoubtedly stronger.

"Daddy, is that woman naked?"

I whip my head around and see a family of four hiking along the edge of the pool. I quickly dive behind Tucker, wrapping my arms around him to hide.

"Oh my god, this is utterly humiliating!" I hiss out. "Tell them to leave! I knew this was stupid. This is why I never let loose and swim without clothes, because shit like this happens," I mutter to myself while Tucker's body shakes with laughter.

"Hi Bob! Hi Lonna! Hey kids… Beautiful day for a hike!"

"Tuck, is that you? Great day for a hike and a swim! Maybe we'll join you! Come on, kids!"

The man toes off his shoes.

"Good god, no! Tucker, *say something!*" I squeal into his shoulder blade.

"Is Annie with you? Or Stacy? I can't see…" Bob bends his knees and shades his eyes to get a better look. Lonna pulls out her bird-watching binoculars.

"No, Bob, she has blonde hair. I think that's Jenna Stevens."

"No, Jenna is with Tad Klein now. Maybe it's Susan from over in Johnsonville."

"No, no, no…didn't Susan have a baby with Darren Smart?" She passes her binoculars to her son. "Remember all the controversy over it?"

"Oh yes, you're right. Let's hope it isn't her."

Could this be any more humiliating? "Can you please tell them to stop Roladexing through your girlfriends and move along?" I pinch his arm for emphasis.

Tucker's chest rumbles with laughter. "Good to see you all, but Patty is correct. My friend is naked."

Oh. My. God.

"I hate you right now!" I hiss. "Why couldn't you say *you* were naked?"

"No need to scare Patty Parker. She's only eight."

I peek over his shoulder and see Bob covering Patty's eyes while Lonna yanks the binoculars out of her son's hands.

"Oh! Erm, rightee-oh, Tucker! See you at the poker game next week! Run along kids, nothing to see here. Troy! Put your iPhone away." Bob puts his shoes back on in record speed.

"Oh my god, I am so humiliated." I rest my forehead on Tucker's back. "Patty Parker will be scarred for life because I was reckless, and Troy Parker has probably sent a grainy photo of me to all his prepubescent friends."

"The cameras on iPhones these days are pretty top notch. Probably not grainy."

"You're *not* helping. Why are they walking out of here slower than a herd of turtles?"

"Troy is hoping for one more shot." He pats my hand wrapped around his chest.

"Ugh, I can't believe you threw me under the bus like that."

"Look, as much as I love the position we're in, I'm super

hard and am about to place your hand around it."

I gasp, realizing I'm clinging onto his back like a naked octopus. With more force than I intend, I push off him, shoving him down into the water. I quickly backpedal away from him. Gone is the confident, sexy woman who wanted to kiss him under the waterfall twenty minutes ago.

I try to think of something funny and flirty to say back to him, but my mind blanks. Why can't I be assertive and tell him I want to taste his lips, to feel his fingers caress my skin? *Because you're a scaredy cat*, the little voice inside my head pipes up.

Here I have the sexiest, available, naked man right at my fingertips, and I'm not bold enough to lean in and kiss him. *You're not adventurous enough for him.* The voice whispers. I want to be adventurous, but I'm nervous. What if...

"Blakely, I don't know what's going on in that pretty head of yours, but stop."

I look up and get lost in his intense grass-green gaze. They make me think of sweet-smelling meadows of clover. He reaches up and smooths a strand of hair back from my cheek and tucks it behind my ear. I nod once and avert my eyes so he can't see the raw insecurity lurking there. I hate that it's there. I'm embarrassed it's there.

"Look at me." His voice is gruff and commanding. I have no choice but to let him see me. *Don't cry, don't cry, dammit, don't you dare cry.* "I'm proud of you." My eyebrows rise, and I release an embarrassing honk, sounding like a strangled goose. His thumb swipes over my cheek, catching a traitorous tear. "I'm serious, Blakely. You went out of your comfort zone and did something you've always wanted to try. Not many people can say they've done that. You let go of all your inhibitions and let your freak flag fly."

I smile tremulously. "My freak flag?"

"Yeah, and it was sexy as hell." He stares at me for an intense moment, gliding his thumb over my lips. I've never wanted someone to kiss me as much as the man standing in front of me. He drops his hand and my heart sinks. "We should get back and finish setting up camp. I'll make you a campfire rollerdog."

I wrinkle my nose. "I'm picturing the nasty hotdogs you see in gas stations, rotating on metal rollers for weeks on end."

He smirks and shakes his head. "Put on your swimsuit and let's go. I think you've had enough 'new me' experiences for one day."

He turns his back on me and swims toward the shore to grab his trunks. Averting my eyes, I swim to the rock where I left my suit. Emotions tangle and knot inside of me as I mull over everything that happened today.

A month ago, I never would have ventured out of my comfort zone like I did today. He's right, I should be proud. Another step in the right direction, but something in the pit of my stomach feels unsettled. All arrows point to Tucker Greyson, but I'm not sure what to do about it.

"Blakely, let's get a move on!" Tucker shouts from the shore. I hastily tie my top and climb out, hoping my boobs aren't being drooled over by a bunch of twelve-year-old boys tonight.

Chapter 17

Under the Stars

Blakely

I DOZE OFF on the ride back to our campsite, utterly exhausted from the hiking and the swimming. I just want to put on some comfy clothes, have a glass of wine, and relax by the fire.

A hand gently skims down my cheek. "Blakely, we're here. Why don't you go change first and I'll get a fire started? I haven't put our air mattresses in the tent yet." Tucker hands me my bag from the back seat.

"Okay, thanks," I reply groggily, trying to acclimate myself. I hop out of the truck and head toward our tent. Stopping, I turn in a circle, looking for the blue tent Tucker had erected earlier. I swear it was right here. Turning in another circle, I spot a crumpled blue tent by Bhodi's car that looks exactly like the one Tucker brought.

"Blake, what are you doing?"

I jump at the sound of Tucker's voice right behind me. "I think something happened to your tent." I point at the heap of canvas and metal.

Tucker's brows knit in confusion. He has the cutest little

crease when he does that. He stalks over to the broken tent and holds up a bent pole. "What the hell happened?"

"Dude!" Bhodi slides his kayak next to his car. "Sorry about the tent. Had a little accident."

"A little? My tent is demolished!"

"Bruh, sorry." Bhodi runs a hand through his hair, looking chagrined. "I accidentally put my car in reverse and ran over your tent. I'm so sorry. I'll replace it."

Tucker's expression is murderous as he looks from the crumpled tent to Bhodi's car, his fists clenched.

"See, there was this girl and—"

"I don't give a fuck about the girl. You've totaled my tent!"

"My bad, bro, really, but if you saw her, you'd understand…" Bhodi makes a curving motion with his hands.

"Bhodi, where are we supposed to camp tonight?" I ask, stepping in front of Tucker, who looks like he's about to reverse his truck over him.

"Man, I didn't even think about that. I'm sure Cherise won't mind if you two crash in her tent with us."

"Wait, who's Cherise?" I ask.

"I'm guessing she's the girl he ran our tent over for," Tucker bites out, looking like flames are about to come out of his flaring nostrils. "And no, we won't be sharing a tent with you."

"Well, if you change your mind, it's the red one over there." Bhodi salutes before jogging off toward Cherise's tent. How on earth did he meet a girl he's going to hook up with in the three hours we were gone this afternoon? Then again, I did witness him playing tonsil hockey with two women in the hot tub.

"Unfucking believable," Tucker curses, kicking the mangled heap of canvas.

"Maybe we should pack up and head home."

Tucker stands up and shakes his head. "Is that what you want?"

"I mean, at the beginning of the trip, I would have hitchhiked home if I wasn't so paranoid about being picked up by a serial killer, but now…"

"But now?" He picks up a pole bent in half, examining it.

"I don't know." I shrug my shoulders and stuff my hands into the pockets of my shorts. "I'm kind of enjoying this experience. I don't want it to end yet."

"Well, we have two choices. We can pack up and drive back home or…"

"Or?" I prompt, causing him to smile.

"Or you could expand your bucket list and we can sleep under the stars."

"On the ground?" I look around nervously for snakes and bugs.

"I can put the air mattress in the bed of the truck with lots of blankets. I have s'mores…" He waggles his eyebrows.

"I've never had a s'more, and I am feeling kind of hangry." I struggle to keep my lips from curving. "Fine, you win. Make me a rollerdog, a s'more, and blow up the mattress. I'm going to live on the edge."

He grins. "I knew you had it in you." He throws the pole down and slings an arm around my shoulders, walking me away from the crime scene. "How on earth have you never had a s'more?"

"I know this is hard to believe, but I'm not exactly the outdoorsy type."

He snorts, shaking his head, and pulls me to his side, causing my heartbeat to quicken as we walk back to the truck. And I let him, because for once in my life this feels right.

"OH MY GOSH, I'm so full." We're lying on the air mattress cocooned in blankets as we stare up at the night sky. I made a blanket barrier between us so he doesn't get any ideas. Okay, okay, it's totally for me. I don't need to be groping him in the middle of the night if I have another sex dream about him.

He turns his head and smiles at me. "How was your first s'more?"

"Once I got past the stickiness of it on my fingers, it was amazing. I wonder how Bhodi is faring."

He grunts. "Let's not ruin this beautiful night. I'm sure he's having fun with his…date."

"Can you really call her a date? He picked her up at a campground."

He grins and I watch the little lines around his eyes crinkle. "Where did she come from, anyway?"

"Some questions are best left unanswered," I say dryly.

He chuckles, nodding his head in agreement.

"The stars are so beautiful tonight," I sigh. "They seem so much closer up here than back in the city. Do you know the constellations? I only know Orion's Belt and The Little Dipper."

"Yeah. See over there? That's Libra, the scorpion's claw." He picks up my hand and grabs hold of my pointer finger, and traces whatever he sees in the night sky. I don't see anything, because I'm completely entranced by him. His nose with the little bump and his sharp jawline accented by the moonlight. I want to run my finger along the plains of his cheeks and the rough stubble around his square chin. He drops my hand and looks at me, smiling. "Not in the mood for astronomy?"

"I don't know." I sigh and look back up at the sky. "It kind of takes the mystery out of it. Sometimes, I just want to look up at the sky and see them twinkle and not think about what else they could be. I do like the names of them though. How did you learn all of them?"

"My grandfather taught me."

"Is he still alive?"

"Yeah, he lives up at the ranch with my mom."

"It must be nice to have your family all around you."

"It is and it isn't. Hard to get away with anything when everyone knows all your secrets." He smiles ruefully.

"When I was little, I'd wish on the stars that I secretly had a big family somewhere out there looking for me. Big holidays with lots of laughter and cousins to play games with." I shrug. "It never happened, of course. My parents have always been pretty self-involved. They are partners at a high-profile law firm in Atlanta. They travel a lot, so I don't see them much. Both sets of grandparents passed away before I was born."

"Sounds lonely."

"It's all I've ever known." I look back up at the stars.

"What's your biggest fear?"

"Oh, we're getting deep here, Mr. Greyson." I turn my head and smile at him.

"You're being evasive, Ms. Mayfield."

I huff out a laugh and swallow my pride. "My biggest fear is failure. But I think you already know that."

"Yeah." He's silent a beat while he looks up at the stars. "That's my biggest fear, too."

"Really?" I sit up on my elbow and smile down at him. "You put off an air of not really caring what others think."

"I don't. I don't want to fail myself or my family. I have goals...dreams. I don't want to let them down."

"That's pretty honorable."

He turns on his side and props his head in his hand, mirroring me. "What makes you happy?"

I giggle nervously. "What is this, twenty questions?"

He smiles devilishly. "I'm just trying to see what makes my roomie tick."

"You already know what makes me happy."

"Do I?" He arches an eyebrow and it takes all my self-control not to lean in and mash my lips to his. I plump up the blanket in between us and take an unsteady breath.

"Yes."

"Organization makes you happiest?"

I blow out the breath I didn't realize I was holding. "Bingo. Pretty pathetic, huh? Does that make me boring? I mean, does it take the mystery out of me as a woman?"

The little crease between his eyebrows appears, and I want to take my index finger and smooth it out. "I'm not sure what you're asking."

"Well, if being organized is what makes me happy, that's kind of pathetic, right? Being organized is my way of controlling the chaos."

"You know what I think?" He waits for me to look at him. "I think you might hide behind your need to be organized. I don't think you've truly found what makes you happy. That's the mystery."

I stare into his clover-green eyes, mesmerized by their crystal-clear beauty. His dark lashes are long, almost feminine, as he closes them and they brush against his cheek. He opens them again, the playfulness there seconds ago now replaced with something more raw and intense. Something I saw earlier when we were by the waterfall.

"You're right, I haven't found what makes me happy yet," I whisper, moving closer to him. "What makes you happy, Tucker?"

"Baseball," he says without a second thought. He slides his hand over my hip. There's a magnetism between us my body refuses to ignore. His pupils darken as I shove the barrier blanket away. I'm not going to be scared this time.

I tease my lips over his. Petal-soft butterfly kisses turn deeper, more complex, as his lips move against mine. I may have started the kiss, but he effortlessly takes over, pulling me into him, his hand lightly trailing from my hip down to my thigh. He pulls my leg over his, bringing me flush against him. All the noise in my head disappears, leaving only my senses to navigate my way through the intoxicating kiss. He tastes like peppermint from his toothpaste and smells like campfire.

His lips coax mine apart and I can't stop my hands from gliding up under his t-shirt. The hard ridges of muscle feel like satin under my fingertips as I blindly explore his magnificent body. His tongue expertly dances with mine while his fingers thread through my hair and tug me closer. I whimper, wanting more…needing more. My fingers edge the band of his sweatpants. I run a palm over his hard length, igniting a low growl from him.

"Hey, do you guys have any more s'mores left? My girl's hungry."

I swear I can hear a record player screeching as the needle slides off.

I untangle myself from Tucker as he sits up, running his hands through his hair. "What the fuck do you want, Bhodi?"

"Oh…hey there, whoa, didn't see you had the roommate back there with ya. Nice, man. Can I borrow your keys?"

Someone please drown this guy in the river.

"What for?" Tucker grits out.

"Just looking for the s'mores you were talking about on the hike earlier. I can grab them. Are they in the back of the truck?" He tries the door, but it's locked. He jiggles the handle like it will miraculously open.

"Motherfucking idiot," Tucker seethes under his breath, chucking his keys at him. "Bhodi! We don't have any. Go bother someone else."

He roots through the bags, moaning. "Dude, yes, this is

perfect." He slams the truck door, breaking the peaceful silence. "Bruh, chillax. I found some chips instead." He wanders off into the dark, the rustling of the bag followed by the crunch of chips echoing in the night. He didn't just break the spell Tucker had me under. He plowed his kayak right through it. He backed his Subaru over it and crunched our moment like he did the tent. I wrap the blanket around myself and look back up at the stars. Tucker settles in next to me. I'm half expecting him to lean over and whisper, *now where were we?* But he doesn't. He lays back and stares up at the stars.

"Why did you invite that idiot again?"

"I don't know," I say miserably. "I'm sorry. Lesson learned."

"Thank God."

I burrow down into the blankets. Tucker reaches out and pulls me into him, leaving his arm draped over me. I like snuggling next to Tucker Greyson. I like it a lot. Perhaps camping isn't so terrible, minus Bhodi Mills. And maybe, just maybe, I'm right where I belong after all. Would it be so bad living here and snuggling against Tucker every night?

"Goodnight, Blakely May."

"Goodnight, Tucker."

He stares up at the sky and I covertly watch him, my eyelids growing heavy. And for the first time, I don't want to strangle him. I want to kiss him some more.

Goal: *Kiss Tucker Greyson again.*

Problem: *I'm confused by my feelings for him.*

Stress: *Wondering if he thought the kiss was as magical as I did.*

What's the best thing that happened today: *Skinny-dipping and kissing Tucker. It's a tie.*

What I am grateful for: *A night under the stars with him.*

Chapter 18

Fruit Flies

Tucker

COLD WATER TRICKLES down my cheek. I must have a damn leak in my ceiling. I roll to the side and pull my blanket with me, shivering. Why is it so damn cold in my house? I peel one gritty eyelid back and sit up with a start, the blanket sliding off my chest. The flint-grey sky drips rain down on us, while fog and rain crawl over the surrounding mountains, making the trees and craggy landscape disappear. I look around for Blakely, gathering my bearings, but all that's peeking out from under the covers is a blonde topknot. The rain has picked up, falling at a steady rate.

"Blakely." I shake the blanket mound next to me. "Blakely, get up. We have to get in the truck." She groans under the covers but doesn't stir. "Blakely, wake up. Come on darlin', it's raining." I shake her again. She slowly sits up and shivers, pulling the blanket up around her.

"It's so cold… Oh my god, it's raining!"

"I've been trying to tell you. Come on, let's get in the truck."

I hop down and help her out, and we grab the blankets

and pillows. The rain is like needles against our skin as it falls from the darkening sky. I reach for the back door, but it's locked. "Blakely, do you have the keys?"

"I don't have them," she shouts from the other side of the truck.

"Did Bhodi give them to you after he opened the door last night?"

"Oh no. Oh god no!" she cries, cupping her hands around her face, peering in. "He left the keys in the back seat and locked the door."

I say a few expletives under my breath. I'm usually a pretty even-keeled kind of guy. People normally don't get under my skin, but Bhodi Mills has tested my patience to the max. Blakely shivers as she grips a rain-soaked blanket over her head. I'm going to kill Bhodi.

Luckily, I keep a spare key in a magnetic case under the truck when I go camping in case I lose my keys on a hike. I reach under and locate the small box, extracting the key. I quickly unlock the car and we bundle into the front seat.

"Thank God for your boy scout skills or we'd be screwed."

I grunt, turning the heaters on full blast. "I think it's safe to say Bhodi Mills is an idiot, and you are never allowed to invite him camping with us again."

Blakely chuckles and holds her hands up to the heater. "Never again."

"Is that to camping or Bhodi?"

"Both." She laughs. "Okay, fine, camping wasn't horrible. I *might* be talked into going again." She sends me a sly grin and I can't help the smile curving my lips.

"I promise next time, we'll be in the comfort of a tent shielding us from chilly rain."

If she gets pneumonia because that jackass needed s'mores at midnight, I will shove his kayak so far up his ass he won't be able to walk again.

THE RIDE BACK flies quickly as heat blasts against our frigid skin. Blakely playfully reminds me it's a good thing she brought an extra pair of long socks. I think back to last night. How easily I could have pulled her under me and touched her soft skin. The kiss was like a drug to my bloodstream, crazy good and addictive. But then that tool, Bhodi, broke the spell she had me under and I realized getting involved with Blakely Mayfield would be a bad idea. I need to keep things light and simple, and that kiss was complicated as hell. It opened up possibilities and a future together, and that's not conceivable between us.

I pull into my driveway and notice Annie waiting by the front door with Hershel. She gives us a little wave as I put the truck in park. Here's the other woman in my life who made light and simple impossible. I exhale heavily, get out of the truck, and walk over to Blakely's side. Hershel comes bounding off the steps and practically bulldozes into me.

"Hey, Annie, what are you doing here? Where's Ben?" I ask, helping Blakely down.

"Oh, he's with my mom. I saw your sister walking

Hershel on the street and asked where you were. She said you went camping and you'd be back this afternoon. I didn't realize you had company. I'm sorry for popping by, but I offered to bring Hershel back."

"Annie, this is Blakely. She's a friend of Junie's from Atlanta. She's here visiting for a bit."

"Oh, hi, nice to meet you." Annie smiles, but it doesn't quite reach her eyes.

Blakely returns her smile and shakes her hand. "Nice to meet you, too. I'm going to go inside and unpack, shower, tidy up, maybe do some laundry. Unless you need privacy in the house? I can drive…somewhere. Or walk…I like to walk."

I hand Blakely her bag and smirk. Like I would tell her to leave. "No, you're fine. It's your house too."

Annie's eyes bounce back and forth between us.

"Okay, well, it was so nice to meet you, Annie." She smiles.

"What? Oh yes, so nice to meet you."

Blakely scurries off and Hershel bounds after her.

"She seems nice. She's really pretty," Annie says.

"Yeah…do you want to come inside?"

Annie looks at the front door wistfully. "Oh, I shouldn't…I only have about thirty minutes before I need to pick Ben back up. I was actually wondering if you wanted to come over for dinner Wednesday night? Unless you're busy with work…or if you have plans with Blakely. I mean, she could come too, I guess, although she probably doesn't want to hang out with your ex and her four-year-old." She giggles nervously.

"I'm sure she wouldn't mind. Ben is a pretty cute guy. Besides, it would be good for her to get out and meet more people. I think she's lonely."

"Oh, sure, I'd love to help...okay, so Wednesday night, it's a date. I mean, not like an actual date... I'll make dinner for the four of us then."

"Thanks Annie, that's really nice of you to include Blakely."

"Of course!" she says cheerfully before she kisses me on the cheek and scurries to her car.

"Thanks for bringing Hershel back."

"Anytime!"

Bhodi's Subaru pulls onto the road. I quickly jump the porch steps and run inside before I get stuck talking to the idiot. It took all my self-control not to murder him this morning. I walk into the kitchen and huff out a laugh when I hear the vacuum going. She doesn't waste a single minute, does she? Following the loud whir of the vacuum to the living room, I stop short.

"What the hell are you doing?"

Blakely looks up from bending over Hershel, her lips forming a perfect O. "Don't be mad, it's doing wonders for the hair and drool." She sweeps the vacuum attachment back and forth over Hershel's back.

I look at her incredulously, folding my arms over my chest. "Are you seriously vacuuming my dog right now?"

"He likes it! And look at all the hair in the canister. I don't know why I didn't think of this before."

Hershel stands there pitifully while my Mr. Clean-obsessed roommate vacuums him. "Jesus, bud, have some dignity."

"You'll thank me later when he's not shedding a pound of hair on the couch!" she shouts over the vacuum. I shake my head and head to the kitchen to unpack the cooler. The vacuum stops and I hear her murmuring *good boy* to Hersh, which makes me grin.

"Hey, do you want a beer?" I walk back in and find her spritzing him with Febreze. "Did you just spray my dog with air freshener?"

"It's not air freshener…exactly. It's odor control spray…for furniture." She looks at the front of the bottle and shrugs. "Trust me, he needs it."

"He's a dog. He's supposed to smell. It's his *job*."

She wrinkles her nose. "His job is to smell?"

I rub my forehead. "Look, Hershel doesn't need perfumes or sprays. Come here, Hersh, don't let her turn you into a frou-frou dog. The next thing I know, you'll be wearing bows."

"Ooh, which reminds me, can you pick up some breath mints for him next time you're at the pet store?" She scrunches her nose while he licks himself. I extend the beer to her, ignoring her breath mint comment, but she shakes her head. "Got any wine?"

"I don't think so, but we could head over to my sister's pub."

"I still need to get out of these clothes and take a shower," she sighs before sitting down on a barstool at the kitchen island. "So, are we going to talk about…you know."

I lean back against the counter on the opposite side. "No, I don't know." I pop open the beer and take a pull. "You want to talk about taking showers? You want to take one together?" I waggle my eyebrows suggestively.

"About the kiss!" she growls irritably.

I love that this conversation is making her cheeks flush. "What about it?"

"You are making this super awkward right now," she grumbles. "I mean, are we going to pretend it didn't happen?"

"Do you want to pretend it didn't happen?" I arch an eyebrow. Pretending the kiss didn't happen would be impossible for me. It's all I can think about. I couldn't sleep last night knowing she was inches away from me and I couldn't touch her.

Her fingernail scrubs at a spot on the granite. "I mean, it was good...right? Or was it forgettable? Oh god, pretend I didn't just ask that." She looks up at me with a look of horror on her face. She's so damn cute. I can't help but smile. Her eyes narrow. "Are you laughing at me? You know what? Forget I ever mentioned it. Forget the whole thing happened."

She gets up from her seat, but I quickly stride over to her and cage her in. Her golden eyes widen as I lean into her. "I'm not laughing at you, Blakely May. I'm laughing because you're so fucking adorable. Do I want to kiss you again? Hell ye—"

She puts her hand behind my neck and pulls me to her lips before I can finish my sentence. I was going to tell her it probably isn't the best idea since we live together, but all thoughts of turning her down go right out the window once her lips touch mine. She whimpers right before my tongue sweeps over hers, deepening the kiss. I push the fruit bowl over on the counter, picking her up and setting her on top of it. Her legs wrap around my waist as we feverishly pull our shirts off. I run my fingertips down her arms, causing little goosebumps to pebble on her flesh.

Her light touch whispers over my stomach and around to my back, burning a fiery path. I need to be closer to her. I break the kiss and run my tongue along the swell of her breast. She runs her fingers through my hair, tugging deliciously while she moans. I reach around and release her clasp, freeing her from the lacy bra. I bend my head and capture her pert nipple in my mouth, while my other hand massages her other breast. She whimpers, pulling me closer to her. My aching hard-on hits her right in her core.

"Oh my god, yes Tucker, yes," she whimpers as I run my tongue over her other rosy bud. I pick her up and carry her to my bedroom, where I gently lay her down. I shed my sweatpants and she shimmies out of her leggings.

"Are you sure about this?" I ask, leaning over her, dipping my head and running my nose along her neck. She smells so fucking good, like summer-ripened strawberries and rain. "Because there's no going back. I'd like to say this won't change anything between us, but it will." *Fuck, who am I trying to talk out of this, her or me?*

"I can't believe I'm saying this, but yes," she breathes out. "I want this."

"Thank fuck." I dip my head and kiss her bruised lips. I don't think I could handle one more second without feeling her underneath me.

"Tucker...you home? Oh, hey Hershel, where is everyone? Tuck! Blakely?"

I close my eyes and curse under my breath, holding my position over Blakely. Her eyes bug out, looking almost cartoonish while she tries to wiggle out from under my arms.

"Oh my god, who is that?" Blakely hisses, swiftly throwing a blanket around herself.

"Yeah, hold on!" I shout back, hopping up and slamming the door shut. *Worst timing ever, Whitney.* I knew I shouldn't have given her a key. I pull a pair of athletic shorts on while Blakely flails around the room looking for her clothes. "That would be my sister. Welcome to having family in a small town."

"Crap, all I have are my leggings…no!" she gasps, her cheeks turning rosy pink. "My bra and shirt are on the kitchen island! I can't hide in here all night. Can I? What if she comes in here and finds me? What then?"

I chuckle. "It's okay. I'll distract her and take her out on the back porch while you run upstairs and get dressed."

"Okay, good plan. One, two, three, go!"

"We're not going on a military mission." I smirk back at her. "You're pretty cute when you're frazzled."

"Tucker? Where are you?"

"Oh my god, stop flirting and go!" Blakely turns me around and shoves me out the door before I can grab a t-shirt.

I stumble into the alcove by the stairs. "Hey Whit, what brings you by?"

"I wanted to hang with my big brother and his roomie since my new manager is on tonight. Thought maybe we could order Chinese. Is Blakely home?"

"She's uh, upstairs. I think she's napping. Let's not wake her yet. You know her, she'll start vacuuming or something weird like that."

Whitney laughs. "Were you working out?" Her face goes slack as her eyes sweep over the kitchen island, zeroing in on Blakely's bra and t-shirt. "Oh my god, did I interrupt you with someone?" she whispers. "It's like five p.m., I didn't think I'd be interrupting anything at five p.m."

"I wasn't with a woman. I was about to take a shower. Let's go out on the back porch and have a beer."

"Yeah, sure, sounds good." She looks at the bra one more time and raises an eyebrow.

"Must be Blakely's." I shrug nonchalantly, quickly grabbing it and throwing it in the laundry room. I grab a clean t-shirt neatly folded in a basket. I look down at the pleated crease in my shirt. Did she starch my t-shirts? I shake my head and grab a beer from the fridge for Whit and the one on the counter I opened earlier.

Whitney dramatically collapses into a deck chair, plucking the beer from my outstretched fingers. "I've had such a long week. How was camping? I'm so sorry about Annie, by the way. She showed up at my house and asked where you were."

"She told me she ran into you on the street walking Hershel."

"I mean, if you consider my front yard the street…"

I smirk, stretching out in an Adirondack chair. "She asked Blakely and I over for dinner Wednesday night."

"What? Oh, the drama that could ensue!" She waggles her eyebrows and then pouts. "I wanna go. Sometimes I hate being a responsible adult with a business to run."

"What do you think's going to happen?" I chuckle. "Annie and I are friends, that's it."

"Does she know that?"

"Yes, of course she does."

"Uh-huh. That's why she was stalking me today, looking for you. Tucker, you are so clueless sometimes. Put the poor girl out of her misery."

"The writing was on the wall when she had another man's baby," I bite out.

"Yeah, a baby, which you're practically a surrogate father for."

My jaw ticks in annoyance. "Stay out of it, Whitney."

She puts her hands up in surrender. "I'm out. I just think things might get sticky now that you have a new roomie."

"Things are clean as a whistle around here. Blakely is…"

"What? Please tell me Jason owes me fifty bucks."

"She's—"

"Hi, Whitney, how are you?" The door opens and Blakely steps out.

Whitney jumps in surprise. "Blakely, hey! I'm sorry I haven't come over sooner. The pub is kind of a mess right now and I've had to be there twenty-four-seven. Ugh, I was just telling Tuck how much it sucks to own a business. Oh, hey! I heard Etta hired you. Congrats! Looks like you'll be staying longer. Cute top!"

I side-eye my sister. "Jesus, take a breath," I mumble before getting up to pull a chair over for Blakely to join us. Her hair is wet and pulled up in a topknot, so she must have taken a quick shower.

"Thanks," she murmurs, sitting down with a glass of wine. "Found some."

"Hey everyone, thanks for the heads-up we were having a get-together." Jason steps up on the back deck.

"It wasn't exactly planned. Whitney showed up on her own, like you." I smirk.

"Eh, well, I wanted to see how camping went." He raises his eyebrows. I shake my head, suppressing a smile. *No, dude, you did not win fifty bucks.*

"It was fun, actually." Blakely beams at Jason. "Hi, I'm Blakely."

Jason shakes her hand. "Nice to meet you, Blakely. I'm Jason. I'm sure you've heard *all* about me. I'm the hot single cousin."

I snort and hand him a beer. "So he likes to think. He's been single since we were in diapers, and not by choice."

Jason smacks the back of my head before sprawling out in a chair. "Don't listen to him. He's just jealous I'm prettier."

"I've heard a lot about you from Junie." Blakely smiles. "So, you guys were both adopted?"

"Yep, Junie and I are twins."

"It's a shame she got the good looks and the brains." Whitney laughs. "What did you get?"

"Talent." Jason smiles confidently.

Whitney and I both crack up, but Blakely looks at him seriously.

"Oh, what do you do?"

"What don't I do?"

"I mean, do you have like an actual talent? Could you go

on *America's Got Talent?*"

"He's going out on tour next year." I grin.

Whitney is laughing so hard she has tears coming out of her eyes. Jason glares at us before flashing a smile at Blakely.

"Really? What is it?" Blakely looks expectantly at Jason.

"Uh…"

"He's really good at sitting on his couch playing video games. Didn't you beat that twelve-year-old the other weekend in some championship?" Whitney asks.

"Hey, I can do other stuff like backflips off the boat."

Blakely looks sorely disappointed. "I was hoping you could sing or do magic tricks or something."

"It's a shame he can't magically make my fifty bucks appear," Whitney says.

"So, back to what we were talking about before we were so rudely interrupted." I clear my throat and glare at my sister. "What's this about a job with Etta Bird?" I look at Blakely, wondering why I'm just now hearing about this.

She waves a hand nonchalantly in front of her face. "Oh, it's nothing. Just some mornings. She kind of blackmailed me into it."

"Oh yeah, that sounds like crazy Etta," Whitney says.

"Wait, is she really crazy? Because I was wonder—"

"She's harmless," I say gruffly, mulling over what it means to have Blakely here on a semi-permanent basis. "But don't tell her anything. It will be all over town in a matter of minutes. I thought you weren't easily swayed by blackmailing threats?"

She gives me a flat stare. "I'm only immune to you."

Whitney's eyes bounce back and forth between us. Jason

coughs, stifling a laugh.

"I thought you were only going to be here a couple of weeks?" I ask.

Whitney hits my arm. "Don't be rude."

I arch an eyebrow at Blakely, ignoring my sister while Jason ducks inside.

"No, it's okay. I did tell you I'd probably only be here a couple of weeks." She gives me a wan smile. "But unofficially, I'm leaving in September."

There's no way I can go two and a half months and not sleep with her. Not when we're constantly in each other's space. It's obvious we're attracted to each other. I wonder if she'll be able to keep it light and fun or if she'll want more from me. Something tells me light and fun isn't on her checklist.

"Earth to Tucker…" Whitney says.

I look up from my beer bottle. "Sorry, did you ask me something?"

"We're talking about getting Chinese for dinner. You in?"

"Oh yeah, whatever you three want. I think there's a menu in the kitchen drawer."

"I'll go look for it." Blakely gets up. As soon as the door clicks shut, my sister turns to me.

"Oh my god, you two had sex!"

"What are you talking about?"

"The sexual tension is palpable, and as your sister, having to feel it pinging between you two is gross. She can't stop staring at you. Not to mention I saw her bra and t-shirt on the kitchen island. You were shirtless. She's acting all weird…"

"Slow down, Columbo. Do you ever wonder if you'll pass out from lack of oxygen while talking? We did *not* have sex because a certain annoying sister might have interrupted."

She gasps. "I knew it! You know what this means? I won the bet!"

Jason reappears, shaking his head. "No, no way. If Tucker says nothing happened, then I believe him. She does not look like a woman who just had sex."

Whitney side-eyes Jason and smirks. "Like you would know what that looks like."

I run a hand down my face. These two drive me nuts. "You did not win the bet, Whit, and furthermore—"

"What bet?" Blakely asks, sitting back down in her chair. The three of us shift uneasily in our seats.

"Jesus, Blakely, you're like a damn ninja." Whitney laughs lightly. "We were talking about the bet between Jason and I, that I won, by the way. We bet Tucker couldn't—"

"Couldn't get you to go camping," I effectively cut her off, glaring at her. Sometimes I want to strangle her. If Blakely knew Whitney and Jason had a bet I couldn't get her in my bed, she would go ballistic, and I can't say I'd blame her. We have enough on our plates to sort out as it is.

"Ah, so that's why you were pushing it so hard." She smirks. Guilt punches me in the gut. "Well, I didn't want to go, but Tucker didn't leave me much of a choice."

"I bet he didn't." Whitney laughs lightly under her breath. "Sounds cozy."

Hershel jumps up, growling.

"What is it, Hersh?" I smooth back his ruffled fur, looking around for a threatening animal on the bank of the river. Whitney perks up in her seat. "Oh well, hello there Mr. Muscles! Who is that and why haven't I been introduced?"

I look up to see what my sister is referring to and almost choke on my beer. Dipshit Bhodi Barracuda Mills is doing air squats on his back deck, shirtless.

"That's a hard no. You are not getting involved with him. He cost me a five-hundred-dollar tent."

"I agree. Trust your brother on this one, Whitney." Blakely grimaces. "He's a slimeball."

"Who isn't these days?" she murmurs, arching her neck to get a better look. "He's so yummy. Why haven't I seen him before?" As if pulled by an invisible string, she gets up from her seat and goes over to the deck railing.

Jason looks over and rolls his eyes. "He was at the kayak competition. He talked a big game, but then turned over on the first rapid."

"Sounds about right." I shake my head. "Whitney has the worst taste in men. They are like fruit flies around her. Once they show up, they're hard to get rid of."

"Is she going to talk to him?" Blakely whispers, patting my sister's empty chair. I move over so I can get a better view.

"God, I hope not. Hopefully, she's just silently stalking him. She's good at that."

"Hey there, neighbor! Haven't seen you before." Whitney waves to Bhodi, who stops mid-squat. He straightens up and grabs a water bottle.

"Hey there yourself, gorgeous. Haven't seen you around

these parts either."

Whitney titters, making me want to punch this guy's lights out.

"Great, here we go," Jason grumbles. "Let's hope she doesn't hire him at the pub."

"She's not going to take our advice?" Blakely's eyes widen while she watches the train wreck unfold.

"Nope."

"We're ordering Chinese. Want to join us?" Whitney asks.

"No!" Blakely, Jason, and I shout in unison.

Whitney glares at us over her shoulder. "Don't be assholes," she hisses. "Be nice!"

Blakely grabs my hand, squeezing it tight.

"Be over in fifteen!"

Whitney bounces on her toes while the three of us groan. "Awesome! I'll be waiting."

"Fucking great, another fruit fly," I mutter before standing up to go inside and place the order.

Goal: *Try camping again.*

Problem: *No problems here…okay, maybe I have a slight problem. I got completely naked with Tucker Greyson and was going to let him do the dirty.*

Stress: *We're roommates. Doing the dirty is a BAD idea.*

Best thing to happen today: *Getting naked with Tucker. No, no…that was a bad thing…but damn, he's sinfully sexy and hands-down, the best kisser.*

What I'm grateful for: *I survived skinny-dipping, tubing, sleeping outdoors, eating a rollerdog and s'mores, and making out with Tucker Greyson. Oh god, maybe I'm having another breakdown.* ☹

Chapter 19

Ed Barker

Blakely

THE BELL CHIMES when I open the shop door. "Etta? Good morning," I shout. "Are you here? It's Blakely!"

"Jesus, I can hear you. I'm old, not deaf!"

I look around the shop. "Where are you?"

The curtain by the side window ripples. I walk over and slowly move it aside. Etta is standing at the edge of the window with a pair of binoculars glued to her face. "What are you doing?"

"Watching Ed Barker mow his lawn in his underwear. He's got quite the er, lawn mowing equipment, if you know what I mean. His blade is *sharp*."

"Ew, Etta! I don't want to know about his…tools. That's an invasion of privacy," I chastise.

"Oh Blakley, stop being so uptight. It's not like I'm groping the man in public. Look for yourself. I may be old, but I'm not dead. Perhaps Ed is a little too young for me, but this is a free country. If he's going to mow in his skivvies, I'm gonna watch."

I gingerly take the binoculars from her and raise them

up, mentally preparing myself for a wrinkly old man in dirty white bikini briefs...if one can sufficiently ready themselves for that.

"Wow," I breathe out, studying his tanned skin glistening in the morning sun. His dark hair ruffles in the morning breeze while he pauses, wiping his brow. Ed Barker isn't wrinkly. Ed Barker is fucking dreamy. Sexy is an inadequate word to describe him mowing his yard in black shorts, which could be considered underwear through seventy-year-old eyes.

"Told ya so. He's the fire chief for Greyson Gap."

"He's so beautiful."

"Those hips don't lie, Shakira. His father had some Cherokee in his blood. His mother is from Venezuela." Etta stands on her tippy-toes to get a better look. If anyone passed us on the side street, they would think we were kissing the glass. Etta wipes the condensation our breath is making on the glass with her scarf.

"He's...wow. He's perfection. He should be on the cover of GQ," I murmur.

"Give me those back, this ain't a free showing of *Magic Mike*." She wrangles the binoculars away from me. "You have your very own GQ model right under your nose. Let me have Ed."

"I don't have anything under my nose." I move away from the curtain and look around the shop. One thing is for certain, Etta can never find out Tucker and I almost had sex. Not only would I never hear the end of it, but it would be splashed all over Greyson Gap within minutes. "Where should I start?"

"Well, you're late." Etta regrettably lowers the binoculars and wipes a smudge off the window.

"I'm ten minutes early," I cry, double-checking my watch.

"I have paperwork for you to fill out. Then I'm going to skadoodle on out of here and let you run the shop."

"Wait, aren't you going to train me first?"

"Train you? What are you, a seal at the zoo? Someone comes in, they buy something, you ring it up. Battabam, battaboom."

"Uh, Etta, I think it's a bit more complicated than that. What about the computer and credit card machines? Where do you keep extra tissue paper, cash, in case I run out or need to make change?"

Etta sighs heavily, her bangles jingling as she raises a hand to her forehead. "You're more complicated than I expected. Fine, we'll do a mock run-through so you feel good about yourself."

"I…"

"I'll be the customer." She waves her hand dismissively at me. "You just be…you." She walks out of the store. The bell jingles when she walks back in with her nose in the air. She fingers a bracelet on a table by the window. She glances at me and looks away. *What on earth is she doing?* She clears her throat and glances in my direction, one eyebrow raised. She huffs out a breath, her body sagging dramatically. "Good grief! I am the customer, Blakely. Welcome me."

Oh…she's in character. "Oh, yes, sorry. Welcome to Tidings. How may I help you?"

"I need to use the restroom."

"Of course, it's right back here."

"No!" Etta barks, startling me with her sharp tone. "Blakely, we never *ever* let customers use the restrooms. They're like wild animals who pee all over everything. And especially don't let Betty Doliver use it. Trust me, she tries every Friday morning after she's been to The Bagel Bin. Ten cups of coffee would make anyone have to bomb the bowl. One time and I had to air out my shop for three days."

I grimace in revulsion. "No Betty Doliver. Got it."

"If you take away anything from our little lesson, it's this. No bathrooms. I don't care if they look like they are about to pass out because they have to pee so badly, that's not my fault. They make Depends for that reason. Got it?" She looks at me sharply, her nostrils flaring.

"Got it." I nod. "No bathrooms, no Betty Doliver, wear Depends."

"Good, now, I'd like to purchase some stationery. Is anything on sale?"

"I have no idea."

"Heavens to Betsy. No, nothing is *ever* on sale. Sales are for nincompoops and coupon-cutters like Lonna Parker."

I nod. "Sorry, ma'am, we have nothing on sale."

"Good." She lifts her chin and sashays over to a bookcase housing stationery. She picks up a box. "May I take these home and if I decide I don't like them, bring them back?"

"As long as the package hasn't been opened."

"Hallelujah. Finally, she gets something right," Etta grumbles. "Can I order my own monogram stationery?"

"Yes?"

"Yes, the book with ordering instructions is under the

computer." She picks up a bracelet on the way to the computer and pulls out a large white binder. "There are also instructions on closing and opening in here."

"Oh, good. Would you like to purchase the bracelet you just put on?"

Etta smiles at me brightly for the first time since I've met her. "I thought I was going to have to send you over to the Gas N Go, but I think you are going to do just fine here, my dear."

The bell jingles and we look up to see Tucker duck into the store. "Good morning, Ms. Etta. How are you on this lovely morning? It's gonna be a hot one. I was wondering if I could steal Blakely for a second?"

"Oh, why Tucker Greyson, no need to steal from me, honey. This fresh ray of sunshine is free for you." Etta smiles at him coquettishly before pushing me forward with amazing arm strength. I huff out a laugh, stumbling into Tucker. He catches me easily and smiles, his cute little dimples popping. It takes my breath away and I'm pretty sure Etta sighs from behind me.

"Hi, how did you know I was here?"

"It's a small town, Smiles. Everyone knows you're here."

"Oh, kind of creepy, but okay. What's up?"

He's still holding me in his arms and it feels...intimate. Flashbacks of the almost-sex we had the day before make my cheeks feel hot. He smells incredible, and I want to stay tucked against his chest and gaze into his clover-green eyes for the rest of the day. *Focus, Blakely, the man is trying to talk to you, not throw you down in the middle of Etta's store.* I take a step back and smooth my hand over my hair.

"I forgot to tell you last night. We've been invited over to Annie's house for dinner Wednesday night."

"Oh, I don't know, Tucker..." I look over my shoulder to see if Etta is listening. She's pretending to fold scarves, but I know the sneaky geriatric has her hearing aid turned up to ten.

"You need to get out and meet people. It will be fun, I promise."

I swallow past wanting to tell him no because he's right. I *do* need to get out more. I've been here a few weeks and so far my circle consists of Tucker, Whitney, Barracuda Bhodi, and Etta. Maybe the Parkers since they've seen me naked. I definitely need to expand my circle.

"Okay." I nod, convincing myself this is a smart plan.

He squeezes my arm and gives me a disarming smile. "Cool, have a great day. See you later, Etta! Thanks for hiring my girl here. She'll have this place running like a well-oiled machine lickety-split."

His girl?

"Mmm, stay out of trouble, Tucker Greyson."

He winks and flashes his all-star smile, making my knees turn to jelly. "Yes, ma'am. Y'all have a nice day."

The bell rings and he exits into the sunshine. We both silently watch the golden boy walk away.

"Wow," I breathe out.

"Indeed." Etta fans herself next to me.

I shake my head. "I meant wow, what an easy customer." I smile brightly, trying desperately to hide the effect Tucker has over me.

"Mmm, hmph. So, you're going to Annie's for dinner.

That should be interesting."

"Why? Should I be worried? What do you know?"

"If you're going to live by the river, make friends with the crocodile," Etta says mysteriously before she walks away.

"What the heck does that even mean?"

"You should worry about your hair if you need something to agonize over. My girl in town, Tanya, over at Suzie Q's is excellent. She's been doing it for years. In fact, she might have an opening this afternoon."

"What's wrong with my hair?" I touch my hair and turn to look in a small mirror by the scarves. Maybe I need a trim, but the color isn't bad.

"It needs some oomph. Go to Tanya. She'll fix you right up. Better than those fancy high-dollar salons in Atlanta. Here's her number." Etta hands me a card before she walks back over to the computer. "Why don't you check me out so I can show you how to do it?"

Oh, this woman is infuriating! "Etta, so help me God, if you don't tell me what you know about Annie, I will march over to Ed Barker's house and tell him you are a pervy old lady with binoculars and a lawn mowing fetish."

"Oh fine," she says grumpily. "Annie, as you know, is Tucker's ex-fiancée. You also know she had a one-night stand and, as a result, had Ben."

"Yikes, I didn't know it was one night."

"Well, the silly girl has been in love with Tucker Greyson since she was in pigtails. Wherever he went, she was trailing right behind him. She's never gotten over him. And I'm guessing she's invited you over to size up the competition."

"Oh, no, I'm not the competition."

"Honey, if you're not the competition, then Ed Barker is the ugliest man on this side of the Eluwei River."

I worry my bottom lip. "So, should I not go?"

"The Cheyenne say, 'The first teacher is our own heart'."

I mull over her words, not sure what she's trying to tell me. She audibly sighs. "Oh, for God's sake, do I have to spell it out for you? *Listen* to your heart, Blakely!"

"I don't know what my heart is trying to tell me." I whine pitifully.

Etta shakes her head and opens the cash register. "That, my dear, is a bigger problem than Annie."

Goal: *Figure out what my heart is trying to tell me.*

Problem: *I don't have a clue.*

Stress: *Apparently, my hair is a mess and there are crocodiles in the river.*

What's the best thing that happened today: *I saw Ed Barker mowing his lawn.*

What I am grateful for: *I'm grateful to have Etta Bird on my side.*

Chapter 20

Suzie Q's

Blakely

I TURN DOWN an old dirt road ten minutes from Main Street, positive I'm lost. If I were a hair stylist, I'd be in the center of town, or at least by the Gas N Go where everyone can see me. There's no signage, so I keep trundling along, my car bouncing over potholes. I cringe, listening to the pops of gravel and small rocks ping off the side of my car. Add on a new paint job, along with fixing the dent from Tucker's tractor. I pull up in front of an old trailer home with a small front porch. A yellow wooden sign badly in need of new paint reads *Suzie Q's*.

I'm already kicking myself for listening to Etta and letting her get into my head. There's nothing wrong with my hair. I went to Clair Michelles, an upscale Atlanta hair salon that would charge a hundred dollars for a trim. Now I'm sitting in front of Suzie Q's which looks like it's about to fall down the next time a thunderstorm rolls through, having a mini freakout.

I breathe in deep through my nose and out through my mouth. It's only hair, I can do this. Besides, it couldn't hurt to get a little oomph, right? Look at Whitney, Annie, and even that angry Stacy lady who wanted to poke Tucker's eyes out with a dart. They all have nice hair. Rule number one, don't judge a book by its cover.

I get out, lock up my car, and step onto the rickety front porch. "Hello?" I knock next to the open screen door. Great, this means no air conditioning. Country music plays softly, and what sounds like ten small dogs start yapping from somewhere in the back.

"Cinnamon, Harley, Sugar, Dusty, Gary, Jay, Joe Don, shush it! Come on in, honey," a woman from the back room shouts, her voice growing closer.

That was either seven or eight dogs I counted... I tentatively open the screen door and step in. "Uh... Hi, I'm Blakely Mayfield. I have an appointment at four. Etta Bird referred me?"

An older woman with foil in her hair and sunglasses on sits motionless in one of the chairs. She looks like the dead guy from the old movie *Weekend at Bernie's*, where they prop him up at parties and pretend he's alive. God, I hope she's alive.

I look around the open one-room shop. There's a salon chair in front of a mirror, a washing station, and some hair dryers. An old green couch that's seen better days sits against one wall. Tables littered with magazines and hair products sit between two chairs. Well, at least it's set up like a salon and it's clean-ish, although it does smell like cigarettes, hairspray, and dog pee.

"Oh yes! Hiya darlin', I'm Tanya." She steps out from the back room. Tanya's a busty, curvy, bleached-blonde with

her hair tied up in a topknot on her head. She's wearing a
tie-dye tank top, capri leggings, and kitten-heel sandals. I
wouldn't be able to guess her age if my life depended on it.
"Had to cage up the vermin!" She cackles while lighting up a
cigarette. She takes a deep drag and rolls her eyes heaven-
ward. "Jesus, that's good. Sorry hon, just give me a sec…had
a rough afternoon. Doris Plunkin's dog was fit to be tied
today when I had to put bows in his ears. Nearly took my
face off." She grimaces before taking another deep drag, then
stubs the cigarette out in an ashtray on the counter. "Well,
aren't you cute! Have a seat, have a seat. Now where did I
put my dang apron?" she mutters as she throws some towels
off a chair. The dogs yip again. "Sugar, I know that's you!
Pipe it, sister!" She unearths a purple cape from behind a
throw pillow. "I love my little pup-pups, but dang can they
yap. Want to see them?"

"Oh, uh…not much of a dog person." Afraid she's going
to unleash the hounds from hell, I quickly take a seat in the
chair. She whips the cape around my neck and shoves a
scrapbook in my hands.

She opens the book to the first page as she leans over me
and points with a neon-pink lacquered nail at a picture of a
white furball. She smells like baby powder and cigarettes.
"That's my beloved Dolly. That fucker Ron, my ex, took her
with him when he left, just to spite me."

I look down at the little white dog with about ten pink
bows in her hair.

"Here's my baby Cinnamon, and her sister, Sugar. Same
mama, different daddy, if you know what I mean." She
laughs. "Then there's Harley. Bless it, he's so dang precious."

Her hot-pink lacquered nail draws a heart over a black scruffy terrier thing. "Then there's Dusty. Now he's a miniature poodle, but you wouldn't know it. He weighed in at the vet last week at forty-five pounds."

She flips a page. "This is Gary, Jay, and Joe Don." She pauses and looks at me expectantly. "You know who I named them after, right?"

"Uh…"

"Rascal Flatts! I'm a huge Rascal Flatts fanatic. Even got Joe Don to sign a sweatshirt for…you guessed it, Joe Don!" She laughs, slapping me on the shoulder. "They're basset hounds."

"Wow, that's a lot of dogs, Tanya."

"Oh, they are my precious babies! We miss Dolly, but we don't talk about it much because if I cry, they start a howlin'. But I have trained Harley to bite Ron's nuts off if he ever tries to show up on my doorstep."

"Yikes." I cringe, scared to ask how you train a dog for such a thing.

"I do dog grooming here too, so if you ever need a dog groomed, I'm your gal. One-stop shop!" She laughs, which turns into a coughing fit.

Jesus, help me. I'm getting my hair cut by a dog groomer? She pops some bubblegum in her mouth while she checks her hair and makeup in the mirror.

"All right, Sugar, let's see what we're workin' with." She winks at herself before her eyes flit down to me. "Oh wow, okay. It needs some TLC from Auntie Tanya, but don't worry, sugar, I gotcha. I can cut off about four inches, maybe give you angled bangs…ooh, a shag cut would look killer on you, like Pat Benatar!"

"Uh, I'd like a trim please, and maybe some highlights? No bangs, no shag cuts."

Tanya nods. "Mmm-hmm, yep, you betcha, darlin'. Don't you worry about it. Just sit back and relax and let Tanya do her thing." She walks over to the fridge and takes something out.

"Maybe this isn't a good idea…" I try to get up, but she gently pushes me back down and angles the chair back.

"Shh, now you let Tanya do what she does best." She pops her bubblegum and places a cooling mask over my eyes. She massages my temples, which would normally be relaxing, but it's hard to relax while Tanya talks a mile a minute and smacks her gum like a cow chewing cud.

"Oh my goodness, Etta tells me you're new to town and you're living with Tucker Greyson. Woo-wee, now there's a man I'd like to ride like a bull for eight seconds, if you know what I mean."

Unfortunately, I do, and now I'm picturing Tanya hanging on to Tucker for eight seconds. Scarred for life.

"He has always been such a looker. If I weren't ten…ish years older than him, I'd sink my teeth into that delicious tush of his. Girl, you better get steppin' on that if you want a chance because he has women lined up around the block, and they are waiting like drunk girls at a bar bathroom. They will wait that shit out until either their bladders burst or the men's room opens up. Know what I mean?"

I inwardly cringe, my bladder suddenly making me squirm in my seat. I'm not really drawing on the comparison since I've never had to 'wait it out' outside a bar bathroom, but it doesn't matter, because Tanya keeps talking.

"Isn't that right, Lolly? Women *lined* up!"

"Mmm-hmm." The woman who was sleeping when I walked in suddenly chimes in. Thank you, baby Jesus, she's alive.

"So, how *do* you know Tucker? Watch out for that one, honey. He's got the lady parade following him wherever he goes. Am I right, Lolly?"

Wait, wasn't she just telling me I better hop up on the Tucker bull? I'm getting whiplash trying to keep up with her.

"Lady parade," Lolly croaks, lighting up a cigarette. I recoil from the plume of smoke hanging in the air like a stale cloud.

"I heard Stacy Reeger slashed his tires at the beginning of summer. Now that girl, woo-wee, she is trouble. Watch your back with that one." She sits me back up and sprays down my hair. She gives herself one last smile in the mirror before she turns my chair to face the kitchen.

"Just an inch off, Tanya, please." I fidget in my seat, my eyes darting over to Lolly, worried the cigarette hanging precariously out of her mouth might ignite this whole place like a cherry bomb.

"Yes, ma'am. So anyway, Stacy is hell bent on marrying Tucker. Watch out for her because she'll stick you in the back with a shiv quicker than you can say *Orange is the New Black*. Woo-wee, I'd hate to get on her bad side. She's one scissor blade short, if you know what I mean."

"She'll cut ya," Lolly wheezes.

"Then there's sweet Annie Deal and her precious baby

Ben. Now I love Annie, but she messed up big time with Tucker."

"Big time," Lolly chimes in around a cloud of smoke.

"I mean, who cheats on that hunky-hunkadoodles? With a one-night stand, no less. Please, that's just waiting for karma to bite you in the ass, and oh boy did it... Cinnamon! Quit it," she screams suddenly, causing me to jump out of my skin. "Sorry darlin', I can hear her pawing at the cage and it drives me bonkers. So anyway, where was I? Oh yes, Annie... I sure wish they had worked out because they were so adorable. The whole town wishes they were together, but some things aren't meant to be. Poor Tucker, he needed to have someone hold him to their bosom during that difficult time. I would have been up for the job if I weren't with my ungrateful fucker of an ex, Ron. But now he's single and ready to mingle."

She takes a much-needed breath before she slurps Diet Mountain Dew from a straw. I'm trying to keep up, wondering if she means Ron is single or if we're still talking about Tucker.

"Well, you're single now..." I hedge.

She slaps me on the shoulder. "Girl, you're so bad! I'm past my prime now, but tell me what's he like to live with? Does he strut around the house naked?"

"Uh..." Images of Tucker walking shirtless around the kitchen, lifting my shirt over my head and making me almost orgasm on the spot when his tongue flicked my nipple. "I um..." I look over at Lolly and she waggles her eyebrows from underneath her sunglasses.

"Girl, you don't have to say a word. I can see it in your

eyes. Woo-wee, I'm blushing just looking at you!" Tanya gushes. "Aren't you, Lolly?"

"Mmm-hmm."

"Oh no, it's not like that. We're just friends," I say.

"Uh-huh, like I'm *just friends* with the mailman." She winks.

"How long have you lived in Greyson Gap?" I ask, desperate to get off the Tucker topic or, God forbid, the mailman.

"All my life. Ain't that right, Lolly?" She squirts some gel in my hair, which smells strongly of chemicals.

"Mmm-hmm."

I look over at Lolly, worried for her safety, watching the cigarette butt reach the end. "Maybe...um...perhaps she should put that out?"

Tanya looks over at Lolly. "Honey, put your cigarette out before you snooze off. You know I'd rescue those dogs first!"

I sigh in relief as Lolly stubs out the nub in a soda can.

"Shouldn't you be brushing it on and foiling it in sections?" I ask Tanya as I try to swivel in my chair to get a glimpse in the mirror. Tanya holds the chair, not letting it budge.

"What do you do, Blakely?" she asks sweetly.

"I'm an event planner." I bite my lip while she rakes the product through my hair with her long fluorescent-pink fingernails. "I mean, I was. I'm taking some time off."

"Uh-huh, and would I show up at your party and tell you how to run things?" She snaps her gum and slaps my shoulder, tittering. "Oh, who are we kidding? I totally would! But my point is, I've been doing this for twenty years, hon, I gotcha."

I give her a weak smile, trying to calm the terrifying scenarios about what's happening to my hair in my head. She's been doing this for twenty years. Tanya knows what she's doing, even though her home smells like Joe Don's tour bus after a weekend bender with dogs. *God, stop being so judgmental, Blakely. You don't even know what Joe Don's tour bus smells like.*

Besides, Etta wouldn't have recommended Tanya if she didn't trust her, and Etta's hair is lovely. Look, she even has a happy-ish customer in here. Quit trying to micromanage everyone. Just sit back and relax. I close my eyes as Tanya prattles on, slurping her Dew and snapping her gum. I'm jolted out of my semi-relaxed state as a car pulls up and the dogs bark hysterically.

"Let's move you to this dryer and sit while my next appointment is here. Can I get you anything, darlin'?" she yells over the crazed barking. I shake my head no and sit down. She throws an outdated *People* magazine in my lap and greets her next customer.

"Racquel Dewbury! How's my girl?"

Racquel trudges across the porch, hunched over her walker, the tennis balls on the bottom making a thump-squeak noise. She's a petite woman with skin the color of rosewood and perfectly coiffed jet-black hair, her lips turned down into a permanent frown.

"Hey, Lolly." She eyes me suspiciously as she enters. "Who's she? I've never seen her before."

"That's Blakely. She's the one living with Tucker Greyson over in the Greyson Gap house," Tanya shouts loudly.

"Quit screamin' in my ear! I ain't deaf. Tell those damn mutts to shut up," Raquel grumbles as she slowly eases into the seat next to me. She peers up at me from thick square glasses secured by a gold chain looping around her neck. She pulls a crumpled tissue out of her purse, blowing and honking her nose. I smile down at her magnified eyes. It's like looking through a fishbowl. She gives me a once-over. "What's your name?"

"Blakely Mayfield."

"From the Junieanna County Mayfields?"

"Um, no ma'am, I don't believe so."

"Hmph. No one knows where the hell they come from these days, nor do they care. It's a damn shame, I tell you. That's the problem with society. No one gives a damn. You should know your ancestry. You probably don't even know where your mama was born," she mutters as she watches Tanya sweep around her chair. "My mama was Diana Ross. Not the music performer, mind you, but she sure could sing like her. We like to say Diana was named after her."

"Okay, Racquel, ready for ya, honey!"

"Well now, I just sat down here next to May and I'm a talkin', so you wait your turn," she says sourly. I bite down on my lip to keep from laughing. "Do you smoke?"

"No, ma'am."

"Good. That tart over there does. Nasty habit."

"I can hear you, Racquel. Lolly, let's get you fixed up."

Lolly slowly gets up from her chair and shuffles over to the rinsing station, where Tanya takes the foils out. "So, Racquel, do you have plans tonight?" Tanya asks, rinsing

Lolly's hair.

"You know I do. Got me a *hot* date!" She slaps her knee and smiles for the first time.

I smirk, looking over at the elderly woman hunched over next to me in her thick stockings and orthopedic shoes.

"I need you to fix this up ASAP, Tanya."

Racquel unpins her wig and tosses it across the room like a frisbee, causing me to choke on my saliva as it lands next to Lolly's chair.

"All right, Racquel, no need to get all huffy!" Tanya wheezes, leaning down to pick up the wig. "The usual?"

"I was thinking of dyeing it like a rainbow and adding flowers to it." She hits my arm hard and shakes her head, giving me the *can you believe this nutjob* expression. "Of course, the usual, you ninny. Do I ever get anything else?" Racquel snaps back before returning her attention to me. "What do you do, May? I don't see a ring on your finger."

Rubbing the sore spot on my arm, I almost wish Tanya would fix Racquel's wig first so I could catch up on two-year-old celebrity gossip instead of getting the Spanish inquisition from this elderly hard-ass.

"I was an event planner, but I'm currently working at Tidings."

"Oh yes, I know. Etta is my best friend. She's told me *all* about you."

"Oh, not much to tell." I laugh lightly, feeling slightly uneasy at what Etta might have divulged.

"Everyone has a story." Racquel leans in, looking me over.

"Now, Racquel, leave the poor girl alone and let her

relax!" Tanya chides. "I heard Ed Barker was out mowing in his underwear again."

"Ooh girl, you know I got the 4-1-1 on that from Etta!" She slaps her knee and cackles. She turns to me, patting my knee. "Now that young man is one fine specimen, if I do say so myself. My grandson is going to let me borrow his photography equipment, so Etta and I can do a little reconnaissance mission. He even has a zoom lens! He thinks I want to take pictures of the moon." She grins widely. "Little does he know it's Ed Barker's full moon I'll be processing in the darkroom. I live in a house one block over from Ed. Have you met him?"

"No ma'am, but I walked into the shop while Etta was…uh, studying his lawn-mowing technique."

"Tee-hee-hee. I bet she was. We have a wager going on who will ask him out first."

"You and Etta have a bet to ask out Ed?" I look over at Tanya, but she's lost in her own world as she hums along to the music, blow-drying Lolly's hair.

"Not us!" She side-eyes me. "Girl, were you dropped on your head as a youngin'? Nothin' but watermelon seeds floatin' around in there. We have our very own *Bachelor* show happenin' right here in Greyson Gap. Ed Barker, Jason Thorton, and Tucker Greyson are our most eligible bachelors."

"Do they know this?" I bite back a smile.

"Of course not, you ninny!" Her eyes appear huge in her Coke-bottle glasses. She looks at me like I just asked her to do cartwheels across the floor. "My bet was on you being the bachelorette, but now, after meetin' you, I'm not so sure."

Part of me wants to be offended by her statement, but the other part wants to laugh because Tucker Greyson and I will never be Greyson Gap's *Bachelor* entertainment.

"Don't put your money on me, Racquel."

I watch in horror while Tanya throws clumps of Lolly's overly bleached hair which has fallen out behind her as she dries it. She quickly puts some product in it to make it spiky and then turns to work on styling Racquel's wig. Lolly gets up and shuffles back to her chair.

"Hmph, Ike and Beauford warned me you were as sour as turnip greens toward him, but I couldn't believe it. Who would ever be stupid enough to turn down Tucker Greyson?" She clucks her tongue and whispers, "Unless, of course, you're the L-word."

"What's the L-word?"

"Lesbian, you fool!" she shouts, pursing her lips.

"Like Maebry Evans," Tanya pipes up. "Loud and proud, she always says."

My head swivels between Racquel and Tanya. "Uh, I'm not—"

"So, you don't find Tucker attractive?" Racquel arches a penciled-in eyebrow.

"No, I do, it's just, I'm—"

"So, you *do* find him attractive?" She leans toward me. "What's the problem then?"

How long does it take Tanya to style a wig, for Pete's sake? Like a dog with a bone, Raquel is not giving up on this. "I'm not in the correct frame of mind right now to be looking for a boyfriend, not that it's any of your business. I'm here for a little R and R, a summer vacation if you will."

"Ooh, summer flings are the best!" Tanya pipes up from across the room. "I'd drop my panties for some piña coladas, Rascal Flatts' 'Summer Nights' playing, and a hot man giving me eyes as he slides his stick over a pool table."

"That certainly paints a picture," Racquel mumbles next to me. "Are you done yet, Tanya? I need to change into a hot little number I picked up at Dahlias."

"Who ya going out with?" Tanya slurps her Dew while Lolly quietly snores in her seat.

"Double-date with Etta and the boys. Ike and Beauford are taking us to bingo over at the Hawk's Nest Club."

"That sounds fun." I smile, but Racquel's expression says she doesn't agree.

"It's going to be a bear to get through. Beauford is meaner than a possum stuck in a grill plate. But that's okay, I can dish it right back."

I remember the two elderly gentlemen from the pub on my first night. Damn, to be a fly on the wall of the Hawk's Nest.

"Alrighty, Ms. Racquel, got you fixed up all nice and purdy." Tanya halts as she looks at me, her eyes widening. "Oh crap, I forgot to set the timer!"

"What does that mean? Is my hair going to be okay?" I nervously touch the towel clipped to my head. Images of Lolly's hair coming out in clumps ratchets my anxiety into overdrive.

"Oh sure, yes, no problem. Let's get you rinsed real quick." She kicks some stuff out of the way and pushes me down into a seat attached to a sink. "Racquel, give me a quick sec and I'll have you on your way to your date."

"Oh, no, I can wait. I need to see this."

My nerves are at an all-time high as she moves me over to the chair and swivels it around before I can get a glimpse in the mirror. "Let me get it dried and styled so we can see the correct color before you peek at it."

"It's going to be okay, right?"

"Of course!" Her grim expression doesn't put me at ease. "And if you don't like it, Dawn fixes everything. That's the great thing about hair."

"Does Dawn work here too?" I squeak out, praying to God she's talking about another stylist who is off today.

"No, silly, the dish soap! Dawn gets anything and everything out." She smacks her gum and smiles proudly, like she invented the soap herself. I'm not the least assured. She gets out a diffuser and adds mousse to my hair.

"Oh, I don't wear my hair curly."

"Hmm...well, I tried something new. Picked it up the other day at the drugstore." She quickly dries my hair, then sprays about a gallon of hairspray in it before she takes a teaser comb to the top. She swivels the chair around and rips off the cape around my neck. "Ta-da!"

I'm speechless...

"Is her hair *pink*? You look like a damn Easter egg! Is that the new style these days? I'll never understand why y'all trying to make your hair all colors of the rainbow." Racquel arches her neck to get a better look.

"What do you think? I tried a new thing called streaking the hair. I also gave you a temporary perm. It will come out in a week-ish, or so...if you don't love it." Tanya smiles at me, her eyes a little crazed.

"It's…uh, it's curly…and pink."

She snaps her gum and swigs her Mountain Dew. "I love it!"

"My hair is pink," I say, unable to tear my eyes away from the image in the mirror. I look like I'm wearing a bad eighties permed wig. Electrocuted pink Confetti Fun Easter grass is sticking out in all directions from my head.

Tanya smacks her gum. "Tucker is going to love it."

"Tucker is going to laugh his ass off," Racquel snickers.

"Now, Ms. Racquel, you hush! Let's get your hair set. Blakely, that will be sixty-five, hon. Tip is already included in the price. I didn't cut it today. I can fit you in next week after my schnauzer trim if you want the inch off."

"But I just wanted a trim and highlights…" My lip trembles while I try to keep the tears at bay. I will *not* cry in front of these women.

"Yup! Next time." Tanya winks at me.

"But…my hair is pink." My hands are shaking and my neck prickles with sweat. Or hives…I'm not sure. I don't know whether to laugh or scream.

"Has she turned into a robot? That's all she can say," Racquel mutters.

Tanya shrugs. "Tell Tucker we said hi!"

They both turn their backs on me. I look over to Lolly for help, but I think she's asleep…or dead. Hard to tell with the sunglasses on. I get my cash out and leave the money on the table, not sure what else to do.

My fucking hair is pink.

Chapter 21

Like a Ninja

Blakely

I'M NOT SURE how I drive home without getting in an accident since my eyes are glued to the rearview mirror and my pink frizzed-out hair. I can't let Tucker see this. I mean, I can't let *anyone* see this, but most of all him. He'll never let me live this down. I pull up Whitney's number on my cell and pray she can help.

"Hello?"

"Hey, Whitney, it's Blakely. Um, I kind of have a situation and I'm hoping you can help?"

"What's up?"

"So…Etta recommended I get my hair done by Tanya over at Suzie Q's—"

"Oh no, Blakely, tell me you didn't."

"I did. It's awful, Whitney! I want to put a bag over my head," I cry.

"Look, I love Tanya like a long-lost black sheep aunt working on the carnival circuit, but she almost lost her license about a year ago. Went crazy wackadoodles. Her boyfriend left her. There was a downward spiral. It was bad."

"What?! Why the hell would Etta refer me to her?"

"Well, the older ladies try to support her. The rest of us drive to Asheville to get our hair done. I can get you an appointment with my girl if you need it."

"Yes! I mean, I don't know if she can fix this...but I'm desperate. I'm about to pull into the drugstore and grab the darkest hair dye they have."

"Don't do that. Your blonde is gorgeous."

"Not anymore," I whimper.

"Awe, I'm sure it's not that bad."

I take a selfie at the red light and send it to her.

"Oh, oh my...is your hair..."

"Pink. It's fucking Easter-egg pink, Whitney. What do I do?"

"Okay, okay, I'll call my girl right now. Don't worry, Blakely, we'll fix this."

"You're the best, Whit. Thank you so much."

"No prob. I'll send you a text with your appointment time."

I hang up with Whitney after effusively thanking her, and call Junie next, only to get her voicemail.

"Hey Junie, it's me, your friend Blakely. The one living in your mountain retreat? I miss you. Things have been interesting, to say the least...um, the town folk are...unique. Your cousin has been...accommodating. Oh! I met your brother. He's adorable." I clear the guilt building up in my throat. I can't tell Junie I had a hot make-out session with her cousin. She'd be so disappointed in me. "So yeah! Just wanted to catch up. Dr. Cooper thinks I'm progressing nicely, so that's good. Anyway, I know you're busy with Dr.

Reed going on maternity leave, but call me soon!"

I pull into the driveway and grab a plastic grocery bag out of the glove compartment, putting it over my head as I run into the house. The kitchen is dark and I thank my lucky stars Tucker isn't here. I grab the bottle of Dawn dish soap and sprint upstairs, hoping Tanya is correct and it will wash it right out. The steam in the shower smells of cigarette smoke, hairspray, and acrid dye. After five rounds of lathering and rinsing, I get out and towel-dry my hair. The pink is still vibrant and so is the stupid perm.

"Tucker? Hersh?" I shout down the stairs. With no answer or jingle of a collar, I grab my flower-arranging book and put on a ball cap to cover my hair and run downstairs. I need to do something productive because my anxiety is off the charts, so I pull out the flowers I bought from the store earlier and get to work. My phone chirps with an incoming text.

Whitney Greyson: *So I told her it was an emergency, but she can't get you in until a week from Thursday. She's really good.*

Crap, it's only Tuesday! An entire week and two days? I'll have to wear a scarf over my head. I can make it look fashionable again, right? Ugh, I'll look like an idiot, but what else can I do?

Me: *Thanks Whit, I'll take it!!*

I clip the ends of the flowers and take out the vases I purchased the other day, poring over the pages I've already read and tagged. After an hour, I clean up the mess and beam at my arrangements. Martha Stewart doesn't have anything on me. I scarf down some leftover Chinese and run back upstairs when I hear Tucker's truck pull in. Opening up my journal, I write furiously.

> *Goal:* Make it until next Thursday with pink hair and not murder Etta.
>
> *Problem:* My hair is pink for nine more days.
>
> *Stress:* Having pink permed hair like a poodle on top of my head and running into Tucker. Well, running into anyone, really.
>
> *What's the best thing that happened today:* ~~Nothing good happened today.~~
>
> *Be positive, Blakely.*
>
> *What's the best thing that happened today:* Lolly didn't burn down Suzie Q's with her cigarette and I made some pretty flower arrangements.
>
> *What I am grateful for:* I don't have a shag haircut like Pat Benatar.

I toss my journal to the side and grab my laptop, settling back against my pillows when there's a soft knock at the door.

"Blakely, you in there?"

"Don't come in!"

"Why?" He pauses, the door cracked. "Does this have something to do with the fifty flower arrangements in the kitchen?"

"There aren't fifty." I roll my eyes even though he can't see me.

"I counted. There are fifty-two, to be exact."

Oh.

"Ha, uh, must have gotten carried away...just experimenting with flowers." The door opens a touch more. "Don't come in! I'm serious, Tucker. I'm not feeling well and I look atrocious. I don't want you to see me like this."

"Okay...do you need anything from the drugstore?"

Hair dye in the darkest shade available. Maybe some clippers to shave it all off like Britney Spears did during her public meltdown. "Nope, I'm good."

"Uh, okay. I'll be downstairs if you need me."

"Okay...thanks."

Phew, that was close. I get up to go to the bathroom and cringe looking at myself in the mirror. My hair has turned into a triangular-shaped frizz, and yep, it's still pink. I brush my teeth and head to bed early, thinking up different ways I can hide my hair. A beanie would work, but would be hot in this weather. I never understood how some guys can stand wearing one all summer. Scarf it is, I guess. Nine days.

ANXIETY OVER MY hair has me tossing and turning, so I sneak downstairs for a glass of milk around midnight. It's quiet except for the hum of the refrigerator. I don't want to wake up Tucker or Hershel, so I keep the lights off while I feel my way into the kitchen, waiting for my eyes to adjust to the pitch black. The French door opens with a click and I throw myself down behind the island, tucking and rolling, stifling a groan as my hip hits the floor. I crawl on my belly and peek around the island.

Biting my lip, I hope to see Tucker's cowboy boots come into view. I almost call out his name when Hershel growls from the hallway. Oh god, not Tucker. Is someone breaking into the house? I peek over the island but can't see anything because of all the damn vases of flowers. I duck as I see a shadow creep toward the stairs. My heart is pounding in my ears.

"Jesus fucking Christ, I almost clobbered you! What the fuck are you doing?" Tucker bellows as the hall lights come on.

A female voice yips. "Crap! You scared the shit out of me." *Is that Whitney?*

"What the hell are you doing here sneaking into my house at midnight?"

"Oh, god, this is so embarrassing. I was hoping to wake up Blakely."

"Well, she's not feeling good. What could you possibly want that couldn't wait until morning? Wait, why are you wearing Bhodi's bike shirt, barefoot...Jesus, you're fucking kidding me."

I sink back down to the floor, not wanting to be seen, because now it would be weird I've been hiding in the kitchen this whole time.

"I was at Barracuda's and we ran out of—"

"No! I don't want to hear it. I don't even want to *think*

about what you need at midnight. Gross, Whitney. That guy is a slimeball. I can't *believe* you're sleeping with him."

"Hey, I like him! Besides, it's none of your business who I sleep with."

"You made it my business by breaking into my house."

"So dramatic, it's not a B and E if I used my key. So…um, do you have any?"

Tucker mutters some choice words as he stomps off to his room. "I'm only giving you these because I don't want you to get a disease from that dirtbag."

"I don't understand why you dislike Bhodi so much," Whitney grumbles. "It's not my fault you have spare condoms to give out."

"I really can't handle you or this conversation right now."

"What's up with all the flower arrangements? Who died?"

"You, if you don't leave," Tucker growls.

"Okay, okay, I'm going. Jeez, someone really needs to get laid."

"Out."

The door to the back shuts with a thud and the lights switch off. I'm about to stand up and race upstairs when Tucker walks around the other side of the island, heading for the fridge. I curl up into a tight child's pose. *Please don't see me, please don't see me*, I silently pray. I'm not sure how I would explain myself.

He takes a glass out of the cabinet and fills it up from the water dispenser attached to the fridge. He takes a long drink and fills it again. What lasts ten seconds feels like an hour.

Hershel slurps loudly from his water bowl. His nails click on the floor as he draws closer to me. I don't look up, hoping he'll mosey along back to Tucker's room. Water drips all over my elbow and head while he sniffs my neck and gives me a lick. Desperately trying not to make a peep, I shove him away, but he doesn't take the hint. He licks my arm and paws at my side. Tucker refills his glass and I wonder how much damn water a man needs at night.

"Come on, Hersh," Tuckers says. I try to gauge which direction he's heading when his foot connects with my head and he grunts as he topples over me. The metal cup bounces loudly off the floor, water sloshing everywhere. Hershel barks, dancing around us.

"What the fuck?" Tucker rolls and grabs me, pinning me under him. I suck in a surprised breath, feeling his hard muscles on top of me. He arches an eyebrow, surprised. "Smiles? What the fuck are you doing? Were you lying in wait like a ninja trying to kill me?"

Our breaths co-mingle as I try to calm my racing heart. "I… I was, uh…cleaning the floor."

The flimsy lie sounds ridiculous and we both know it.

"You were cleaning the floor in the middle of the night…in the dark?" He arches an eyebrow and I have to bite down on my lower lip to keep from smashing it to his sexy smirk.

My body begs for friction as he lightly presses into me and it takes Herculean strength not to wrap my legs around him and pull him closer. I press my fingers against his warm, bare chest and inwardly smile, thinking of what Tanya would do in this situation. She'd hug him to her busty bosom is what she would do. My heart rate kicks up a notch as his eyes drop to my lips. I dart my tongue out, wetting them in anticipation. He dips closer, his lips parting. We haven't kissed since we almost had sex, and it's killing me. Just one kiss...is that asking too much?

He pauses and I squirm underneath him. He's moving at snail-speed and it's driving me mad. My pheromones are practically screaming, *give it to me now!* Why isn't he taking advantage of our prone position?

I decide to take matters into my own hands. Wrapping my hand around his neck, I pull him to me. He lowers his head at the same time I lift mine, our foreheads smashing into each other in the most unarousing thud.

"Ow, shit!" I yelp.

"Dammit, that hurt. Did you really just headbutt me?"

"Not on purpose," I mumble. "Why did you move your head?"

"I was moving to get off of you. I figured you didn't want me breathing in your face when you're not feeling well. Are you okay?" He pulls back and sits in a squat position, rubbing his forehead. Concern washes over his face when I don't move. My head is pounding from his rock-hard skull. He pulls out his phone and turns on the flashlight, blinding me as he shines it in my eyes.

"I'm fine." I swat his hand away and sit up, irritated and embarrassed.

"Okay, if you're sure," he says, looking dubious. "Are you feeling better?" He stands, flipping the kitchen lights on, and grabs a cloth from the drawer. He throws it over the water on the floor before his eyes fix on my hair and he freezes. "What the hell happened to your hair?"

I self-consciously smooth down the frizzy mess and hold it to my shoulder. "Minor accident at Suzie Q's."

"The dog groomer?"

I'm going to murder Etta. "Well, she cuts human hair too..."

"Maybe back in the early nineties... It's pink." He looks at me quizzically, his hands planted on his hips. At least he's distracted from my midnight-cleaning fib.

"I'm aware."

"But...why?"

"I was held hostage by Tanya and Racquel Dew-something."

"Racquel Dewbury?" He holds a hand over his mouth, covering his laugh with a cough.

"Go ahead, laugh. I know I look like an Easter egg."

"I was thinking more like a pink poodle..."

I pick up the wet rag and chuck it at him. "Ugh, I knew you'd make fun of me."

He helps me up off the floor and holds me before I can make an escape. "I'm only making fun of you a little."

"Is that supposed to make me feel better?"

"Were you really sick earlier?"

"No, I was trying to avoid you." I push against his chest, but not before I see the quick flash of hurt in his eyes. "It's not just you. I'd like to avoid the whole town for nine days before Whitney's stylist can fix it, but I can't."

Before I can get loose, he kisses me softly on the lips, but now I don't want the tender caress he's offering, my pride thoroughly wounded.

"I'm sorry, Blakely May, it's not that bad. What can I do to help you?"

"I'm going back to bed," I mutter, wiggling again, and he drops his arms. He stops me in my tracks at the top of the stairs.

"Blakely, for what it's worth, I think you're perfect. Pink hair and all."

I scowl down at him, surprised by his confession. Before I can reply, he heads to his room and shuts the door.

Chapter 22

Meatloaf with the Mayor

Blakely

MY GAZE STAYS fixed on Annie's door while I clutch one of my flower arrangements to my chest. I didn't really want to come, especially with my pink hair, but backing out this late in the game would've been rude. Tucker steps up behind me, forcing me through the door Annie holds open.

"Hi, Blakely, welcome! I'm so glad you could come tonight. Wow, these are beautiful," she says warmly, her eyes quickly perusing my hair. "Oh, you colored your hair. It looks...uh—"

"Terrible, it's okay. No one warned me not to go to Tanya over at Suzie Q's. Thank you so much for having me."

"The dog groomer?" She looks over at Tucker, confusion written across her face.

"I told you." Tucker coughs in his hand, and grunts when I jab him with my elbow.

"Yes, well, I wasn't aware Tanya was a woman of many talents." I smile sheepishly, looking around her small, but immaculate, home. My kind of girl. She leans in and kisses

Tucker on his cheek. A flush of jealousy heats my skin, startling me. Why should I be jealous? It's not like they're a couple. It's not like *we're* a couple, but still... Jesus, I'm a hot mess.

The little boy I saw fishing with Tucker the other week comes running down the hallway and jumps into his arms. He clings to Tucker's neck, not letting go. It makes my heart explode. Annie's eyes light up with love and I suddenly feel like a voyeuristic outsider, the obvious fourth wheel. I shouldn't be the person putting a wedge in this relationship, because even though Tucker has said Annie and he are just friends, Etta was right. She wants to be more.

And what am I to Tucker? We haven't discussed what happened Sunday before we were interrupted by his sister. We spent the most painful evening listening to Bhodi talk endlessly about kayaking stories, with Whitney hanging on his every word. Later that night, we both went our separate ways, too exhausted to talk. And last night ended badly when he teased me about my hair.

"What can I get you to drink, Blakely?" Annie asks, pulling me back to the present.

"Oh, water is fine, thank you."

"Are you sure? I have wine...red or white. I'm going to have a glass, don't make me drink alone." She laughs lightly, warmly smiling. She's so damn nice it makes me feel worse.

"I'll have whatever you're having."

"Great! Dinner should be ready soon. Tuck, you know where to get the beer."

He winks at me before Ben drags him over to the toy bin and shows him a new monster truck his Mimi got him.

Unsure of which direction to go in, I decide to take the more intimidating route and follow Annie into the kitchen.

"Can I help you with dinner? It smells amazing in here."

"Oh, you're so sweet. I'm making Tucker's favorite, so it shouldn't take long."

"Okay." I smile, but my stomach lurches as I sit down at the kitchen table. She hands me a glass of red, which I gratefully accept. I don't even know what Tucker's favorite meal is. I live with the man, but I don't have a clue what he likes. "I don't know Tucker that well. What's his favorite meal?"

"Oh, sorry." She laughs as she opens the oven and pulls the pan out. "We're having meatloaf, mashed potatoes, and green beans."

"My favorite." Tucker materializes out of thin air. He bends and kisses the top of my head before grabbing a beer from the fridge. Annie's eye subtly twitches before she turns to drain the potatoes.

"So how do you know Junie?" she asks, aggressively mashing the potatoes.

"We met at a seminar for Women in Business a few years ago and hit it off immediately. She was staying with me while she was getting her kitchen in her condo remodeled. I had some time off and needed to get out of the city, so she offered her place here." I smile at Tucker as he uncaps the beer and winks at me. No need to divulge I had a nervous breakdown and Junie ordered me to take a little R and R.

"We haven't seen Junie in ages, have we, Tucker? So busy down there in Atlanta slaying it as a doctor."

"She likes her life in the city." Tucker looks down at his

beer, frowning.

"I guess. Just hope she doesn't forget about us back here in Greyson Gap." She places the potatoes on the table. "Ben? Put your toys away and come in for dinner! Blakely, you'll have to excuse him. He hasn't quite mastered his table manners yet."

"Oh, don't worry about me. I love kids."

Kids scare the crap out of me, but I give her a bright, reassuring smile.

"Benjamin! It's time for dinner," Annie yells abruptly, causing me to jump in my seat. "Sorry, it's been a long day."

"I'll go get him," Tucker says easily, sliding out of his chair.

The dark circles under her eyes are either from lack of sleep or smudged makeup. Either way, I feel bad she's catering to us. "Annie, you should have let us cook for you. You have enough going on."

"Oh nonsense, I love to entertain. I haven't done it much since Ben was born. Tucker comes over for dinner at least once a week, so that's nice. I love cooking for him because he scarfs it down, unlike my little picky four-year-old. Do you enjoy cooking?"

I gulp my wine. "If there's a recipe, I can follow. I need precise measurements. I could never wing it and throw in a dash of this or that."

"Oh, but that's the fun of it!"

"Ha, I'll take your word for it."

Tucker comes back in with Ben upside down over his shoulder, giggling. My ovaries somersault. Damn, he'd make a hot dad.

"Down!" Ben screeches, and Tucker rolls him over and flips him into the seat across from me. I smile at Ben, who eyes me suspiciously. "Who are you? Why do you have pink hair?"

"Ben, that's rude. This is Ms. Blakely. She's our guest tonight," Annie chastises. I smile at him, but he doesn't return it.

"Yuck, I hate green beans." He picks a green bean up from his plate and chucks it over his shoulder. The clean freak in me shudders.

"Ben, dude, you need green beans to grow up big and strong like me." Tucker snatches a green bean off his plate and pops it into his mouth. Ben giggles and mimics him. Tucker fist-bumps his little hand. "Nice."

Tucker is so good with him. I wonder if he wants a whole van full of kids or if he's happy being a single guy. He looks pretty comfortable at Annie's table while they chat about the Greyson Gap Fourth of July River Festival this upcoming weekend.

"You should come with us, Blakely. Right, Tucker?" Annie hands me a plate.

"Oh, actually Whitney asked me—"

"Cool, we'll all go together." Tucker shovels a bite of mashed potatoes into his mouth.

"It's settled then," Annie says, taking a dainty bite of her food. Ben chatters on about his new monster truck, while Annie asks Tucker about some new business off of Main Street, and I can't shake the feeling from earlier that I'm intruding.

"Did you all grow up together?"

"Yes, Tucker and I were high school sweethearts. He was two years older than me. An All-American baseball god." Annie laughs. "That seems like forever ago, doesn't it?" She looks across the table at him dreamily.

Tucker smiles, but it doesn't reach his eyes as he moves food around on his plate. "Annie and Junie were pretty inseparable, always following Jason and me around on the weekends to different ballgames around the state."

"Remember the time we got stuck in that monsoon in the tent?"

Tucker nods, but doesn't pick up the story thread.

"That sounds adventurous and fun." I smile, mentally kicking myself for triggering a stroll down memory lane.

"It definitely wasn't glamorous, but we were kids in love. I'd have followed him to the ends of the earth," Annie sighs as she stares across the table at Tucker. I sneak a peek at him, but his eyes are focused on his plate.

"So, Annie, what do you do?"

"Oh, I work for Tucker's construction company. I want to be his personal assistant when he's elected Mayor, but he hasn't asked me yet," she teases.

Choking on a piece of meatloaf, I quickly take a sip from my wineglass. "I'm sorry. I think I misunderstood you. Did you say mayor?"

"Tucker James, did you not tell Blakely you're running for Mayor of Greyson Gap? He's always shying away from it."

My eyes dart from Annie to Tucker. I feel like I've been sucker-punched. "You're going to be the *mayor?*"

"Well, not yet, but it will happen. Everyone loves Tucker, he's our hometown celebrity," Annie gushes. "He's so perfect for the job. And his father and grandfather were Mayor, so it's meant to be."

I want to stick my hand up in her face and tell her to take a back seat for a moment so Tucker can meet my eyes and answer for himself. "Tucker, why didn't you tell me?"

Tucker frowns, looking up at me. "It's not—"

"This is gross." Ben picks up a piece of meatloaf and throws it across the table, smacking me right between the eyes with it before it drops to my plate.

"Oh!" I quickly bring my napkin up to my face and wipe off the grease and ketchup.

"Benjamin Tucker! We do *not* throw food! I am so sorry, Blakely, are you okay?" Annie gets up and yanks a protesting Ben from his chair. "You are excused to your room, mister. No dessert for you tonight."

"But I'm hungry," Ben whines as Annie drags him to his room.

Benjamin Tucker? She named him after Tucker even though he isn't his kid? That's got to be a kick in the balls.

The man in question looks over, concern etched across his features. "Are you okay? Jesus, I've never seen him act like that before. He's usually a great kid."

"It's okay, I mean, I'm okay." I frown down at the piece of meatloaf wedged into my mashed potatoes on my plate, losing my appetite. "I hate that he's still hungry."

"He'll be fine. He's acting like a little shit." Tucker moves over to my side, crouching down beside me. He lifts his napkin to wipe the tip of my nose. "There's some ketchup here."

His grass-green eyes scan my face for any other traces of ketchup. It squeezes my heart. I want to smooth out the cute little crease between his eyes and kiss his lips and tell him I'm okay.

"Why didn't you tell me you were running for Mayor of Greyson Gap?" I ask softly.

"Because I didn't think it was that big of a deal." He stands and turns to the sink, breaking the moment.

I scoff as I turn in my chair to look at him. "It's a big deal, Tucker."

"Well, I'm sorry. I didn't think it was. I'm not even sure it's going to happen. I'm running against Bill Doliver and he has a following in this town. I'll be lucky to get a handful of votes."

I bring the plates over from the table and set them next to the dishes he's washing. "Hmm, I doubt that. It seems like something you would have mentioned to your roommate in passing, like I'm not doing your chore chart because *I'm going to be the goddamn mayor!*" I hiss next to him as I roughly dry a bowl.

"I didn't mention it because I'm *not* the mayor."

"Semantics."

Tucker side-eyes me. "Can we please drop it?"

"Fine."

"Good."

We work side by side, the air between us thick with tension. He washes and I dry. I want to say something, but my feathers are ruffled. How could he not tell me about his important career aspirations? I thought we were friends.

It's not really about him running for Mayor, is it? Dr.

Cooper's voice echoes in my head. *No, Dr. Cooper, it's not.* I'm jealous that Annie knows everything going on in his life. His favorite meals, his career aspirations... I feel disconnected from him. Every smile I garner from him, every story he tells me, makes me feel connected to Tucker and this town. I *want* to belong. I'm stressed over seeing him interact with Annie and Ben tonight and I'm purposefully picking a fight.

Furiously, I dry the plate in my hands until I can see my reflection in it. He breaks the silence first, taking it from my hands.

"I can tell Annie likes you."

"She's really sweet. It must be hard to be a single mom," I answer begrudgingly.

Tucker's jaw ticks. "Yes, well, sometimes life throws you curveballs."

Realizing how difficult this situation must be on him, I sigh, the tension leaving my shoulders. "I'm sorry, Tucker, that was callous of me to bring it up."

He shrugs. "It's life, Blakely. You can't predict how it's going to go. Just when you think everything's going exactly as planned, God throws a wrench into it. Annie and I made our choices."

"Did you know Ben wasn't yours?"

"Not until halfway through the pregnancy."

I stare at him slack-jawed.

"Thanks for cleaning up. I'm sorry about Ben. He must have been tired," Annie says from behind me. I fumble with the plate I'm drying, wondering how much she heard. "Anyone want coffee or dessert?"

A look I can't decipher passes between Tucker and Annie, and I know that's my cue to exit stage left. I knew about Annie and Tucker from Etta and what Tucker shared, but I didn't realize how strong their relationship was. What a joke to think I could fit in around here. That I was beginning to really like Tucker and think there was a possibility brewing between us. Seeing him with Annie and Ben tonight...well, as the old westerns go, this town ain't big enough for the both of us.

Decision made, I smile at the two of them. "Uh, you know what? It's such a pretty night. Why don't you two hang out and catch up over dessert and I'll walk home. It's not too far."

"Blakely, it's like five miles." Tucker gives me a strange look as I sidestep away from him.

"Five miles, really?" Crap, I'll get home around midnight wearing these wedge heels. "Well, that's okay. I should walk off the amazing meal you cooked... I didn't get my exercise in today. You know me, if it was on the schedule, it must get done." I laugh awkwardly.

Tucker folds his arms over his chest and squints. "I'm going to take you home. Stop being ridiculous."

"No," I shout before lowering my voice, glancing down the hall. "I mean, you can't because Annie made dessert. Stay and chat with her." But he's not listening to me as he grabs his keys from the hall table. Ugh, this is hopeless. "Fine, take me home, but only if you promise to come back and have dessert with Annie."

"Oh Tucker, you don—"

"*Yes*, he does." They both give me strange looks. I can't say I blame them; I'm acting like a lunatic. "Please, it would make me feel better since you worked so hard on tonight's dinner and dessert."

"It's just mini cheesecakes. It's not a big deal."

"Mini cheesecakes?" I squeal. "That sounds super complicated and delicious. Tucker, you are *not* going to miss out on dessert."

Tucker side-eyes me. "Okay, Blakely, got it. Annie, I'll be back in a bit."

I wrap Annie in a light hug, surprising us both. "Thanks for dinner."

"Oh anytime, thank you for the beautiful flowers. I'm so sorry Ben threw food at you. I'm so embarrassed."

"No, it's fine, kids being kids. See you at the festival!" I wave, rushing out to Tucker's truck. I get in before he can open the door for me. He slides in next to me and stares at me for a beat.

"Want to tell me what the hell that was all about?"

I exhale the breath I was holding. "Look, it's really obvious Annie still has feelings for you. I think you two need to hash it out, and you don't need me in the middle confusing things."

Tucker's jaw tightens, his teeth grinding as he starts the truck. "We have. There's no confusion on my part."

We ride in silence for a bit before I can't stand it any longer. I need to say my piece.

"She seems lonely. And although it was nice of her to invite me, she didn't really want me there. And she wasn't rude or mean about it, it's just the vibe I was picking up. Maybe you two should reconnect?" He looks over at me, his expression shuttered. "She told me you come over for weekly dinners. She works at your company. You clearly have a strong relationship with her son since he's named after you."

"Blakely—" He stops the truck in front of his house.

"You guys have a history together. Even Tanya said the whole town wishes you two were together. You were the quintessential All-American couple. Go talk to her." I pause and glance at his silhouette. "And Tucker? No one will blame you if you want to pick up where that dream left off."

I hop out of the truck and slam the door before he can respond. I'm silently kicking myself for throwing whatever we had under his truck tires. Did we even have anything to begin with? We've kissed twice. Okay, and there was some heavy petting…and maybe I was about to have sex with him if Whitney hadn't interrupted, but it's not like I could call him mine.

God, get a grip, Blakely Mayfield. I shake my head, muttering to myself. I need to burn off this weird energy before it spreads like wildfire in my veins.

Chapter 23

Meant to Be

Tucker

"DESSERT?" ANNIE STEPS out onto the porch carrying two small dishes.

"Sure." I smile, placing my beer on the porch banister. "Is Ben asleep?"

"Yeah. I don't know what got into him tonight. I hope he didn't scare Blakely off."

"That was probably my fault. I was trying to pump him up about her before dinner, calling her my special friend. He must have gotten jealous." I spoon some of her dessert into my mouth and groan in pleasure.

"Hmm...maybe. She's nice." Annie smiles, rocking the swing with her toe.

"She said the same thing about you."

"Are you two...dating?"

The swing creaks in the deafening silence. Dammit, I think Blakely and Whitney were right about Annie.

"No, but I think I'd like to." I set the dessert next to my beer. "Listen, Annie, I think I've been doing you a disservice."

"How's that?"

"We never really talked about what happened between us after you had Ben."

"Uh, I remember the fight and the consequential breakup pretty well."

"No, I mean, when I moved back here and had to take over my dad's business. I saw you struggling as a single mom. You were isolated and it made me sad and protective. I hung out with you and Ben because I wanted you to know you weren't alone and I cared about you. You were a safe place for me when I was at my most vulnerable. And perhaps I leaned on you a little too much after my dad died."

"Tucker…"

"I'm your friend, Annie. That's all I'll ever be. You and I were never meant to be more."

"How can you say that? After all the years we were to-gether? Jesus, if I could take back that one stupid night, I would in a heartbeat. I'd never give up Ben, but you know what I mean." She quietly sobs, curling into my chest.

"Shh, I know what you mean. There's a reason you had that one stupid night. You were lonely and needed attention. I was so focused on my career, I couldn't be there for you. I was selfish in that regard. You know I love you, Annie, but in my heart, it's always been as a friend. It was never more than that." I rub my neck. "You deserve someone who loves you completely."

"Why would you ask me to marry you if you didn't love me?"

Looking out across her front yard, my conscious battles with my heart. The truth will sound callous and hurtful, but

I can't keep leading her on to spare her feelings. That's what got us to this point in the first place.

"I felt pressured to take the next step with you, not because I was head over heels in love, but because it was my duty. We were going to have a baby together. It seemed like the right thing to do. I was excited about the pregnancy and was convinced my feelings would grow. But then when I found out he wasn't mine..." I shrug. "I'm sorry, Annie."

She clings to me, tears soaking through my shirt. "I always felt like I was more in love with you in our relationship. I was always competing against baseball."

"I know, I'm sorry." I stroke her arm, not sure what else to say. I'd say I'm sorry a million times over if it would take the hurt away. "I was a selfish ass who led you on. You know I adore Ben, and I'll always be here for both of you, but I'm not the one for you, Annie. He's out there, waiting for you and Ben."

We rock while she cries against my chest, listening to the crickets make their music, the warm breeze drifting over us. I know this is difficult for her. Whitney and Blakely were right. After everything, she was still hoping we'd be together. I'll always feel protective of her, but part of me died when I found out Ben wasn't mine. It was the closure I needed to move on from her. She squeezes me before she lets go and sits up, rubbing her eyes, sniffling. "So, what do we do now?"

"It's up to you. I'm hoping we can stay friends, because I don't want to lose you or Ben. Would that be okay?"

She nods, looking down at her hands. "It's going to take time, but I don't want to lose you either."

"I understand." I hug her to my side and squeeze her. "I hope you can find the guy who will sweep you off your feet and be an amazing dad to Ben."

"Not in Greyson Gap." She sniffles and shudders. "Unless it's Creepy Carl, he's the only single guy left."

I chuckle. "Creepy Carl is definitely not who you're going to end up with. There are lots of single guys here, you just haven't been noticing."

"Do you think Blakely is the one for you?"

I contemplate her question while we rock. "I don't know. I think she might be a possibility, but probably not. She's leaving at the end of summer."

"That's too bad. I like her. I'm not going to lie. It stings it's not me, but at least it's Blakely and not Stacy Reeger."

I choke on my beer. "Stacy Reeger slashed my tires. I think it's safe to say I will never end up with her."

"She and Creepy Carl would make a good fit." A watery laugh erupts from her as she snuggles back against me. "Whoever you end up with, Tucker, she better treat you well or else I'm going to have to kick some serious ass."

I smirk as I kiss the top of her head. "Thanks, Annie, you're a good friend."

"Thank you for always being there for me and Ben. Whoever she is, she better not fuck it up like I did."

"Hey, don't think like that. Everything happens for a reason. Us parting ways was inevitable."

"Yeah...I guess."

We have never been this honest with each other, always skirting around the elephant in the room. I pretended things were good between Annie and me because she was struggling to be a single parent. But I never meant to give her false hope. Now I can finally breathe easy around her again. We're finally at peace with each other.

I OPEN THE front door about an hour later and the smell of bleach singes my nose hairs.

"Blake?" I call out to the empty kitchen and family room. Both rooms are spotless and freshly cleaned. Hershel bounds down the stairs and meets me at the bottom.

"Hey buddy, is she on a cleaning bender?" I take the steps two at a time and find her in her bathroom scrubbing the shower tiles. "Blakely, what are you doing?"

"Oh, hey." She sits back on her haunches and wipes her brow with her arm. She's changed into a tank top and denim overall shorts, and her hair is tied up in a messy bun with a bandana. She's up to her elbows in lime-green rubber gloves holding a scrub brush. "Just doing a little light cleaning."

The sparkling white subway tile practically blinds me. "Uh-huh. It's nine p.m."

"Already? I should be done in about an hour. I can't seem to get this grout clean." Blakely furiously scrubs a white spot.

"Let's step away from the cleaning products, darlin'. I think the bleach has gotten to you."

She laughs lightly. "I'm fine."

I pick her up by the waist and swing her around when

she refuses to stop. Throwing her over my shoulder, I stomp down the stairs when she doesn't stop protesting. I set her down on the couch and peel her gloves off, throwing them on the floor, folding my arms over my chest.

"I'm not sure what's going on with you, but I'm pretty sure scrubbing the entire house was not on your chore chart today. Do you want to talk about it?"

"I'm fine! I'm just—"

I swoop down, cradle her head, and kiss her before she tells me she's doing a light clean, again. Whatever is going on in that active head of hers, behind those golden eyes, needs to be calmed. I'm hoping she'll let me help her. Baseball used to crawl into my head and camp out, leaving me exhausted. If I had a terrible game or the coach screamed at me, I'd let the voices tell me I wasn't good enough. I'm not sure what her trigger was, or what the voices are telling her, but I want to help.

I break the kiss and sit down on the couch next to her. Breathless, she watches me warily while I pick her feet up and put them in my lap, running my knuckles along her arch. She leans her head back on the couch and sighs.

"That's heaven right there."

I smile. "Why does our house smell like it was dipped in bleach?"

"Not our house, *your* house."

"Well, it's your house while you're here."

"But it's not permanent," she says. "*We're* not permanent. And I feel like I'm holding you back, or I might be in the way."

"In the way of what?"

"You and Annie. I mean tonight, you looked like a family and there I was, a splinter in a sore thumb. Even Ben knew I was an outsider. And Etta said I was competition and I should up my game."

My thumb glides along her arch. "Annie and I are just friends. I made that point crystal clear tonight. If I thought you were holding me back or I was confused about my feelings for her, I certainly wouldn't be sitting here rubbing your feet." My thumb slides up her silky-smooth calf, causing her to softly moan.

"But the whole town wants you two together, except for Etta and Racquel. They have their own Bachelor Nation thing happening in Greyson Gap. Everyone says you guys were meant to be."

I stop kneading for a second, irritated I have to defend what I want versus what the town wants. "That doesn't mean it's what my heart wants. I promise you there's no miscommunication or confusion between Annie and me. She is my friend. That's it, plain and simple. As for the town of Greyson Gap, they don't get a say in what I want."

She raises herself up on her elbows and wiggles her feet for me to continue. "What *do* you want?"

"You. I can't stop thinking about you."

Her breath catches. "I'm not staying."

"I'm not asking you to." She nods, her eyes shimmering with unshed tears. It confuses me. "Do you want me to ask you to stay?"

She tries to pull her foot away, but I hang on.

"No, of course not. That would be silly. We don't even know each other. We don't even *like* each other."

I arch an eyebrow. "Really? I like you." I tug her down so she's lying flat on the couch. I hold myself over her. "I like you a lot."

Her gaze falls to my mouth. "But I drive you insane, and you don't tell me important things, like wanting to be Mayor. I clean too much, I have pink hair, and I write hateful things about you in my journal."

I rear my head back. "I thought your journal was about personal growth goals?"

Her eyes flicker to the side as she shrugs. "It is…"

"So, you're upset because I didn't tell you I was running for Mayor of Greyson Gap?" I stare down into her golden-honey pools. "I didn't tell you because you had this image of me in your head as some ex-baseball player who could barely string two sentences together. You would have laughed if I said I was running for Mayor."

Her eyes cloud with guilt. "You really think that's what I thought?"

My mouth tightens. "Just like I thought you were an uptight snob when I first met you. I would've told you, eventually. Honestly, I didn't think it was a big deal."

She traces her finger along my jaw. "For what it's worth, I think you'd make a great mayor."

"Hmm, we'll see. I have to get elected first. And for what it's worth, I don't think you're a snob." I lightly kiss her lips, her body feeling way too good underneath me. "Look, Blakely, I like you. I like you a lot, but I'm not looking for anything serious and you're not permanently staying here. We're both attracted to each other, we can't deny that. Why can't we call it what it is and have some fun?"

"Wow, not exactly swoonworthy," she grumbles, looking away from me.

I gently pull her chin back, her eyes connecting with mine. "I never said I was a hearts and roses kind of guy, darlin'."

"I know...*darlin'*." She smirks. "You're more of a let's go fishing, hiking, make out in the back of a truck, take-me-on-the-kitchen-counter-sex kind of guy."

I smile and shrug unapologetically. "YOLO."

"You and your stupid YOLO." She smiles and bites her lip. "So, how do you want to do this? Schedule rendezvous and—"

I shake my head. "No plans, Smiles. No set appointments or writing it down in your calendar. Just you and me, whenever the fuck we want. Think you can handle it?"

She swallows, the apples of her cheeks pinking. I feel like the big bad wolf cornering Little Red Riding Hood. "Look, there's no pressure on my end. If you just want to be roommates, I understand."

"I think..." She swallows and looks away. "I think I need to sleep on it."

"Good." I gently run my finger down her cheek. "Get some sleep. Write about how much you want me in your journal. No more cleaning...even I'm feeling a little loopy from the bleach. And when you're ready? I'll be waiting." I gently kiss her lips and smile to myself as I head to my bedroom, alone.

Chapter 24

Beehive Betty

Blakely

FLIPPING THE SIGN on the shop door to open, I turn and survey the pristine store. The candles have been rearranged to my liking, my favorite scent already burning. It's finally Friday and I'm excited to go to the kickoff for the Fourth of July River Festival tonight.

Last year I spent the Fourth running around like a chicken with my head cut off for an event we were hired to plan. It went off spectacularly, but by the time the fireworks rolled around, I was mentally and physically spent. Come to think of it, every holiday has been like that. Always planning an event for someone else and being so tired, I'd spend the next day in bed recuperating. I can't remember one holiday I actually enjoyed for myself.

Straightening some stationery, realization kicks me hard in the gut. I haven't been living life. I've been killing myself to please others and make sure everything was perfect for them. Literally making myself sick to create a flawless event. Living a life to please others, I convinced myself I was happy, but the truth is, it was exhausting. I can't wait to discuss this huge breakthrough with Dr. Cooper and Tucker.

Ugh, Tucker. I've been avoiding him since our little talk about being roommates who have sex when the mood strikes us. I tried to drive him and his ludicrous offer out of my mind, but he was all I could think about during my morning yoga. *Friends with benefits is ludicrous, right?* Luckily, he's been busy with a construction project on the other side of town and prepping for the election, so evading him hasn't been too difficult.

Casual sex with Tucker. Just thinking about it makes my skin break out in a cold sweat. The thought of being spontaneous and not being in control of the situation makes me nervous as hell. But the real stressor for me is what will happen *after* our one night of sex?

Ugh, I can't think about this right now. I'm at work. I've counted the cash drawer twice, vacuumed, color-coded the scarves... Okay, I'm totally going to think about it, obsessively, since there's no one around to distract me. Tucker's face when he leaned over me the other night and kissed my lips, asking me to be his friend with benefits, is forefront in my brain. Who does that anyway? Who thinks it's totally okay to have a casual fling with their roommate? Didn't Junie say he was a player? The only two women I've seen him interact with are his ex, Annie, and I-want-to-gouge-your-eyes-out Stacy Reeger.

"Be honest with yourself, Blakely Marie Mayfield. You *want* to have hot, steamy, no-strings-attached sex with Tucker Greyson."

There, I said it out loud. The one man I vowed I'd never sleep with has me all tied up in knots, wondering what it would feel like to have him make me come undone—like loosening a satin bow from a present. Images of Tucker between my legs, his hands gripping my thighs while running his tongue slowly along my seam. My fingers thread through his hair, pulling tight as I buck against him, until I lose control.

I lean against the counter and fan myself with a Tidings order form, feeling weak in the knees. Great, now I'm having sexual fantasies during the day, *at work*, about the man. What is wrong with me? He said he liked me...a lot. Three little words and my resolve crumpled like one of Racquel Dewbury's used tissues. So then, what's my problem?

Don't get me wrong, I was so damn close to sealing the deal when he was hovering over me, his biceps bulging, muscles straining against his t-shirt. His pretty, green mischievous eyes kept drifting down to my lips. I wanted it to happen, but Lord knows I can't do casual.

I'm the least relaxed person I know. I've never had a one-night stand. I'm floundering, not knowing what's supposed to happen next. Do we go out on a date? Do I make the next move? Am I supposed to pretend our talk never happened? What the fuck does casual sex even mean?

Furthermore, how does one even act after casual sex? Do I give him a high-five or a pat on the bum and call it a good game? Will we snuggle after, or will he say, *later babe*, and kick me out of his bed? Living together definitely makes the whole situation sticky, but at least my walk of shame is only a couple of stairs up to my room.

But isn't this the whole point of my *new me* experience? Step out of my comfort zone and try new things? Tucker has been nothing but transparent. If I don't like it or I've changed my mind, I can stop it at any time, right? *Right?*

Jesus, I'm spiraling. We haven't even had sex yet, and my mind is on a runaway train going straight off a cliff. This is exactly why I can't do casual. I have no clue what I'm doing.

The bell rings, blessedly bringing me out of my head. Turning around, I paste on a smile, excited beyond belief to have a customer to take my mind off Tucker. "Good morning! Welcome to Tidings!"

The woman eyes me suspiciously, her gaze lingering on my pink hair. I tried tying a scarf over it after watching several how-to videos, but it looked ridiculous.

"Is Etta here?"

"Oh, no, I'm sorry. She'll be in this afternoon. Can I help you with something?"

The older woman is wearing a pink visor with "Greyson Gap Ladies" stitched in silver. Her banana yellow hair is piled high into a hair-sprayed beehive sitting on top of her head, the visor sufficiently holding it in place. It looks like Tanya's handiwork. She fans herself with a menu, her large bag held against her purple velour tracksuit. She edges closer to the candles near the desk.

"That's right. Etta told me she hired someone new. I love the smell of these." She picks one up and grimaces, quickly setting it back down.

"Oh yes, one hundred percent soy with a burn time of sixteen hours. I have the lily water burning right now."

"Mmm, that's nice." She picks up a box of stationery and checks the price.

"Is there something in particular you're looking for?" I

ask.

"Just browsing."

She's got to be sweating bullets wearing a velour tracksuit in July. "I see your hat says *Greyson Gap Ladies*. Is it a local club?"

"Oh yes, dear. We mostly gather for bunco or bridge. I'm going to pop into the bathroom, if you don't mind. Won't be a sec."

Alarm bells go off in my head. Etta's number-one rule was no bathroom. "Oh, I'm so sorry, but our bathroom isn't available to the public. I think there's one in the coffee shop you can use."

"Oh, okay, thank you." She checks another price on the back of a stationery box as the bell rings, announcing another visitor. I turn my back on Beehive, ready to greet the next customer.

"Good morning, welcome to Tidings," I say cheerfully to two women who saunter in holding coffees.

"Good morning, we're just browsing. Got into town last night and saw this cute store while at the coffee shop."

"Well, of course! Come on in and let me know if you have any questions. Welcome to Greyson Gap." I turn to check on Beehive, but I don't see her. I know she didn't leave through the front door because I've been facing it. I quickly look behind the counter. "Uh...hello? Miss?" The two women in the shop look up at me. "Sorry...did y'all see the woman who was in here when you walked in? Purple tracksuit?"

"I saw her go into the back." The short brunette smiles. My smile slips, my stomach suddenly queasy.

Shit, shit, shit! Etta is going to kill me. Who the fuck is this woman and why is she lurking in the back office? Oh, no...oh god, it can't be. It's Friday...and she was fanning herself with The Bagel Bin menu. It's the woman Etta told me under no certain circumstances to ever let in the store. Not only did I let her into the store, but she's using our pristine bathroom. Goddammit!

Why is this happening to me? What is wrong with the people in this town? I can't go bang on the door and yell at her to get out because I have customers in the store. Should I text Etta? She's going to be so pissed. My forehead feels clammy as I paste on a sickly smile, trying to figure out what to do.

Okay, calm down, Blakely, what's the worst that can happen? She's just using the bathroom. It's not like she's stolen a bunch of merchandise and run off with it.

"Can I ask you a question?" the short brunette asks me.

"Of course," I squeak. "Oh, I love the stationery you're holding. There's a matching planner over here. Oh, and we even have a candle to complete the set." I quickly grab it.

She shoots a look at her friend. "I wanted to ask the price of the stationery. It's not on this one."

Whoa, take it down a notch, Blakely. You're scaring this poor woman. I place the candle back on the counter. "Of course, it's sixteen for twelve cards."

Her friend takes the planner from me. "Ooh, this is pretty. I need a new one."

"I love this one because it has a little section at the bottom for notes..." I wrinkle my nose.

The two women look at each other and mimic my facial expression. "What is that smell?" the tall brunette whispers.

This can't be happening. I quickly grab the lighter from behind the desk and light another candle, but the scents are so soft, meant to enhance, not overpower a room.

"It smells like a sewage break. Do you think a pipe burst?" The friend holding the planner fans her face, looking at me expectantly.

"No," I say flatly. "I almost wish it was." I go to the front door and prop it open, letting all the air conditioning out into the sticky, humid morning. The women place the planner and cards down on a table, exchanging whispers. No doubt talking about the disgusting smell emanating from the back of the store.

"We'll be back. We're here all week." They quickly rush out of the store, their faces crinkled in disgust.

I march to the back bathroom and loudly rap on the door with my knuckles. "Um, excuse me? I thought I asked you not to use the bathroom." I'm met with silence, so I bang on the door. "Hello? I know you're in there."

"Oh, hi." Her voice is muffled from the other side of the door. "I'm so sorry, I couldn't wait. And your tissue paper is so much softer than the coffee shop. Your bathroom is cleaner too."

"Yes, because we don't let the public use it!" I shrill, wanting to wring this woman's neck.

"Well, I wouldn't tell Etta about this. She'll be *very* angry with you." Beehive has the nerve to giggle.

"GET OUT OF THE BATHROOM!" I bang on the door for good measure. "Or I'm calling the police!"

A customer walks in, wrinkles her nose, turns and walks right out.

"Oh wait! I can help you!" I run after her, but she's gone. Jesus, this woman is driving customers out even with the door open.

The toilet flushes and Beehive comes out, a guilty smile stretching her flabby lips. My gut reaction is to tackle her like a linebacker, but I hold my ground, fuming. She waves as she rushes by me.

"Thank you! Have a great Fourth weekend! Oh, by the way, I think it's leaking." She disappears out the door with her large bag. I stare after her, dumbfounded. Did she say it was *leaking*?

I run back toward the bathroom with my fingers pinching my nose shut. I kick the cracked door open with my foot. The toilet seat is down, but water is overflowing all over the bathroom. I quickly push down on the handle, but there's no resistance. No, this can't be happening! Panicking, I grab a bunch of paper towels and throw them on the floor. What the hell am I supposed to do? Etta will find out I let Beehive use the bathroom and fire me. It's the senator's party all over again. I don't know how to fix this and the anxiety is crippling.

My vision blurs while I make my way to the back room, my heart thundering in my chest. I grab my cellphone from my purse and call Tucker, the edges of a panic attack on the horizon. *Breathe, Blakely. It's not your fault.*

"Hey Bla—"

"Some lady with a beehive came in the store and took a monstrous...I can't even say it, but now the toilet is clogged and there's water overflowing and I don't know how to stop it and Etta told me not to let her use it because she's a repeat offender, but she snuck back here when my back was turned and now Etta's going to fire me!"

"Whoa, whoa, slow down. Can you turn the water source off?"

I stare at the phone incredulously. "Do I look like a goddamn plumber?"

"Okay, hold on. I'm calling Mervin Kinicki to see if he's available. He's the local plumber. Give me a second."

"I'm sorry. I didn't mean to snap. It's just...Etta's going to be furious. She'll fire me and then I'll have to go back home. I'm overwhelmed and humiliated, and a big fat failure." I sniffle, tears tracking down my cheeks.

"Hey, it's going to be okay, babe, don't cry. You're not a failure. I've got you. I promise Etta won't fire you. Do you need me to come down there? I'm over at The Calhoun House, but I can be there in twenty. Mervin just texted me back and says he's on his way. Don't cry, Blakely." His calming voice is like a balm over my frazzled nerves.

I've got you. His words squeeze my heart. I've never had someone tell me they had my back before. It's comforting. "No, don't leave your jobsite. I'm okay."

"Call me when Merv gets there."

"Okay, I will." I sniff, blotting my cheeks with a tissue. "Tuck? Thanks for helping."

"I'm here if you need me."

I hang up, dreading my next phone call. I just wanted a simple job. Was that asking too much? Maybe the Gas N Go would have been a better fit. No one would be *dying* to use their restrooms.

I dial her number, my fingers shaking. Etta answers on

the third ring.

"You let her use the bathroom, didn't you?"

"What…how did…she snuck past me and locked herself in! I had customers in the store. What was I supposed to do? Oh god, Etta, I'm so sorry." I cry, disappointed in myself, angry at Beehive lady, all the horrible feelings of failure from my last job rising to the surface. "It started overflowing. Tucker called Mervin the plumber to come check it out. He should be here shortly. I didn't know what to do."

Etta sighs, her voice softening. "Now don't go getting your knickers in a knot and fall apart on me now. I should have known she'd try to pull a fast one on you since you're new. She's been trying to sabotage my shop for years. It's not your fault, it's a long-standing feud between us. Now stop your crying. How were you to know she was a sneaky poop-slinging ninny?"

"But Etta, I failed you…"

"Now, now, hush that nonsense. It's nothing that can't be fixed. Someone once said, 'Each misstep is still a step. Another lesson learned, another opportunity to get it right the next time.' This is another lesson learned, Blakely. Now get a hold of yourself, because Merv doesn't like criers. I'll be there soon."

"Thank you, Etta."

I try to fan around the store and light another candle, but it doesn't help. Twenty minutes later Plumber Mervin shows up. Merv is in his fifties with thinning grayish-brown hair, a handlebar mustache, and a potbelly peeking out of his gray t-shirt. His low-slung jeans are loaded down with a tool belt, and I'd bet my Container Store stock if he bent over,

I'd see an impressive plumber's crack.

He's not very chatty, so I point him in the bathroom's direction. He smells like sour milk, beer, and cigarettes. I've hit my quota on pungent lingering odors for the week, so I leave him to it. He lays out all his tools and gets to work while I sit miserably at the desk, wishing it were three instead of eleven so I could race home, shower, and call Dr. Cooper.

By eleven forty-five, Merv puts his tools away, grunting as he puts the bill on the counter. "Looks like someone tampered with the pipes. Your hall carpet needs to be replaced. Might need to replace the linoleum in the bathroom, but I'm no floor expert. I cleaned it up as best I could."

"Got it, thank you, Merv. You're a lifesaver." I wave while he trundles out of the store. I go back to the bathroom. Luckily, the smell is gone and the floor and toilet cleaned up. Unfortunately, the carpet is soaked. I'll have to replace it. I might as well work for free the rest of the summer.

The bell dings and a harried woman with her two children rush in.

"Good morning, welcome to Tidings." I muster a perfunctory smile. The last thing I want to do is deal with customers right now.

"Can my son Billy use your restroom?"

I look at Billy as he picks his nose and cups his shorts with his other hand. Billy looks like he'd pee all over the wall. "No! No one can use the bathroom!"

"Jeez, sorry for asking," she mutters, giving me a strange look, wrangling her kids back out the door.

"I'm sorry! You can use the coffee shop next door!" I

shout after her, but she's already gone. I bury my head in my hands and slump against the desk. Great, I'm turning into Etta Bird.

Goal: *Become more forceful with customers.*

Problem: *I didn't know Beehive Betty was the Bagel Bin pooper.*

Stress: *Having Beehive Betty lock herself in the bathroom and take a dump.*

What's the best thing that happened today: ~~Nothing good happened today.~~ *Tucker came to my rescue.*

What I am grateful for: *Not grateful for much these days. Dr. Cooper is now on speed dial.*

Chapter 25

Mr. Mayor

Tucker

WALKING INTO THE offices of Greyson Construction, I make a beeline for my cousin's open door. He's absorbed by something on his phone, his brows creased in concentration. He doesn't even hear me enter.

My father started Greyson Construction in the early nineties after he stepped down as Mayor. The company started small, renovating mountain homes and building luxury cabins for city dwellers who needed an escape. After he died, I stepped in as CEO of the company, and Jason took over as COO. It's been a learning curve for both of us, but we've grown the company exponentially by expanding our territory to Asheville.

Running for Mayor was my grandfather, GT's idea, not mine. I never wanted to get into politics, but he and my mom pushed the subject until I caved. As a Greyson, it was only natural to follow in my grandfather and dad's footsteps. I can never say no to GT, but I worry if I become Mayor, I'll have to give up the day-to-day duties of Greyson Construction. I guess I'll cross that bridge *if* I get elected.

"You shouldn't be watching porn on company time." I flop down into a chair across from Jason. He doesn't even flinch.

"It's hard not to when I get it free from your account." He leans back in his chair and smiles. "How can I help you on this fine Independence Day, Mr. Mayor?"

"God, please don't call me that," I grumble.

"Better get used to it. According to town gossip, you're a shoo-in. In other news, I've spent the last half hour trying to straighten out the Carter Property shithole. Danny said the owner changed his mind about the stair railing after it was installed. He said it was three quarters of an inch too tall. I swear this guy likes to complain about the stupidest shit. Last week the stone walls were a quarter shade too light."

"I'll stop by the house this afternoon and check it out. I just got back from the Calhoun house. At least it's right on schedule."

"That's good. Eddie and I are meeting at Surf and Turfs for lunch if you want to join us. As long as you don't draw a mob being the town celebrity and all."

I chuckle. "As much as I'd love to make you and Eddie uncomfortable, I have to head up to the ranch."

"Everything okay?"

"Grandpa wants us to move the cows soon."

Jason sighs. "I need to be more present up there. I'm thinking about selling Surf and Turfs."

I nod in agreement. "I think we both have too many hands in the pot."

"What time are you going to the festival tonight?" he asks, twirling a pencil.

"Depends now on when I get finished cleaning up your crap at the Carter house." I duck, laughing when the flying pencil misses my head. "I was going to meet Blakely and Whit at the pub at six. You coming?"

"I'll meet you guys at the festival."

"You going with someone?" I raise an eyebrow.

He shrugs. "So, what's going on with you and Blakely?"

"Nothing. Everything. I don't know."

Jason grins. "You like her."

"I like her."

"Fuck, I hate losing to Whitney. Can't you pretend to hate her until I get my fifty bucks?"

I rub my hand along my jaw, chuckling as I shake my head. "I asked her if she wanted to have no-strings-attached sex."

Jason laughs. "Seriously? That was ballsy."

"Well, it's not like she's sticking around. She's here for the summer."

"What did she say?"

"She said she'll think about it."

"Ouch. Did that bruise your tender ego?"

"Nah, she'll come around sooner than later." I smile, but it quickly falls. "I don't know, man, there's something about her. I think I'm fucked."

Jason gives me a knowing look. "So now, Romeo, even though you vowed to make it casual, your heart's involved and you can't stop thinking about her. So much for no strings."

"What do you think I should do?"

He leans back in his chair, clasping his hands behind his

head, a new tattoo peeking out from the arm of his t-shirt. "What do you want to do?"

I scrub my face with my hands and groan. "I don't know. What the fuck is wrong with me? What am I waiting for?"

"Uh, I don't know. What are you waiting for?"

"She's not a woman you can sleep with and quickly move on from. She's different. I don't want to spook her."

"So why in the hell did you put casual sex on the table?" he asks.

"I don't know. I don't want to get involved."

"But you already are."

"Right...exactly. I'm so fucked."

He drops his hands. "Sounds complicated."

"You have no idea."

"You really want my opinion?" Jason picks up his phone and spins it on his finger like he's a Harlem Globetrotter. "If this is something you want, go slow with her. Let her come to you. She'll be worth the wait."

"It's going to be torture." I grimace.

"The best things usually are." He grins, his phone crashing to the table along with my heart.

Chapter 26

The Festival

Blakely

"NEIGHBOR GIRL. ANYONE sitting here?"

Super, just what I need after today's shitshow. I grit my teeth and turn on my stool. "Hey, Bhodi, go ahead…my day can't get any worse," I mumble under my breath as I look around the pub.

His gaze flicks over me. "Didn't your hair used to be blonde?"

"Yes, but now it's pink."

"Haven't you heard blondes have more fun?"

"Thanks for the heads-up." I roll my eyes and take a sip of my white wine.

"Being stood up?"

"No," I huff. "I'm waiting for someone."

"Who?"

Bhodi Mills is the cherry on my fucking disaster sundae today. "Whitney."

"Is she here?" Bhodi stretches his neck, looking around.

I look at him oddly. You would think he'd know she owns the pub since he's been sleeping with her. "Of course, she's here. Why?"

"She and I kind of hook—"

"Stop right there, please. You don't need to finish that sentence."

His leg bounces like he's hopped up on Red Bull. "It's cool," he says, more to himself than me, checking his watch for the third time since sitting down.

"Are *you* meeting someone?" I ask suspiciously.

"I have a Viphut date coming here, but now I'm a little nervous. Whitney might freak out if she sees us together."

"Uh, you think?" *What an idiot.* "Why would you have your date meet you at Whitney's pub?"

"I didn't really think it through."

"Clearly." I bite my lip to keep from laughing. This moron is clueless.

Tucker strolls in wearing a sexy grin. I pop up, surprised, because he texted earlier that he was stuck at a jobsite and would have to meet us later at the festival. His eyes light up as they land on me and it does a funny thing to my heart. I'm really glad to see him after the day I've had, but I'm also nervous about our whole "casual" situation.

I never resolved how I should handle my roommate with benefits in public. Do I kiss him, hug him, give him a jovial punch to the arm? My heart rate speeds up as he draws closer. Dr. Cooper's advice wasn't exactly helpful, either. She told me to go with what made me feel comfortable. *Nothing is making me comfortable, Dr. Cooper!* My skin itches with all the indecision.

His appealing smile garners the attention from everyone in the room, but he only has eyes for me. The title of Mayor would suit him well. He nods his head in greeting to a couple sitting by the front door. Ike stops him to chat, while another table waives him over. Everyone wants a piece of Tucker Greyson.

I still feel a pang of guilt, assuming the sweaty shirtless mechanic I met over a month ago was a dumb, skirt-chasing Neanderthal. He's the exact opposite. He's kind, attractive, smart, funny...and right in front of me asking if I want to have no-strings sex. *What the hell is wrong with me?* I squirm in my seat and take a gulp of wine. I can't believe I'm about to ask the Barracuda for advice, but if anyone's an expert on this topic, it's him.

"Bhodi, how do you handle friends with benefits? I mean, do you hang out with them afterwards? Call them the next day? Let her sleep over?"

Bhodi's gaze dips to my legs and slowly travels up to my face. "Are you asking me to be friends with bennies?"

"What? No! God, no. I'm asking for a friend."

He looks at me suspiciously. "I mean, you're not really my type, but I'd be open to it if you wanted to."

I roll my eyes. Ugh, this was such a bad idea. "Can you focus on the question at hand and tell me how you handle your friends with benefits?"

He shrugs. "I don't ask them to hang around, if that's what you're asking. As soon as we bang it out in bed or on the counter, couch, wall—"

"I get the picture." Grimacing, I roll my hand for him to hurry. He's such a slimeball, and I'm seriously questioning Whitney's taste in men.

"Afterwards, I either ask them to hang out and hope to

get another sesh in or I tell them I'll catch them later. They're usually cool with it." He shrugs. "It's kind of like pizza. Sometimes it's great cold the next day, sometimes you want it hot and ready in fifteen minutes."

Did he really just compare sex with women to pizza? Do all guys think like this? Am I a fucking piece of pizza to Tucker?

Bhodi looks at his phone restlessly. "For once in my life, I hope this Viphut date is a no-show."

"Well, that would be good, considering Whitney's older brother just walked in and he's heading this way." I smile into my wineglass. "Are you sweating?"

"No…shit, I don't know. Play it cool, here he comes."

I'm amused he actually thinks I'm on his side.

"Bruh." Bhodi holds up his hand for a fist-bump, which Tucker ignores. He leans in to kiss my cheek. I sigh, relieved he's made the first move.

"Hello gorgeous, I like the hair."

I self-consciously touch my hair, which I've pulled back into a fishtail braid. "Thanks. One more week and I can say goodbye to Easter-egg pink."

"I think I might miss it. Let me grab a beer and I'll join you. Need anything?"

"Yeah, bro, I'll take a beer." Bhodi checks his phone, missing the insipid stare Tucker sends his way. He raises two fingers to the new bartender. Grabbing the beers from the bar, he leaves a twenty, sliding one to Bhodi, who, thankfully, is engrossed on his phone.

"I want to hear how the rest of your day went." He sits down in the chair on the other side of me at the high top.

My heartstrings tug a little that he cares. Maybe I'm

more than pizza...god, I hope so. "Etta didn't fire me. She let me go home early."

"Did you ever figure out who the woman was?"

"What woman?" Bhodi looks around the bar anxiously. I pat his hand but think better of it, grabbing some hand sanitizer from my purse.

"Beehive Betty, whose real name is Betty Doliver." I wrinkle my nose, thinking about the foul woman.

"Yeah, I know her." Tucker rubs a hand along his jaw. "The Greyson Gap Ladies Club hangs out at the coffee shop on Fridays. Her husband, Bill, is running against me for Mayor."

"I can't imagine her being the mayor's wife. She's awful. The rugs are ruined and the linoleum needs to be replaced in the bathroom. Etta wasn't too happy."

"I'm sure she realizes it's not your fault." Tucker links his hand with mine. What I really want for him to do is wrap me in his arms and hold me, but that's definitely not something casual roommates do.

"Hey guys! I'll be ready in a few!" Whitney heads over to the bar and talks to the bartender before coming back to our table. "Oh, hey Barracuda, I thought you had plans."

Bhodi looks like a deer caught in headlights. "Plans...with you!"

"Real smooth," I mutter.

Whitney smiles brightly. "Great! Give me ten minutes and I'll meet y'all out front."

"Where's Annie, isn't she coming?" I ask Tucker.

"She's going with her mom." He smiles, squeezing my hand.

I squeeze back, feeling a tad guilty Tucker had to spell out his feelings for her, but in the end, it's best for both of them. We finish our drinks and head out front to wait for Whitney. A tall man with a buzz cut passes by us.

"Carl." Tucker nods.

Carl nods his head, entering the pub without a reply. Besides Stacy Reeger, Carl is the only other person in this town who doesn't appear to like Tucker.

"Who was that?"

"Carl is a state trooper who lives at the end of Willow Drive. I have no idea why, but Hershel loves to hang out in his yard. He has some sort of dog sense and knows how much Carl hates dogs."

"Are we talking about Creepy Carl?" Whitney comes up behind us.

"Why do you call him Creepy Carl?" I ask.

"Because something about him screams creepy, like he buries dead bodies on his property. He's always been very intense and weird."

"Yikes, stay clear of Creepy Carl, got it." Trying to keep up with all the unique personalities in this town makes my head hurt.

"I'm ready if you guys are." Whitney loops her arm in Bhodi's. A cab pulls up to the curb. A woman with long brown hair gets out wearing a red dress and heels. She looks over at us before entering the pub.

"Bhodi? Bhodi Mills?"

"Shit," he breathes out. "Tammy?"

"Yeah, hi. Nice to meet you. Sorry I'm late. I didn't realize how far this place was from Asheville." She smiles at the four of us, frozen on the sidewalk. Bhodi looks like he's about to throw up, while Whitney is turning an interesting shade of magenta. She flings her arm away from him.

"Are you…is she…" Whitney fumbles. "Are you on a *date?*"

Tammy takes a step back, her smile sliding off her face. She looks back to see if her cab is still there, but it's already pulled away from the curb.

"Whitney, it's not what it looks like." Bhodi tries to grab her hand, but she wrenches it away. "Tammy and I—"

"No, no need to explain," Whitney cuts him off, stalking down the street. "God, I'm such an idiot!" she yells to the dusky sky. "Come on guys, let's go. Have fun on your *date.*"

"Whitney, come on! You're blowing this way out of proportion. We're having fun."

Whitney whirls around. "Oh, *I'm* blowing this out of proportion?" She stalks back up to him and knees him in the groin. He doubles over and yelps in pain, crumpling to the ground. "How's that for fun, Bhodi fucking Barracuda?"

"Call me later? Whit?" Bhodi wheezes as poor Tammy rushes into the bar.

Whitney holds her hand above her head and flips him off without a backward glance.

Tucker grabs my hand and we step around Bhodi, hurrying to catch up with her. "Another fruit fly bites the dust."

"Are you okay, Whitney?" I ask. "We can skip the festival if you want."

"I can't believe you guys let me get involved with that idiot!"

"Whoa, try again. We warned you against sleeping with

him," Tucker points out.

"Can't you be on my side for once?" she gripes while we walk onto the street where the festivities are being held. "I'm so tired of asshole guys who sleep with every girl in sight. Why can't I find one nice guy who won't sleep around on me, or isn't married, or isn't a swinger who wants a three-way with you and your best friend, or doesn't have a secret pregnant girlfriend in another town?"

I raise my eyebrows, looking over at Tucker. He shakes his head, tight-lipped, as we follow Whitney into a wine tent.

"Is that asking too much?" Whitney continues. "Because if it is, then I'm swearing off men for good! I will never sleep with the likes of Bhodi the Barracuda again! Is Maebry Evans single? I'd switch teams for her if she'll have me." She slams cash down on the folding table. "Hey, Angie, can I buy a whole bottle?"

Angie, a dark-haired, middle-aged woman wearing thick glasses, giggles nervously and picks up the cash. "Ah, hey Whitney, how's it going? Um, I'm really sorry, but we can only sell by the glass tonight," she says, her cheeks turning rosy as she glances over at Tucker.

"Got it, always playing by the rules, Angie." Whitney nods. "Angie is Pastor Ken's assistant. Angie, this is Blakely Mayfield."

"Nice to meet you." I smile and shake Angie's hand.

"Okay, well, if I can't have the bottle, I'll take four glass-es. Blakely, I'm gonna need you to order a couple. I'm buying."

"Oh, um, well, there's a two-drink maximum, Whitney." Angie glances anxiously between Tucker and me, shifting uneasily on her New Balance shoes. I'm guessing Angie isn't experienced in handling jilted women who want to drown their feelings in wine.

"Two-drink maximum? How am I supposed to get drunk off that?" Whitney leans over the table, causing Angie to take a step back and adjust her glasses. "Angie, just between you and me? I'm having a bit of a crisis. Give me the maximum for all three of us…add the guy standing over there. Oh, and the woman over—"

"Just get one glass, Whit, and stop harassing poor Angie. You can always come back," Tucker says testily before he walks away.

"What crawled up his butt? Fine, since we're *playing by the rules*, give me two each for the three of us, Ang," Whitney grumbles. "Heavy on the pour."

"Do you think guzzling cheap wine is the best idea right now?" I glance quickly at Angie. "No offense, Angie."

"Yes, Blakely, I do. If you had some sleazebag you're sleeping with roll up to the Fourth festival with a random chick he met online, wouldn't you want to guzzle all the cheap wine you could get your hands on?"

Angie's eyes widen as she pushes the cups toward Whitney.

I nod. "Point taken."

"Don't have too much fun tonight, ladies." Angie giggles uncertainly, wiping her hands on her pants. "It was nice to meet you, Blakely."

"You, too." I smile brightly, grabbing some cocktail napkins.

"Don't worry, we are going to have *so* much fun. Tell

Pastor Ken I'll be in for confession on Sunday." Whitney winks before picking up the three cups filled to the brim with white wine and motions for me to grab the other three. Craning my neck, I look for Tucker, but I don't see him in the crowded tent.

"There's Jason talking to...oh god, Stacy Reeger. We need to go rescue him," Whitney shouts over her shoulder and I reluctantly follow, alarm bells going off in my head.

Stacy Reeger might cut me with a shiv, according to Tanya and Lolly. Hopefully, she doesn't realize I'm Tucker's new roommate or else I might be the next face on her dartboard.

"Jason, so glad you're here!" Whitney shouts.

Jason peers at our wine and laughs. "Wow, you guys aren't messing around tonight."

I smile and shrug. Stacy gives me a head-to-toe perusal, and not in a smiling, I-love-your-outfit, kind of way. I take a sip, needing the liquid encouragement. Whitney grins at her while handing two of her cups of wine to Jason.

"Hold these for me. Don't go sneaking off with them," she says before turning to Stacy. "So, Stacy, have you met Tucker's girlfriend, Blakely?"

I spit out the wine I just sipped. Oh god, oh no, I don't want to die tonight. "Not girlfriend, just roommate," I swiftly explain, blotting my shirt with a napkin. Stacy's eyes narrow.

"I thought it was a rumor."

"Awe, now darlin', no need to be shy over us being to-gether." A muscular arm wraps around my waist, pulling me to a granite-hard chest. I shiver when he kisses my neck and whispers *'play along'* in my ear, but I'm too focused on Stacy's claw-like talons as she cracks the plastic wine cup in her hand.

"I heard you were working for Etta, but I didn't realize you were *involved* with Tucker as well. Isn't that...cozy?"

I gulp. *Oh god, she's heard about me and knows where I work?*

"Involved...haha, it's such a complicated word..." The words die on my lips watching Stacy's nostrils flare, the bitter contempt flaring in her eyes. Her jealousy pings off me, like hail in a rainstorm. I hand some wine to Whitney and try to peel Tucker's arm off my waist, but he's like a damn koala, tugging me tighter.

"Blakely May, if you keep squirming, I may have to carry you out of this tent and have my wicked way with you," he growls in my ear.

"Oh, ha! You're so funny, *roomie!*" I elbow him in the ribs. He grunts, letting go of me, and moves over into a conversation with Jason and some other guy, but not before he lands another kiss on my cheek.

"Right...don't you make a cute couple." The word 'cute' rolling off Stacy's tongue like she swallowed curdled milk. "Have you met Tucker's Annie? She's the sweetest girl."

"She's not his dog, Stacy," Whitney mumbles into her wine cup.

"Yes, I had dinner with Annie this past week." I give her a sugary smile, knowing she's trying to needle me. "She shared her meatloaf recipe with me. It's Tucker's favorite." *Liar, liar, pants on fire.*

Stacy looks perturbed but refuses to walk away. "So, how

long have you and Tucker been living together?"

"I arrived in June, so a little over a month." I swallow some wine, looking everywhere other than Stacy.

"Hmm, so…convenient. Has he taken you to the ranch yet?" she asks innocently. "It's *so* much fun."

The ranch? I subtly try to signal Whitney for help, but she's guzzling the wine she took from me. "No, not yet."

Stacy gives me a pitiful look. "Well, then you're not *really* a couple." She walks away, leaving me wondering what the hell the ranch is and what it has to do with making us a couple.

Whitney throws her three empty cups in the trash and plucks the last cup out of Jason's hands, taking a large gulp. "Ugh, thank God that mood-killer finally took a hike. I for sure thought she was going to punch you in the face when my brother wrapped himself around you."

"Thanks for the heads-up," I grumble.

Whitney smiles breezily. "Come on, let's mingle, 'cause, well, I'm suddenly single!" She tugs me out of the tent back into the street where vendors line the sidewalk, funnel cake and BBQ permeating the air. She loops her arm through mine.

"Whitney, do you want to talk about what happened back there with Bhodi?"

"Nope," she says, popping her 'p'. She finishes another cup of wine and I pass her one of mine. We weave in and out of the crowd. "Fun fact, he likes to have his nipples pinched hard during sex."

Ew, no, please no. I don't want to know any vomit-inducing facts about Bhodi Mills.

"That's not—"

"And he calls me his little cookie and himself Big Daddy during sex, but guess what?" she whispers loudly. "He's *not* big."

"Uh, okay, listen, I don't really—"

"Listen up, Greyson Gap!" she shouts, pulling us to a stop. "Bhodi Mills has a small penis!"

Oh. My. God.

A family of five gives us a wide berth, another couple snickering as they look over their shoulders at us.

"Whitney!" I hiss. "You can't shout that."

"I just did. Whoopsies." She giggles. "Ooh, there's Eddie Barker. Isn't he dreamy?"

"You need to date a nice guy like Eddie. He's hot as hell." I smile and wave as we pass by the Greyson Gap Fire Department booth, where he's handing out plastic fire-fighting hats and stickers to little kids.

"Oh, believe me, I've tried, but he's not interested. It's probably for the best. He's too shy and quiet for my taste. Keeps to himself mostly, like a goddamn disciplined monk. I think I'm too much woman for him." She chucks her empty cup into the trash and grabs the one I was drinking out of my hand.

"Go ahead, I didn't want that," I deadpan. "That's too bad about Eddie."

"Tell me about it." She laughs before she throws back the last of the wine.

"You better slow down on those, tiger."

"Why?" Whitney shrugs. "I'm trying to erase Barracuda's memory."

"This isn't going to end well."

I smile and wave to Lonna Parker and her son as we pass on the street. My smile slides off my face when she dramatically drags Troy to the other side of her, like I'm going to pounce on him.

"God, Lonna Parker is so uptight. Why is she acting like we're going to show little Troy our boobies?" Whitney says loud enough for Lonna to hear.

Do I tell her the whole Parker family saw me skinny-dipping with her brother? I'd like to forget it happened myself. I know there's some prepubescent kid out there that has salivated over a grainy photo of my boobs. Jesus.

"Whit, why did Stacy ask me if I've gone up to the ranch? She said Tucker and I weren't a couple unless he's taken me there…not that Tucker and I are a couple. Your brother and I are most definitely *not* a couple. I guess I'm confused by what she meant."

"God, she's such a jealous B," Whitney snorts. "She's talking about our family ranch where Mama and my grandfather, GT, live. Tucker has a house on the property too, but he's renting it out this summer."

"Oh yeah, he mentioned it." Dammit, why isn't she answering the question?

"Oh, hi Blakely! I hope the self-help books have been enlightening," Laura Twinkle shouts from her bookstore booth, causing several people to turn their heads. "You've inspired me to start a self-help group on Wednesdays. Hope to see you there. Maybe you can be my first guest speaker!"

"Oh…okay, Laura, I'll get back to you." I awkwardly wave and smile, tugging Whitney along. "Wow, small towns, gotta love them." I giggle nervously. "Why would Stacy say we aren't a couple if I haven't been to the ranch? And again, let me clarify, I'm not your brother's girlfriend, I'm just curi-ah!"

A neon-pink lacquered nail clutches my wrist and pulls me to the side. "I heard you made an appointment in Asheville to change your hair. What's wrong with it?" Tanya's eager eyes about pop out of her head. She's about to be pulled down by the eight dogs wrapped around her legs with leashes. One of them growls at me while the rest yip and howl. I try to pull away, but she isn't about to let go. I look to Whitney for help, but she's wandered over to another wine tent.

"Hey, Tanya, are these all your cuties?" Maybe I can get her talking about the dogs and get her attention off my hair.

"But it's so pretty! You don't like the pink?" Tanya whines, looking crestfallen in her red, white, and blue sequin jumpsuit. I almost feel bad about making an appointment to get it fixed.

"Oh! Um...I love the pink...I just want to go darker for fall, you know?"

"Ooh, I'm picturing BBQ sauce red with a stripe of purple. Or are we talking more fuchsia? Either way, I think I can squeeze you in after Mrs. Mertleman's poodle on Monday if you want a darker pink. Ooh, or eggplant might be fun for fall. Gary, Joe Don, quit it!"

I look down, and one basset is humping the other. The thirty-pound black poodle growls, his beady eyes locked on my jugular. Is he the one who can take Ron's nuts off? I can't remember, but I don't want to stick around to find out.

Tanya drops my arm, distracted by Joe Don and Gary, and I take a step back.

"Uh, okay…I might be working that day, but I'll call you." I wave goodbye before she can grab me again. "Whitney's waiting for me. Have a happy Fourth, Tanya!"

"I'll see you next week, sugar! I'll show you my purple color chart!"

Crap, why couldn't I tell her the truth? Now I'm going to have to avoid her or be honest and hurt her feelings. I grab Whitney's arm and steer her away from the wine.

"Thanks for leaving me with Tanya, *friend*."

"Oh, she's harmless." She waves a hand and sips wine from a plastic cup. "They would only give me one glass. Can you believe that bullshit?"

"She wants me to come in and have the pink redone. I can't even tell you the colors she described… BBQ sauce red?"

Whitney laughs loudly, dragging me down the street. "Don't let her get those claws near your hair. Small towns can be really great, but they can also be very stifling with everyone's nose up in your business. You'll quickly learn who you can trust." She side-eyes me. "Like my brother. He's the most trustworthy guy I know."

"Hmm…" I say noncommittally.

"What's going on with you two, anyway?" She drunkenly clings to my arm while we stop and look at a booth selling photographs of the beautiful Blue Ridge Mountains.

"Nothing's happening."

"Well, something should! You guys have sparks flying whenever you're together."

I look at her dubiously. "We do?"

"Yes! I've never seen Tucker look at a woman the way he looks at you."

"Yeah, with annoyance," I scoff, flipping through a bin of waterfall photographs.

"With sparks and sparklers and fireworks," she says, dreamily.

"How much wine have you had?"

"And you"—she points her finger, ignoring me—"you want to lick him like a lollipop. But I'm gonna warn you. If you hurt his heart, I'll make Stacy Reeger look like a sweet, innocent angel."

Whitney gives me a stern look for a few seconds before her features melt into joy. "Ooh look! Soft pretzels, I need one now. Let's go." She drags me off before I can utter a word, too stunned to know what to say, anyway.

FAMILIAR HANDS WRAP around my waist while I watch the Fourth of July fireworks burst overhead. I start in surprise, but easily melt into Tucker's hold. It feels so right.

"I've been looking for you all night," he whispers against the shell of my ear, causing goosebumps to rise on my skin.

"I know, I'm sorry. Whitney was a mess. They finally banned her from the wine and beer tent. I got cornered by Racquel and Etta with their plans to marry off Greyson Gap's most eligible bachelors. By the way, you're at the top of their list. Unfortunately, I lost track of her during that."

Tucker chuckles, kissing me right under my jaw. "I asked Eddie Barker to make sure Whit got home okay, which means you and I have the rest of the night to ourselves."

Nerves clench my stomach. "Ha, hardly. Stacy Reeger has been on the prowl looking for you."

Bursts of color shower down from the sky while the surrounding crowd *ooh*s and *aah*s.

"Let's go watch these from the house."

I look at him over my shoulder. "You can see them from there?"

"The roof has a little balcony we can watch from."

I spy Etta waving to me, dragging Racquel with her. I definitely don't need those two nosy nellies up in my business if they've seen Tucker's arms wrapped around me. "Let's get out of here." Before my nerves can climb up my spine, I wave goodbye to Etta and pull Tucker through the crowd.

"What's the big hurry?"

"Etta and Racquel are hot on our heels."

"They're in their seventies." He chuckles. "I think it's safe to say they aren't going to catch up."

"Listen, they're more agile than they let on. Racquel only uses the walker to get a close parking spot at The Market Stop and to hit people with it if they're in her way. Her words, not mine. Besides, I've had enough talk about rose ceremonies and Greyson Gap's eligible bachelors and bachelorettes to last me a lifetime. Trust me, this is for the best."

Tucker gives me a devastating smile as another firework

breaks apart overhead. I press my hand to my stomach as I look up at the bright colors fizzing in the sky. The feeling something is about to change sparkles in the air, brighter than the fireworks.

Chapter 27

Fireworks on the Balcony

Tucker

I LEAD HER up the stairs to a door at the end of the hall and up another set of spiral stairs to a smaller door I have to unlock.

"I've always wondered what was behind this door. This isn't like a Christian Grey thing where you're going to spring it on me you're a BSDM freak, is it?"

"What?" I laugh. "Who's Christian Grey?"

"Er…never mind." Blakely pushes me forward as we step out onto a small balcony on the roof of the house overlooking the river. The fireworks shoot up brilliantly before spiraling back down against the inky sky. I pour her a glass of wine I grabbed on my way up and dust off a lounge chair. Sitting down on it, I motion for her to sit between my legs.

She hesitates, her shy smile tightening my chest, before sitting down. She scoots back and rests her head on my shoulder. "This is amazing. Way better than standing on a crowded street."

We watch the fireworks, but I'm achingly hard with her butt snuggled up against me. I know I'm supposed to take things slow, but this is painful. Lazily drawing my finger in a figure-eight pattern on her arm, I breathe in her soft floral scent and nuzzle her neck right behind her ear. She squirms against me.

"What are you doing, Tucker?" she asks huskily.

"Your scent is driving me crazy."

"My *scent?*" She laughs. "Whatever rocks your boat, Tucker Greyson."

"Hmm...you do." I gently pull her earlobe between my teeth. She squeaks in surprise, but quickly melts into me. "I want you, Blakely. Have you made a decision about us?"

"I..." She pulls away and turns to face me. "I want you too, but I need to be honest. I'm not really sure how to do casual." Her golden-brown eyes distract me from what I really want, her vulnerability shining brightly behind her mask of feigned indifference. *Don't spook her.*

"Do you trust me?" The fireworks sparkle in the sky behind her. I brush my thumb along her jaw. She nods, leaning toward me, her gaze never faltering. I cup her face, pulling her down to me, skating featherlight kisses over her soft skin before she tilts her lips up to mine.

Her body slowly melts against me, surrendering to the kiss. Fingers tentatively lift my shirt, almost as if she's afraid I'll stop her and tell her no. Taking control, I pull my shirt off in one fell swoop. Her fingers explore the planes of my chest, but I'm greedy and want to feel her skin against mine. I lift her shirt over her head and gently cup her breasts, running my thumbs along the smooth lilac satin of her bra. "God, you're beautiful, Blakely."

Her skin tastes like sun-ripened strawberries and I have

to tell myself to slow down while I drop kisses from her shoulder to her breast, sliding her straps off. I unclasp her bra and capture her tight bud in my mouth. She moans in pleasure as she rocks into me, threading her fingers through my hair, and I silently curse the stars when I almost come in my pants. It drives me wild, seeing how responsive she is to my touch.

I pick her up and lay her down on the padded chair. She wriggles out of her jeans and tries to neatly fold them before I grab them out of her hands and toss them to the side. I swallow her protest with a kiss and slowly drop kisses down her breasts to her quivering belly, skimming the satin of her matching panties. I hook my fingers into them and press my lips right over her apex. She bucks against me.

"Blakely, I'm going to make you come with my mouth. Is that okay?"

"Yes," she breathes out and it makes me want to fuck her six ways to Sunday. I glide a finger into her and watch her arch off the chair. She's so fucking beautiful. I replace my finger with my tongue and suck on her sweet clit. She writhes underneath me, her legs clamping my head.

I chuckle. "Beautiful, you're going to have to hold still and try not to take my head off with your legs. Relax, I've got you."

"It's just, I mean, I've had oral sex before, but it's been a while. Charles didn't like to do this. You don't have to if you don't want to."

"Charles didn't like to taste your sweet pussy?" I arch an eyebrow and her rosy cheeks deepen. "He's a fucking idiot. Trust me, Blakely May, I *want* to lick every inch of you and eat you out until you scream for release. Relax and let go," I murmur, holding her thighs apart.

"Relax and let go, ha! You do realize who you have underneath you, right?"

I spread her legs wider and slide my tongue into her. I groan against her because I can't fucking get enough of her. Charles is an ass-hat loser to make her feel like her needs and desires weren't worth his time. I'd go down on her every day if she'd let me. She tastes sweet like honey, peaches and cream, as I lick and suck on her. She pants, making the hottest little moans while I work her over. It's the fucking sexiest sound I've ever heard and I'm so fucking hard I can't see straight. Her muscles contract and I know she's close.

"Oh my god, Tucker, yes, don't stop," she pants, grabbing my hair. She screams my name seconds later as she comes hard, the fireworks drowning out her cries while they burst in the sky behind us, and I don't stop until she's boneless.

I wipe my mouth off and grin, taking in her glazed, golden-brown eyes and satiated smile.

"Wow, that was unbelievable." She smiles up at me, but it slips a little when I slide her panties back on.

"Are you okay?"

"I'm just never that...impulsive." She shrugs, her cheeks blushing, and I know she's overthinking it. "Why did you put my panties on?" She bites her bottom lip.

"Because tonight was about you. I meant what I said. We'll go slow." Kissing her lips, I get up and painfully adjust my hard-on.

"That's your version of going slow?" she squeaks, her

cheeks flaming.

I sit on the chaise lounge and wait while she gets dressed.

"Did you not enjoy it, Smiles?"

"Oh, no! I did. I was just thinking we'd start with heavy petting. But it was, um…really great. Amazing, actually." She bites her bottom lip, buttoning up her jeans.

"Heavy petting?" I try not to laugh. She's fucking adorable. "I think you've been hanging out with Etta and Racquel too much. I'm going to go take a cold shower, and then watch a movie."

Her eyes flicker from me to the dark sky and back.

I reach for her hand and pull her to me, kissing her lips. "Tasting you tonight? It's my new favorite addiction. Do I want more? Hell yes. But I can wait."

She swallows and another crack crumbles my wall.

"You're overthinking it, Smiles." I kiss her lips. "Watch a movie with me."

"I'm always overthinking it," she mutters, grabbing the wine before following me back downstairs. "So, Tucker, what's your stance on pizza?"

Chapter 28

Sexy Kitten Oil

Blakely

THE DOOR CHIMES announcing a customer. A thin woman with long wavy hair, dressed in a peasant blouse, leggings, and Birkenstocks, walks into Tidings carrying a black tackle box. I saw her last week at the festival on Main Street selling candles and oils. She tried to engage Whitney and me in conversation, but Whitney roughly tugged me away from her booth. This must be the candlemaker. Etta said a rep for the company would stop in today with a shipment. She gave me permission to add other scents if I think they'd sell. She was impressed I sold the lily water candle out of stock in a week. I'm obsessed with the candles.

"Hi, how are you?" I smile as she approaches the counter.

"Hi, I haven't seen you in here before. Are you new?"

"Yes. I'm here for the summer. My name is Blakely."

"Oh, nice to meet you, Blakely," she says airily, placing her tackle box on the counter. She steps away and walks around the shop. "Mind if I light this?" She holds up a brown stick resembling a cigar.

Hmm, odd, but maybe she's doing a demonstration for a

new scent. I hand her a lighter. "Of course. I can't wait to see what you've brought."

"Wow, lots of bad juju in here." She frowns at me before she lights the stick and waves it around, chanting, "Cranberries and cakes, sparrows and rakes, let's get the wind to blow to the fates."

What on earth? I nervously look around to see if anyone else is witnessing this, but it's just me and the candle lady. I honestly can't see Etta putting up with this, but her candles are bestsellers...

She stubs out the stick before I can interrupt her. "There, now that I've saged the place, let's get down to business."

"I'm sorry. What was your name again?"

"Oh...it's Linseed."

"Nice to meet you, Lindsey. Why don't you tell me what you've brought today? The lily water scent was a big hit."

"No, Lin-seed, like the oil."

"Oh, my apologies." I shift on my feet, my spine tingling with unease. Etta deals with her monthly, it's fine.

Linseed opens her box, but I can't see around the lid. "I have lots of products which would be great in the store—"

"Oh, I'm only supposed to approve one new scent, maybe two. The others are doing well."

Linseed shrugs. "Okay, my favorite is oregano. It's earthy and pungent, but grounding." She sets several dark brown vials on the counter. Uh-oh, Etta definitely didn't mention oils.

"Um, Linseed—"

"Or I have patchouli, which is a classic, or bergamot, which everyone favors."

"Linseed, I don—"

"But what's really the best is my homemade mixture of sandalwood, seaweed, and grapefruit. I call it my frisky kitty oil. You look like you could use a little frisky kitty in your life."

Ugh, that sounds like a horrible combination. I didn't even know seaweed was an oil. She babbles on about the health benefits of her oils and how great they would be for the store. I can't get a word in as I look around helplessly while she continues to unload bottles on the counter, talking a mile a minute. My pulse spikes, panic inching along my spine. This has already gotten out of control and I'm feeling like a car coasting without a driver.

"Linseed... Linseed!" I shrill, which finally closes her trap.

"So how many do you want to buy?" she asks absently, dabbing oil on herself. "Or would you rather do a sexy kitten party? Your vibes are screaming for your inner sexy kitten to be let loose on the prowl."

"A sexy what? Wait a second, are you even a rep for Cottage Home Candles?"

Her face twists in disgust. "Ugh, over my dead body would I ever be a rep for those soy-loving, honeycomb bee-killing, bunny-murdering miscreants."

If she's not the rep, who the hell is this woman? "Um, okay...there's been a slight misunderstanding. Who do you work for?"

"Linseed's Oils." She rolls her eyes like I'm the biggest moron to step foot in Greyson Gap. "I make the oils myself. I use vegan products and don't test on animals like those hideous candles you sell. I also have an oil-of-the-month club, Linseed's Luscious Oils, for when you're needing a little help in the bedroom—"

"Wait, then what's frisky kitty for?" *Why do I even care?* I shake my head, exasperated. "You know what, never mind. I'm sorry, I thought I was meeting the rep for Cottage Candles." I gather her bottles and push them toward her box. "I don't have the authority to approve new purchases, so you'll have to come back another day when Etta is here."

She reaches out and grabs my wrist. "Try this oil on. It will calm your inner chi."

Before I can tug my wrist, she rubs some oil over my pulse point. It does not soothe my inner chi. It makes my pulse skyrocket with anxiety.

"First of all, you don't just grab someone's wrist without their permission and pour oil on them. I could have had an allergic reaction. Second, we don't sell oils here, so you need to pack up your stuff and leave...now!"

I get a tissue and roughly rub the oil off my wrist. I can't stand strong pungent perfumes and this one smells like my decrepit old piano teacher, Mrs. Snoop. It brings back terrible memories of her using a ruler on my knuckles when I hit the wrong key.

"Jeez, you don't have to be so rude," she sniffs, quickly placing the oils back in her box. "A simple 'no thank you' would have sufficed. I knew there was bad chi when I walked in here. You could use the frisky kitty. You seem a tad high-strung."

I fold my arms and glare at her, a headache forming at the base of my skull. I'm beginning to understand why Etta is the way she is. The people in this town are certifiable, and they all want to come to Tidings.

Linseed looks at me serenely once she locks her tackle box. "That will be fifty dollars."

"What will be fifty dollars?" I drum my fingers on the counter in annoyance.

"I saged your store."

"I never asked you to!" *The nerve of this wackadoodle.*

"Trust me, it needed it. You gave me permission when you gave me the lighter."

"If I had known it would have been fifty dollars and you weren't with Cottage Candles, I would have told you to get the hell out!"

She sits down on the carpet and crosses her arms. "I'm not leaving until I get paid."

I roll my eyes to the ceiling. *Why the fuck is this happening to me? Universe, what lesson am I supposed to be learning here?* Dare I say this is worse than Beehive Betty Doliver?

Linseed hums some off-key tune I don't recognize. At least Betty got the hell out of the store. Now, I have a squatter trying to swindle me out of fifty bucks. The humming increases the pressure of my headache. What would Etta do? She'd probably chase her out of here with the vacuum. Should I call Etta? I don't really want to bother her because she's at a doctor's appointment. What would I do if this were taking place at one of my events? I'd call the police, that's what I'd do.

I pick up the phone and dial the non-emergency number.

"These doughnus are fabuwous, Doween," a muffled

voice says over the line.

"Uh, hello?" I cover the mouthpiece and turn my back on Linseed.

"Gweyson Gap Poe-weece Station," a woman answers, sounding like she just stuffed one of those fabulous donuts in her mouth. "Cherwool speaking."

"Uh, yes, hi Cheryl, I have a woman who is refusing to leave Tidings Gift Store. I need a police officer to come over and help me escort her out."

Cheryl chews thoughtfully for a moment and then slurps her drink. Good thing this isn't a true emergency...yet. "Is it Linseed?"

"Yes! How did you know?" Cheryl must be the town psychic.

"Just pay her and she'll be on her way. No need to send the sheriff over."

I turn around and look down at stupid, carefree Linseed while she does yoga poses in the middle of the store. "But...but that's ludicrous!"

"Honey, listen to me." Cheryl takes another bite and thankfully chews her food before continuing. "If you pay Linseed now, she won't bother you again. If you don't, she'll come by every week and sage your place, charging you for each time. It's best just to get it over with."

"What? That's blackmail," I hiss into the phone. "Aren't you supposed to serve and protect?"

"I mean, I can send Jerry over there, but he'll tell you the same thing." The line goes dead and I stare at it incredulously. What the hell just happened? I hang up and furiously dial 9-1-1, my fingers bludgeoning the poor buttons on the phone.

"9-1-1, what's yo emorjuncy?" Cheryl says around another mouthful of donut.

"Oh, for Pete's sake," I grumble. Just my luck, Cheryl works both phones for the police department.

"Ms. Mayfield, if you tie up the emergency line with a problem I have already given a solution to, then I am going to have the Greyson Gap Police Department fine you."

"What?" I screech, trying to remember if I gave her my name. I don't believe I did. "Cheryl, I have someone trespa—" The line goes dead. A patron opens the door, sees Linseed doing downward dog, and immediately backpedals out. "Agh, that's it!" I yell, completely losing my shit. I dig in my purse, grab fifty dollars and throw the bills at Linseed, who smiles smugly. "Get out!"

I point toward the door. She grabs her tackle box and scoots out the door. "Let me know if you want to carry oils in the shop!"

"Never!" I shout back. The balls on this woman.

Deflating against the counter, I spy a couple vials of *Linseed's Sexy Kitten Oil* set and *Linseed's Inner chi* next to the candles. I know without a doubt she'll come back to collect money for these. Opening the sexy kitten bottle, I sniff the oil and gag. No one is getting their sexy on with oil that smells like bad aftershave mixed with skunk. I get a paper gift bag and put the oils in it. I'll find out where she lives and drop them off. I can't believe I had to pay fifty fucking dollars to have her say some quack about cranberries and wind while she waved around a stinky stick and the police department didn't even care. It could have been a cigar for all I know.

The bell rings and a gentleman with light-brown hair, pressed khakis, and loafers comes in holding a box. "Hi, I'm Greg with Cottage Home Candles. Are you Blakely? Sorry I'm late, I had to stop for gas. My darn teenager took the car out last night and, wouldn't you know it, left it on empty."

He shakes his head, placing the box on the counter, giving me a '*kids, what are you going to do*' grin.

"So tell me, Blakely, what's your favorite candle scent?" His smile is friendly and I want to wrap him in a big hug for being so normal, but I don't want to make the situation awkward.

"Tell me, Greg, what's your opinion on saging?"

Goal: Not to let any more chaos enter my work sanctuary.

Problem: What the hell is in the water in Greyson Gap? There are some strange people in this town. It's going to happen again, I know it. Everything comes in threes, right? Cranberries and wind will inevitably make me unhinge...now I'm chanting like freaking Linseed.

Stress: Cheryl at the police station would rather eat donuts than protect the citizens of Greyson Gap. I will definitely be reporting her. Must find out where she got those donuts from...

What's the best thing that happened today: I got to pick out the most glorious jasmine and green tea candle.

What I am grateful for: Cottage Home Candles. It turns out they don't murder bunnies, beehives, or perform animal testing. Their products are vegan and all natural. I wonder if Greg knows Linseed is bad-mouthing his company...

Chapter 29

Lay It on the Line

Blakely

IT'S BEEN TEN days. Ten torturous days of hot kisses and stolen glances. I'm addicted to him and I haven't even gotten a real taste. Damn, can the man dish it out. I've never had an orgasm make me feel higher or glow brighter than the fireworks in the sky that night. I've been waiting on pins and needles for Tucker to make his move, but he always stops himself before it goes too far. I even had my hair fixed in Asheville, hoping it would spur him into action, but he just smiled, gave me a quick kiss and said it looked great. Something has to give because I'm wound tighter than a Yo-Yo that's about to unravel and crash to the floor.

Doubt claws its sharp nails, digging me into an old familiar hole. Charles always said how unimaginative I was in bed. Maybe it's true. Maybe Tucker doesn't want me like he initially said, because something turned him off. Perhaps he realized what a headcase I am and why it would be a bad idea to get involved with me. He's only teasing me with kisses to appease me.

I talked to Junie a few days ago, but I never got around

to telling her about Tucker. Okay, I was a total chicken shit and quickly changed the subject when she asked how he was as a roommate. Now I'm kicking myself because I need her advice. How would I even start off the conversation? Oh hey Junie, thanks for letting me stay at your house for free while I sort through my shit. By the way, do you think having sex with your cousin would help my healing process? I could call Dr. Cooper, but she would ask what I'm feeling. *Sexually frustrated, Dr. Cooper! That's what I'm feeling!*

I can't talk to Whitney because who wants to talk about their brother's sex life? And Annie? Well, she's a big-old hell no, and then there's Bhodi the Barracuda who compared casual sex to leftover pizza. If I had the *cojones* Tanya had, I'd smash Tucker to my bosom and suffocate him until he surrendered.

Sighing, I spray down the front door with window cleaner, wiping the sticky fingerprints off the glass, and flip the sign to open. I guess there's only one person left.

"Etta, what do you think of casual relationships?"

"How casual? Wham-bam-thank-you-ma'am casual? Are you having relations with your new neighbor, Bhodi Mills?"

"What? No! Eew, why would you think that? Unless…" I gasp, my back going ramrod straight. "Oh my god, is that the gossip going around town?"

"Oh no, I was making my own deductions." She takes a pencil and writes while she mumbles, "Racquel owes me twenty dollars."

This was a bad idea. I must be really miserable, definitely desperate. Defeated, I walk over to where she's working at the computer, and grab her canister of pens to color code.

"See a friend of mine called the other day needing help because she has suddenly found herself in a precarious situation. She wants to sleep with her roommate, but he wants to keep things casual and—"

"Is the roommate good-looking?"

"Uh, yes, but that's not the point."

"Well then, get to the point. I'm not getting any younger here."

I flutter my hands, knocking the cup of pens over. Etta eyes me over her readers, her lips pressed in a firm line.

I quickly pick the cup up and shove the pens back in. "Uh, okay, so this friend of mine is now feeling scared. What if she starts a casual fling and then decides she wants more?"

"Well, your friend is a dumbass. She should never start a casual fling if the stakes are too high for her."

"Jeez Etta, you don't mince words, do you?" I grumble. "I mean, she doesn't think she'll want more, but what if she does? It's a pretty risky decision. What happens if she sleeps with him and then can't handle it?"

"She's worried she's going to develop feelings for this roommate? Who's to say she hasn't already?"

"She hasn't. I mean, that would be silly. She hasn't known him for very long. She doesn't even like him."

"Well, what ying-yang would sleep with someone she doesn't even like?"

"Maybe she does like him…" I chew my bottom lip. "She's confused."

"Well, why doesn't the idiot just tell him?"

"Because, Etta, he told her to keep it simple! He was upfront and honest with her. But it's been almost two weeks...two weeks! And nothing. He hasn't tried anything and now she's wondering if he's lost interest. Now, if she tells him she might have feelings for him, it will blow up in her face and she'll have to move out."

"Ah-hah. Will the sex be good?" Etta takes a pencil from behind her ear and casually writes a note in her calendar as if we were talking about the weather.

"So unbelievably good." I blush, realizing my blunder.

Etta clucks her tongue, peering at me over her purple and blue readers. "Unrequited love is for nilly-willies. Don't be a roadside weed, Blakely. Be a centerpiece statement-making flower!"

My mouth slightly agape, I stare at her. "I'm not sure what you're talking about... You think she should tell him?"

She huffs, getting out her label maker. "Do you have wax in your ears? An ancient Native American proverb says, 'Certain things catch your eye, but pursue only those that capture the heart'."

"That's beautiful, but I'm not sure how it pertains..."

Etta stops tagging the stationery boxes and looks at me like she wants to throttle me. "Racquel was right about you," she mutters. "No gumption. Certainly, won't be receiving a rose at this point."

"I think we're getting off topic, Etta."

"For Pete's sake, Blakely, get your head in the game! Now I know you're a tad uptight and a bit of a traditionalist, but let's get into the twenty-first century here and have sex with the man!"

"Oh, this isn't about me," I say quickly, my cheeks feeling like they are on fire. She gives me a withering stare rivaling the Queen of England when Prince Harry said he was going to Megxit. "Oh, jeez…okay, it is about me." I nervously bite my lip. "But what if he says no?"

"Tucker Greyson is a gentleman with a capital G. He will not say no."

"Okay, and then what?"

"And then you lay it on the line. Trees start with seeds, Blakely." She gives me one last pointed look right before the bell rings, announcing a customer.

Lay it on the line. The thought makes me want to clean…vigorously.

Goal: Lay it on the line with Tucker Greyson. Trees start with seeds. Be a statement flower, not a roadside weed.

Problem: I'm scared I won't be able to handle casual sex.

Stress: Not having sex with him is slowly killing me, and I look and feel like a roadside weed.

What's the best thing that happened today: I had the most amazing chocolate donut from Greyson Gap Bakery, AKA donut haven. Thank you, Etta, for the treat.

What I am grateful for: Stacy Reeger hasn't stabbed me with a shiv yet.

Chapter 30

The Declaration

Tucker

SURPRISE CATCHES IN my throat as I stroke my tongue against hers, matching her frenzied pace. She practically jumped me when I walked through the door seconds ago. Although I wasn't prepared for the zealous kiss, I'm not going to deny I like it. I like it a lot.

Catching glimpses of Blakely when she lets her guard down is a high all unto itself. I'll admit, I shouldn't have pushed her on the night of the Fourth, but seeing her come apart in my hands was worth the risk. She's slowly drawing out of her uptight shell and I'm patiently waiting, killing myself in the process.

I've discovered blue balls are real and quite painful and cold showers chafe your skin. There's no denying how badly I want to take things to the next level, but I'm waiting for her to take the initiative. If she can't do casual, then we can't get involved. If she were staying, it would be different... No, I can't let my mind go there because she's not staying.

I ease back from her and hold her face in my hands. I run my finger from her temple to her lips, smoothing out the frown between her brows. "What's going on?"

"What do you mean?"

"I barely got in the door tonight before you mauled me... I'm not complaining," I quickly amend as her eyes narrow.

"I didn't *maul* you." She tries to push away from me, but I quickly gather her into my arms. I might as well be holding an ironing board, she's so stiff. Her cheeks bloom a rosy pink before she turns her head away. "Have you ever thought maybe I was trying to seduce you? I must suck at that, too."

"Blakely, relax. I liked it." I chuckle, rubbing her arms. "I'm sorry, maul was a poor choice of words. I was just curious. Tell me what's got your brain running a million miles an hour right now."

She gives me a flat stare. "My mind is blank at the moment."

"I can see it in your eyes, Blakely May. You are itching to vacuum something, color-coordinate the fridge, or starch my t-shirts."

"Fine," she huffs, averting her gaze. "What's going on between us? I mean, what am I to you? No, don't answer." She smashes her finger against my lips. "What are we doing right now?"

I arch an eyebrow. "We're kissing?" I manage to say with smushed lips.

"Exactly." She takes a deep breath, removing her fingers. "It's great. It really is, but I want more. No, I *need* more."

I crack a smile and lean in to kiss her again, but she puts her palm on my face. "Wait, I'm not done."

I laugh. "Okay..."

"Be a statement flower, Blakely," she whispers to herself and stands taller, clearing her throat. "I like you... I think you like me? Oh god." She covers her face with her hands.

I lower her hands. "I like you, Blakely May. A lot."

"Okay, that's good...a relief, really. Don't worry, I'm not going all super stalker on you and slash your tires like Stacy..." She laughs lightly and it sounds a tinge unhinged. "You know what? Forget I brought it up. This is getting weird."

I'm perplexed by this conversation because I'm not sure what she wants me to say. I feel like I'm walking through a minefield to get to the answer. One wrong step and I'm blown to smithereens. "Blakely, what's going on? Tell me what you want."

"I want sex!" she says with exasperation. "I *need* sex, Tucker. With you." She exhales, her shoulders sagging. "There I finally said it. Shit, I can't believe I just shouted that." She rubs a hand across her forehead, her gaze focusing on something over my shoulder. "Look, I may not be the best lover in your history of sexual partners, and I'm sure there's a lot I need to learn. My confidence is totally shot because Charles made me feel inadequate. Gah, I need to stop talking about him and how lame I am in bed. Who wants to hear, *hey I'm terrible at sex, so it will suck for you, too.*" Her eyes widen. "Someone please tape my mouth shut."

She tries to back away, but I hold her caged in my arms, keeping her from completely falling apart. "Blakely..."

"Well, there's some baggage for you to unpack." She laughs lightly, her eyes darting nervously around the room. "The truth is, Tucker, I want sex...with you. Wild and crazy, dogs-howling, earth-shattering sex." She bites her bottom lip nervously. "I'm not sure I can swing being casual, but I'm going to try because it's what you want. I may have fee…" Her gaze slams into mine but quickly shifts. "I may have favors to ask of you down the road, but I promise you I will be the best damn casual sex of your life if you'll let me. And I know I sound totally unhinged at the moment, but I promise I'm not. I'm really nervous and you know, there's YOLO so…"

Her eyes suddenly shift to mine, her gaze imploring me to say or do something. This is the moment. I can either shut this down right now and we can go back to what we were. She'll leave and my heart will still be intact. Or I can take the proverbial hand she's holding out to me and leap with her. Fuck my heart.

Grinning, I pick her up and carry her to my bedroom. "I thought you'd never ask, Smiles."

I gently put her down and pull her sundress over her head, running my hands down her silky-smooth arms. She shivers when I dip to kiss her, my tongue sliding sweetly over hers. She unbuttons my shirt and slips it over my shoulders until it drops to the ground. Her fingertips glide down my chest, slowly tracing over hard muscle quivering under her touch. I unclasp her bra and let it drop to the ground, cupping her soft breasts in my hands. I'm aching to suck on her rosy peaks as they tighten with the graze of my thumb. She sucks in a breath, arching in to me. I love how responsive she is to my touch.

She gasps as I bend and capture her nipple in my mouth, sucking on her pert bud. She runs a hand down my chest to the top of my jeans and flicks the button open, lowering the zipper until I feel her warm hands clasp around me, gently pulling. I groan and thrust into her hands, her thumb gliding over the tip.

"Lay down," I say gruffly, shucking my pants. She quickly shimmies out of her panties and I can't help but skim my fingers over her valleys and curves, dipping into her wet heat. She arches off the bed, whimpering while I lavish her breasts with my tongue, slowly dragging kisses down, spreading her legs. "So wet for me," I growl, dipping my head and slowly running my tongue along her slit.

She yanks my hair, pulling me to her. "Yes, Tucker, more."

I insert a finger and feast on her sweetness, slowly dragging my tongue and finger back and forth until she's writhing underneath me, screaming my name. "Oh god yes, Tucker, I'm coming," she moans, bucking underneath me before her limbs grow heavy.

I sheath my throbbing cock with a condom I grab out of my side drawer. "Are you sure about this, Blakely May?"

She smiles lazily up at me. "Yes, I want this."

Thank God. I flip her over onto her stomach and pull her ass into the air. I squeeze her ass cheek and then smack it lightly, causing her to jump. She huffs out a laugh, her eyes narrowing as she looks over her shoulder at me.

"What was that for?"

"I've been wanting to spank that ass since the day you stormed off and hit my tractor." I smirk, positioning myself behind her, and slowly slide into her wet heat, letting her adjust to my thick length. Damn, she feels so good. I slowly drag out, trying to control the overwhelming sensations which make me want to plunder her.

"Please, Tuck. Go faster," she mewls beneath me.

I buck into her and it feels amazing, like sliding into home plate after stealing third base. She's so fucking wet and warm for me. I grab her hips and start a steady rhythm.

"Harder, Tucker," she moans, and it takes all my control not to come. I slam into her again, groaning when I bottom out.

"Jesus, you're so fucking tight," I grit out.

She cries out while I pump in and out of her. I reach around and draw fast, tight circles over her clit, causing her to unravel. Her moans have me going wild, sweat trickling down my back as I pound into her sweet pussy. It's all I can do to hold it together when she cries out she's coming. She shudders, her walls tightening around me like a vise. I hold her before her muscles go lax and ease her down.

"Turn over for me, Blakely. I want to see your brown-sugar eyes when I make you come again."

She slips over and I ease myself back in slowly, wanting this to last longer, but I can't. I bend her knee and pump in and out of her. Her tits bounce with every thrust and my balls tighten. I circle her clit with my fingers and she cries out, convulsing again around me. It's all I can do to hang on. Her swollen lips part while her glazed eyes watch me. I'm mesmerized by the way I slide perfectly into her.

"You're so fucking beautiful, Blakely. I'm going to come," I groan, jerking into her over and over, never having come this hard before. "So fucking beautiful." I kiss her breasts and gently ease her leg down, kissing her calf.

"Wow, that was…" she pants. "I've never had an orgasm rip through me with so much intensity before."

"So good."

"Better than good," she agrees. "Can we do it again? I mean, not right this second, but maybe in fifteen minutes? Will that give you enough time, you think?"

I huff out a laugh, trying to calm my racing heart. "Give me a couple of minutes." I get up to throw the condom away and crawl back into bed gathering her into my arms. She feels so fucking good, her soft lips placing kisses along my chest. Warm satin skin, soft thighs… I could get used to this. It's been a while since I've wanted to hold and cuddle with a woman after sex. *Don't get attached.*

She nips my chin and climbs on top of me. I run my hands over her thighs. I'm already hard for her again, a record time for me. "Okay, Blakely, you win."

She grins down at me. "You should know by now I'm a perfectionist. I think I did well the first go-around, but I know I can do better."

"Jesus, woman, you climaxed three times."

"Mmm, practice makes perfect," she says, kissing down my chest.

I suck in my breath and close my eyes while she shows me how much better she can do.

Goal: Not to have sex with Tucker Greyson again.

One and done. I got it out of my system and that's that. Go back to being flirty roommates.

Problem: The sex is amazing. I don't think we can go back to what we were.

Stress: Continuing the amazing sex and not falling for him.

What's the best thing that happened today: When Tucker did the thing with his tongue... I'm blushing just thinking about it.

What I am grateful for: I'm grateful for hot sex with Tucker Greyson. Jesus, whoever would have thought I'd write that! Dr. Cooper will have an aneurism when she reads this.

Chapter 31

Creepy Carl

Blakely

I LET HERSHEL out the back door and open a letter addressed to me on the counter. A single white piece of paper falls out. Unfolding it, I huff out an incredulous laugh. The town of Greyson Gap is fining me a hundred and fifty dollars for false reporting on an emergency line. You have got to be fucking kidding me! My blood pressure goes through the roof. I'm not paying a fine because I tried to have Linseed removed. If anything, someone should pay *me* for emotional trauma.

I don't know who Cheryl thinks she is, but this is war. I'm so angry I can't even think straight. I turn the vacuum on and vigorously push over the carpet in a diagonal pattern.

Okay, calm down, Blakely. If anyone can fix this mess, Etta can, or maybe Tucker, since he's running for Mayor. Although I would die if my Linseed drama became a stain on his election campaign. Damn Linseed and her frisky kitty oils! I'm still pissed she tricked me. Ugh, I can't think about Linseed right now.

What would Dr. Cooper do in this situation? She'd ask

me why I'm so angry. *Because it's not fair, Dr. Cooper!* Etta
would tell me to flow like water and let it go. I channel my
inner yogi and breathe in and out while pushing the vacuum
back and forth. But instead of an even-keeled lungful of air,
my breathing comes out choppy and wheezy, like a smoker
doing pushups.

Redirect, Blakely. Think about something else, anything
besides a bogus charge and hippy Linseed. I put the vacuum
away and dig through the bags of groceries I dropped on the
counter. Tucker will be home soon, and I have a new fish
recipe from Ina Garten I'd like to try tonight. The ladies
were raving about it the other day during Laura Twinkle's
book club happy hour.

My curiosity is still piqued about going to the ranch, and
I'm hoping I can bring it up tonight over dinner. Truthfully,
I've been wanting Tucker to ask me. Not to announce to
Greyson Gap we're a couple, but to get to know him better.
It's a part of his life I haven't seen yet. A part of him I don't
know. Inviting myself seems pushy and desperate, but maybe
I can ask him a few questions which will lead to a date up
there…just as friends, of course. Easy-peasy lemon-squeezie,
right?

Yeah right, there's nothing easy-lemony about any of
this, especially after I made such a fool out of myself the last
time we had a heart to heart. The real question is, *why* do I
want to feel closer to him? Why do I even care? Friends who
have casual sex *don't* get emotionally attached. Cold pizza,
Blakely, that's all you are to him. I wash my hands and get
out the chopping board and a knife, my thoughts going back
to Tucker.

Hands-down, the sex has been amazing. We can both agree on that. The root of the issue stems from what Stacy Reeger said when she loftily put it out there, that if I'm really in Tucker's life, I'd be invited to the ranch. I know I should blow off her comment like a dandelion seed in the wind, but it's burrowed itself under my skin, slowly festering.

Even though this town is Cocoa Krispies crazy, I'm finding myself drawn to staying here more and more each day. No, I'm not the successful entrepreneur I always pictured myself to be, living in a glitzy metropolitan city, but maybe it's because Greyson Gap has changed me. Maybe *I've* changed me, and I no longer want my old life back. Would it be so bad to start over here? I can see myself making a life here, working with Etta, maybe opening a flower shop. Having coffee with Laura Twinkle and getting my nails done with Whitney. Coming home each night to Tucker.

I hold my breath, nervous to entertain those thoughts any further in my head. Concentrating on the task at hand, I slice the onion into precise quarters. A loud banging noise causes me to jump, the knife clattering to the floor. The pounding starts again, and I realize it's coming from the front door. I open the door a crack.

"Yes? Can I help you…" The words die a quick death on my lips. Creepy Carl stands there with his fists on his hips, wearing a shirt so starched it looks like it could stand up on its own, tucked into stiff pleated pants and shiny black shoes. "Oh, hello, officer…uh, Carl. Would you like to come in?" *Please say no.*

"Your dog defecated in my yard," he seethes, his fists clenched tight. His dark gelled hair doesn't move a millimeter out of place.

"Oh-uh, not my dog per se..."

Creepy Carl isn't creepy. He's downright scary as hell. "You live in this house. The dog *came* from this house. So, that makes him *your* dog."

"Well, hmm...are you sure it wasn't someone else's dog? I mean, I literally just let Hersh—"

"I know it was *your* dog, Miz Mayfield," *Gah, he knows my name?* "I have pictures."

"You took pictures of my dog pooping? Er...can I see them?" I'm wondering if he's going to fling grainy Polaroids in my face, because a psycho killer like Carl would have a Polaroid camera, but he doesn't move a muscle. His left eye twitches and his nostrils flare.

"Miz Mayfield—"

"Look, I don't really like dogs. I mean, I like dogs, don't get me wrong. I'm not a dog hater. They are cuddly and cute, but the drool is a bit much and the hair, don't even get me started on the hair. Sometimes, okay, well, most of the time, they really smell. I honestly think I'm more of a fish per—"

"Miz Mayfield!" He effectively shuts me up while he shoves his cellphone in front of my face, causing me to pee a little in my pants. There's no doubt it's Hershel hunched over on his front lawn.

"Oh, okay hmm...well, it *looks* like it's Tucker Greyson's dog, but one can never be sure with Photoshop. Are you a Photoshop wizard? I, for one, am not..."

His blotchy purple complexion doesn't look healthy.

I clear my throat. "What would you like me to do, Creearl?"

Creepy Carl looks at me with absolute loathing. Jeez, if anyone could use some inner chi, it's this guy. Maybe some fun-time sexy kitten oil thrown in there, too.

Questions tumble through my brain at lightning speed. If I don't comply with his wishes, can he arrest me for Tucker's dog doing what dogs do when nature calls? Am I liable for feces smeared on his lawn? Will he lure me over to his house, kill me, and bury me in his backyard? Why is Hershel so hellbent on crapping in this guy's yard?

He waggles the phone in my face. "I want you to go pick up the dog poop, Miz Mayfield. That's what I expect you to do, and make sure it doesn't happen again." Spittle lands on my shirt and I cringe, thinking of all the germs parachuting down on me. I curse Tucker under my breath.

"Of course, no problem. I'm so sorry he pooped in your yard. Let me grab a bag."

"I will wait here and escort you to the evidence left at the crime scene."

This guy has been watching a little too much *CSI*. Carl's disdainful glare moves my feet into action. "Right, I'll be right back." Grabbing my rubber gloves and three plastic grocery bags, I text Whitney I have to go down to Carl's house in case he decides to bury me next to the poop. I pull on my wellies and begrudgingly follow Officer Carl a few doors down to his house.

Bhodi's front screen door is open as we pass by, but he's not hosing off his gear or flexing his muscles, annoying the shit out of me, like every other time I'm outside. Go figure, when I need him most, he's nowhere to be found.

We walk in silence past a few houses, and it's awkward as hell. I feel like I'm being marched right into my untimely death in front of a firing squad. I chance a peek at Carl's profile. His brows are furrowed in thought as he looks down at his shiny polished shoes.

Maybe everyone has Carl wrong. Perhaps he's just shy and a bit intimidating. What Carl really needs is friends to let loose with. Ooh, I could throw a neighborhood block party and introduce everyone. Carl would be the life of the party doing cannonballs into Barracuda's hot tub.

He'd no longer be creepy. He'd be Crazy Carl. He'd be so grateful he belongs to a community of friends in the neighborhood, he'd be less uptight. Less likely to care if Hershel likes to take his morning coffee out on his lawn. If anyone knows how to throw a killer party, it's me. *Carl, prepare to be dazzled!*

I rub my hands together, excited about this new project. "So, Carl, how long have you lived in Greyson Gap?"

"It's Officer Sheldon."

Okay, so it may take some time to unwind this tight ball of yarn. "Officer Sheldon—"

"We're here."

He grabs a bucket and shovel left on his porch and strides back over to me. Is he going to make me dig my own grave? *Jesus, pull it together, Blakely. He's not really a serial killer...that you know of.* He points down at the pristine grass, but I don't see anything.

"Uh, okay...this is it?" I squat down to find the offense in question. A magnifying glass would be helpful. I'm about to take a plastic bag and pretend to pick up air when I finally spy it on his perfectly manicured lawn. It's the size of a quarter.

Now look, I am a woman who likes things neat and tidy, and I wouldn't want someone's dog leaving dookies in my yard either, but the fact he marched down to the house for me to pick up something a squirrel could have produced is a little ridiculous. Squatting down, I put a bag over my gloves and pick it up. Movement to my left startles me. Carl's down on his knees beside me, tilting his head to make sure I got it all.

"Do you need to take samples to send off to the crime lab?" I ask sweetly. "I can take a picture if you'd like…" *It will last longer.*

His nostrils flare while he stares at me like he's debating whether to shove my nose in the spot. Don't push him, Blakely. They call him Creepy Carl for a reason.

He stands back up, and I follow suit. "Unnecessary," he says curtly. "Make sure your dog is on a leash at all times. I have cameras, so I *will* know if he does this again, Miz Mayfield. And I will take legal action."

He quickly strides up his driveway, leaving me holding a bag of squirrel poop with my mouth hanging open. Guess there aren't going to be any hot-tub parties for Crazy Creepy Carl.

Goal: *Not to have another run-in with Creepy Carl.*

Problem: *Hershel likes to take dumps in his yard.*

Stress: *Being arrested for not picking up after Hershel. Especially when he's not my dog.*

What's the best thing that happened today: *Ugh... not much.*

What I am grateful for: *I'm grateful I won't have to plan a hot-tub party for Carl after all...*

Chapter 32

Popping the Question

Tucker

"TUCKER, WAIT UP!" Whitney waves to me in the parking lot.

"What are you doing here?" I hold onto the door of my truck.

"I was on my way to the pub and was hoping to catch you before you left. I called your office, but the new girl said you left already."

I groan. "Whit, I can't help you tonight. Blakely has something planned."

She shakes her head. "No, no, Brian is working out okay. I wanted to see if you were going up to the ranch on Sunday for dinner."

"You tracked me down to ask if I'm coming to dinner on Sunday?"

She pushes her hair over her shoulder. "Um, well, that and to see if you were going to bring Blakely with you. I think you should. I know you don't like to bring anyone up there because it's your *sacred* place, but I think Mom and GT should meet her."

"Why?" I lean against my car, folding my arms over my chest. "You know Mom. It will give her hope. She'll get ideas in her head and start planning weddings and knitting things for her future grandkids."

"Would that be so bad? Giving her hope, I mean?"

Irritation races down my spine. "Yes, that would be bad, Whit. In case you've forgotten, Blakely isn't sticking around. She has a life back in Atlanta that she will return to soon. She's *leaving*. Am I the only one who remembers that?"

Whitney cocks her hip and arches an eyebrow. "You know, Tucker, for being so smart, sometimes you are so stupid. Stop being a stubborn son of a bitch and invite her to the ranch."

"You don't get it." I shake my head.

"Yeah, you're right. Stupid me for seeing how happy this woman makes my brother. How his eyes light up when she walks in a room. I'm the idiot for wanting him to be happy."

She turns and stomps back to her car. If only she knew I was hanging on by a thread.

"Whitney...come on," I call after her, but she ignores me as she gets in her car and peels out of the parking lot.

THE MUDROOM IS filled with packages when I get home from work. I wait for Hershel to greet me, but he never comes. Probably can't get past the boxes.

"Hey, where's Hersh?"

"What am I, a big fat zero?" Blakely pouts over her shoulder.

"Sorry, how was your day, beautiful? What's up with all the boxes?" I come up behind her and wrap my hands around her waist, leaning in to kiss her neck and breathe in her signature scent. I could definitely get used to coming home to her every day.

"Surprise! I hope you don't mind. I had flyers and buttons made too." She turns around and I can't help but laugh. She's wearing a gray Tucker Greyson for Mayor t-shirt with my smiling face printed across her chest. It reads, *If he can't do it, no one can.*

"I kind of like my face on your chest."

"Perv." She giggles, swatting me with her dish towel. "I was thinking we could pass them out at the Pub."

"Thank you, Blakely May. That was really sweet of you to have these made." I pull her into a hug and kiss her lips. "What's all this?" Mouthwatering smells waft through the kitchen.

"I thought I'd make you dinner. Kind of like a date. We haven't had one yet."

I scoff. "We've been on lots of dates." She arches an eyebrow. "We went camping, we've watched Marie Kondo, and had several movie nights. We've—"

"Yeah, you can stop right there. Camping was *not* a date. Watching TV and movies is something roommates do. Face it, you've become complacent and we're not even really dating...anyway, come see Hershel's new pen."

"His new pen?"

"Yes, I got it for him and he loves it. Oh, and I got this

fabulous contraption called the Scooper 2000. It picks up poop and you don't even have to touch it! I never thought I'd ever get so giddy over a pooper scooper."

"Why does Hershel have a pen?" I grab a beer out of the fridge and uncap it.

"Well, when Creepy Carl, which is the perfect name for him by the way, threatened to arrest me if your dog poops in his yard again, I decided a pen was necessary."

I rub a hand down my face, leaning against the counter. "Oh no, I'm so sorry. I don't know what his obsession is with Carl's grass."

"Hershel thinks Carl's lawn is the softest greenest grass he's ever walked on. It makes perfect sense to me. Exactly like Betty Doliver wanting to use the shop's bathroom because we have the softest toilet paper."

"Can we not talk about Betty Doliver and her bathroom preferences? I've had a horrible day as it is." I grimace before taking a drink. Turning, I look out the deck window to check on Hershel. "Uh, Blakely? Is this your pen?"

She joins me at the door and gasps. Hershel greets us at the back door, dragging a mangled metal pen attached to his collar. His tail wags a mile a minute like he didn't just have a battle to the death with a dog pen.

"Oh my god, it's made of metal. The guy at the store told me it was indestructible. How on earth did he destroy it?"

"He could have been strangled," I say irritably, opening the door. "You can't lock him up."

"I'm sorry, but I didn't know what else to do. Maybe you should go pick up his dookie next time!"

"Dookie isn't even a word."

She glares at me while I release his collar, freeing poor Hershel from the pen. "Look, Carl threatened me. If you don't like my means of keeping *your* dog at the house, then get a fence, or better yet, move him back to the ranch!"

"Where I go, Hershel goes," I say through gritted teeth.

"Splendid! You can go with him!" She storms back into the kitchen.

I follow her, itching to start a fight as my head battles with my heart. My conversation with Whitney earlier still raw and biting.

"And when do you plan on leaving, huh, Blakely? Why do you want a date night when our time together has an expiration? We're halfway through August, and you're still working at Etta's, making friends, no talk of returning to Atlanta—"

"Do you have a problem with that?" She whirls and pins me to the spot.

"What I have a problem with is you inserting yourself into our lives only to get up and walk away in a few weeks."

"*You're* the one who told me to insert myself! You're the one who told me to make friends and put myself out there. Now you're pissed because I did? Make up your fucking mind!"

I drag both my hands down my face, feeling miserable and defeated. She's right. I told her to make friends. I'm purposefully being a dick and picking a fight with her because I'm feeling things which could rip my heart to shreds when she leaves.

The truth is, I don't want her to leave. Coming home to

her each night has made me realize I want more from her than just a romp in my sheets. I want to take her out on actual dates—wine and dine her, and snuggle up next to her every night. Take her camping again and sleep under the stars. I want her to be mine.

I laugh to myself, incredulous over the situation. I'm the one who kept chanting over and over to keep it simple. But now my heart has complicated the hell out of things and the thought of her leaving sits in my gut like an empty wasteland.

Deflated, I set my beer down and walk over to where she's furiously scrubbing a pan. "You're right, I did. I'm sorry. You're only here for a few more weeks. I don't want to spend it fighting with you." I nuzzle her neck, hugging her from behind.

"I'm sorry too. I should have called and asked you what I should do with Hershel. I would have never forgiven myself if he hurt himself with the pen."

I kiss the top of her head. "What are you making?"

"Chilean sea bass with glazed sweet potatoes and sauteed broccolini."

"I'm allergic to fish." I smile ruefully as she turns in my arms.

"Ha, ha, ha. Nice try. Don't worry, I've followed the recipe to a T."

"No really, I am."

"But…you took me fishing! You said lake fish was some of the best around." She gasps, "You made me *touch* a fish!"

My smile hitches. "All true. At least, that's what Jason tells me. He owns the best seafood and steak restaurant in town."

"Wait, I thought he owned a construction business with you."

"He does. We dabble in a bit of everything."

She rolls her eyes. "Is everything in this town owned by the Greysons?"

"Not everything." I smile.

"Are you seriously allergic?"

I nod apologetically. "But I can eat the potatoes and broccoli."

"Ugh, I'm such a failure! I'm never going to learn your likes and dislikes, your allergies, what your favorite color is…"

I stare at her, perplexed. "What does it matter? It's not like we're a couple, Blakely." The knife digs a little deeper, twisting.

"Right, because I'm leaving," she says sullenly, taking the fish out of the oven.

I gather her into my arms, because I'm a glutton for punishment. "Thank you for trying." I kiss her lips. "Blue."

"Blue?"

"Is my favorite color."

She gives me a lopsided smile. "Mine is white."

"That's not even a color." I laugh. "It's the color of…clean."

"White is order and balance." She shrugs a shoulder.

I chuckle, capturing her lips with mine. She wraps her arms around my neck and I pick her up and place her on the kitchen island, stepping between her legs. I slide my tongue over hers, tasting her over and over again. "Come up to the ranch with me this Sunday. I want you to meet my family."

Her eyes widen. "Really? It won't complicate things?"

"I want you there." I kiss her tenderly, knowing I just blew apart the wall I held around my heart. It's going to fucking complicate everything, but I don't care. I teeter on the edge of hope, knowing it's a dangerous place to be.

She breaks the kiss and smiles up at me, her eyes glazed and dreamy. I cup her breasts and run my thumbs over her hardened nipples. "Dinner will get cold," she moans as I lift her shirt and close my mouth over her sheer bra, teasing her nipple through the gauzy material.

"Then we'll microwave it, or order pizza. Honestly, I don't give a fuck about dinner right now," I say gruffly, unsnapping her bra. She sighs with pleasure when I graze my teeth over the sensitive skin, swirling her tight bud with my tongue.

"Oh god, yes." She arches into me, her fingers grabbing a hold of my t-shirt, tracing over my lower abdominal muscles. I yank my t-shirt over my head with one hand and she greedily zeros in on my chest.

"You're like Mr. April."

I chuckle, leaning down to nibble her jaw. "Who is Mr. April?" I kiss my way down her neck.

"He's the hot firefighter on my esthetician's wall calendar."

"Hmm, I was in a similar calendar for charity, except I was just holding a baseball glove," I mumble, sliding my hands up her thighs. She leans back on her elbows and throws me a saucy smile when I tug her panties down.

"I think I'm gonna need a copy. I should have put that

picture on the t-shirt. You would have been a shoo-in for Mayor. Oh my god," she gasps when I slip a finger into her. I groan in anticipation, hooking her satin-smooth legs over my shoulders. My tongue delves into her sweetness as she cries out my name. I love how responsive she is. Her legs shake, her orgasm drawing closer, but I don't want her to come yet. She tastes so damn good. I tease her with my tongue, soft strokes against her velvet heat, but she quickly grows impatient. Her fingers tug my hair, her soft little moans driving me wild while she rides her hot pussy against my tongue, taking no prisoners. I suck her clit, my finger driving in and out of her. The waves of her orgasm wash over her as she cries out she's coming. I feast on her until she's done. "Damn baby, you taste so fucking good."

I gather her in my arms and bring her over to the couch, where I lay her down and strip off my pants.

"That is so hot," she mumbles, her eyes raking over my body. I grab a condom and roll it on before I place a knee on the couch beside her.

"You're picturing me with just a baseball glove, aren't you?" My smug smile grows when she nods yes. Pulling her to me, I watch while I slowly sink into her hot wetness. I bend her knees and spread her legs wide open. Slowly pumping in and out of her, fascinated by the way her body takes me completely. I pinch and tease her nipples while she meets me thrust for thrust. But it's not a frenzied pace. I'm taking my time, enjoying every gasp, every moan, the slap of our skin as I make love to her.

"Oh my god, Tucker, yes! Oh, I'm coming again," she cries out, tightening around me. I growl and bend to kiss her bee-stung lips.

"You're so beautiful," I whisper. I turn her around and tell her to hug a pillow while I lift her ass in the air so I can take her from behind. I hold onto her hips as I start a steady rhythm, talking dirty to her, which makes her even more wet, if that's possible. She's so fucking beautiful with her hair splayed out against the couch. It slams into me as I come hard. I want more than just casual with Blakely.

I want it all.

Chapter 33

The Ranch

Blakely

WE DRIVE PAST the old barn, the spot I pulled over when I first met Tucker. The broken-down tractor is still in the same spot. I smile despite myself. We've come a long way since then.

"There it is, the place where you fell head over heels in lust with me."

I look over at his profile and scoff. "You wish."

"Don't think I didn't catch you staring at my ass that day."

"Can you blame me? It's a pretty fine ass," I begrudgingly admit. "But then you opened your mouth."

"And pure poetic prose came tumbling out." He grins.

I laugh. "Hardly. More like never-ending bullshit."

"You liked me."

"I hated you." I bite my lip, trying to hide my smile.

"My, how the tides have changed, Blakely May."

"Have they?" I ask, arching an eyebrow. "I still hate that name."

"I know." He chuckles as he pulls the truck through

gates with Greyson Gap Ranch arching overhead. We drive down a long, paved road lined with trees.

Tucker's truck pulls to a stop in front of a beautiful, sprawling two-story log cabin with enormous picture windows and a wraparound front porch. Bright green grass rolls downhill into a crystal-blue lake with pastures filled with cattle dotting the landscape. It's the most beautiful house I've seen in Greyson Gap. "Wow, this is breathtaking, Tucker."

"The Eluwei River, which runs by our house in town, starts in the mountains on our property. It means *the quiet river* in Cherokee."

Tucker hops out and opens my door for me, helping me down. Hershel bounds out, tongue lolling, without so much as a 'roll tide' command from Tucker.

"He's a ridiculous dog."

Tucker grins. "What? He's excited to be home."

"Well, why the heck wouldn't he get out of the truck at the other house?"

"Because I wasn't getting out of the truck."

I roll my eyes, turning toward the front steps as Tucker hefts the box of campaign t-shirts under one arm. "You two idiots belong together."

He playfully grabs my butt before turning me to him. My knees go weak when he nips my lips. "You better watch your smart mouth, Blakely May. You're about to meet my mama and she thinks I'm the smartest, handsomest man in Greyson Gap."

"Mama's boy, got it." I reach up and run my finger over the rough stubble on his cheek, his grass-green eyes dancing with mirth. "Maybe she dropped you on your head when you were a baby. She feels guilty, so she placates you with feel-good words like smart, handsome, and sensitive."

He laughs, tugging me up the front porch stairs. "Hey, I *am* smart and sensitive. Handsome is a given." He winks at me and I roll my eyes. He opens the solid front door. "Mom? GT?"

"Who's GT again?" I whisper.

"Grandpa Tucker. We call him GT for short."

I nod my head and paste on a bright smile when a vivacious blonde comes running out of the kitchen. "Oh my god, I've missed you! You've been gone so long!"

"I saw you last week." Tucker towers over his mom. He drops the box right before she wraps him in a bear hug. Patting his chest, she turns toward me with a wide smile. "Mama, this is my friend Blakely."

"Oh, Blakely! Aren't you as beautiful as my homemade apple pie. It's so nice to meet you. I'm Linda." She squeezes me into a hug. She smells like fresh cotton and apples. "Come in, come in, you two. What did you bring me? Your sister should be here soon. Aunt Janice is wandering around here somewhere. Hasn't helped me a lick with dinner, but that's nothing new. Did Tucker warn you about GT?" She grabs my hand and pulls me through the house.

"Uh..."

She sighs and shoots an exasperated look over her shoulder, her suddenly quiet son trailing behind us. "Tucker James Greyson, were you going to throw poor Blakely to the wolves?"

"She can handle herself just fine, Mom." Tucker winks at

me.

"Well, he's in a *mood* tonight. Uncle Beau is coming to dinner with Patricia and Jason. Patricia is my late husband's cousin, Blakely, and Jason and Junie's mom."

"Wow, sounds like the whole family will be here." I wring my hands while Tucker's mom guides me into the kitchen.

"Almost everyone. We're missing our June Bug, of course. I heard that's how you met Tucker, through Junie?"

"Uh, yes, informally."

"We haven't seen her since Christmas. Down there in the big city, making her way. We're so proud of her, but we wish she'd come home more." Tucker has his mom's pretty green eyes, but that's where the similarities stop. Whitney favors her mom more with their naturally blonde hair and pert little nose. "Blakely, do you like to cook?"

"Um, sure, if there's a recipe I can follow."

"Ha, I like this one, Tucker." She squeezes me before she dons an apron and pulls on an oven mitt. Another petite blonde who resembles Linda walks into the kitchen and stops in her tracks when she sees us.

"Oh, my stars! Is that Tucker Greyson? Bless it. It's been so long I've forgotten what you look like, sugar. Come over here and give your long-lost auntie a hug. Have you grown an inch? I thought I'd never see you again."

"Aunt Janice, I saw you last week. Funny how you and Mom suddenly have amnesia." Tucker rolls his eyes before he wraps his arms around his aunt and gives her a quick squeeze. Linda smirks, fiddling with the charcuterie board.

"Feels like forever now that you're living in town. I never

know when you'll grace us with your presence, your excellency," she says dramatically, curtsying. She turns to me and smiles. "Hi, I'm Tucker's favorite, Aunt Janice. You must be Blakely? I hope you're the reason he hasn't been up to the ranch in years." She winks at me, and I can't help but like her.

"Hi, it's nice to meet you too." I shake her outstretched hand.

"Blakely, I'm going to be honest. I'm glad you're the reason Tucker has suddenly abandoned his family. Whitney told me y'all are holed up in a little cabin on the water like sex-crazed rabbits in their—"

"Wow! How much wine have you had tonight, Aunt Janice?" Tucker rubs a hand down his face as heat floods my cheeks.

She laughs. "Just a smidge. Anyhoo, I'm so happy to meet you. Lord knows Annie was trying her hardest to win back our boy, but she was an honest-to-god dingaling, if you ask me. I mean, who lies about—"

"No one asked, Aunt Janice," Tucker growls between clenched teeth. She throws me a wink.

"Isn't she adorable, Janice?" Linda smiles affectionately at me. "Maybe we should have her up to the ranch every week, so Tucker will visit more."

Tucker snorts, folding his arms over his broad chest. "Okay, message delivered, you two. Whitney hasn't come up to the ranch in a month. You don't harass *her* like this." He pops a piece of cheese from the charcuterie board into his mouth and his mom slaps his hand.

"That's because we love you more than Whitney." Janice

smiles sweetly, topping off her wine.

Tucker sneaks an olive off the tray and laughs. "Yeah, that's why you're always slipping money into her purse."

Linda glares at her sister. "Oh, for heaven's sake, Janice, Whitney will never learn if you keep giving her money."

"You know I have a soft spot for my little Whit-Whit. She works too hard at that pub of hers. A girl needs to have her nails done and a new dress to make her feel put-together."

"She needs to be a responsible adult."

"You're too hard on her, Linda."

"Hmm, and you're too soft," Linda grumbles. "Tucker, why don't you go introduce Blakely to GT before everyone gets here? Once Uncle Beauford arrives, it will go downhill pretty quick."

Tucker kisses his mom on the cheek before we slip out of the kitchen.

"I like your mom and aunt. They're really funny."

"They're pushy as hell is what they are."

"At least they want to see you. My mom is more concerned about her next Botox appointment than what I'm doing." Tucker frowns and squeezes my hand. "Does your aunt live here too?"

"No, she lives up the road, but she's always here keeping my mom company. She was married to a wealthy surgeon, but he died of a heart attack and left her with a hefty estate. They never had kids."

"Why does your grandfather hate Uncle Beauford so much?" I whisper.

"Well, Uncle Beau was married to GT's sister Margaret.

We called her Aunt Margie. She was so much fun to be around. Uncle Beau too." I arch an eyebrow, thinking about the grumpy curmudgeon I met my first night at the bar. "I know. It's hard to believe. Anyway, Beauford was Grandpa's best friend. Apparently, he got Aunt Margie pregnant out of wedlock. GT didn't know they were involved and it was quite the scandal back then. They eloped and were happy, but GT felt betrayed and has never forgiven him."

"Wow, that's a long time to carry a grudge."

"He always thought Beauford held Margaret back from her true potential, although she never saw it that way. When my grandmother and Aunt Margie passed away, Uncle Beau turned into the salty old bugger he is today, and GT needles him endlessly. Now I should war—"

"What the hell are you dawdling out in the hallway for? Get in here!" a grumpy voice floats out from the great room.

"Here we go." Tucker squeezes my hand again before stepping down into a large room with floor-to-ceiling windows. It has the most breathtaking view of the lake, pastures, and mountains. "Hi, GT, how's my old man?" He releases my hand and walks over to a leather chair and leans in, kissing GT on the cheek. He's a handsome gentleman with thick snow-white hair and a tanned, weathered face. He has a blanket thrown over his legs, which makes me wonder if he's ill.

"You and Jason need to come back up here and help me with the cattle."

"I will, GT. A couple more weeks and I'll be up."

"Is this the reason you've been hiding out in town?" He lifts his chin toward me, his ice-blue eyes assessing.

Tucker smiles, and it warms me like the sun. "Grandpa, this is my friend Blakely Mayfield."

I nervously step forward and extend my hand. "Hi sir, it's nice to meet you. Thank you for having me up to the ranch. It's beautiful."

"Anytime," he says, his eyes twinkling. "Are you the one who busted my tractor?"

Oh god, oh no, he knows about the tractor? I feel my cheeks fire up as I glance over to Tucker for help, but he just laughs.

"I'm so sorry, sir, it was an accident—"

"No matter, it needed an overhaul. Let's blame it on that good-for-nothin' skunk Beauford." He smiles at me.

"Yes, sir." I smile shakily in return and look over at Tucker. "I'd love to see the cattle. Maybe I could come up with you—"

"No," Tucker says sternly. I'm momentarily taken aback by his sharp tone.

"Well now, Tucker, if the young lady wants to see how we herd the cattle…"

"It's dangerous, and I'd bet the ranch she's never ridden a horse."

I narrow my eyes at him and stick my nose in the air. "Well then, I guess you'd lose the ranch. Five-time dressage champion, thank you very much."

"We're not prancing and jumping fence posts, Smiles." Tucker sticks his hands on his hips in annoyance as we square off. "It's dirty, smelly, and sweaty work. You could get thrown from your horse, crushed by the cattle. No, and that's my final word."

"Well, with English riding, you could get thrown from a

horse and you'd get sweaty, dirty, and smelly, so what's the difference?"

GT laughs, clapping his hands. "I like this one, Tucker. Reminds me of your grandmother. Have her up this week and we'll take care of it." He stands up and strolls out of the room wearing nothing but his plaid button-down, boxers, and cowboy boots. My eyes widen in shock as I turn toward Tucker, who looks furious. He shakes his head.

"Don't say I didn't warn you, Blakely." He strides out after GT while I quickly gather my wits. Maybe this wasn't such a great idea.

AUNT JANICE AND Linda insisted everyone wear Tucker's campaign t-shirt at dinner. It's been really hard not to laugh seeing his face around the table, but it's cute to see how proud and supportive they are.

"Pass the salt, you good-for-nothing scrub brush!" GT yells at Beauford across the table. These two are a different matter. Whoever thought it was a good idea to sit these two across from each other clearly skipped taking their medication this morning.

Patricia, Junie and Jason's mom, walks into the dining room and sets a basket of warm rolls on the table in front of me. "Can't believe I forgot to set these out. They're sourdough rolls, Blakely, made from scratch." She smiles warmly and gently pats my shoulder before sitting down next to me.

"Fresh bread right out of the oven is the best. You'll have to come over next weekend and help Linda and me make my mama's banana-nut bread recipe."

"Oh, I'm not much of a baker."

"Patty is the best baker in Greyson Gap!" Linda gushes from the head of the table. "She owns the Greyson Gap Bakery in town."

"Oh my gosh, you own the bakery? You make the most amazing donuts!"

Patty blushes. "Oh well, thank you. You'll have to make those with me, too."

"Dagnabbit, I said, pass the salt and stop pretending like you can't hear me, you cod oil liver face orangutang!"

Beauford throws the salt grinder, aiming for GT's face, but luckily Jason's quick reflexes catch it in midair.

"Daddy, be nice and act like a gentleman," Patricia scolds Beauford.

"I'll act like a man when this buffoon wears pants to the table!"

"I'll wear pants to the table when hell freezes over!" GT gripes back.

"Hell will freeze over the day you step through its gates, you crotchety old bastard!" Beauford snarls.

"Who are you calling crotchety, you cow-towing free-loader!"

Oh boy. I look around the dinner table nervously as their sparring escalates, but everyone seems oblivious to it. Whitney is animatedly telling a story about her new bartender, but I can't hear a thing with GT breathing fire out of his nose across from me. Tucker's hand slides over my thigh, grounding me. He leans in and whispers against the shell of my ear, causing goosebumps to break out along my arm.

"Don't mind them. This is all just fun and games for them."

I smile to reassure him and take a bite of the delicious beef stew his mom prepared. In all honesty, this night has been filled with love and laughter despite the two old men squaring off across the table. It's something I never grew up with. Tucker's mom, her sister Janice, and Patty have been kind and welcoming, making me feel like I'm part of the family. I see how important family is, and how desperately I've needed it since I arrived. Well, if I'm honest with myself, how desperately I've needed it my whole life.

"So, Blakely, when are you going to start popping out grandbabies for me?" His mom smiles down the table at me. Everyone freezes, their gazes locking on me. The beef stew lodges in my throat and I have to take a drink of water, grateful for the reprieve.

"Mom!" Tucker barks. "Cut it out. Blakely and I are just friends."

"Oh, I know, but I can always dream." She winks at me. "You two would make some gorgeous little babies." Frozen to the spot, I'm not sure how to respond. *Why, yes Linda, I'd like to screw your son's brains out daily until we produce a child.* Whitney smirks at me across the way, as if she can read my thoughts. Tucker stares down at his food, frowning.

"Oh, my gosh yes! We need some grandbabies running around the ranch," Aunt Janice chimes in. Jason coughs in his hand, trying to keep from laughing.

Jesus, this is awkward.

"Hey you horse's ass, you owe me money for busting my tractor," GT yells at Beauford. I look up, surprised. He winks at me while Beauford slings an insult right back about the old rusty bucket. I return his smile, grateful for the change in conversation, and dig into my stew, the chatter flowing around me like a warm hug.

I know I have a home and responsibilities I need to get back to in Atlanta, but perhaps I could stay a little longer.

Goal: *Prove Tucker wrong and show him I can herd a cow.*

Problem: *I don't know how to herd a cow.*

Stress: *Having to pretend like I know how to herd a cow.*

What's the best thing that happened today: *Meeting Tucker's family, even GT in his boxers.*

What I am grateful for: *I'm not Uncle Beauford.*

Chapter 34

The Quiet River

Tucker

MY MOM HUGS Blakely before handing her a dozen Tupperware containers.

"Oh, oh my, okay, thank you." She juggles the Tupperware awkwardly, patting my mom on the back. "Thank you, Linda."

"You will never go hungry if I'm cooking." She winks. GT walks into the kitchen and motions with his chin for me to follow him.

"Mom, don't squeeze her to death. Blakely, I need to talk to my grandfather. I'll be right back and then we'll go."

"Don't worry about Blakely, Tuck. We'll entertain her!" Aunt Janice yells over her shoulder, where she and Whitney are washing dishes.

"That's what I'm afraid of," I grumble before being shooed out of the kitchen by my mom.

I meet my grandfather out on the front porch. I'm thankful he's finally put some pants on. This little feud he has with Uncle Beau is ridiculous. "GT, did you need something?"

"Take a seat, son." He motions to the rocking chair next to him.

I sigh. "Look, if this is about Blakely coming to the herding, I think it's a bad idea."

"Noted, but I think it will be good for her. An eye-opening experience."

I scowl as we rock in silence, looking out over the pastures and lake. Once my grandfather makes his mind up about something, it's hard to talk him out of it.

"But that's not what I wanted to discuss." GT leans back in his seat and bridges his fingers together. "How's the election coming along?"

"I think Bill has a leg up with some of the council members because he wants to put Pat Reilly in as police chief. Rumor has it he wants to clear out the old mill and build a Walmart over there."

"That sneaky son of a bitch. He's going to destroy this town if he's elected. Pat Reilly is nothing but a puppet. My sources tell me he's Betty's half-brother. Grew up in Kitquah County."

I lean forward. "I didn't know that."

"They don't want the town folk to find out."

I scratch my jaw and smile. "It would be a shame if Etta Bird got wind of it."

"Indeed." My grandfather chuckles. "This town is your responsibility, son. We need you to win this election more than ever. The Dolivers are hellbent on turning this land into a giant strip mall, and the current mayor elect stopped caring months ago."

"I know, Grandpa."

"On a personal note, I wanted to let you know I like your girl, Blakely."

"GT, she's not my girl."

Grandpa drums his fingers, the silence hanging heavy between us. "Son, when your father passed, it hurt me something bad. But I knew he was up in heaven with your grandmother, and that brought me some comfort. I know it's been hard on you, your mom, and Whitney. As a father and grandfather, you want your loved ones to be happy. Tucker, it's plain as day you haven't been happy."

"Grandpa, I'm fine."

"I should have said something sooner, but I didn't realize how bad it was until seeing you with Blakely tonight. You have a light in your eyes I haven't seen in a long time. Now I liked Annie, but she hurt you something bad, and that's hard for family to forget. I never thought she was the right one for you, but I see something in Blakely."

"GT, she's *not* staying," I grind out. *Why can't everyone understand this?*

The blood-orange sun dips behind the Smokies, painting the sky a rich portrait of purples and pinks.

"Have I ever told you the story of how the Eluwei River got its name?"

"Blakely is waiting for me, Grandpa. Can't this wait?"

"No, son, it can't. My grandfather told me this story a long time ago and now I'm passing it along to you. The Eluwei River, as you know, means the quiet river, but it's not very quiet, is it?"

"No." I scowl. "Look, GT—"

He holds up a hand, silencing me. "The Cherokee believe the river, or the 'Long Man', as they call it, is a living, breathing heart. Its purpose is to bring life and cleanse our bodies and souls, washing away any sadness.

"Some say that a boulder can stop the flow of water, making the river's heart die. But the Eluwei was different. It quietly snaked its way through the valleys, spreading its fingers through the earth, claiming the rocky terrain without the earth's permission. The earth was furious when it heard of the river's deceit and placed a boulder in its path, blocking the Eluwei's heart.

"But the Eluwei didn't want to die. It was determined to carry life, so it pushed against the boulder, carving a new path until it could flow, its heart beating once again. The earth recognized the river's resilience and strength, honoring it with the gift to protect the mind, body, and spirit. The Eluwei flows in all of us, son. It's in the quiet where the answers lie. You just have to move the boulder and your heart will beat again."

We sit in silence, letting the story soak in as we watch the cattle graze the pasture in the early evening light.

"Hey, Tuck, you better get inside," Whitney says behind the screen door. "Mom has the baby photos out."

I sigh and stand, placing my hand on my grandfather's shoulder. "I better go rescue Blakely. Thanks, GT. For everything."

GT nods and rocks, patting my hand once. "That's what I'm here for."

I PULL THE truck into the driveway of the river house and turn off the ignition. Blakely is wedged against the passenger door with her mouth slightly open, softly snoring. Well, she didn't run screaming for the hills after meeting everyone, so that's a plus. Especially when my mom brought up having babies in front of everyone. It was almost worse than the time she and Aunt Janice gave me and my date the birds and the bees talk before my eighth-grade dance. Talk about being scarred for life.

My mom pulled me to the side after dinner and hugged me. She got misty-eyed when she told me my dad would have absolutely adored Blakely. I told my mom for the hundredth time we were just friends. She said that's how the greatest love stories start. I know my mom misses my dad and wants to see Whitney and me settle down, but it worries me she'll get attached to Blakely.

Like I have.

"Blakely May, we're home," I whisper, unbuckling her seat belt. She stirs but doesn't open her eyes—stubborn little mule. I'm not happy she insisted on coming up to watch us move the cattle. It's not that I don't think she can hang with us, but I would die if anything happened to her. She's my responsibility when she's at the ranch. I silently curse as realization slams into me. I'd protect Blakely from anything or anyone ever trying to harm her, on or off the ranch.

Hershel whines, grabbing my attention. Letting him out,

I walk around to Blakely's door and gently open it so she doesn't fall out. "Come on, babe. I'll carry you."

She wraps her arms around my neck, snuggling into my chest. "But what about the apple pie and ten Tupperware containers of food?" she mumbles, her voice drugged with sleep.

"I'll get it later." I chuckle. My mom always sends Jason, Whitney, and me home with enough food to feed an army. She thinks we'll starve to death without her cooking. I shoulder the car door shut and open the front door with one hand. Hershel trots in behind me. I carry Blakely to my bedroom and gently lay her down. Undressing, I climb into bed next to her, pulling her into my arms. I slide her silky hair off her shoulder and kiss the tiny little freckle on her back. "Blakely May?"

"Mm?"

"Thank you for coming tonight. It meant a lot to me."

She squeezes my arm wrapped around her. "Thank you for inviting me. I loved your whole family, especially your mom."

"She loved you, too. She'll probably expect you up for the next one."

"I'd like that."

"Yeah, me too." I swallow past the sudden lump forming in my throat. My brain is having a hard time keeping up with my heart. GT's story seared like a brand over my heart. "Blakely?"

"Yeah?" She turns over, facing me. She smiles sleepily while she runs her thumb right between my eyebrows. "You okay?"

I'm falling for you, and I don't want you to leave. Seeing you with my family tonight solidified you belong here in Greyson Gap with me. I wish you could see how wonderful you are and how happy you make me. For a guy always surrounded by people, I didn't realize how lonely I was until you ran into my grandaddy's tractor. Don't go back to Atlanta. Stay here with me.

"I'm good," I say, gently kissing her lips. My tongue sweeps over hers. We have a deal, one which doesn't include me falling for her. I can't tell her how I feel, but I can show her. She sits up as I pull her top off and unhook her bra, making quick work of the rest of her clothes. I run my nose down her neck, grazing my teeth over her shoulder. My fingers map her soft skin, making her moan my name. Rocking into her, I hiss out a breath. I gaze down at her full breasts with their rosy peaks, her nipples begging to be sucked. Her cheeks are flushed, and her golden-brown eyes glaze over with lust as she parts her full lips. She's fucking beautiful, and she's mine, at least for tonight.

"You're gorgeous." I bend my head and suck on her nipple, causing her to whimper. I rock into her again. Her fingers trace the line of muscle on my arms while she wraps her legs around me, pulling me to her.

"Tucker, I need you," she whispers, arching in to me.

"I'm here."

She plucks my heartstrings with each moan and cry of my name. I make love to her slowly, allowing my heart to fall in deeper with her than I've ever allowed it to go before. The connection between us solidifies. The boulder my grandfather spoke of pushed aside, allowing the river to flow through and wash over me. It cleanses my soul while the current slowly pulls me under, carrying me home.

Chapter 35

The River

Blakely

WE SIT IN silence while the truck bounces down the old dirt road. I know Tucker is annoyed I've tagged along, but also resigned to the fact I'm here and we're doing this. When he tried to put his foot down this morning and squash the idea of me helping out, I promptly reminded him he was the one who encouraged me to try new things.

"Remember, don't tell my mom we had to throw out all the food."

I smirk. "Don't worry, I don't want to explain how we forgot to get it out of the car because we were having a marathon sex night."

He gives me a wink before he turns into the ranch. I used to roll my eyes at those eye winks and dimpled smiles, but now it makes me want to straddle him in this truck and do naughty things. *My, how the mighty have fallen, Blakely Mayfield.*

We arrive at the main stable and he helps me out of the truck before letting Hershel out, who barks and runs around the paddock like a maniac. Grandpa Tucker walks out of the stable, holding a coffee cup. Thankfully, he's wearing pants today.

"Mornin', kids. Tucker, why don't you saddle up Pokey for Blakely. I'm gonna take Dugan and you can have Buck." Tucker nods, heading into the barn. "Brody, Tom, Wiley, and Jason are going to help us out today."

"So GT, what exactly is involved when we herd the cattle?"

"Well, we're moving them down to a lower pasture before winter gets here."

"I'm really impressed you still work the cattle."

"Ah well, it's in my blood. I don't get after 'em like I used to, and we're half the size of what we used to be. The ranch was supposed to fall to Tucker since he's the oldest grandson, but with his baseball career, he couldn't take it on. Then his daddy got sick and he came back home to help, but he had other obligations as well."

"I'm sorry. It must be hard not knowing who will carry on the legacy."

"Nah, between Tucker and Jason, they'll get it figured out. Tucker needs to concentrate on the election and Jason needs to turn the reins of that fancy restaurant he owns in town over to someone else."

Tucker leads a large stately black horse out of the barn followed by a pinto who's half the size. "You should do well on Pokey. He's easy-going." His grin is wide and sexy and I'm tempted to kiss it right off his face.

"Why do I get the horse named Pokey?"

"Be lucky I didn't insist on GT giving you Slowmo. Now this is a western saddle, Smiles. It's different from your fancy riding." He grins. "Need me to help you up?"

"I got it." I bat his hand away, grabbing the saddle horn, and place my foot into the stirrup while Tucker holds the reins.

"Easy."

"Are you talking to me or Pokey?" I hop up and Tucker puts his hand on my ass, shoving me forward so I land with an unrefined thump in the seat. Pokey turns his head, but seems nonplussed. "Gee, thanks for that."

Tucker hands me the reins and chuckles. "Sorry, Smiles. I couldn't help grabbing your butt in those tight jeans." He slides his hand over my thigh, and it takes all my self-control to ignore the sudden ache to have him between my legs. *What is wrong with me?* It's like I crave Tucker Greyson twenty-four-seven these days.

"Blakely, I need you to listen to me. I know you want to show off and go all 'I can ride this horse like a pro' just to prove me wrong, but I don't want anything to happen to you today. I'll be distracted with the cattle, and I don't have the luxury of wondering if you're okay while I'm working. It's dangerous out there, and I'll need to know you're safe. Okay?"

I nod, watching him slip on his leather gloves and I can't help but drool over his tight jeans, leather chaps, and black cowboy hat. Lord have mercy. He needs to do another calendar for my eyes only.

"Good. We'll take the horses out on another day and you can show me what you got, but today just take it easy. Pokey loves GT's horse Dugan, so I want you to stick with him today. GT can't hang with the boys like he used to, even though he tries. Let him feel like he's taking responsibility for you today, okay? No need to go YOLO on me and chase a cow down so you can check off another box."

I smile. "Chasing down cows isn't really on my YOLO list, anyway."

He smirks and runs a hand down my thigh. "You look good on Pokey, Blakely May."

I sigh deeply as he effortlessly gets on his black steed. GT saddles up and we walk toward the pasture where the other ranch hands are waiting for us. Hershel and GT's blue heeler, Chief, run ahead with Tucker while I hang back with GT and breathe in the crisp mountain air.

"It's so beautiful here, GT. Have you lived here all your life?"

"All my life. I was born and raised here. Never had a desire to go anywhere else."

"I can see why."

"Most city folk get bored here after a while. They're drawn to the beautiful mountain scenery and the small-town charm, but they start to miss their overpriced Starbucks crap and big-box stores selling them everything under the sun. What seemed like relaxation to them at first turns into sheer boredom and they miss the fast-paced city life. I've seen it more times than I can count." He eyes me from under the brim of his hat. "I wouldn't blame you if you had to go back to the city."

"Oh, I don't think I'd ever get bored here. I'm finding the quiet and slow pace actually suits me. I was only supposed to be here for the summer, to take some time off from my job, but I don't know... My business partner is probably wondering what the heck happened to me. Junie's undoubtedly killed all my plants in my condo by now. I'll have to return to Atlanta soon."

"You have to or you want to?"

"I…" The words die on my tongue because I'm not sure of anything anymore.

"My grandson is quite taken with you, you know. He acts like he doesn't have a care in the world and he's living life in the moment, but he's a tender heart, that one. He really took it hard when his daddy died. We all did. I see a difference in him since you've arrived. The light is back in his eyes."

Guilt pitter-patters on my heart like tiny raindrops. "Oh, we're just friends, GT." I look away from his penetrating stare, afraid he'll see right through my lies.

"That's what they all say, darlin'." GT chuckles.

We ride in silence for a few minutes along a trail up into the mountains where the cattle have been moved for the summer. The pines covering the sloping mountainside are dotted with wild azaleas, maple, and magnolia trees. It's so incredibly lush and green. Wisps of smoke-like clouds linger among the pines in the distance, giving the Smoky Mountains its namesake. GT points out a spot on the mountain where they had a fire last summer.

"Thankfully, the river cut off its path before it burned the ranch. Rivers are funny like that. They can save you or pull you under and drown you." He stares off over the pastures. "Sometimes they stop you from getting to the other side, cutting your journey short, and sometimes they move you along to your next destination when you're ready." He's silent for a beat, the clopping of the horses' hoofs rhythmically tugging us along. "Where's the river taking you, Blakely?"

I feel like this isn't a question I can brush off lightly. GT waits patiently for my answer while the boys ride ahead. "I think"—I swallow and run my hand over Pokey's coarse mane—"I think I would like the river to take me home where I belong."

"And where is that?"

Goosebumps break out along my arm as we mosey along. The answer is on my tongue before I can swallow it back down. "Here. I belong here."

"Yes, you do."

TUCKER'S PROFILE CATCHES the golden light and shadows from the setting sun through the window of the truck. My eyelids are heavy and all I want to do is curl up and sleep, but I can't take my eyes off him. I'm completely in awe of the man.

There's no doubt who was in charge while herding the cattle today. He and Jason guided the others and moved the cattle down from the hills, across the river and into the lower pasture, all with Hershel and Chief nipping at their heels. I relished watching Tucker in his element. His hard muscles straining while he maneuvered his horse, his jaw tight with concentration. I'm pretty certain Cowboy Tucker will star in my dreams every night from here on out. I even got to canter with Pokey and feel the wind through my hair, which was completely exhilarating. But I especially enjoyed talking to GT.

He gave me a full history of the land and how the Greyson clan came to be here. They traveled to the Colonies from Scotland with some other families and landed in North Carolina. His grandfather settled on the land with the river and raised his family alongside it, building Greyson Gap into what it is today. We talked about Tucker's dad, Grant, and I got the impression he was a gregarious, beloved member of the community. When he passed away from colon cancer four years ago, it left an indelible mark on the family and the town. A lot of loss and tragedy, but happy memories, too. We briefly talked about my parents and my job back in Atlanta, but I found myself not wanting to talk about a place I no longer wished to return to.

Pokey stuck by GT's side, which was perfect because I got to watch the action from the sidelines. Correction, I got to watch Tucker from the sidelines. Normally, I would obsess over the dirt and grime on his clothes and what kind of pretreatment I would use to remove the stubborn stains, but not one OCD thought went through my head. Okay, maybe a few when Hershel rolled in cow manure...but I really considered it a new leaf turned over.

Linda made us lunch once we got back. I sat with her on a beautifully crafted wood bench swing on the front porch, talking about everything under the sun. She showed me photos of Tucker's baseball career, and I experienced a rollercoaster of emotions, seeing how gifted he was, and learning how devastated his family was when he had to give it all up.

The men brushed and fed the horses and hosed down Hershel at my insistence. Six months ago, if you had told me I'd be on a ranch watching my man herd cattle, I would have dribbled sauvignon blanc down my chin.

I memorize Tucker's profile, the setting sun turning his caramel brown hair to a reddish-gold. He makes me feel giddy and out of control. Not something I'm used to, but I kind of like it. He makes me feel like I don't always need a plan.

"Tucker?"

"Yes?"

"Thank you for today. I know you didn't want me to tag along, but I'm grateful I did." I smile drowsily up at him. "You looked pretty good up on your horse."

"It's not that I didn't want you tagging along. I never would have forgiven myself if something happened to you, but I shouldn't have worried. You handled yourself like a pro on Pokey." He looks at me tenderly for a second before his gaze returns to the road, his thumb drums a steady beat on the steering wheel. "I'm glad you came up today, Smiles."

"Me too." My eyes want to drift shut, but I struggle to keep them open. It was an amazing day I never would have gotten to experience if I hadn't come to Greyson Gap and gotten lost. I glance at the handsome man sitting beside me, and an overwhelming tenderness for him grabs my heart and squeezes it hard.

Goal: *Find a way to stay in Greyson Gap.*

Problem: *I have responsibilities back in Atlanta.*

Stress: *I don't want to return anymore. I want to stay and I don't know how Tucker will feel about that.*

What's the best thing that happened today: *Watching Tucker take command at the ranch—so damn sexy. And getting to ride again. I've missed it.*

What I am grateful for: *GT wore pants today, and I'm grateful for finding a place that feels like I finally belong.*

Chapter 36

Welcome Back

Blakely

I FLING MY purse on the island and grab a bottle of white wine from the fridge. I had a peaceful day at Etta's shop today, but I'm grateful to get off my feet and sit out on the back porch with a glass of wine. Well, okay, it wasn't exactly quiet because Etta and Racquel were there with me strategizing about how they can throw a rose ceremony in the center of town. I told them it might be beneficial to their cause if they clued the participants in on their wild little fantasy. Racquel looked at me like I asked her to throw knives at me blindfolded and called me watermelon seeds for the rest of the afternoon.

I pour a glass and sit in the afternoon sun, soaking up some vitamin D, watching the river run its course like it has for centuries. Slipping off my sandals, it beckons me to feel the cool rush of water over my toes. The bank is a little rocky, but I pick my way down and plunge my feet into the cold water. The current sweeps over my feet, carrying away my anxiety. It's kind of crazy to think this little town has been here for over a hundred years and I may never have discovered it if Junie hadn't ordered me to come stay here three months ago. And the crazy part? I listened to her, when my M.O. would have been to bury my feelings with work and ignore the problem. I was pretty broken.

Inhaling the crisp mountain air, I close my eyes and smile. I don't feel broken anymore. I feel strong and independent. Like I'm finally in control of my life, which is ironic because it's never been more out of control.

I have an eclectic community who has embraced me with open arms, as if I've always belonged here. It's nice to walk down the street and be greeted by your first name, and asked over for dinner.

What's even better is falling asleep watching Marie Kondo (I know, complete blasphemy) and waking up snuggled in Tucker's bed next to him. Those mornings have become my favorite. No, I'm not a completely changed person—I still obsessively clean and I get anxiety, but I am trying to manage those feelings when they start to itch under my skin.

I go on long walks by the river, or meet Whitney to get our nails done, or arrange flowers, which I've become quite accomplished at. I bring new arrangements to Etta and Laura Twinkle's bookshop weekly. And of course, one to Greyson Construction. Whitney says I need to charge people for them, but it's just a hobby to keep me busy. Dare I say I'm actually happy living the simple life?

My phone rings from the back porch. I'm expecting a call from Tucker to tell me what time we're going to Jason's place for dinner. I race back to the porch and swipe it open before it goes to voicemail.

"Hey, sorry, I was down by the river—"

"Blakely, thank God you answered."

"Liz? Wow, I wasn't expec—"

"I need you back here, Blakely, ASAP. We have a new VIP client who insists she won't do her event without you at the helm. We need this account to bring us back afloat."

"Oh, wow, Liz, I... I'm honored, but—"

"I won't take no for an answer, Blakely. If I have to drive to North Carolina and pack your bags myself, I will." She laughs.

"Liz, I don't know..."

She's silent for a beat while my heart thunders in my ears.

"What is there not to know?" she asks incredulously. "Look, I'm sorry I asked you to take a step back, but let's be honest, you needed a break and I had to clean up our image."

I wince, the truth taking a swing at my ego. "I'd love to come back, but I—"

"Great, we have a meeting at noon on Friday."

"But Liz," I stammer. "That gives me no time to wrap things up here. It's Wednesday!"

"Do you know the mess I've had to deal with since you've been on hiatus? The headaches, the canceled parties and events because we've lost our clients' trust in us? I've had to call *all* our former clients and beg them to let us plan their next event. *Beg*, Blakely! Do you know how humiliating that is? You owe me this."

Before I can utter another word, she's disconnected. I stare at my phone in disbelief. I knew my time was quickly drawing to an end with September right around the corner, but having her call me out of the blue has thrown me for a loop. I haven't heard from her in the last three and a half months, not a single peep to see how I was doing. I didn't realize how resentful she was over the mess in May, but she's the one who pushed for me to take a step back so she could salvage our brand.

A tear slips down my cheek and I quickly brush it away as the truth pounds along with my heartbeat. Responsibility versus what I really want wars within me. I don't want to leave Greyson Gap and the new life I've created here. I don't want to leave Etta high and dry at Tidings. Who's going to keep Whitney from getting back together with Bhodi the Barracuda? And who will vacuum Hershel and keep his breath fresh?

I have a petition I'm working on to ban Linseed from saging stores in Greyson Gap. Who will take over if I go? What's going to happen with the Greyson Gap Bachelor/Bachelorette? Currently, I'm Etta and Racquel's only, somewhat willing, participant. Okay, not really willing, but who's going to say no to those two?

And the thought of leaving my charming, messy, undeniably sexy ex-baseball player roommate, Tucker Greyson, makes my heart want to shrivel up and die.

I call Dr. Cooper while I pace back and forth. She'll steer me in the right direction. Her voicemail picks up and I curse, leaving her an SOS message before I hunt down my journal. I'll get my thoughts organized before she calls back.

Goal: *Call Liz back and tell her I'm not returning. Tell Tucker I love him and I'm staying.*

Problem: *I have to return. My heart wants to stay, but my brain is telling me I owe it to Liz. If I return to my old life, there's no point in telling Tucker how I feel.*

Stress: *I don't want to return. I don't want my old job back. I'm scared I'll hurt Tucker.*

What's the best thing that happened today: ~~I can't think of a single thing.~~

What I am grateful for: ~~I'm grateful for~~

Chapter 37

No Time for Goodbyes

Tucker

TAKING THE STAIRS two at a time after a quick scan of the kitchen and living room, I open her door without knocking and skid to a stop. "So, the rumors are true." My heart sinks in my chest as she gently places a folded sweater wrapped in tissue in her bag. She looks up at me, her cheeks tear-stained. She gives me a wobbly smile.

"Word gets around town fast. I let Etta know twenty minutes ago."

"I told you never to tell Etta something you didn't want the whole town to know." We stare at each other, the uncomfortable silence making my ears ring. So many unanswered questions pinging back and forth between us. I don't want her to go. I've fallen in love with her and it will shatter my soul into a thousand pieces if she returns to Atlanta. I reach for her wrist and pull her into my arms. I kiss her cheeks, her lips. "Don't go," I whisper, knowing she's already gone.

She clings to me, desperation written across her features, but ultimately pushes away.

"We both know I have to get back to my life in Atlanta, Tucker. This...this was all just summer fun—a distraction. I can't work at Etta's shop forever. Staying longer will only prolong the inevitable. Besides, you'll be busy with the election and the construction business... I'd be in your way. This never would have worked between us. I mean, I can't even kayak." She sits down on the bed and busies herself by picking up a folded shirt and refolds it. "This is for the best. Now you can have your house back without the annoying clean freak leaving you Post-It notes everywhere or making your bed with military corners."

"I could give two shits you can't kayak." I sit next to her on the bed and take her hand in mine. "I've grown to like my OCD roommate, and the military corners guarantee I can't kick off my covers anymore. Hell, I can't even move my legs," I joke. She gives me a watery smile. "I look forward to the Post-It notes, the dozens of flower arrangements everywhere, and watching you vacuum my dog."

"It really removes a lot of the hair."

"I have no doubt. You've become a part of this town, Blakely, a part of me...can't you see that?"

"It's easy for you to belong, Tucker," she sighs. "Your whole family is here. When you came back, you could fall right back in with ease. Everyone knows and loves you. I'm an outsider. I don't have family to help me get through the difficult times or the hard decisions."

"But you *do* have family here," I say, squeezing her hand. "Sometimes family isn't about a blood bond, it's about friendships and connections. They are the people who will have your back when life gets hard, who will fight for you when you're backed into a corner, who will share a laugh with you when all you want to do is cry. Those are your people, Blakely, and whether you realize it or not, they are right here in Greyson Gap."

She wipes a tear from her cheek. "My partner, Liz, called me this afternoon and said there's an important client who won't hire us without me heading up the project. Our business needs this job to stay afloat."

I look down at our joined hands. "Do you feel like you're ready?"

"Ready or not, I owe her for leaving her to clean up my mess these past three months."

I hold her watery gaze. "If you feel like it's the right thing to do, then you need to go."

"Honestly? I don't know what's right anymore."

"Is it what you want?" I ask.

She hesitates and looks down at her bag. "It's my duty." She looks at me sadly. "I own half the business, Tucker. I have a condo back in Atlanta, responsibilities I've ignored while I was here."

"You're not answering me. Is it what *you* want?"

"Yes."

She can't look me in the eye. I know she's lying and it's killing me inside. I had the same indecision written across my face when I told my manager I was leaving baseball for good. She's convinced herself she has to return, and nothing I say will talk her out of it.

"When are you leaving?"

"As soon as I'm done packing."

I stand up and pace. "That's it? Were you even going to

say goodbye?"

Another tear slides down her cheek. "Sometimes it's easier for everyone involved if there aren't goodbyes."

"That's bullshit, and you know it." Anger floods my chest as I roughly run my hands through my hair. "You mean everything—"

"Look, what we had was incredible, but it's run its course." She stands up, effectively cutting me off. "You wanted a casual fling and I needed to find myself. I think we both got what we wanted." Her words sting, hitting their mark. Her features soften, reading the heartbreak clear as day on my face. "I'll never forget this summer or you, Tucker. Let's be honest, we always knew this was how it would end. I'm going to miss you and Hershel and Greyson Gap more than you'll ever know, but in the end, it doesn't change the outcome."

She twists the rusty knife she's slid into my heart.

"Blakely, don't give up on us." The zipper closing on her suitcase drowns my words. I clear my throat and pause in the doorway, knowing nothing I say will change her mind. "You know where to find me when you're ready, Blakely May."

Her shoulders slump in defeat before I turn and thunder down the stairs, out of the house and out of her life.

She's right. I knew this day was coming, but it's still a complete fucking punch to the gut. Like a summer flash storm, it blew in and swept away what I was trying to protect, leaving behind a path of destruction. I thought my biggest fear was never falling in love, but I was wrong. My biggest fear should have been having my heart broken.

I pause in the driveway and hang my head, my fists

clenched. Even though it's clear we're not on the same page, I still want to tell her I love her. To come back to me when she finds her way. To live here and be mine. I shake my head and climb into my truck, reversing out of the driveway before I change my mind. Sometimes you have to let the bird fly away and hope like hell she comes back to you.

Chapter 38

I'm Fine

Blakely

MY FINGERS TREMBLE while I scroll for her number, keeping one eye on the road while semitrucks thunder past me in the slow lane. I roll down the window, hoping the breeze will clear my senses.

"Oh my god, Blakely! I'm so sorry I've been MIA. I swear, I listened to all your messages. It's been a whirlwind having to cover for Dr. Reed while she's out on maternity leave. Enough about me. How are you? How is Greyson Gap treating you? Etta still on your case about The Bachelor?"

"Junie..." I croak out. Hearing her voice releases the dam. Fresh tears roll down my cheeks.

"Oh my god, what happened?"

I take a deep, shuddering breath. "Liz called and said I needed to come back immediately for a client."

"Okay, well, that's good, right? I think it's a great sign she's reaching out to you, begging you to come back."

"It's awful!" I blubber. "I don't want to come back home. I fell in love with Tucker and Greyson Gap, and that's where I belong because GT talked about the river and it's supposed to bring me home, and he said no to Annie because he wanted me. And now Etta will be lost without me, and who will help Laura Twinkle with her self-help Wednesdays?"

"Whoa, whoa, slow down, sister. Grandpa Tucker turned down Annie because he wanted you?"

"What? No!" I blow my nose loudly, erratically steering with the other hand. "I'm talking about Tucker," I sob. A guy in a white Chevy truck flips me the bird while he leans on his horn, shouting a few choice words.

"Are you *driving*? Oh god, pull over, Blakely. You are not safe on the road right now."

I wipe the tears from my eyes as I pull off the highway. "I'm fine, I'm fine..."

"You are not fine."

"I'm..." I cry. "I'm heartbroken, Junie. I've screwed up so badly. I kept telling myself to rip it off like a Band-Aid. Just get it over with, he'll be fine—but Junie, he wasn't fine. I told him we were just a casual fling, and I threw it in his face like he didn't mean anything to me, but he does!"

"Wait, *who* are we talking about?"

"Tucker!"

"Oh...oh no, I was afraid this would happen. You fell in love with Tucker?"

"Yes!" I blow my nose again. "Sorry. I wanted to tell you, but I was afraid you'd be upset with me. I hated him at first. He was so annoying, but there was this undeniable sexual tension between us we couldn't ignore. We tried to be casual, but the sex... Oh my god, the sex was unbelievable. Junie, I've never felt so connected with a man before Tucker."

"Did he feel it too?"

"I mean, we never exchanged I love yous, but he invited me up to the ranch to meet his mom and GT. I don't know Junie. He was so infuriating at first, but eventually we became friends, and then it turned into something deeper. Did I mention the sex was off the charts?"

"Uh-huh… I can't believe he asked you up to the ranch."

"Stacy Reeger told me he asks all his girlfriends up to the ranch. She's been there." I sniffle before blowing my nose.

"Stacy Reeger probably crashed a BBQ Jason was throwing," Junie snorts. "No, Blakely. He's never asked a girl up there. It's his sacred place. I think it's safe to say he has feelings for you, too."

My heart plummets. "Oh god, I've fucked it all up. What am I going to do, Junie? Liz called and ruined everything."

"Whoa, okay. Let's take this one step at a time. You and Tucker had a fling and developed feelings for each other. Then Liz called. Is this the first you've spoken to her?"

"Yes."

"Okay, so Liz calls out of the blue and demands you get your butt back to Atlanta. You packed your bags and ended things with Tucker, but you didn't want to."

"Right." Fresh tears spill down my cheeks.

"Can I be Dr. Thorton for a minute?"

"Yes, please!"

"You need to return to Atlanta and talk to Liz in person. Figure out if you want to stay in Atlanta and revive your business. You and Liz need to have a sit-down about expectations from here on out."

"But—"

"As your best friend and cousin to the idiot who let you leave, I'd tell you to call Tucker and tell him everything. Tell him you messed up and you want to make it work."

I look out the window at the pines lining the highway. The mist-shrouded Smokies, creating a border between earth and sky, to my left. I'm only a half-hour outside of Greyson Gap, and I'm already homesick, the pain tugging at my gut. It would be so easy to turn this car around and tell Tucker I want to stay and be with him. But there are so many unknowns. What if he's changed his mind and decided he doesn't want complicated? What if I move there and our feelings fizzle out, or God forbid, I become an Annie to him? Unknowns scare the shit out of me.

"I can't."

"Why on earth not?"

"Because I don't know what I'm going to do. I can't string him along if I decide to stay in Atlanta. Besides, he needs to focus on his mayoral election. I'll be a distraction for him."

"Isn't that a decision you need to let him make?"

Resolute and focused for the first time since Liz called, I accept my fate. I've already hurt Tucker, possibly beyond repair. Once he realizes I was a diversion, he'll stay on course and concentrate on the election and his business.

"You're right, Junie. I'm coming home to straighten everything out," I say with renewed determination. "It's time."

Chapter 39

The Dream

Blakely

PEACH STREET IN downtown Atlanta is crowded on this unusually warm fall evening. I pull my purse tighter, bustling past tourists window shopping and people walking home from their jobs, before quickly ducking into my favorite florist shop. I immediately breathe in the cool floral mix of fragrances, my mind easing.

It's been two months since I left Greyson Gap. Two months since I've spoken to Tucker. Not a call, not a text, nothing. There were half a million times my finger hovered over his name in my contact list, but I could never quite gain enough momentum or courage to actually press it.

Apparently, he never could either.

An agonizing sixty days…one thousand four hundred and forty hours, I sit and wait for my life to return to the way it was before I ever stepped foot in Greyson Gap.

"Can I help you?" a man behind the counter asks politely.

"I'm just looking, thanks." I smile, perusing the buckets of fresh flowers and pick out a few apricot roses, some cream and purple freesia, and a few sprigs of greenery. "I'll take these."

My heart is already returning to a normal beat since I got off the phone with our demanding client a few minutes ago. Is it terrible to say I no longer want to bend over backward for people anymore? I don't care if she wants her party at The St. Regis instead of The Omni. I don't care this is the fourth time she's requested a new location or that she wants a different theme. I just don't care.

Eighty-six thousand four hundred torturous minutes have ticked by, and I've spent them all longing to be back in his arms.

I pay for the flowers and walk home from my appointment with Dr. Cooper, calling Junie on my way.

"Hey girl! I was about to call you. Can you meet for drinks later?" she asks.

"Not tonight, Junie, I'm tired."

"Uh-oh, what's going on? You sound down."

"I had the dream again."

"The one where Etta Bird hired Betty Doliver and Linseed and they locked you out of the shop? And they were throwing all the candles away and messing up the color-coordinated scarves?"

"Yes, but last night Tucker was in it again. He made Creepy Carl handcuff me and shove me in a patrol car and stuck his tongue down Stacy Reeger's throat while everyone cheered and threw red roses at them. Then Linseed poured oil all over my pink hair and I woke up gasping."

"That's...a lot to unpack. Why was Linseed in the patrol car with you?"

"She wasn't. I was back on the sidewalk at that point. It doesn't make any sense, so don't try to figure it out."

"Have you told Dr. Cooper about these dreams?"

"Good god, no. We have enough to discuss without delving into why Linseed is attacking me with frisky kitty."

"I see your point. So listen, I'm going home for Thanksgiving. Why don't you come with me? Although Freud would call that dream a warning *not* to come back. At least we won't be serving turkey and mayo sandwiches." She laughs at her own joke, but it quickly dies when I don't join in. "Shit, too soon?"

I chew my thumbnail, a nasty habit I started as soon as I crossed the Georgia border. I stress-chew my nails down to the nub and then freak out because they look so bad. It's a vicious cycle.

"Thanks for the offer, but it will be too awkward. I haven't spoken to Tucker at all. Besides, I have an event scheduled for Thanksgiving Day."

"I see Liz is back to her old tricks and scheduling you to work all the holidays again."

"I still owe her."

"Blakely Marie Mayfield, you don't owe her anything. It was an accident. Spoiled mayo! Who could have predicted that? I saw such a change in you the first week you were back, but now...it's like you're the shell of the person who came home. Your job and Liz are literally sucking the life out of you. Why can't you see that?" She sighs as someone says something in the background. "Shoot, I've got to go. Let me know if you change your mind about Thanksgiving. I know everyone would welcome you with open arms."

"Okay, thanks, Junie," I say miserably, ending the call.

I know Junie means well, but I can't show my face back in Greyson Gap after I practically ran out of town and left everyone high and dry. I especially can't face Tucker again. These past two months have been like a jail sentence. All the work for self-improvement went right out the window the minute I left Greyson Gap.

It was like all the colors that filled me with light immediately left my body when I came back, and now I'm wandering through each day leached of life, utterly miserable. I couldn't even tell Tucker I had fallen in love with him. God, I was so fucking lame to tell him I enjoyed our time together. I deserve to be alone.

Burying my nose in the beautiful bouquet, breathing in the soothing scent, I close my eyes. Junie and my flowers are the only things that bring me joy these days. The flowers crush against a human chest I walk straight into.

"Oof."

"Excuse me, I'm so sorry...Blakely? Is that you?" The man I blindly walked into clears his throat, stuffing his hands in his pocket.

They say the universe throws you a bone when you need it most. It gives you lemons to make lemonade. It sends rainbows after the rain to let you know everything is going to be okay. The universe is always in your corner looking out for you.

But not for this girl. Nope. The universe is throwing me one big obnoxious F-U middle finger in the form of Charles Pinkerton the Third. My ex. *Think shit's bad now, Blakely Mayfield? Think again.*

"Wow, Charles, it's been a while," I say, looking past his shoulder, hoping he'll want to end this conversation quicker than I do. But life isn't letting me off that easily.

He wraps his hand around my upper arm. "I'm so glad I bumped into you. Susan called me the other week to see if you and I could have a sit-down. She'd call you herself, but she thinks it would be better coming from me. Shall we go get a glass of wine to discuss?"

Indignation crawls up my throat. I yank my arm from his grasp. "My *mother* called you?"

"Don't cause a scene." Charles looks around, but no one is paying any attention. He latches my arm again and pulls me over to a vacant storefront window. "Susan is concerned, and frankly, from what I've heard, I am, too."

"Concerned about what?" I pointedly stare at his hand touching me.

"Your escapade this summer. Your direction." He looks down his nose at me. "But most of all, your reputation. I think you need an intervention, Blakely."

"My... Are you *serious?*"

"Your parents are going to the Mediterranean for the holidays and, to be honest, they don't want your behavior to upset their vacation. Are you depressed, Blakely? Is Liz concerned? She was always the brains behind the operation."

The black hole I lived in while dating this douchebag creeps in, threatening to swallow me whole while Charles babbles on. *Be a wildflower, Blakely, not a roadside weed.*

"Remove your hands from me, Charles, immediately." I roughly shove his hand off my arm. "You don't have any say in my life. You never did. So, you can take your intervention and shove it up your ass."

"Blakely—" He clamps his hand around my bicep again as I attempt to slide past him.

YOLO, Blakely.

With that singular thought in mind, I turn and take a page from Whitney and knee him right where it counts. It feels so damn good. Charles doubles over on the sidewalk, his face turning purple.

"Oh, and Charles? Give my regards to Susan and tell her I'm doing just fine."

Feeling like a million bucks, I leave him gasping against the brick wall and walk toward home. My phone dings with a message from Whitney.

Whitney: *Hey girl, you might want to get back up to North Carolina. Etta is in the hospital.*

Chapter 40

Brown Bag Sandwiches

Blakely

I RUSH DOWN the hallway, the nose-bleed smell of disinfectant not bringing me any kind of comfort. This type of disinfectant is used to cover up death and discomfort. Room 211. I slump against the doorway. Tubes run in every direction while machines beep in a steady rhythm. Her frail body is swallowed up by the hospital bed. Her personality is too big, too loud to be subjected to this tiny, beige and blue room with one small window. I quickly swipe the tears I didn't even realize were falling from my cheeks with the edge of my blazer.

"Well, don't dawdle there in the doorway. Get your fanny in here so I can yell at you."

I straighten and reluctantly pull myself into the room. "Oh, Etta…" Fresh tears spring from my eyes.

"Now don't go boo-hooing all over my blanket." She shoves a tissue box in my face, eyeing my gift over her readers. "There better be French fries or chocolates with those flowers."

I set the bundle of fresh flowers down on the table and

lean in to gently kiss her papery cheek. "Now why did you have to go and try and die on me, Etta? Don't you know you're not supposed to do that?" My voice wobbles as I wipe my cheeks with a tissue, giving her a watery smile. She purses her lips and tosses the word puzzle she was working on to the side of her bed.

"Hmph. If I had known it would have taken a heart attack to get you back to North Carolina, Racquel and I would have hatched a plan way sooner than this."

"Color me surprised." I laugh and sit on the edge of her bed. Smiling, I reach for her hand. I've missed her so much. "How are you feeling?"

"Tired and old, but mostly tired. There's a handsome doctor, so at least I have that working in my favor, but the food here is the pits. Racquel snuck me in a Rueben sandwich the other day." She chuckles. "No one was about to question what was in her paper bag after she ran one of the nurses out with her walker."

"Now, Etta, you can't eat food like that anymore. You need low salt and low fat."

"Don't be a ninny-poop, Blakely," she grumbles. "How is life in that big, fancy city of yours?"

I smile and lie right through my teeth. "Fantastic."

"Horse crap and you know it." She shakes her head. "You're miserable."

I sigh and deflate. Etta can always see right through me. "You're right, I'm miserable. I hate my job, I hate my business partner, I hate my condo, I hate the city."

"That's a lot of hate."

"It is, but Etta...I don't know how to change it."

"There's an old Native American proverb that says, 'The journey between who you once were and who you are now becoming is where the dance of life really takes place.' I think, Blakely, you're ready to dance."

"I'm a terrible dancer," I try to joke, but it falls flat. I look down at our joined hands. "I don't know, Etta. I just feel…stuck."

She pats my hand. "My doctor said I can go home in two days."

"Oh, Etta, that's wonderful news! Do you have someone at home to help you?"

"Yes, my niece is coming from Greensboro to help out. And everyone in Greyson Gap has already stocked my fridge full of casseroles. You don't have to ask for help. They just know when you need it."

"Well, that's good." I smile.

"I need you to watch the shop."

My smile slips. Is Etta going senile? Does she not remember I moved back to Atlanta? "Etta, remember I moved…" I tread carefully.

She gives me a pointed look and huffs. "I had heart damage, not brain damage, Blakely. I know you moved, but now I'm telling you, you need to move back."

"Now don't raise your heart rate, you'll set off alarms." I smooth her blanket down, my gaze fixed on the newspaper beside her. "I can't move back. My life is in Atlanta. I don't belong in Greyson Gap."

"Pish-posh. You just told me you're miserable and, from what I can tell, you have no life."

"I have a life," I huff. Etta arches an eyebrow, causing me

to retract. "Okay, so I don't have a life. That doesn't mean I should pick up and move to Greyson Gap. Say I run the store for you while you're recouping, then what? What am I going to do after you return to the store?"

Her fingers crimp the edge of the blanket. "I won't be returning to the store."

"But Etta, you love the shop!"

"Blakely, I'm seventy-six. I'm tired and I think God and my handsome doctor are trying to tell me it's time to enjoy my life. I'd like to sell the shop to you. I've been thinking about it for a while and there's no one else I'd rather turn it over to. Perhaps you could even sell your beautiful flower arrangements."

"Oh, Etta, I mean…I'm honored, really."

She pats my hand. "Just think about it, dear, but don't think too long. Word has gotten out and that conniving, two-timing, bathroom-flooding ninny-head Betty Doliver has her eye on the shop to turn it into a Cracker Barrel."

"Why would Betty Doliver…wait, you mean she really has been trying to sabotage your business all along?"

"Of course! She only lives a block off Main Street. She could make it home faster than the time it takes to sneak into my shop. Why else would she try to stink up my business every week?"

A throat clears behind us, and I look over my shoulder. I almost press Etta's emergency button because my heart feels like it's about to burst out of my chest. Leaning in the doorway with one arm raised casually against the door, dressed in a plaid button-down, jeans, and cowboy boots is the sexiest ex-baseball player my eyes have ever feasted on.

"Tucker." I swallow, my hand knocking the newspaper off the bed. Nerves zip along my skin as I quickly sweep it up, placing it on Etta's side table. "I, uh, better get going anyway. Etta, I'll think about it." I squeeze her hand and she rolls her eyes.

"Don't leave on my account." Tucker walks into the room with a paper bag and sets it on Etta's table.

"Is that the good stuff?" She grabs the bag and peers into it. "Tucker Greyson, you are missing three quarters of the sandwich and what the hell are baked chips? I asked for fries! Some Mayor you've turned out to be."

Mayor? That means he won the election! Of course, I missed it. I've missed everything. Sadness scratches down my heart with its sharp claws. I get up to leave, but Tucker gently grabs my arm. "Can I talk to you for a moment?"

"Oh, uh—"

"Go ahead, you two go talk. Lord knows I'm not going anywhere. I'll be eating a cardboard baked chip with a...what the hell is this? *No-sodium* turkey? Tucker Greyson, I asked for corned beef!" Etta gripes, throwing her paper bag back on the table.

I chuckle. "Sounds like you're in trouble."

"Hmm." Tucker guides me out of the room and down the hallway outside to a little courtyard with a bench. The cool air feels good, the leaves rustling in the tree above us.

"Wow, congratulations on becoming Mayor! How have you been?" Dread fills my belly as I try to inject false cheer into my voice. I'm not sure I'm ready for what he has to say.

He hunches against the cold, sticking his hands in his pockets. "Thanks, I've been good. How about you?"

"Oh my gosh, so great. Super great... I'm really happy."

His eyes travel from the crown of my head all the way to my toes. He cracks a smile, which has my heart doing a double under. "Your hair is back to its original golden-blonde. It suits you."

"Yeah, my stylist almost fainted when she saw my ashy hair." I give him a half-hearted smile. "Listen, I know you're busy and you don't really want to talk about my hair. I've got to get on the road, so..."

He places his hands on my arms. "You're not going to stay a few days in Greyson Gap and see everyone?"

"Tucker..." It hurts to look into his grass-green eyes. "I just came to see how Etta was doing. If I knew you would be here, I wouldn't have..." My words trail off, looking for the closest escape route. My heart can't handle all of Tucker Greyson standing right in front of me. He looks too good. He smells freaking amazing, and his touch makes me want to beg him for forgiveness.

"Do you want to know what I see?"

God, no. Just let me go because I'm about to fall apart.

"Sure, be my guest," my traitorous brain says, overriding my heart.

"I see right through you, Blakely May. I see someone who is too scared to take the leap. Too scared to search for happiness. Someone who feels she is unworthy of finding out who she really is and how she can affect the lives of everyone around her."

I scoff, anger curling its dirty fingers around my heart. "Affect everyone's lives? So, if I move to Greyson Gap and set up shop there, I'm going to be changing people's lives?

That's ridiculous."

"Is it?"

"I'm not curing world hunger by taking over Tidings, Tucker, that's for damn sure."

"What about the people in Greyson Gap? Don't you think you impacted them in your brief stay? Whitney misses her girl time with you. Etta thinks of you as family. Laura Twinkle's self-help group has doubled in size every Wednesday evening because you gave her the courage to help others, and Tanya has teenage girls coming to Suzie Q's getting their hair dyed different colors."

"Oh god, that shouldn't be a thing."

He chuckles. "It's given Tanya her confidence back. Laura too. You've given these women a chance to show their shine. Don't you think it's about time you did it for Blakely Mayfield?" He lets go of my arms and rubs a thumb down my cheek. "And don't think for one second you haven't turned my world upside down. I miss you like crazy and I need you now more than ever."

His footsteps crunch over the leaves as he walks away, leaving me speechless.

Goal: Figure out what truly makes me happy.

Problem: I'm scared. I don't want to let everyone down, worst of all, myself.

Stress: Living a life that doesn't make me happy.

What's the best thing that happened today: *Seeing Tucker.*

What I am grateful for: *Etta survived her heart attack.*

Chapter 41
Liz
Blakely

LIZ'S EYES NARROW, and her chin lifts, the lines bracketing her mouth deepening with displeasure. The words on the menu blur as I stare at them with the intensity of a thousand suns. Avoiding eye contact with her is my only chance of surviving this moment.

"You can't be serious." She sets her menu to the side, taking a long pull of her iced tea.

"Look, the business is doing great. You have your clientele back and to be honest, Liz, I don't love it anymore. I'm not passionate about it."

"It's not about being passionate, *Blakely*. It's about business. You can't leave *now*!"

I drum my fingers on the table, annoyed she's not hearing me. "I don't want to work holidays anymore or have every weekend tied up with someone else celebrating life. I don't have it in me anymore. I spent Thanksgiving by myself because I had to work an event that day. It was lonely and depressing as hell. It's time I live my life. It's *my* turn."

"So, we'll hire someone to work those events. There must

be college kids who need internships. I'll call the university this afternoon."

My fists clench in my lap. "Liz, you're not listening to me. I don't want to do it anymore. I'm done."

Her fingertips drum on the table. "So what? You're just walking away, leaving me to hold the proverbial bag yet again?"

"I understand you're upset. I do," I say soothingly. "I need to make changes in my life for my health and well-being."

"Well, what about me? What about my well-being? It's always been about you, Blakely. I've slaved *hours* at the computer advertising and talking to clients. Hours I'll never get back."

"We can dissolve our LLC if you don't want it, Liz."

"Of course I want it! Don't think you're the only event planner in Atlanta. You *are* replaceable," she snaps, and I blanch. "I'm sorry, that wasn't nice. Clearly, I'm upset. Can't you stay for a little longer until I find a replacement?" Liz's tone turns soft and pleading. The old guilt rears its ugly head.

It's your turn to dance, Blakely. Etta's voice echoes in my head.

"I've stayed long enough, Liz. Like you said, I'm easily replaceable. My lawyer drew up these papers, which I'll need you to sign." The manila envelope shakes in my fingers. I place it on the table before I cave and give in to her demand for more time.

"So that's it? I can't convince you to stay?"

"No," I say firmly. "Upon our agreement, you have first

right of refusal if you don't want to buy my half. I'll work the golf outing this weekend and then I'm done."

"And then what am I supposed to do?"

"Well, you managed for three and a half months without me when you agreed I should take a leave of absence because I was an embarrassment to the company image. I'm sure you'll figure it out." Folding my napkin on the table, my appetite long gone, I grab my purse and stand up to leave. "Sign the papers, Liz, and mail them to my lawyer. It's pretty cut and dry."

It's almost comical, the way her eyes bug out and her mouth hangs open. I quickly exit the restaurant before I crumple. It turns out Liz and I were never great business partners. I did all the work and put the time into the events and she did the bookings. What really sold our business was my work ethic and attention to detail. She's taken advantage of me for the past seven years and I finally decided enough was enough. I've got bigger things ahead.

I pull my cellphone out of my purse and look up the contact.

"Hello?" the familiar voice answers.

"Etta, I'm ready to come home."

Chapter 42

Every Rose Has Its Thorn

Tucker

I'VE BEEN UP at the ranch a lot these past few months, pouring all my energy into helping Grandpa with the cattle and being the newly elected mayor while I tried to keep my mind off Blakely. I was sure she would have contacted me after seeing her at the hospital, but she hasn't. I've wanted to reach out so badly, but I knew I couldn't. If I forced her hand, she would've retreated.

Whitney thinks I'm a dumbass for not going after her, but she doesn't know Blakely the way I do. Having been through a similar experience after my dad died and leaving baseball, I know no one else can help you find your happiness. It has to come from within.

The pastures dotted with cattle stretch endlessly below me, the Smokies behind me breaking into the low-hanging clouds. I zip my jacket up, the winter evening chilly and damp, and follow the Eluwei River down the mountainside wishing it would bring me peace like Grandpa said it would. Maybe she'll never get there, I don't know. I'm hoping she does, and I hope she'll find me when she's ready.

My horse, Buck, moves down toward the gulch, as I make my way back home. There's a new episode of Marie Kondo on tonight. Watching it makes me feel like Blakely is still with me. Pathetic, I know, but the lady really does know her stuff. I've managed to clean out half my closet.

Whitney's white jeep is in my turnaround when I approach the house. It's odd for her to be up to the ranch on a weeknight. I hope she doesn't need me to tend bar tonight. I don't have it in me. Pulling out my cellphone, I check to see if she tried calling me, but it's dead. I unsaddle Buck and feed him before heading in, Hershel right on my heels.

Hershel barks and bounds into the family room. "Hey, Whit, what are you doing here?" I toe off my boots at the door, a habit Blakely Post-It-noted into me.

"I tried calling you on your cell like fifty times. Where have you been? I need you to come to the pub tonight. We've got this holiday thing and I need help."

I groan. I'd do anything for my sister, but I'm exhausted. "Come on, not tonight... I just—"

"Look, you've been moping around here for months like a sad sack. You barely squeaked by in the election, *Mr. Mayor.* You don't even have a Christmas tree up! Even baby Jesus thinks it's depressing." Her eyes sweep over my bare family room as she picks up a wooden piece from a manger scene my mom put on my counter to bring some Christmas cheer into my house. "I promise, I won't ask you to help me out again...for at least a month."

I groan again, flopping down on the couch. "Why can't you keep a bartender? Are you *that* difficult to work for? What happened to the last guy? Brian? He was cool."

Whitney bites her bottom lip. "He got clingy…"

I roll my eyes as I lean forward and hold my head in my hands. "You slept with him, didn't you? Have you ever thought of hiring a female bartender? Or here's a tip, don't get involved with your employees?"

"You're full of great ideas and I really appreciate the insight, but I need help tonight. Pleeease? With a cherry on top? I'll do your laundry for two weeks."

"Two months."

"Ugh, fine."

"And I want my t-shirts pressed."

"What? That's weird. Who irons t-shirts?"

I smile to myself. Blakely does.

"Fine. Two months, and t-shirts pressed." Whitney pouts, folding her arms over her chest.

"Let me go take a shower."

Whitney fist-pumps the air. "Yes! Thank you!"

"Yeah, yeah. Feed Hershel while I get ready. He's coming in with me tonight."

"Fine, but if he growls at a customer…"

I roll my eyes. "He only growls at Creepy Carl, Uncle Beau, and Bhodi."

Whitney bends over to kiss him. "Such a good boy," she coos. "Hurry up!" she barks at me.

WE PULL INTO the parking lot of The Greyson Gap Pub and

park in Whitney's spot. "Wow, it's crowded for this early on a Thursday night."

"Exactly why I needed you. I told you, there's a holiday party."

Whitney pulls the pub door open, and I hold it for her while she walks in first. A spotlight blinds me, freezing me to the spot. People cheer and clap, shouting *surprise!* Disoriented, I clutch Hershel's leash tighter. What the hell is going on? It's not my birthday... Is it a ribbon cutting ceremony I forgot about?

"Whitney, what is happening?" I growl, shading my eyes from the blinding light. The pub looks like Santa's elves vomited every last light and decoration they had at the North Pole in here.

"Tucker Greyson, we thought you'd never get here." Etta's voice booms off the walls of the bar as she talks into a microphone. Several people clap my back while Whitney tugs me unwillingly toward the bar. I look around and see everyone from town. Even my mom, Aunt Janice, Aunt Patty, and GT are at a table near the back.

"Whitney, whatever is going on, I'm going to murder you."

Whitney laughs lightly. "I know." She grabs Hershel's leash from me and veers off, but not before giving me a hard push in Etta's direction. She's standing on a small stage in front of the bar.

"Mayor Greyson, would you do me the honor and join me up on stage?"

Everyone hoots and whistles. There's a small band next to the stage playing a poor rendition of Poison's song, "Every

Rose Has Its Thorn". Definitely not anything close to Bret Michaels' version, but I do a double-take because the lead singer has an uncanny resemblance to him. Sweat trickles down my back. I'm about to step up on stage when Linseed cuts in front of me, squirting me in the face with some kind of spray. A mist of citrus and something akin to motor oil blocks my sinuses.

"What the hell?" Disoriented, I turn in a circle, the spray stinging my eyes. *What is going on?*

Etta rolls her eyes at Linseed before she grabs my hand, yanking me up on stage. "Good evening, everyone!" She beams. "Tonight is a special night. Do you know what tonight is, Tucker?"

"I have no clue what's going on." Bleary-eyed and befuddled, I look out at the crowd. I try to catch Jason's eye, but he's laughing his ass off. He's dead to me, along with my sister. Is Junie standing next to him? No, it can't be. She said she wasn't coming home for Christmas.

"Aw, he's crying!" someone from the front row gushes, bringing my attention back to the nightmare I'm suddenly in. Racquel appears out of thin air, hitting my shin with her walker, and shoves a tissue in my face.

"Tonight is Greyson Gap's first annual *Bachelor!* Racquel, hand me a rose." Etta snaps her fingers while Racquel shuffles across the stage, handing Etta a red rose.

All I can think about is how much I want to kill Whitney for bringing me here. I'm so pissed I can't even see straight. That and the oil Linseed sprayed.

Etta continues, "Now, things are a little different from the show on television, because we're searching for only one bachelorette."

"I'll volunteer as tribute!" someone shouts from the crowd. God, this is so humiliating. The last thing I want to do is go on a date Etta and Racquel conjure up for me.

"Pipe it down, Tanya," Etta says sourly. "Now, Tucker, hold this." She shoves a small black velvet box into my hand. I look down at it and swallow thickly. Another drop of sweat drips down my spine. Is this what I think it is? I don't watch *The Bachelor*. Do they end it with a promise of marriage? Please let it be earrings or a brooch. Jesus Christ, this is getting out of control. "Racquel and I want to thank Edie from Edie's Diamonds for donating to the cause."

Etta turns to me, her gracious smile dropping as she gives me a stern look. She holds her hand over the microphone.

"Tucker Greyson, can you please smile and pretend like you're having the time of your life? Racquel and I worked really hard to put this together. If you ruin it like your sourpuss expression says you're about to, I will tell your mama and your grandpa you upset this whole thing! Don't forget who used to change your diapers, young man."

"Yes, ma'am," I reluctantly mutter, shoving the box into my pocket. I may be a grown adult and Mayor of this town, but Etta still scares the crap out of me.

"And now it's time for Tucker's bachelorette to come out."

Please don't let it be Stacy Reeger. Please God, I will move to the ranch and take over the business, just don't let it be her.

Racquel hits me with her walker again, causing me to look up as the crowd erupts with cheers and whistles. Blakely timidly steps up onto the stage. How had I not seen her in the crowd? I can't stop the smile from spreading across my face. She returns my smile, biting her bottom lip and wringing her hands.

"What are you doing here?" I whisper in her ear, pulling her into my arms. She's here, standing before me like a mirage, and I'm not going to let her go. I've given her enough time to sort out her shit, and now it's my turn. Hell or high water, I'm not going to let her run away again. "We need to talk," I say gruffly, pulling her off the stage. "Etta, have a drink. We'll be right back."

Chapter 43

Puzzle Pieces

Blakely

TUCKER WHISKS ME away from the crowd while champagne is popped and the band plays another depressing eighties heartbreak song.

"What is this?" Tucker asks.

"I'm no expert, but it sounds like Bon Jovi's 'Never Say Goodbye'."

"No, I mean, what are you doing here?" He drags me outside into the beer garden, where we have some privacy. He tucks a loose lock of hair behind my ear. "We haven't spoken since the hospital. Are you visiting, or are you here to stay?" His green eyes are so vulnerable, it makes my heart crack.

"Tucker, I owe you an apology. I—"

"Blakely, you don't owe me anything."

"But I do. I practically ran out of Greyson Gap with my tail between my legs. A deserter, a coward, a chicken…I was all of it." Shaking my head, I sit down and try to explain my feelings for him. "Have you ever tried to do a jigsaw puzzle?"

He looks at me quizzically. "Yes…my grandma loved

364

them."

"I feel like love is a lot like a jigsaw puzzle." I take my finger and stroke over the cute little crease between his eyebrows. "You sort out all the pieces and start with the corners. It's daunting and exhausting trying to find the right pieces to match together. Sometimes you think you've hit the jackpot, but then the edges don't exactly line up. You try to jam those pieces together because you want it to work so badly, but the puzzle knows.

"The piece isn't the right one, so you throw it back into the sea of cardboard and search again. And you're tired. So damn tired of looking, Tuck, you want to walk away from it all. Until suddenly, you realize the perfect piece has been sitting right in front of you the whole time. It fits into your piece perfectly.

"You're my puzzle piece, Tucker. You've been right under my nose the whole time, but I couldn't see how perfectly you fit with me. This town, the people here…they complete the whole puzzle. I just couldn't put it together until I knew you were it for me."

He reaches out and pulls me up into his arms. "Remember when we were lying under the stars and you asked me what makes me happy?"

I nod. "You said baseball."

"I was lying. I even knew I was lying in that moment because the first thing that popped into my head was you, despite my best efforts to run you out of town. Whenever I'm around you, I'm incredibly happy. Baseball was a boyhood dream. I did it, I conquered it, I retired from it. My new dreams include you, Blakely May."

"Even if I'm a neurotic germaphobe, Type-A maniac who loves to color-coordinate her clothes, has a label-maker in every room of her house, and Post-It notes in her fanny pack?" He raises an eyebrow and smirks, but I keep going. "Even if I get an orgasm walking down the kitchen pantry aisle of The Container Store, which, by the way, I have a lot of stock in. God, they have such great containers. You can label flour to granola bars, crackers—"

"Getting off track, Smiles." He chuckles.

"Sorry." I shake my head. "The thing is, I love made beds and scheduled times to brush my teeth. I'm trying to let it go, but I'm not sure I can. I beat the mantra YOLO in my head with every breath I take, but it's not always easy. I don't know if I can ever be messy and carefree, but I'm in love with my frustratingly sexy roommate who makes my heart flutter every time he smiles. Even if he refuses to do my brilliant chore charts."

Smiling, he kisses my lips. "He's in love with her, too. Does this mean my queen of clean is here to stay?"

"Yes, if you'll have me."

He picks me up and twirls me around. "You realize I'm going to make you step out of your comfort zone, right?"

I laugh and nod. "I'm counting on it. I've fallen for you, Tucker Greyson, despite my best efforts not to. Somehow you winked your way into my heart and I've missed you...so damn much."

My lips touch his and the puzzle piece slides into place.

"You two finished out here?" Racquel gripes from the patio door. "The band is about to sing their last song of the set, and it's a godawful racket! Whoever gave that string bean, bandana-wearing, sweaty fool on stage a license to sing is beyond me. No one appreciates the good old songs of Motown anymore."

Tucker pulls back and gives me a shit-eating grin. "Sounds like we've got some unfinished business inside."

"Can't we go hide?" I whine. "I'm pretty sure Stacy Reeger is waiting in the parking lot for me with a shiv."

He laughs as he tugs my hand and ushers me back inside. "Step one of stepping out of your comfort zone. Let's go finish what Etta and Racquel started."

"Ugh, fine, only because they've been plotting this for months. I've missed you, Tucker Greyson." I stop him and place a hand on his chest and kiss him thoroughly. He groans, sliding his hands under my shirt. I break the kiss and pull back. "Wait, what did you mean you tried to drive me out of town?"

Chapter 44

The Rose Finale

Tucker

WE STEP BACK through the crowd, all eyes trained on us as I guide Blakely back up onto the stage.

"Cheese and biscuits, it's about time," Etta huffs, turning the microphone back on. "I may look sixty, but these almost-eighty-year-old legs can't wait around for you two to figure out what we already know."

I wink at Etta, holding Blakely's hand tight in mine. "Sorry, Etta. Please continue on with your uh…show."

"Thank you to Blade and his band, The Queen's Right-eousness, for our intermission entertainment." Etta nods in his direction. "As I was saying before, we had to take a brief break"—Etta glares at us—"Ace, would you all be a dear and give us a drumroll please?"

Blade's drummer plays like he's in the middle of a one-act solo during a live concert. My eyes glaze over and I'm about to check my watch when he bangs his symbols six times before silence engulfs the crowd. Etta and Racquel stare at me expectantly.

"Give her the ring, you nincompoop!" Etta says impatiently into the mic.

"They both have watermelon seeds in their heads. We're gonna have nothin' but watermelon seed babies from the two of them," Racquel gripes beside Etta.

I smile at Blakely, who looks like a deer in headlights, seconds from bolting the scene. I look around at the people who have been in my life from the beginning, and I decide right then what I want to do.

"Blakely Mayfield, without a doubt, there is no one else I want standing beside me in this life. I know this is sudden, but you're right, we are two pieces which fit together in the puzzle that is Greyson Gap."

She smiles shakily as I wipe away the tears from her cheeks. I get down on my knee and pop open the velvet box I didn't even know I would need, but thank my lucky stars it's in my hand.

"Blakely May, I love you. I think I loved you the moment you huffed back to your car and peeled out, hitting GT's tractor. There is no one else I want pressing my t-shirts or bleaching my grout. I never knew how much I needed you until you showed up in my life. Will you make me the happiest man on this earth and marry me? YOLO, Blakely."

"YOLO, Tucker," she whispers.

"That was one weird way of askin'," Racquel gripes to Etta. "What the hell is Yolo?"

"Well? We're not getting any younger here, Blakely." Etta waves her hand impatiently.

Blakely laughs, rolling her eyes at Etta and Racquel. "Yes, Tucker Greyson. I want all of those things and more." She throws her arms around my neck and kisses me senseless. I slide the beautiful square-cut diamond on her finger and see Etta and Racquel high-fiving each other out of the corner of my eye.

"Count on you to propose in front of the whole damn town." She laughs in my arms.

"Rumors run faster than the river current in this town, Smiles. Best to let everyone have their version of how it happened."

The crowd erupts while we kiss and they rush the stage, giving us hugs and congratulations all around.

Edie from Edie's Diamonds is the first to reach us. "Congratulations, Mayor Greyson. Uh, I'm gonna need for you to pay for the ring," she whispers quietly beside me.

"Of course, Edie. I will settle with you tomorrow." I wink at Blakely.

"Oh, my gawd! I'm so excited for y'all. I knew this was going to happen!" Tanya grabs me in a hug and squishes my face to her bosom, the most traumatic eight seconds of my life. "Blakely, you'll have to let me do your hair and makeup for the wedding. I have so many ideas!"

"Oh, uh…" Blakely turns to me with wide eyes while Tanya wraps her in a bear hug, lifting her off her feet.

"We'll get back to you, Tanya. Let's give Blakely a little air." I pull her off right before Junie and Jason squeeze us into a hug.

"That was something." Jason gives me a shit-eating grin.

"Were you in on this?" I growl.

He holds his hands up. "Swear to God, I was an innocent bystander."

I eye him doubtfully, squeezing Junie into a hug. "What

are you doing all the way up from Atlanta, Doc?"

"Here to watch two of my favorite people fall in love." She squeezes Blakely into a hug and whispers, "I'm so proud of you."

Whitney grabs me around the waist and kisses my cheek, handing Hershel's leash over to me. "Congratulations, big brother. You forgive me?"

"Just this once." I squeeze her tight. "Pain in my ass."

"Blakely, thank God you're back. Are you here to stay? Because Tucker said I have to do his laundry and press his t-shirts for two months! And we have to go get our nails done so I can tell you about this new guy. Wait, oh my god, this means we're going to be sisters now!" Whitney squeals, causing Hershel to bark.

Blakely laughs as I lightly shove Whitney away. "Go away, pest."

"I'm here to stay," Blakely murmurs against my lips and I can't wipe the permanent grin off my face.

Chapter 45
Belonging
Blakely

THINGS HAVE BEEN amazing since I followed my heart and moved back to the small mountain town of Greyson Gap six months ago. Etta handed over the reins of Tidings about a month after I moved back. The transition went smoothly and I've even added fresh flower arrangements as a service. I'm gathering up the courage to buy the space next door to turn it into a full florist shop, but I'm not quite ready. Waving hello to Hilda, the coffee shop owner across the street, I open up the door to Tidings, the familiar chime of the bell sounding like home to me.

"Hey, Annie, how was the morning? I hope I'm not too late. Setting up the booth for the flower festival took longer than I expected. You'll never believe who they put me next to."

"Oh no, who?"

"Linseed."

Annie grimaces. "Keep an eye on her. She'll try to sage your booth. We were busy this morning with all the tourist traffic." She smiles as she pulls her purse strap over her shoulder. "I'm sorry to run, but I've got to grab Ben from school. See you tomorrow."

"No worries. Thanks for your help today." I smile while I unload the bags I was carrying onto the counter. Sighing with relief, I grab a bottle of water from the mini fridge.

I hired Annie to help me at the shop in the mornings after her schedule changed and she couldn't work the hours needed at Greyson Construction. She's turned out to be a really great friend and has been a much needed addition to Tidings. It's become my mission to set her up on a date with Eddie Barker.

I walk over to the front door and flip the sign Mrs. Thurston, a sweet woman who owns a needlepoint shop, made for me to closed. It reads, *No public restrooms, no saging.* I think she's my new favorite town member.

The beautiful summer evening beckons me to sit and relax for a minute before heading home. I'm in love with the vintage blue bench I found at a local antique shop and put in front of the shop, along with some potted red geraniums and a dog bowl for when Hershel comes to the shop with me. Betty Doliver apparently made his growl list and hasn't shown her face around in months. He keeps all the riffraff out.

Sitting down, I sigh, content with my life. Tidings has become an important little corner of this world, inviting people in to chat, shop, or just hang out. Etta and Racquel swing by the shop on Wednesday mornings before their weekly standing appointment at Suzie Q's salon and pet grooming. They're vigorously planning their next *Bachelor* show and have been waiting with bated breath for warm weather so they can watch Ed Barker mow his lawn again. God help us all.

Two teenagers walk by with pink and green hair and wave hello. I smile and wave back. "I like your hair."

"Thanks! Lolly did it," one of them chirps.

Tanya's been so busy, she's hired Lolly to help out. I think I'd rather get trapped in a tent with Bhodi the Barracuda than let Lolly touch my hair, but to each their own. I still haven't figured out how to tell Tanya she will not be doing my hair and makeup for the wedding. She keeps sending me sparkly lavender eyeshadows and matching hair color samples.

I pull my cellphone out and press Tucker's name.

"Hey babe, how did the booth set-up go?" His smooth voice makes my stomach flutter, itching to get home to him.

"I'm next to Linseed's booth, but I have Eddie's booth on the other side of me, so that's a plus. He can always shoot her with the firehose if she gets aggressive."

"People would pay money to see that happen. I'm at the new house. It's coming along well, so I should be home soon."

"I can't wait to see it completed!"

"A couple more weeks and it will be done. Funny thing though, the guys keep finding Post-It notes with specific instructions everywhere. Know anything about that?"

"Nope."

"Uh-huh."

Tucker and I are living together at the river house until our own place on the lake at the ranch is built. Greyson Construction is doing an amazing job, and I've let Tucker take total control of the project, which hasn't been the easiest for me. I haven't even gone to see it, because I want to be totally surprised.

Okay, that's a lie. I may have gone up there once or twice...okay, a few times a week, to check on things after the workers are gone and leave little notes on how I want things done.

"Can we order pizza for dinner? Then maybe some Marie Kondo and hot sex?" I ask to get his mind off the notes.

"Whatever you want, babe. It's your world, I'm just living in it. By the way, your parents sent a package. I left it on the kitchen island."

"Thanks, it's their housewarming gift of jelly from England."

"Well, they're trying. Oh hey, sorry, Jason's calling. Gotta run, love you."

"I love you, too." I hang up and sigh. Susan and my father were furious when I quit my job and got engaged to someone who isn't Charles Pinkerton the third. Once they realized I wouldn't be returning to Atlanta or breaking off my engagement, they begrudgingly became more accepting of my new life. They semi-retired and moved to the English countryside a few months ago and told me they'd pencil my wedding into their schedule when we decided on a date. Dr. Cooper called it baby steps in the right direction.

My smile grows and I wave to my best friend, Junie, walking down the street, swinging a shopping bag. She waves back enthusiastically.

"I'm glad you're still here." She plops down next to me on the bench, her long black hair sliding over her shoulder.

"I was afraid you closed the shop early because of the festival tomorrow."

"Thought I'd take a moment to breathe. How did the search go today?"

Junie groans, stretching her legs. "I didn't realize there were so many dives in Greyson Gap."

"I take it you didn't find a place?"

"No, but I'm confident I will. Got a cute dress at Dahlias, though."

"Ooh, let's see it." She pulls out a beautiful red sundress. "Perfect color for you. Have I told you lately how happy I am you moved back home to Greyson Gap? I wouldn't be here if it wasn't for you."

"Like I'd really let you leave me behind in Atlanta? You weren't getting rid of me that easily." She smiles. "Ooh, do I hear Eddie Barker's lawn mower?" She stretches her neck, causing me to laugh. No one can resist Eddie Barker in shorts.

"Thanks, Junie."

"For what?"

"For everything." I squeeze her into a side hug.

"You did it all on your own...with a little help from some friends." She winks, squeezing me back.

Epilogue
Blakely

Three months later

LIGHTS FROM THE sheriff's patrol car cast red shadows on
the walls of Tidings, the siren blaring loudly down Main
Street. *What the heck is going on?* Sheriff Jerry hefts his
bulky body out of his patrol car and ambles up to Tidings.
Shit, shit, shit! Did I ever pay the fine for calling 9-1-1?

I quickly duck down behind the counter, hoping he
didn't see me. My chances of making it to the bathroom are
nil as the bell chimes on the door.

"Ms. Mayfield, it's Officer Poole. I know you're in here.
I just saw you."

Dammit. I slowly rise and put on my brightest smile.
"Why Sherriff Poole, aren't you a sight for sore eyes!
Whatever brings you into my little ol' store?" *Why do I sound
like Blanche from Golden Girls?* I clear my throat. "I mean,
how can I help you today?"

"I'm supposed to escort you to the town square."

"What? Why?" My eyes dart around the shop. "On what
grounds?"

Jerry sighs, placing his hands on his gun belt. "Please
don't make me handcuff you to get you to cooperate. Lord

knows I don't want to go and taser you to the ground. That didn't go so well last week for a drunk tourist."

I gulp and hold up my hands, my nightmare suddenly playing out in real life.

"No need to taser, I'm coming. Don't I get a phone call?" I ask, locking up.

Jerry looks at me strangely before opening the back door. "I'm not arresting you."

I question the non-arrest when he puts his hand on my head, guiding me into his vehicle. Staring at the plexiglass separating us, the bars on the window staring ominously back at me, I wonder for the umpteenth time if I'm dreaming. The stench of lemons and puke is infused in the faux-leather seats. Sweat pricks the back of my neck and all I can think about is what kind of funk is in this car. *Don't touch a thing. Keep it together, Blakely.*

He drives me down the block to the town square. I could have walked this in five minutes and not have fried my sense of smell. A crowd has gathered and I'm wondering what on earth is going on? Before I can question Jerry, he heaves himself out of the car and helps me out.

"Jerry, I'm not sure..." My voice peters out when Etta and Racquel suddenly appear in front of me. One of them reaches out and ties a bandana around my eyes. I'm guessing it's Etta. She's much speedier than Racquel. "Oh my god, what are you two up to now?"

"Stop questioning everything for once, Blakely, and go with the flow."

"Yeah, you only live once, Watermelon Seeds. Just go with it," Racquel gripes from my other side, hitting my shins with her walker.

"Ow, Racquel! What is going on? We've already done *The Bachelor* thing."

"We have, haven't we?" Etta sounds like she's smiling. *Traitor.*

Laughter and chatter surround me as they shuffle me through the crowd. The smell of funnel cake permeates the air. "Etta, are we at a town fair I wasn't aware of?"

Etta laughs in my ear. "No dear, now is the time to practice some patience. Go right through here." I feel Racquel drop my other arm as Etta helps me navigate.

"Go get 'em, Watermelon Seeds!"

"Etta, I swear to God, whatever you two have cooked up, I'm going to murder you."

Etta laughs lightly. "A spring chicken never gets plucked."

"What the hell does that even mean?"

"I don't know. I just made it up on the fly. Now stand here and wait. Don't take your bandana off or I'll let Betty into the shop."

Something gets powdered on my face. "Agh! What is that?" I choke.

"Oh lordy! Did I get powder in your mouth? Sorry, sugar," she says, slurping from a straw. "You're sweatier than I expected."

"Tanya?" They've roped Tanya into this scenario? Jesus help us all. This might be worse than my nightmare. "Tanya, will you pinch me? I think I'm dreaming and I need to wake up."

Tanya laughs. "You're not dreaming."

"Do you know what's going on?"

"I'm not supposed to say. Etta and Racquel have been

cooking this up for weeks. Aren't they just hilarious?"

"They're special all right," I grumble as the acrid burn of cigarettes turns my head. "Is Lolly here too?"

"She's here, but she's asleep in her lawn chair." She pulls my shirt off, and I screech, quickly folding my arms over my chest. "Don't worry, hon, no one can see you. Shimmy out of your skirt. Ooh wee, there goes that fine specimen of a man, Carl."

"Creepy Carl? Can he see me?" I cry out.

"I bet he's strict in the bedroom, like handcuffs you to the bed and whips you kind of strict. He could manhandle me anytime he wants. I'm getting chills just thinking about it." She slurps from her drink. I squeeze my eyes tight behind the blindfold. *Don't think about Carl in black leather stirrups with a whip. Don't think about it...* Gah! Some things can't ever be undone.

She shoves something silky over my head and I wonder for the millionth time what on earth is going on? Without a doubt, this has to be one of my weird Greyson Gap nightmares. I'll wake up from it any second now.

"Where's Junie? Where's Tucker?" I ask. "Whitney?"

"All these questions, hold onto the bandana for a sec." She drags a brush through my hair as I hold the bandana to my eyes. "Not much to work with, but I have something that will do the trick."

"Whatever it is, please—"

"I gotcha, hon. Let me just..." She grabs a lock of hair and then places something on my head. She brushes some shadow on my eyelids and reties the bandana. "There. Perfect, if I say so myself."

"Good evening, Greyson Gap!" Etta says, her voice

booming over the microphone. "If everyone can please take their seats, we'll begin." The crowd claps and whistles. I'm trying to think of a reality show where someone was blindfolded or brought somewhere against their will in a cop car and terrorized by the local dog groomer, but I'm drawing a blank.

"Ooh, this is so excitin'!" Tanya giddily claps next to me, but I don't share her level of enthusiasm. She grabs my arm and leads me closer to the people chattering. I hear a few *ooh*s and *aah*s.

Tanya removes the bandana and checks over my makeup. I try to grasp my bearings while I take in my surroundings. What seems like all of Greyson Gap is here, sitting in folding chairs, fanning themselves against the early evening June heat on the town square. *Is that Bhodi sticking his tongue down Linseed's throat?* Ugh, I can never unsee that.

The large oak trees surrounding us are strung with twinkling lights. Someone went through a lot of trouble to get those lights looking so beautiful and perfect, just like I would have. Boxes of wildflowers and candles line the walkway to a flower-covered wooden arch. Twinkling white lights dance in the breeze, while nearby bushes release the sweet smell of honeysuckle.

Everything fades into the periphery as my gaze falls on the most handsome man standing in front of me dressed in a light-gray linen suit which fits him like a glove. I look down at the dress Tanya shoved over me. It's the dress I've mooned over with Junie in one of the wedding magazines I hoard in my closet. The flowing white silk dress with an empire waist and delicate lace cap sleeves fits me perfectly. I touch my head and feel a crown of flowers, just like the model in the photograph. Tucker smiles and winks at me like the first time we met. Junie and Whitney stand off to his right and Jason and Eddie to his left. GT steps up beside me holding a bouquet of delicate pink peonies in one hand and Hershel's leash in the other. Both look very dapper in their bow ties.

"Can Hershel and I have the honor of walking you down the aisle, Blakely?" He hands the flowers over to me.

"I'd be honored, GT." I choke up, realization hitting me square between the eyes. This isn't a crazy show Etta and Racquel cooked up. This is my wedding. We walk down the aisle and I see all the familiar faces I've grown to love. Annie gives me a gushing smile and blows me a kiss. Laura Twinkle holds her hand in the shape of a heart when she sees me. I concentrate on walking so I don't burst into tears. I'm so overwhelmed by the sudden turn of events and the outpouring of love.

"I'm glad the river brought you home, Blakely."

"Me too, GT. Thank you for everything."

"No need to thank me. That's what family does. They take care of each other."

I give him a watery smile. "I'm glad you're wearing pants today, GT."

He laughs. "I usually do, but I find it amusing to get Beau's goat at family dinners." He winks as he comes to a stop. "This is where we part. You take care of my boy up there. He's something special to me."

"He's something special to me, too."

"Well then, I'll gladly hand you off to him." GT kisses my cheek and joins a weeping Linda in the front row. Hershel barks, causing the crowd to laugh. Aunt Janice and Aunt Patty wave excitedly from the front row.

Tucker smiles, gathering me into his arms.

"What on earth is going on?" I giggle into his neck.

"Smiles, I know this isn't exactly what you planned for our wedding, but when Racquel and Etta told me we were taking too long on our wedding plans and they had a new idea for an event, I had to somehow turn it around."

"The cop car?"

"Yeah, sorry. I couldn't talk them down from that, but you'll thank me someday for what I did put a stop to. I had Whitney and Junie help me when I found the closet full of wedding magazines with meticulous Post-It notes under the bed in the Tupperware containers labeled Blakely's wedding."

"It's perfect."

He grins, affectionately teasing a strand of hair between his fingers. "I like the purple."

"Wait, what? My hair is purple?" *Dammit, Tanya!*

"Light purple, and just a lock of it." He chuckles before his expression grows subdued. "Your parents couldn't be here, but they send their love."

"I know. It's okay. My family is here."

He nods and runs his thumb along my cheek. "Blakely, you have shown me how extraordinary each day can be and we shouldn't waste a single one. I want to try all the new things with you and go on all the adventures. I want to chase our dreams together. Today is as good as any to start our lives together. YOLO." He kisses my nose.

Tears leak out of my eyes. "I want that too. YOLO."

Junie steps forward and kisses my cheek before gently taking my flowers from my tight grasp. "I'm so proud of you. You've come so far, Blakely."

Tucker squeezes my hand before we turn to stand in

front of Etta with Racquel assisting her.

"Etta's officiating? Is this even legal?" I laugh nervously.

"Of course it's legal, you ninny. I got ordained online!" Etta winks at me and clears her throat. "Now, let's begin. An old Native American once said, 'Love is the only force capable of transforming an enemy into a friend.' I think you two have proven that to be true."

Everyone laughs as I look into Tucker's crystal-clear green eyes and smile, my heart completely full. "I love you, Tucker Greyson."

"I love you more, Blakely May."

"Oh, for heaven's sake, you two, I haven't gotten to that part yet," Etta grumbles and reluctantly smiles. I squeeze his hand and he squeezes back while Etta talks about love, family, and forevers.

Goal: *To Live Happily Ever After*

Problem: *If a problem arises, I will trust in myself that I have the ability to fix it.*

Stress: *No Stress. I've got this.*

What's the best thing that happened today: *I believed in myself.*

What I am grateful for: *Everything.*

The End

There's an old Cherokee legend that the Eluwei River was once dammed to create the lake up on Greyson Gap Ranch, long before the ranch existed. But the river had other ideas. It wanted to flow and carry on. It could not stand to be a sedentary lake, so it made an alternative path through the hills, carving its way down through the town of Greyson Gap. The river knew that to survive, it had to change course and start over. And so it did.

Junie's Story
Where the River Flows
Coming Soon

Dear Reader,

Music plays a big part in my life and my writing. I post the playlists on Spotify for all my books under their titles.

Ready To Love Again – Lady A
More Than My Hometown – Morgan Wallen
Southern Symphony – Russell Dickerson
About Damn Time – Lizzo
I Will Survive – Gloria Gaynor
All By Myself – Celine Dion
Til It's Over – Old Dominion
Complete Mess – 5 Seconds of Summer
She Likes It – Russell Dickerson
Pick Me Up – Gabby Barrett
Nobody – Dylan Scott
I Wanna Make You Close Your Eyes – Dierks Bentley
Independent With You – Kylie Morgan
You're The Only Reason – Gabby Barrett
Never Til Now – Ashley Cooke with Brett Young
Glitter in the Air – Pink
Every Rose Has Its Thorn – Poison
Never Say Goodbye – Bon Jovi
Waiting For You – Russell Dickerson
So Many Skies – Caroline Jones with Matthew Ramsey
Home – Phillip Phillips

Acknowledgments

When they say it takes a village, this book definitely used every member of the tribe and then some to come together. A big thank-you to Allisson for going over the plot with me repeatedly and reading the book probably as many times as I did. It was a lot. Thank you to Lisa, Wendy, and Rachel for being the very first readers and for providing great feedback and cheering me on. Your support means the world to me. I'm sorry Bhodi is so annoying. Thank you to my super important beta readers, MW Nel and Stephanie. Nel, your ability to comb through the book line by line and provide feedback was invaluable. I apologize for all the exclamation marks. Stephanie, thank you for putting up with all my follow-up questions and talking me off the ledge more than once. You can always be my conductor. To Aundreya, thank you for taking the time to read through the salon chapter and giving me your insight. Dawn fixes everything. To Emily, Rachel, Meg, Alison, Addie, and Harlow thank you for always being in my corner, cheering me on. I truly couldn't do this journey without you. To my loyal book-stagrammers, thank you for always voicing your love and pushing my books. I'm humbled by your generosity and love. I love each and every one of you. To Michelle, for having to read and edit yet another one. My writing wouldn't shine without you. Thank you for your patience with me, it's beyond appreciated. Thank you to Holly for loving the opening pages and making me dig deeper into the book. I appreciate your wisdom. To my family, for your support and insisting on reading my books, thank you and I love you. To my husband and kids for putting up with my: just give me one more paragraph, one more minute, one more second! Your patience made this book happen. To Josephine and Richard, thank you from the bottom of my heart for all your love and support.

Other Books by Sophie Sinclair

The Coffee Book Series
Coffee Girl – Coffee Book 1
The Makeup Artist – Coffee Book 2
The Social Hour – Coffee Book 3

The Love Series
Lindsey Love Loves
Patrick Loves Love

About the Author

Sophie Sinclair lives with her husband, two daughters, a boxer-mix named Dunkin Donuts, and a cat named Pickles in Davidson, NC.

You can find me on my website:
www.sophiesinclairwrites.com
Social Media:
Instagram: sophiesinclairauthor
Facebook: Sophie Sinclair Writes
Twitter: @authorssinclair

If you enjoyed this book, please leave a review!

Thank you,
Sophie

—

Made in the USA
Las Vegas, NV
16 July 2022